The Sacrifice

WITHDRAWN

The Sacrifice

ROBERT WHITLOW

THOMAS NELSON
Since 1798

NASHVILLE DALLAS MEXICO CITY RIO DE JANEIRO BEIJING

The Sacrifice

Published in Nashville, Tennessee, by Thomas Nelson. Thomas Nelson is a registered trademark of Thomas Nelson, Inc.

Thomas Nelson, Inc. titles may be purchased in bulk for educational, business, fund-raising, or sales promotional use. For information, please e-mail SpecialMarkets@ThomasNelson.com

Unless otherwise indicated, Scripture quotations used in this book are from the Holy Bible, New International Version (NIV). © 1973, 1978, 1984, International Bible Society. Used by permission of Zondervan Bible Publishers.

Other Scripture references are from the following sources:

The King James Version of the Bible (KJV).

The New King James Version of the Bible (NKJV), © 1979, 1980, 1982, Thomas Nelson, Inc., Publishers.

The Revised Standard Version of the Bible (RSV). © 1946, 1952, 1971, 1973 by the Division of Christian Education of the National Council of the Churches of Christ in the USA. Used by permission.

The New Revised Standard Version Bible (NRSV), © 1989 by the Division of Christian Education of the National Council of the Churches of Christ in the USA.

Publisher's Note: This novel is a work of fiction. Names, characters, places, and incidents are either products of the author's imagination or used fictitiously. All characters are fictional, and any similarity to people living or dead is purely coincidental.

ISBN 978-0-8499-4318-8 (tp)
ISBN 978-0-8499-4520-5 (rpkg)

Printed in the United States of America
07 08 09 10 11 RRD 11 10 9 8 7

To all who pray for students and teachers.
Your sacrifice will not go unrewarded.

I looked for a man among them who would build up the wall
and stand before me in the gap on behalf of the land.
EZEKIEL 22:30

ACKNOWLEDGMENTS

Serve one another in love.
GALATIANS 5:13

My greatest thanks go to my wife, Kathy, for her unwavering commitment to the message of this book and her encouragement to complete it. Thanks to my editors, Ami McConnell, Traci DePree, Wendy Wood, and Keren Kilgore—you skillfully used the pick, chisel, and brush. And special appreciation to my good friend Kent Reynolds for his invaluable insight.

And to those who prayed. You pulled back the veil.

PROLOGUE

The thief comes only to steal and kill and destroy.
JOHN 10:10

Early one morning as the sun was rising, Tao Pang stood at the edge of the river. Thin vapors of mist hovered over the surface of the water. Many years before the river had beckoned as his grave. Today, he thanked the Lord of life.

To his surprise, the Voice responded, *"You are going to America."*

Hmong refugees had been trickling out of Southeast Asia since the 1970s. Tao and thousands like him longed for the chance to emigrate to the United States, but few made it.

"How?" he asked.

No answer.

"Why?"

No answer.

Tao looked across the water. The waterway flowed into a bigger river, the river flowed into the ocean, and the ocean touched the shores of America. If God could take a drop of water from the river swirling at his feet and send it to America, he could do the same with Tao. What he would do when he got there would be revealed in its appointed time.

Nine months later, he arrived in Los Angeles.

———

Darkness has a strategy. For millennia, evil has been associated with chaos, but in reality, it marches in strict cadence to a master plan. Its goals are simple. Its greatest enemy is light. Wherever light appears the darkness rises up to snuff it out.

In a small North Carolina town, a light was flickering.

No one noticed the light. Those who held it did not recognize its significance. It shone in the midst of a new generation, and thus posed a great threat. The darkness saw it and knew it must be destroyed. The plan was set in motion. It was a proven scheme.

Darkness would destroy light.

A willing ally was already on the scene. So willing, that he would sacrifice himself on the altar of deception. But he was not under absolute control. He was not a marionette, and he could choose avenues that didn't serve the lowest purposes of evil. Thus, the plan held risks.

The idea didn't come to the student in a moment of brooding isolation. It came in a crowded hallway at the high school between third and fourth periods. He was making his way from one class to another and stopped at his locker. Leaning over to pick up his textbook, he was jostled and hit his nose so hard against the metal frame that it made his eyes water. He spun around, but the offender had vanished into the anonymous throng.

Surging emotions boiled up inside him. Anger, rage, wrath. There weren't enough adjectives to describe the range of negative emotions that fought to control him. Sometimes, he kept them bottled up, and they seethed beneath the surface. Other times, he opened the door. Never had he given them full reign over his will. He rubbed his nose and closed the locker.

Suddenly, he had an experience unlike anything that had ever happened to him. He saw a massive wall of fire that started at one end of the hallway and rushed toward him like a flaming tidal wave. Frozen in place, he couldn't escape the approaching torrent. The fire swept forward and crashed over him. The magnitude and power of the vision took his breath away. After the firestorm passed, it was immediately followed by a darkness that held an unexpected, surprising calm. Peace came over him. And he knew the truth. The end of life was nothingness. Death held no fear.

Other students streamed past. No one noticed him.

1

Roll, Jordan, roll. Come down to the river and be baptized.
Roll, Jordan, roll. Pass through the waters to the other side.
Roll, Jordan, roll. In dying you'll become alive.
Roll, Jordan, roll.

The members of Hall's Chapel weren't in a hurry. In some cases, friends and relatives had prayed and waited decades for this moment. Prodigals had come home; those wandering in the wilderness of sin had come to the edge of the promised land. The celebration of salvation was a time to be savored. The voices of the congregation gathered along Montgomery Creek flowed over the water in triumph. Refrain followed refrain in affirmation of a faith as unrelenting as the force of the current rushing past the white frame church. Tambourines joined the voices. Hands clapped in syncopated rhythm.

Dressed in white robes, the five candidates for baptism walked forward to the edge of the stream and faced the rest of the congregation. The small crowd grew quiet.

A heavyset woman in a baptismal garment lifted her hands in the air and cried out at the top of her voice, "Thank you, Jesus!"

Her declaration was greeted with a chorus of "Yes, Lord!" and "Amen!"

Bishop Moore joined the converts and introduced each one using their new first name—"brother" or "sister." From this day forward they would be part of the larger family of God's children who had met on the banks of the creek for almost 150 years. The former slaves who founded the church took seriously the command to love one another and passed on a strong sense of community that had not been lost by subsequent generations.

Each new believer stepped into the edge of the water and gave a brief testimony of the journey that had brought him or her to the river of God's forgiveness. The stories were similar, yet each one unique.

When it was her turn, the woman who had cried out shed a few tears that fell warm from her dark cheeks into the cool water at her bare feet. Some who knew her had doubted she would ever let go of the bitterness and unforgivingness that had dominated her life for more than twenty-five years, but the chains had been broken, the captive set free. Other testimonies followed until all five confirmed their faith in the presence of the gathered witnesses.

Bishop Moore waded into the water. Much of the stream bottom in the valley was covered with smooth rocks that made footing treacherous for the trout fishermen who crowded the stream each April, but the church deacons had cleared away the rocks and made a safe path to the small pool where Bishop Moore waited for the first candidate. A teenage boy walked gingerly forward into the cold water that inched up his legs to his waist. His family looked on with joy.

Bishop Moore held up his right hand and said in a loud voice, "Michael Lindale Wallace, I baptize you in the name of the Father, the Son, and the Holy Ghost."

Then, putting his hand over Mike's face, the bishop laid the young man back into the water. Bishop Moore didn't do a quick baptism. He wanted people to remember their moment under the water, so he went deep and stayed long. The five had been cautioned by the lady who gave them their robes to take a deep breath.

After several seconds, the bishop lifted Mike out of the water and proclaimed, "Buried in likeness to his death in baptism; raised to walk in newness of resurrection life."

The sputtering boy managed a big smile. His father shouted, "Hallelujah!"

Mike splashed through the water toward the shore. The next in line was the woman who had shed the tears. She stepped deeper into the water.

The first shot didn't cause a stir. One of the elders later told the police detective, "I thought it was a firecracker."

The second shot knifed through the water about three feet from the woman wading toward the bishop. The bullet left a line of bubbles before disappearing into the sandy bottom.

The third shot shattered the windshield of a car parked next to the sanctuary. At the sound of the splintering glass, pandemonium broke out. The air was filled with screams. People began running away from the water. Some ran toward the sanctuary. Others hid behind cars and trucks. Several children who were not standing near their parents froze, unsure what to do.

The fourth shot passed through the bottom of the new dress Alisha Mason was wearing. At that moment, the teenager didn't know how close she'd come to serious injury. (It was several days before she took out the dress and saw the place where the bullet almost nicked her left calf.) She hid behind a tree.

The fifth shot hit the church above the front door. It was the only bullet recovered by the sheriff's department.

Hurriedly glancing over his shoulder, Bishop Moore scrambled toward the bank as quickly as his aging legs could carry him. Out of the corner of his eye, he saw a figure running downstream through the dense underbrush on the other side of the stream.

Papers from a real-estate development contract were neatly stacked in rows across the wooden surface of Scott Ellis's desk. He ran his fingers through his short brown hair as he searched for a paragraph that he wanted to move from one section of the document to another. Stocky and muscular, the young lawyer had taken off his coat and hung it on a wooden hanger on the inside of his office door. The phone on a small, antique table beside his desk buzzed.

"Harold Garrison on line four," the receptionist said.

Scott didn't recognize the name. "Did he say what it was about?"

"No. Mr. Humphrey talked to him and told me to forward the call to you."

"Okay, I'll take it."

Scott knew from the receptionist's response that Mr. Garrison was a potential client referred down the line from the firm's senior partner. He couldn't dodge the call. Leland Humphrey would ask him about it later. He punched the flashing button.

"Scott Ellis, here."

"Yeah, this here is Harold Garrison. My son is in trouble with the law, and I have to talk to someone today."

Scott looked at his calendar. "What kind of trouble?"

"He's locked up at the jail for teenagers."

"The youth detention center?"

"Yeah. The police picked him up this past weekend. I'm leaving town tonight and need to see a lawyer before I get on the road."

"What are the charges?" Scott asked.

"Uh, the summons from the juvenile court said he's unruly and delinquent."

"That could mean a lot of things. Did anyone at the detention center tell you anything more specific?"

"Yeah, a guy wrote it down on a piece of paper." The phone was quiet for a few seconds. "It says 'assault with a deadly weapon with intent to inflict serious injury, assaulting by pointing a gun, and criminal damage to property.'"

"Those are serious charges."

"Lester says it's a big mistake. He ain't never been in any kind of trouble before."

"Lester is your son?"

"Yeah."

"How old is he?"

"Sixteen. He'll be seventeen in less than a month."

Scott's calendar was clear at three o'clock. "Can you come in at three this afternoon?"

"Yeah, but I need to know you're a fighter. I want someone who can win."

"I've had some success," Scott responded.

Actually, he'd appeared in juvenile court two times since graduating from law school. In his first case, he represented a student who was suspended from school for fighting. The other matter involved a young man charged with illegal possession of a few pills. Scott worked out deals for both clients that involved supervised probation. He wasn't sure that met Mr. Garrison's definition for success, but the juvenile court process was informal and the results predictable. He was confident that he could do as well as any other attorney in town.

4

"How much is this going to cost me?" Mr. Garrison asked.

Scott thought quickly. "Did Mr. Humphrey mention a fee?"

"He said it might be $2,500 if it has to go to a hearing."

"That sounds right."

"Do I have to bring all of it this afternoon?"

Scott hesitated. The cardinal rule of criminal cases was to get the entire fee up front, but he didn't want to lose the chance for courtroom experience.

"Can you do that?" he asked.

"Only if y'all take cash. I don't have no checking account."

"Yes, sir. Cash will be fine."

Scott Wesley Ellis, the newest associate of Humphrey, Balcomb and Jackson, checked the time on the small digital clock that divided his working day into the six-minute intervals billable by the law firm at rates of $115 to $160 per hour. He quickly completed a billing slip: "Initial phone call—Garrison case."

Scott's cream-colored office was at the end of the hall on the second floor of the firm's two-story, brick building. Everything in the office was there for a reason. Scott's diplomas and his law license were framed and hung in a razor-straight row behind his desk. A picture of his father at the main entrance to Fort Bragg stood at attention next to a similar photo of Scott taken at the same location twenty-five years later. Inside the top drawer of his desk every pen and paper clip was in its place. The young lawyer didn't have to look twice when he needed something.

The dark-colored wooden surface of his desk and the small antique table where his phone rested were always shiny. Scott tried to keep clutter in the office to a minimum. There weren't any pleadings or documents on the floor, and stray letters or memos found a home in the proper file or ended up in the trash can without lingering in paperwork limbo. As much as possible in the midst of a developing law practice, Scott tried to manage the flow of work from his in-box across his desk and into his out-box. For him, outward organization was a key to efficiency.

As a child, Scott had ridden his bicycle past Humphrey, Balcomb and Jackson on his way to the barbershop. He never imagined that one day he would enter the building as an attorney himself. The same shiny brass nameplate was still there, but the firm had expanded over the years from three to seven attorneys. Lawyers, secretaries, and paralegals occupied every available inch of both floors.

From his office window, Scott could see the steeple of the First Baptist Church and the southwest corner of the Blanchard County Courthouse. One of the advantages of practicing law in a small town was convenient access to the halls of justice, and all the law firms in Catawba clustered around the courthouse like baby chicks around a hen.

Scott's salary was smaller than his counterparts an hour down the road in the office towers of Charlotte, but at the smaller firm he had the opportunity to sit at the feet of Mr. Humphrey, a true Southern orator whose courtroom demeanor was so compelling that other attorneys would listen and take notes in the gallery when he gave a closing argument. Scott wanted to be a trial lawyer, and if there was courtroom potential in his future, he believed Leland Humphrey could call it forth.

Deciding to give an immediate report to his boss about the call from Harold Garrison, Scott left his office and descended the broad wooden staircase to the first floor. He passed Frank Balcomb's darkened office. The number two attorney on the firm letterhead spent more time playing golf or relaxing at his beach house near Wilmington than practicing law.

Mr. Humphrey's office occupied a large corner on the ground floor. From his chair he could adjust the window blinds and see the sidewalk in front of the main entrance to the firm, thus observing who walked through the door before the receptionist notified him.

Scott knocked lightly.

"Come in!" the older man's voice boomed out.

Leland Humphrey was sixty-nine years old with a full head of white hair, bushy eyebrows, and clear green eyes. Navy blue suspenders framed his ample midsection, and he wore a blue bow tie and white shirt. The older lawyer was leaning back in a burgundy leather chair behind a huge desk covered with mounds of papers. His office was the antithesis of Scott's work area. File folders turned in opposite directions were stacked like paper battlements three feet high on the floor surrounding the chair. More piles of paperwork rested on a long credenza.

It was an organizational nightmare, but when asked about a particular case, Mr. Humphrey could usually thrust his hand into a stack of papers and come up with the answer in a matter of seconds. Orderliness existed in the senior partner's mind, not in his surroundings.

The two men were different in outward habits, but they shared a common dedication to the law and an ability to communicate with each other that was obvious to both of them from their first meeting when Scott interviewed with the firm. Mr. Humphrey's affection for the practice of law was mature and seasoned with wisdom; Scott's interest was motivated by a new challenge and his innate commitment to honor and justice. On a more basic level, both men liked a good, clean fight.

"Have a seat," Mr. Humphrey said.

Scott sat in a comfortable wing chair. "I talked with Mr. Garrison about his son's juvenile court case. He's coming in this afternoon. I told him to bring $2,500 as the fee for handling the case through a hearing in juvenile court."

"Good. It's a chance for some low-key trial experience, and I thought you might enjoy it. If you have any questions, let me know."

"Okay, thanks."

Leland Humphrey sat up straighter in his chair and raised his right eyebrow. "Have you done any pro bono work recently?"

The older lawyer often raised an eyebrow when asking a question. Sometimes it was the left, sometimes the right, sometimes both at once. He had been accused of using the habit as a device to signal a witness the most advantageous answer to a question in court.

"I served as a court-appointed guardian about six months ago," Scott said.

"What type of case?"

"It involved a tenth-grade girl at the high school who ran away from home and accused her stepfather of physical abuse. Now she's back at home, and the man is out of the house."

Mr. Humphrey reached into a stack of papers on his desk and began stirring the mix. "She went to the high school?"

"Yes, sir."

"What a coincidence!"

"What do you mean?"

"A pro bono project I'd like you to consider." The older lawyer found the sheet of paper he wanted. "This is a letter from Dr. Lassiter, the principal at Catawba High School. Was he there when you were a student?"

"No, sir. He came after I graduated."

Mr. Humphrey handed Scott the sheet of paper. "Take a look at this."

Dear Mr. Humphrey,

Each year, the North Carolina Academy of Trial Lawyers sponsors a high school mock trial program. I want to provide this opportunity for students at Catawba High School. The team will participate in simulated trial competitions against other schools in our region. One of our faculty members has agreed to serve as an advisor; however, we need the type of expertise that only a practicing attorney can bring to the program.

Do you have an attorney with your firm who would be willing to serve as a volunteer advisor? The program will involve significant time commitment over the next few months, but I'm sure it will be a rewarding experience for all involved.

I look forward to hearing from you.

Sincerely,
Dr. Vince Lassiter
Principal

While Scott read the letter, Mr. Humphrey continued rummaging through the papers on his desk. He pulled out another sheet and slid it toward Scott.

"After reading the request from Dr. Lassiter, I remembered your résumé. Didn't you participate in the mock trial program at Wake Forest?"

Scott didn't need to read the résumé. His team from Wake Forest Law School had made it to the regional finals, only to lose to Duke in a controversial decision.

"Yes, but I was a team member, not a coach."

"The best coaches play a sport before they coach it. It will be great exposure for you and the firm." He pointed again at Scott's résumé. "You're just the kind of attorney they need."

"I enjoyed the mock trial program in law school," Scott admitted, "but I don't want to end up trying to motivate a group of bored kids."

"I don't think that will be a problem. This type of activity will attract the better students."

Scott paused. He had one other concern. "The principal says the time commitment is significant. What if it takes away from my work here? I need to keep my billable hours at a good level."

The right eyebrow shot up. "I thought you might mention that. I've already called Dr. Lassiter, and he says the meetings will be in the evening after work-hours. You're not married, and I can't think of a better project for you to contribute to the school and community. You'll do great."

Scott managed a wry grin. "It sounds like the verdict was predetermined. Are there grounds for appeal?"

"No, but I have a second reason for encouraging you to volunteer."

"What's that?"

"It's not just to help the kids. In teaching them, you'll end up teaching yourself. Learning to make things simple and understandable is a key to courtroom communication. If you can show teenagers what to do in a legal case, it will help develop your own skills."

As usual, Leland Humphrey was right.

"I'll do it," Scott said simply.

Mr. Humphrey stood up. "Good. Give Dr. Lassiter a call before you leave today; he's expecting to hear from you."

Scott returned to his office and phoned the principal. Dr. Lassiter had a packet of materials for him about the program, and they agreed to meet at the school for lunch the following day.

———

Shortly before 3 P.M., the receptionist buzzed Scott and announced the arrival of Harold Garrison. Scott straightened his tie and picked up the legal pad on which he'd taken notes during their brief phone conversation earlier in the day. Generally, the lawyers in the firm didn't meet with clients in their offices but used one of the three small conference rooms adjacent to the reception area. When he opened the door and saw Harold Garrison, Scott knew it had been pointless to adjust his tie.

"Mr. Garrison," he said. "I'm Scott Ellis."

Harold Garrison was a gruff-looking man with an unshaven face, dark curly hair, and a prominent stomach that was only partially covered by a shirt missing several buttons.

"Come into the conference room," Scott said.

The conference room Scott selected contained a cherry table with a tiny inlaid design around its edge. On one wall hung a painting of a ship approaching the Cape Hatteras lighthouse and on another a portrait of General Robert Frederick Hoke, a Civil War hero from North Carolina who became a major general in the Confederate army at the tender age of twenty-six. Harold Garrison sat down in a chair covered with ivory-colored upholstery.

Scott sat across the table from Mr. Garrison.

"Before I ask you about the case, I need some background information."

"About what?"

"Your family. In juvenile court, a defendant's home life is often as important to the juvenile court judge as the issue of guilt or innocence."

The saga of the Garrison family could have been the lyrics to an old-time country music song. Harold had divorced Lester's mother after she ran off to Phenix City, Alabama, with her boyfriend. Lester was seven years old at the time, and they moved in with Harold's mother. Since then, Harold stayed on the road about twenty-six days a month and drove all over the Southeast and Midwest for a regional trucking company, but avoided Phenix City.

"If I ever see either one of them," Harold said, "I'll probably end up in the chain gang."

"And Lester stays with your mother?"

"Yeah, she's got bad sugar and lost her sight a couple of years ago. I depend on Lester to look after her when I'm on the road."

"What year is Lester in school?"

The question stumped Harold for a few seconds. "I think he has one more year to go. I only made it to the eighth grade, but Lester is pretty smart."

Scott turned over a fresh sheet of paper. "What can you tell me about the arrest?"

"They claim Lester fired some shots at a bunch of blacks getting baptized in Montgomery Creek."

"Was anyone hurt?"

"No, but they had to find someone to blame. And the police will always accuse a white person if there is a complaint by a black church."

Scott ignored the racial slur and focused on the facts. "Was Lester in the area?"

"Yeah, but he hangs out along the creek all the time. Some jerks in a patrol car saw him walking along the road and picked him up."

Scott flipped back to the first sheet of his pad. "Do you know why he was charged with criminal damage to property?"

"I think some cars got hit with bullets. But none of this has anything to do with my son. He's the scrapegoat."

Scott wrote "scrapegoat" on the sheet in quotes and put down his pen. "Okay, let me tell you about the juvenile court process. It's not like a criminal proceeding in superior court. There isn't a jury; it's more informal. Everything is tried in front of a judge who makes a decision and recommends disposition."

"Huh?"

"Punishment."

Harold raised his voice. "Punishment! You make it sound like he's already guilty. I told you I want a fighter."

"Don't take me wrong," Scott said quickly. "I'm just explaining the process. Even though it's in juvenile court, the state still has to prove its case. I will investigate everything and, when the time comes, attack from every angle the law allows. But first, I need to meet with Lester. Tomorrow is Friday. If you hire me, I can go see him in the morning."

Harold calmed down. "That's more like it."

"So, do you want me to take the case?" Scott asked.

"Yeah, I have the money."

Harold reached in his pocket and pulled out a roll of hundred-dollar bills.

2

As thy days, so shall thy strength be.
DEUTERONOMY 33:25 (KJV)

Several days a week, Scott lifted weights at Dixon's Body Shop, a local gym owned by Perry Dixon, his best friend and former high-school classmate. The storefront facility was a throwback to the days before health spas were dominated by rows of stationary bicycles and electronic treadmills. The gym had plenty of barbells, dumbbells, benches, and weight racks, but only two treadmills and a single stair-stepper. Full-length mirrors lined two walls of the main exercise room. No TVs tuned to afternoon soap operas competed with the sounds of metal discs clanging together and the conversations of men who were working out. The gym was open to women for a couple of hours in the morning, then for the rest of the day it was a male-only facility. Perry welcomed everyone from beginners to those who enjoyed watching themselves flex in front of the mirrors.

Scott had little fat on his five-foot-ten-inch frame, and he enjoyed lifting weights, but he went to Dixon's as much to hang out with Perry as to pump iron.

Scott slowly pushed the barbell up from his chest. "Twenty-eight," he said through clenched teeth.

Perry was spotting for him. "Come on, two more. Match your age."

His face red from exertion, Scott arched his back slightly, and his arms, like slow-motion pistons, gradually straightened.

"That's good," Perry said. "One more."

The barbell came down, and Scott took two sharp breaths before pushing up with all his strength. Drops of sweat ran off his forehead and into his eyes. He blinked and his arms trembled as he fought to release the large discs on the ends of the black metal bar from the gravitational pull of the earth. The barbell wobbled as it went up farther on the right side than the left, and Perry, standing behind Scott's head, put a hand out to steady it. Scott continued pushing until his arms passed the point of greatest resistance and pressed upward until his elbows locked in a perpendicular line to his body.

"I guess that will have to do," Perry said as he helped guide the bar onto the supporting rack.

Scott slid forward and sat up. "Whew," he said. "I don't have a thing left. Those last two squeezed out all I had."

Perry threw him a towel. "Good effort. How's the hand?"

Scott opened and closed his right hand. "It cramps, but I can bear it. Let's get something to drink."

The two men walked to the corner of the room and sat down in front of a large floor fan. Scott rubbed his face with a towel. The young lawyer had clean, chiseled features and a square jaw. With sweat running off his face and his muscles expanded from the workout, he could have been a poster boy for the American jock; however, his dark brown eyes revealed a deeper level of both intelligence and feeling.

Perry took a quart bottle of sports drink from an ice-filled cooler and filled two large paper cups. The sandy-haired owner of the gym handed one to Scott and sat across from him in a plastic chair. The fan blew cool air over the two men.

"What's new in the legal business?" Perry asked.

Scott took a long drink from the cup before answering. "Not much. I'm going to be helping with a mock trial program at the high school."

"Mock what?"

"Mock trial. It's a pretend case. The students act as lawyers and witnesses and compete against other schools based on facts given to them. I did it in law school."

"So this is for kids who want to be lawyers?"

"Not necessarily. Most of the students will have witness roles, but they all get a taste of the legal system. There is a teacher who recruits the kids, then I come in and throw lawyer dust on them and hope some of it sticks."

"Is the teacher anyone who taught us in school?"

"The letter didn't say. I'm going to have lunch tomorrow with the principal and find out. Usually, it would be a history teacher." Scott rubbed his head again with the towel, then looked up. "What if it's Mrs. Willston?"

Perry chuckled.

Mrs. Delia Willston had taught American history to generations of students at Catawba High School. Rumor had it that the skinny teacher with a voice that grated worse than fingernails on a chalkboard had lived through the Great Depression. Whatever her age, there was no question that creating depression for students was her specialty. It would be a unique challenge relating to her as an adult.

Perry gave a credible imitation of the teacher's voice calling out, "Mr. Ellis! Mr. Dixon!"

Scott grimaced. "What if I have to deal with her?"

Perry smiled and patted him on the back. "You can handle it. A lot has changed since high school."

———

The following morning Scott stopped by the law office for a few minutes then drove to the Blanchard County Youth Detention Center for his first meeting with Lester Garrison. The YDC was in a wooded area near an industrial park on the east side of town. From the street the modern, brown, brick building looked like a small school, but at the back of the facility there was an open exercise area enclosed by a ten-foot-high chain-link fence topped with a large coil of razor wire. Scott opened the front door and stepped into a spacious reception area that was only crowded on Sunday afternoons when parents and family members came for weekly visits. Today, the room was empty except for a young African-American woman sitting behind a metal desk.

"May I help you?" she asked Scott.

"I'm Scott Ellis, a lawyer. I'd like to see Lester Garrison."

She checked a sheet of paper on a clipboard on her desk. "He's in isolation for fighting. I'll have to check with one of the correctional officers to see if he can be brought out to the interview room."

"Thanks."

Scott waited while the woman went to a solid metal door, punched a sequence of numbers on an entry pad, and went into the secured area of the building. It was several minutes before she returned. He passed the time reading certificates on the wall that recognized the accomplishments of the center's employees and wondering why Lester Garrison got into a fight.

The door opened and the receptionist returned with a large man in a deputy sheriff's uniform.

"Mr. Ellis?" the deputy asked.

"Yes."

"I'm Deputy Hicks. The Garrison boy was in a scuffle at breakfast, and we had to put him in a lockdown cell. I'm not sure he's stable enough to talk with you."

"I'd like to try."

"Are you sure?"

"Yes."

The deputy looked Scott over. "Okay. May I look inside your briefcase?"

Scott put his briefcase on the edge of the desk and popped it open. All he had inside was a legal pad containing his notes of the interview with Harold Garrison.

"Thanks. Please don't let the kid borrow your pen. Follow me."

The deputy opened the metal door, and they walked down a short hall to a second metal door with another numeric padlock. Beyond this door they stepped into a large, spacious room with an elevated ceiling and high windows that let in light but didn't afford an outside view. One side of the room contained eight or nine round tables with four chairs at each table. On the other side Scott could see through two large glass windows into two rooms filled with school desks.

"Have you been here before?" the deputy asked.

"No. My other juvenile clients weren't in detention."

"I didn't think I'd seen you around. What firm are you with?"

"Humphrey, Balcomb and Jackson."

The deputy smiled and tried to raise one of his eyebrows without moving the other one. "Mr. Humphrey has been our family attorney for years. He's the best."

Scott had heard that type of comment before.

The deputy continued, "This is where we feed the kids and allow parental visitation. They go to school in the two classrooms to the side. The girls' wing is down that hallway and the boys' rooms are in the bigger section on this side."

"Where is the interview room?"

"Right here." The deputy stopped in front of another solid-metal door at the beginning of the boys' hall. "Wait inside, and I'll see if I can persuade Mr. Garrison to talk to you."

Scott opened a heavy door that automatically clanged shut behind him. The interview room was a small, windowless cubicle with three gray chairs and a small metal table. The light tan painted concrete-block walls were bare. He put his briefcase on the table and took out his legal pad. Several minutes passed. He began to fidget. The uncomfortably small room reminded him of the simulated interrogation room used during the prisoner-of-war training he received in the army. Finally the door opened.

Beside Deputy Hicks was a tall, skinny young man with a shaved head. The youth was wearing a pair of tight blue jeans and a white T-shirt with the sleeves cut off. He had two prominent tattoos—a swastika on one arm and a pair of lightning bolts on the other. Scott could see that the boy's right eye was puffy and that his left temple area showed evidence of a recent cut that had been closed with a couple of sterile adhesive strips. The deputy guided Lester with a firm grip on the young man's right arm just below the lightning bolts.

"Here we are," Deputy Hicks said. "Only a visit from a lawyer could get you out of lockdown this afternoon."

Scott extended his hand. "I'm Scott Ellis."

Lester didn't reach out to shake hands. Instead, he mumbled, "My hand's sore."

"He cracked his knuckles," the deputy explained. "He took a hard swing at another boy, missed, and hit the wall."

Deputy Hicks released his grip on Lester's arm.

"I'll be in an office on the other side of the assembly room if you need me," the deputy said.

The door clanged shut. Scott sat down and motioned for Lester to take a seat. "Your father hired me to represent you."

"Has he left town yet?"

"I think so, but he gave me your grandmother's name and number. He said you live with her."

"Yeah."

"The best way for me to understand what's happened is to ask you some questions."

Before Scott could begin, Lester started talking.

"When am I getting out? I shouldn't be in here. It's all a frame-up."

"We'll get to that in a minute."

Lester continued, "And they don't allow the races to stay separate."

"What?"

"That's why I got in a fight. They wouldn't let me sit at a table with only whites."

"Wait a minute," Scott interrupted. "Back up. Let's get a few things straight."

"I don't need a lecture. I need to get out of here."

Scott could see traces of his father in the young man's facial features, and even more of Harold Garrison's influence in the young man's attitudes.

"I'm not going to lecture you," Scott said. "As your lawyer, I need to tell you a few things. First, don't talk to anyone, and I mean anyone, about why you are in here. Don't talk to any of the other boys, guards, teachers, caseworkers from juvenile court or anyone else. Second, everything you tell me is between you and me. Nobody else will know about it. I'm representing you, not your father, and I don't have to tell him or anyone else what we discuss. Is that clear?"

"Yeah. I'm not stupid."

"I didn't say you were stupid. I'm explaining how the attorney-client relationship works. Have you ever had a lawyer before?"

"No."

"Then you need to listen. Third, my job is to represent you. I'm not working for the juvenile court authorities. I'm not trying to get the judge to like me. I'm here to give you legal representation. Okay?"

"Yeah," Lester said more quietly.

Scott took a blank legal pad out of his briefcase. "Good. Let's start at the beginning. Your father gave me some background information, but there is a lot I want to ask you."

An hour and a half later Scott put down his pen. He'd taken ten pages of information. Question marks and stars filled the margins next to his notes.

"I'll check with the juvenile court caseworker on my way back to my office and find out if a hearing has been scheduled in your case."

"When do I get out?"

"That will be my second question to the caseworker." Scott leaned across the table. "In the meantime, don't even look sideways at anyone in here. No fighting. No arguing. Understand?"

Lester grunted.

"Getting out is going to depend as much on you as me."

———

At 11 A.M. Scott was sitting in the plainly furnished office of Juan Maribona, the juvenile court caseworker who had prepared the intake information on Lester Garrison.

"A courier from the district attorney's office picked up the Garrison file first thing this morning," Juan said. "I'm sorry you wasted a trip."

"Who's going to handle the hearing in juvenile court?"

"Not us. The D.A. doesn't want to leave the case in juvenile court. They're going to ask the judge to allow Lester to be prosecuted as an adult in superior court."

"As an adult?" Scott asked with surprise.

"It happens," Juan shrugged. "He's almost seventeen, and it was an ugly incident. I was ready to let him go home today and schedule a hearing next week. But somebody wants to teach this kid a lesson. A long, hard lesson."

3

*The youth who loves his alma mater will always ask, not
"What can she do for me?" but "What can I do for her?"*
RUSSELL BRIGGS

September weather in the Piedmont area of North Carolina is un-
predictable. It can be as scorching hot as late July or offer a tantaliz-
ing hint of cool weather ahead in early November. Today was on the
sweltering side, and Scott was glad he could park in a visitor space near
the main entrance to the high school and avoid a long walk across the
black asphalt that had been baking in the morning sun.

Catawba High School had relocated to a new facility two years after
Scott graduated. The old, red-brick high-school building with its steep
rooflines and hissing and popping steam heat had been completely renovated and now served as the middle school. The classroom where Scott
and Perry suffered through Mrs. Willston's history class was now a
brightly painted art studio for seventh graders.

The new high school had a quiet, efficient heating system but none
of the charm of the old buildings. The rectangular tan structures looked
like a series of concrete blocks stacked at random angles on the ground.
Scott pushed open one of the front doors and passed by a male and a
female student who were talking to one another. Glancing sideways, he
saw the glint of sterling silver on top of the young man's tongue.

In the main lobby there was a school trophy case filled with memo-
rabilia from the athletic triumphs of Catawba sports teams. Scott
stopped for a quick look. Football predominated in the glory years of the
1950s and 1960s, but the trophies behind the glass case were now tar-
nished, and several of the young men who played on the great teams that

traveled to Raleigh on cold December nights now had trouble climbing the steps of the bleachers to reach a good seat for the home games. Scott played linebacker on the Catawba High football team for three years. In his senior year they made it to the play-offs only to be soundly defeated in the first round.

There weren't any students in the broad hallway. Scott turned left toward the administrative offices. Inside he was greeted by a tall woman with gray-streaked dark hair who was standing in front of a copy machine.

"I'm Scott Ellis," he said. "I have an appointment with Dr. Lassiter."

"Have a seat. I'll let him know you're here."

While he waited, Scott picked up a yearbook from a small table. Flipping to the teacher section, he found Mrs. Willston's picture and studied it closely. It looked like the same photo she'd used when he was in school. Maybe for the history teacher time stood still.

A short, rotund, middle-aged man with bright, deep brown eyes and a fringe of gray hair around his bald head came out of the office suite and extended his hand.

"Mr. Ellis, I'm Vince Lassiter."

Scott stood and shook the principal's hand.

Dr. Lassiter pointed at the yearbook. "I understand you graduated from Catawba."

"Yes. I was checking the faculty section to see who is still here."

"No bad memories, I hope?"

Scott didn't answer. A bell rang in the hallway signaling the end of a class period.

"We'd better hurry," the principal said. "The cafeteria will be mobbed within the next few minutes."

As they walked down the hall, Dr. Lassiter continued, "I mentioned your name in connection with the mock trial program to Mrs. Willston yesterday afternoon. She remembered you well."

Scott swallowed. "Yes, I took her class when I was a junior. What did she say?"

"That you had a lot of potential. She was pleased to find out that you are a lawyer."

Scott waited for the principal to add that his former teacher was going to be the faculty sponsor for the mock trial team, but Dr. Lassiter kept walking and pushed open a swinging door that led into a cavernous dining hall. The room was quickly filling with hundreds of students who had thirty minutes to eat before going to their next class. Scott followed Dr. Lassiter down the serving line. Ladies wearing hairnets efficiently loaded the plates and set them up on a metal counter. One of the older women dishing out the food looked vaguely familiar to Scott. Dr. Lassiter greeted almost everyone by name.

They left the main cafeteria and sat down at a table in the faculty dining room. Scott stuck his fork into the piece of brown meat on his lime-green plate.

"Is this what I think it is?" he asked.

Dr. Lassiter was already eating. "I don't know. The menu listed it as 'country meat loaf.' Try it. It's not too bad."

Scott followed the older man's lead, and to his surprise, the meat tasted better than similar meals he remembered from his own high-school years. The cook had added just enough pepper to slightly interest his taste buds. But the meat loaf was the culinary highlight of the meal. The green beans tasted like the metal can they'd lived in for many months, and the mashed potatoes were a first cousin to plaster of Paris. Dr. Lassiter seemed to enjoy everything on his plate. Scott didn't complain and pretended he was back at the mess hall.

"Thanks again for agreeing to help with the mock trial team," the principal said. "I want our students to participate in activities they'll remember after they forget the day-to-day grind of the classroom. Who knows? We may have a future trial lawyer in our midst."

Scott took a sip of tea. "I didn't have a clue in high school that I'd be a lawyer someday."

"What did you want to do?"

"Join the army. My father retired from the military as a lieutenant colonel before our family moved to Catawba. He liked army life, and it must have rubbed off on me. Within a few weeks of high-school graduation I was in boot camp at Fort Benning."

"I should have guessed. You sit so straight in your chair. We don't teach that here."

"There are things they do in the military that have a way of hanging around after you take off the uniform. Sit up straight, stand at attention, say 'yes, sir,' and never cry in public."

"How long were you on active duty?"

"Three years. After my initial commitment was up, I didn't reenlist and went to college at Appalachian State followed by law school at Wake Forest."

"Are your parents still in the area?"

"No, they moved to Texas a few years ago to be close to my two older sisters who live in the Dallas area. My dad works as a management consultant, and my mother baby-sits her grandchildren every chance she gets."

Scott decided not to ask about Mrs. Willston's role with the mock trial team. There was no need to confirm that the teacher was going to reappear in his life like a wraith out of the mists of the past.

"What's the high school like now?" he asked.

"I'm sure it's changed some since you graduated, but it's no different from thousands of other schools across the country. There are probably more cliques on campus than in your time. Some groups are bizarre and have to be watched, but my greatest concern is for the students who don't belong to anything or anybody—the loners. No one is looking after them. They are the ones most likely to fall through the cracks and have the worst personal and social problems."

"I never thought about that when I was here."

Dr. Lassiter smiled. "You were probably a popular student. They usually don't look very far beyond their peer group."

"Not really," Scott replied. "I was introverted in high school. I played sports and had a few close friends, but I moved in a small circle. I still enjoy my privacy."

"Then, I especially thank you for giving up your personal time to help with the program. Mrs. Wilson has been recruiting a handpicked group."

At the mention of the teacher's name, Scott's heart sank, and the wraith rode out of the mist. He'd been through a lot in the past twelve years and could cope with almost anything, but there were practical reasons why the history teacher shouldn't sponsor the mock trial team.

He spoke slowly and respectfully. "Dr. Lassiter, don't you think she's too old to take on an extracurricular responsibility like this? Your letter said the time commitment would be significant."

"Too old?" The principal looked puzzled. "What do you mean? She's not that old."

Scott decided it was time to be blunt. If he was going to help with this program, he didn't want it to crash before it got off the ground. No decent students would volunteer for an activity if the history teacher were involved.

"Mrs. Willston taught me," he said. "She was as old as dirt then . . ."

Dr. Lassiter burst out laughing. It reminded Scott of Perry Dixon's reaction—only worse.

"I don't think this is funny," he said. "I want the program to be a success. That can't happen without the right people being involved."

"I totally agree," Dr. Lassiter said, still chuckling. "You didn't hear me correctly. I said Mrs. Wilson, not Mrs. Willston. There's no way I'd ask Delia Willston to work on something like this."

"Oh," Scott said, deflated. "I thought you said . . ."

"It's okay." The principal held up his hand. "And I promise not to tell anyone. The faculty sponsor for the mock trial team is Kay Wilson, a second-year English teacher. I believe she was a student at Catawba High for a year or two before moving to California. You may remember her. I don't know her maiden name."

"I've only kept up with a few of my classmates."

"When we're finished eating, we can go back to my office, and I'll show you Mrs. Wilson's picture in the yearbook. I also need to give you a packet of materials we received from the trial lawyers' association."

After pushing their trays through an opening onto a conveyor belt that chugged its way into the depths of the kitchen, they returned to the administrative area. On one wall of Dr. Lassiter's office Scott saw a large, detailed floor plan of the school. Four blocked areas were labeled A, B, C, and D. The principal pointed to the diagram. "Each of the four grades has all its homerooms in one of the four zones, but the students move from section to section for classes."

Scott saw three small squares labeled "Modular Units" on the south side of the campus. "Are these trailers?"

"Yes. Number three is Mrs. Wilson's regular classroom. That's where you'll meet."

"What days and times would be best?" Scott asked.

"That's up to you. You're the volunteer, so we want to work with your schedule. Do you have any regular commitments on a particular night of the week—business meetings, sports team, church?"

"No, I work out at a gym, and except for the weekends, my evenings are usually free."

"The program will only interfere with your weekend activities during the regional and state competitions. Everything else can be scheduled during the week. I talked with Mrs. Wilson, and she suggested Tuesday and Thursday evenings at seven o'clock. That would avoid conflicts with most other school programs. You'll meet in her classroom, so you can come and go as you please without having to come into the main building."

"That sounds fine."

Dr. Lassiter picked up a thick packet of papers on his desk and handed it to Scott. "This is the information about the competition. With your experience I'm sure you won't have any problems sorting through it, but if you need my help in any way, let me know."

The principal retrieved a copy of the school yearbook from a bookcase beside his desk. "Oh, let me show you Kay Wilson's picture." He flipped through several pages. "Here it is. Top row on the right."

Dr. Lassiter handed the book to Scott. On the opposite page from Delia Willston was a small color photograph of a young woman with long blond hair. Now that he knew her first name, it didn't take Scott more than a second to make the leap back in time twelve years to another time and another place.

"Do you remember her?" the principal asked.

Scott nodded. "Yes, Kay Laramie. She was a couple of years younger than me."

He handed the volume back to the principal.

"She's a good teacher, very creative," Dr. Lassiter said. "I know she'll be a big help."

"Does she know I'm the lawyer who is volunteering to work with the mock trial program?" Scott asked.

"Not yet. I'll tell her later today and ask her to call you."

Scott handed one of his business cards to the principal. "Give her this. I'll be in the office all afternoon."

In the hallway outside the administrative offices, Scott didn't notice whether any of the students brushing past him had studs through their tongues or purple streaks in their hair. He didn't glance at the trophy case. He was deep in the archives of his memory, recalling images in which Kay Laramie appeared.

In the winter of Scott's senior year in high school, a tall, slender, blue-eyed sophomore arrived at Catawba High School and walked through the door of Mr. Myer's English class. Barely sixteen, Kay Laramie was a language whiz who wrote poetry. At first, Scott didn't pay much attention to the new student, but that spring Kay made the magic leap from girl to young woman. And Scott Ellis was sitting next to her in class when the transformation took place.

Everything between them happened fast. In his memory, it was like time-lapse photography. They did the typical high-school things: walking together in the halls, meals at fast-food restaurants, and going to the movies. Scott wasn't much of a conversationalist, but they had phone calls that lasted for an hour, and he surprised his friends by asking Kay to go to the prom. He couldn't remember what she wore, but the pictures from that night were still in a plastic box somewhere at his parents' house.

Kay's father kept her on a short leash. Otherwise, things might have gone farther. Then, after a few weeks, Scott was caught up in the swirling activity of high-school graduation. Kay was there, but his focus shifted to his longtime friends who were about to scatter to the winds. After he marched down the aisle of the auditorium in his cap and gown, Kay's family left for summer vacation. When she returned, Scott and his family were out of town at the beach. They were together for one week before Scott left for basic training. But their relationship was strained, and Scott questioned whether it wasn't better to let it go so they could both move on. How could he expect to hold her affection and see it grow into something more when he could be stationed halfway around the world?

So he was cool. And she thought he was cold. She came to see him on his last day in Catawba and handed him an envelope containing a poem she'd written. He read it alone in his room after she left. She had bared her heart, and it gave him the courage to reciprocate. He dialed her number. It was busy. He tried twice more without success. An hour later he was on his way out of town.

He started four letters to her on different nights while he lay in his bunk during basic training. He thought about her during long marches and while standing guard in the middle of the night. His feelings were real, but he couldn't express them on paper. Her poem had been so powerful; his letters sounded so phony. Frustrated, he decided to wait until he could see her in person and tell her how much she meant to him.

During his first leave at home, he phoned her house as soon as he woke up from a comfortable night in his own bed. Her father answered and told him that she had gone to Charlotte with Bill Corbin. Scott knew Bill. He was a good guy. Scott was devastated. He should have known Kay would go on to someone else. Maybe his doubts were more real than his feelings. He was being trained to fight, but he decided not to fight for Kay. He didn't leave a message.

Now, her last name was Wilson.

4

Summon up remembrance of things past.
WILLIAM SHAKESPEARE, SONNET 30

Kay Wilson glanced up from her desk and checked the time on the clock hanging crookedly on the back wall of modular unit number three. It was the last class period of the day. Several wild strands of the teacher's long blond hair had escaped the grip of the clasp she'd used to gather it together at the back of her head before rushing out of her apartment that morning. Her makeup was an afterthought applied at two stoplights on the way to school, and she'd forgotten to wear the gold hoop earrings that still lay on the corner of the dresser in her bedroom.

Kay enjoyed the popularity reserved for new, young teachers and cultivated relationships with her students by getting to know them as more than names on a seating chart. Friendly and interested in others, she nevertheless kept her personal life private—a practice that fueled the curiosity of female students who wanted to know more about the teacher from California.

"Five minutes!" she called out to the class of twenty-eight eleventh graders writing their final thoughts about Thomas Wolfe's use of imagery in the excerpt from *Look Homeward, Angel* printed on the quiz. While the students worked, Kay continued grading papers from a test given the previous week to another class. She finished Lester Garrison's paper. He made a C, not because his answers were wrong, but because he didn't write enough. His ability to understand and analyze what he read was clear; he just needed encouragement to put his thoughts on paper and improve his understanding of grammar. Lester had been absent from class earlier in the day, and Kay determined to talk to him as soon as possible.

"Time," she announced. "Make sure you've written your name on the top of each sheet and pass your papers to the front."

Janie Collins, a short brunette with brown eyes and a deep dimple in her right cheek, handed a stack of papers to the young English teacher.

"Janie, can you stay after class for a couple of minutes?" Kay asked.

"Yes, ma'am," Janie answered politely with a rural twang that revealed a family heritage on tobacco road. Modular unit three was like home-schooling for Janie. She lived with her mother and two younger brothers in a twelve-by-seventy mobile home in a trailer park.

Kay sat on the edge of her desk. "There is a new extracurricular activity starting next week—a mock trial program, and I thought you might be interested."

"What is it?" Janie asked.

"Pretend court. I've never been involved, but I've read the materials enough to understand the basic idea. A group of students learn about the legal system by acting out a court case. They serve as the lawyers and witnesses based on facts provided to them. After practicing for a couple of months, they compete against students from other schools before real lawyers and judges."

Janie looked skeptical. "I don't like talking in front of groups, and I've never thought about becoming a lawyer."

"It's not limited to people interested in a legal career. You write well and speaking in public is the next step. The first meeting is next Tuesday evening at seven o'clock. If you don't like what you hear, I won't ask you to come back."

"Are you going to be there?"

"Yes, I'm the faculty advisor. Dr. Lassiter is trying to find a lawyer who will help me."

"I'm not sure my mom can bring me to the meetings," Janie said hesitantly. "It depends on her work schedule."

"If you need a ride, let me know and I'll help," Kay offered. "Think about it over the weekend, and we'll talk on Monday."

After Janie left, Kay returned to the tests on her desk. On top was Dustin Rawlings's paper. The football player's perspective on American literature always made her smile. Picking up her red pen, she began. An hour and a half later she was almost to the bottom of her stack when there was a knock on the door. Dr. Lassiter stuck his head inside the room.

"I'm glad I caught you," the principal said. "I had lunch today with a young lawyer who has volunteered to help coach the mock trial team. His card is in your faculty mailbox. Give him a call in the next few days. He knows the first meeting is scheduled next Tuesday."

Kay put down her red pen and rubbed her eyes. "Yes, sir. I need to grade a few more papers, but I'll do it before I go home."

She worked her way steadily through the remainder of the test papers. The final entry was Janie Collins. The young woman wrote a very insightful and fresh commentary on the Wolfe excerpt. Kay wrote "A - 94" on her test.

There was a short, covered walkway from modular unit three to the main building where the teachers' lounge was located. In Kay's mailbox was a sheet of paper announcing a car wash for the Spanish club and a small, ivory-colored business card. It took her a couple of seconds to sort out the names. Humphrey, Balcomb & Jackson - 319 Lipscomb Avenue - Scott W. Ellis - Attorney at Law.

Scott Ellis. She held the card lightly between her fingers.

Scott was still sorting through teenage memories of Kay Laramie when he arrived back at the office. It might take a little effort, he thought, but it shouldn't be too hard to put aside ancient, romantic feelings, especially since the tall, blue-eyed girl with the quick laugh was now Mrs. Wilson, the married English teacher.

He spent the rest of the afternoon preparing for the deposition of an automobile accident reconstruction expert. The firm's client suffered a concussion in a collision with a dump truck and couldn't remember what happened. Scott was finishing up the lengthy memo when the phone buzzed.

"Kay Wilson on line 5."

Scott picked up the phone receiver and in what he considered his friendly, yet professional voice, said, "Hello, this is Scott Ellis."

"Hi, Scott. It's Kay Laramie Wilson from the high school. Remember me?"

The voice was instantly recognizable, just less girlish. Not at all grating like Mrs. Willston.

"Of course, I do," Scott replied. "Your married name didn't register when I talked to Dr. Lassiter, but he showed me your picture in the yearbook. I didn't know you'd moved back to Catawba."

"I've been here a year and a half. How about you?"

"The same. I came back after graduating from law school. When did you get married?"

"Five years ago. And you?"

"Still single. Do you have any kids?"

"About a hundred and ten every day at school but none of my own."

Scott paused. The conversation felt as stiff as a newspaper interview. They were both silent for a moment, and he decided to get down to business.

"I'm looking forward to working with the mock trial team," he said. "At first, I had some reservations about the time commitment, but I'm sure it can be a good program."

"I've been telling the students it will be fun," Kay replied. "But I'm also trying to recruit kids who will be serious about the competition."

That sounded good to Scott. He picked up the mock trial materials he'd put on the corner of his desk.

"I haven't had a chance to look over the packet of information Dr. Lassiter gave me. Have you gone through it?" he asked.

"Yes, but I have a lot of questions."

"Do we need to go over anything before the first meeting?"

"I'd like that. Tomorrow is Saturday. We could meet for breakfast."

Startled, Scott said, "Breakfast?"

"Yeah, someplace in the area would be fine with me."

Scott occasionally ate breakfast at a local restaurant not far from the courthouse. "How about the Eagle?" he suggested.

"Sure. Is 9:30 all right? I don't get to sleep in during the week."

"Okay. I'll look over the materials tonight and see you then."

"Good. We can catch up with one another and get organized."

Scott hung up the phone. It was Kay's voice all right, but a bit more assertive than when she was sixteen and couldn't decide which movie she wanted to see.

It was seven blocks from Scott's office to the one-story brick house where he lived. Built in the early 1950s, the compact dwelling with black shutters had a detached, single-car garage that was barely large enough for Scott's small SUV. He pushed the remote-control button and waited for the garage door to creak slowly open.

Scott bought the house from an older couple who spent the years after their children left home turning the small backyard into a secluded paradise. They built a five-foot-high brick wall around the entire area then carefully landscaped the enclosed plot of ground. It was a perfect refuge for Scott. He lifted the latch on a black, wrought-iron gate and pushed it open. Waiting excitedly on the other side was Nicky.

"Hey, big guy." Scott knelt down and rubbed the curly white fur that covered the dog's head and neck. Nicky, a two-year-old, twelve-pound Bichon Frise, rested his front paws on Scott's leg and closed his eyes in contentment.

It was only a few steps from the gate to the back door of the house. Scott set his briefcase on the kitchen floor and took a dog treat from a glass cookie jar on the counter. When he saw the treat, Nicky sat down and waited until Scott tossed the little bone-shaped biscuit in the air. The dog expertly caught it and scampered from the kitchen to his favorite spot on a narrow oriental rug in the foyer, where he proceeded to munch his reward with as much relish as his ancient, wolfish ancestors would have crunched a deer bone.

Scott turned on the oven and put a frozen pepperoni pizza on the kitchen counter. Ever since he was a little boy, Scott had fixed frozen pizzas. He'd graduated from the cardboardlike varieties of his childhood to the fancier versions in the deli section of the local supermarket. He would eat anything from anchovies to zucchini on a pizza, but basic pepperoni remained his favorite. By the time he'd changed into a T-shirt and jeans, the oven was ready, and he slid the pizza onto a metal rack he always kept positioned for best pizza-cooking results. He sliced pieces of pepperoni from a long stick he kept in the refrigerator and tossed the extra meat on top of the pizza before the cheese began to melt. Nicky came into the kitchen sniffing the air.

Scott shook his head. "None for you, my friend. Puppies don't need pepperoni."

Nicky ran to the back door, jumped through a dog door Scott had cut in the bottom panel, and, in a couple of seconds, jumped back inside.

"I'm coming," Scott said.

Scott took a bottle of beer from the refrigerator and followed Nicky into the backyard. The little dog quickly checked the area around the base of the trees for signs of the squirrels whose many years of peace and quiet had been shattered when Scott introduced his pet to the backyard environment. The enclosure was an ideal size for the little dog that reigned as the biggest, most fearsome creature in his protected world.

It was still warm in the late afternoon sun. In a few months, the leaves on the two maple trees close to the back wall would explode with red and orange, and the large heart-shaped foliage of an ancient redbud would begin turning a brownish purple. Scott sat on a park bench at the edge of a slate-covered patio and sipped his beer.

The previous owners had built a small fishpond on one side of the patio and stocked it with two large goldfish. Scott tried to introduce some smaller fish to the tiny pond, but his stocking experiment abruptly ended when a blue heron dropped out of the sky one cloudy day and ate the new arrivals as an afternoon snack. The two remaining fish, hoping for a handout, swam toward Scott.

Nicky disappeared beneath a bank of azalea bushes that bloomed in early spring like a great white island in a sea of green grass. Scott could hear the dog rustling through the leaves underneath the bushes. In a few seconds, he burst forth and raced around the patio area in a large circle. Scott watched Nicky's antics until it was time for the pizza to come out of the oven.

Scott ate at a shiny table in the dining room adjacent to the kitchen. The kitchen in Scott's house was built before large, live-in kitchens came into vogue, so there wasn't room to set up the table and chairs his grandmother had given him except in the formal dining room with its tall, narrow windows. The room wasn't designed with pizza and beer in mind, but nobody was around to report him to Martha Stewart.

Scott could easily finish off a medium-sized pizza by himself, and after the paltry lunch he'd eaten with Dr. Lassiter, he quickly devoured his food and drained the last drops of his beer. He read the local newspaper while he ate. Nicky lay passively on the wooden floor near his master's feet.

After supper Scott took his briefcase into the living room. The only fully carpeted area in the house contained two pieces of furniture: a big, gray recliner that Scott had selected after sitting in fifty different chairs, and a large-screen TV whose chief purpose was to display Atlanta Braves baseball from March to October and ACC basketball from November through March. Scott would be making payments on the TV for another twenty-two months. He turned on a baseball game and for the next several hours divided his attention between the game and the mock trial materials. Nicky jumped into the chair and lay down in the open space beside Scott's left hip and the armrest. Within a few seconds he was asleep.

The lawyers who prepared the materials had done a good job. The witness roles were humorous and flexible enough to allow for creativity, and the legal issues weren't too complex. When his eyes grew heavy, Scott escorted Nicky to the backyard before putting the little dog in a small cage in the laundry room. Scott enjoyed Nicky's companionship, but he didn't want a furry bed partner licking his ear in the middle of the night.

———

Lester Garrison had memorized the details of every tree that could be seen from the slit of window that gave his narrow room its only glimpse of the outside world. At night, the glare of a bright light positioned on a metal pole outside the window cut a sharp path across his face if he lay too close to the edge of his cot.

He tossed and turned on the narrow bed. The bare gray walls of his room seemed to close in on him if he stared at them, and with his eyes open, the passage of minutes seemed like hours. He had slept several hours earlier in the day to escape the boredom of confinement but now couldn't will himself to unconsciousness.

So he stayed awake in the silence and released his imagination. Some of the images that flashed through his mind were much more serious than the charges against him in the thin manila folder in the district attorney's office.

5

Happy families are all alike;
every unhappy family is unhappy in its own way.

ANNA KARENINA

Scott was out of bed at 7:30 A.M. After opening the door of Nicky's cage, he fixed a cup of strong coffee and poured it into a plastic travel mug. He'd taken a couple of sips by the time Nicky hopped through the dog door after a quick trip to the backyard. Scott put his cup on the kitchen counter and opened the drawer where he kept a retractable leash. At the sight of the green leash, Nicky jumped up and down with excitement until Scott attached the strap to his collar. He enjoyed walking as much as Nicky. For his eagle scout project when he was a teenager, Scott had designed and built a nature path adjacent to a local park.

Coffee in one hand and Nicky pulling on the other, Scott turned left down the sidewalk that ran along the quiet street. It was cool enough to feel like early fall, but the warning of a hot afternoon lurked in the bright sun that shone through the lower branches of the trees on the east side of the street. They passed several rows of modest houses that had also been built in the 1940s and 1950s.

Scott and Nicky were an odd combination. A muscular young man dressed in black sweatpants and Wake Forest T-shirt, and a little white dog who looked like he should be wearing a rhinestone collar and trotting beside a socialite in Central Park. But Scott's manhood wasn't threatened by his association with the animal he'd taken in when an elderly neighbor moved to Florida and couldn't take her new puppy with her to a retirement center. Scott came to the rescue, and the little dog was never at risk of homelessness. Besides, Nicky's presence could be a conversation starter. Scott had recently dated a woman whom he met when she stopped to pat Nicky's head.

Nicky loved to pretend that he was a fearsome beast. Sometimes when he saw a large dog, he would let a deep growl rumble in his throat and scratch the grass backward with his hind legs like a bull preparing to charge. It was all bluster and show, and Scott kept careful watch until they passed the house where a brown boxer lived. Nicky looked toward the house and growled, but the boxer didn't appear. Scott stood ready to snatch his furry friend up in his arms and keep him from harm. Nicky's grand illusions were safe so long as he stayed close to his master's side. Scott was the great protector.

As they drew closer to Lipscomb Avenue, the houses became older and larger. A few had been in the same family for generations. One of the finest structures, a two-story Victorian with a wraparound porch, had been turned into an accountant's office, and another with dark brown cedar siding had been taken over by a local insurance agency. Mr. Humphrey's home, a brick house in a Federal style, occupied a prominent corner lot.

They stopped when they reached the parking lot for the First Methodist Church, a long white building with narrow stained-glass windows and a sharp steeple. Most local attorneys, including Mr. Humphrey and his wife, were members of the Methodist church. The rest of the lawyers in town were evenly split between the large Baptist church that dominated a whole block beside the courthouse and a small Presbyterian church at the other end of Lipscomb Avenue.

Scott's family had attended the Baptist church, and when he was ten years old, he had walked down the aisle and been baptized. The moral teaching Scott received in Sunday school had been reinforced by his father's strict code of ethics and the influence of the boy scouts, but he hadn't attended church on a regular basis for years. Religion had helped shape his character, and once the mold was set, he didn't see the need to go back for a refresher course in the Ten Commandments. Healing for the deep wound to his heart wasn't in a church sanctuary. He'd talked to a military chaplain after Steve Robinson's death and found no balm for his soul.

After a loop through the empty church parking lot and around a basketball goal, Scott and Nicky headed home. By the time they walked up to the front door, Nicky was panting and ready for a drink of water. Scott watched the morning news until it was time to get ready for his breakfast meeting with Kay. Rubbing the stubble on his chin, he went into his bedroom.

When he was in a good mood, Scott sometimes sang in the shower. Nothing understandable, just loud sounds that he considered musical expressions. After his pleasant walk with Nicky, he tried out a few notes until his voice cracked. Putting on a denim shirt and jeans, he grabbed his paperwork and notes from the previous evening and walked the few blocks from his house to the restaurant. The Eagle was on Lipscomb Avenue not far from the law firm. He sat on a bench in front of a large plate-glass window decorated with a faded bald eagle and waited.

Scott didn't see any sign of Kay. Five, ten minutes passed. He fidgeted. Maybe Kay's jealous husband had told her not to have breakfast with an old boyfriend. Scott decided he should make sure she wasn't already inside. He opened the glass door and quickly scanned the large open room that was half-filled with the late Saturday morning crowd. He heard a car door close behind him and turned. It was Kay.

She was casually dressed in jeans, burgundy top, and white running shoes. Different, yet the same. A woman's figure, but with her hair the same color and length as the last image he remembered. He wondered if she'd ever worn it short during the past twelve years. He couldn't help staring.

"Sorry, I'm late," she said.

"That's okay," Scott said. "Have you eaten here since you moved back?"

"No, but I remember that my father liked this place."

As they wound their way to an empty table, a plump, older woman came out of the kitchen area. Bea Dempsey, the sixty-year-old owner of the Eagle, waved to Scott.

"Good morning, Scott!" she called out.

Bea came over to them. Scott introduced Kay.

"Bea, this is Kay Laramie."

"Wilson," Kay corrected him. "You may remember my father, Bob Laramie. He used to eat here all the time. He would order grits to go in a Styrofoam cup."

Bea smiled, revealing a shiny gold tooth on the upper right side of her mouth. "I can't say that I do. We've served a lot of grits to a bunch of folks over the past thirty years. If he comes to town for a visit, send him by, and I'll fix him up. Can I start you off with some coffee?"

Scott looked at Kay who nodded.

"Yes," he said. "And I'll have The Works."

"What's that?" Kay asked.

Scott counted on his fingers. "Three eggs scrambled, four pieces of crisp bacon, two sausage patties, two biscuits, hash browns with onions, grits, and, uh, what am I forgetting Bea?"

"We have nice cantaloupe this morning."

"And a piece of cantaloupe. The fruit changes with the seasons."

"That sounds a bit heavy," Kay said. "I'll have a piece of cantaloupe."

"No grits?" Bea asked.

Kay shook her head. "I didn't inherit that from my father. I've tried regular grits, cheese grits, and shrimp grits at a nice restaurant in Charleston. No matter how they're fixed, I've never found a grit I liked."

"Okay, I'll make sure you get a nice piece of cantaloupe."

Bea went to the kitchen with their order.

"Sorry about the mix-up on your name," Scott said. "I'll try not to make the same mistake with the students."

"That's okay. Mrs. Willston still calls me Laramie."

"I thought she was going to be the advisor for the mock trial team." "Why?"

Scott told her about his conversation with Dr. Lassiter. Kay laughed, and the sound resurfaced another memory from the past.

When he finished, Scott asked, "When did your family leave Catawba?"

"We were only here for two years. I went to Catawba High through my junior year, then we moved to California."

"Where?"

"La Jolla, near San Diego. My father still works for the local utility company."

"La Jolla? I went surfing there when I was in the army."

"You're kidding? Which beach?"

"I don't remember the name. It was at the base of some cliffs. The water was cold and the waves big."

One of the regular waitresses brought two coffees in heavy, white mugs and set the steaming cups in front of them. Scott took a sip of black coffee. Kay dropped in a spoonful of sugar and a packet of creamer.

"My husband and I met on the beach and enjoyed the waves when we lived in California. Since coming back east, we've visited the Outer Banks, but it's no comparison to the Pacific."

"Where does your husband work?" Scott asked.

"Jake is a swim coach and physiology teacher. His last job was at Davidson College."

Scott could imagine Kay's husband—tall and blond like her with a swimmer's broad shoulders.

"How long did you stay in the army?" Kay asked. "When we were in high school, you talked about a career in the military."

"Three years," Scott said, clenching his right fist. "I decided not to reenlist, and looking back, it was the right decision. Even though I got a late start to college and law school, I'm enjoying what I'm doing. One of the senior partners in the firm is a great trial lawyer, and I've already learned a lot from him."

"I never pictured you as a lawyer," Kay said. "You weren't the most talkative person in high school."

"We had long conversations on the phone," Scott protested.

"You held the receiver to your ear, but I think I did most of the talking."

Scott couldn't remember enough details to disagree. Their food arrived, and he plowed into the scrambled eggs. Conversation ceased. No one is expected to talk while chewing scrambled eggs. Kay began slicing off pieces of cantaloupe with a spoon.

"Good cantaloupe," she said.

"Bea buys from local farmers when she can," Scott said between bites. "You and your husband should eat lunch here sometime. The vegetables are second to none."

Kay didn't respond.

"Where is Jake this morning?" Scott asked as he added a dash of salt to his hash browns. "He could have joined us. I'd like to meet him."

"He's not in Catawba. He's living with his girlfriend in Virginia Beach."

Scott stopped his fork in midair. "Oh, I'm sorry."

"The past eleven months have been tough—"

"I wasn't trying to pry," Scott interrupted.

"Of course you weren't. But I'd rather get it out now if we're going to be working together with the students."

She continued, "We were living in Virginia Beach after we moved east to work at the same school. Everything was fine until he met an attractive woman teacher who was going through a divorce. I think she went after Jake more than he chased her, but however it started, they ended up together. When I found out, he told me it was a big mistake and that he wanted to save our marriage. I agreed to give him a second chance, and we decided to get away for a fresh start. I had happy memories of Catawba, and when we checked on jobs in the area, Jake received an offer from the athletic department at Davidson. He'd never coached or taught at the collegiate level before, so it was a great opportunity for him. Then a position opened up for me here at the high school. It looked like we were going in the right direction." She paused. "He stayed seven months."

Scott knew there were always two sides to a marital breakup, but it was hard for him to imagine that much of the blame for this one lay at Kay's door.

Kay sighed. "I've bounced back and forth between wishing things could work out to wanting it to be over. It's been an emotional roller coaster."

"Do you have a lawyer?"

"Yes. Nate Grange. Do you know him?"

"Not really."

Scott had met Grange once or twice. The divorce lawyer was inexpensive and affordable for someone on a teacher's salary but didn't have the best reputation for keeping track of details or taking care of clients.

"He never returns my phone calls until a couple of days later," Kay added.

Scott didn't handle divorce cases, but he suddenly had an idea. "There is a female partner in our firm who specializes in domestic law," he said. "She's one of the best in the area. If I talk to her, she might help you at a reduced rate."

Kay responded to his gesture with an appreciative smile. "Thanks, but I don't think there is much left to do on the legal side of things. Jake filed the papers right after he left, but because the North Carolina law makes him wait a full year before he can get a divorce, there hasn't been a final hearing. We don't have a lot of property, and except for the furniture in the apartment and my car, there isn't anything I want."

"Okay," Scott said. "But let me know if I can help or if you need to talk to someone. I can still hold a receiver to my ear."

Scott's offer stopped Kay in her tracks. Not sure how to respond, she looked at him for a moment before continuing. "I don't want to spend all of our time on my troubles. I have some questions about the mock trial program."

"Sure. I read the materials last night."

Thirty minutes later they parted company. Kay had a much clearer picture of the mock trial process. Scott's insight into how he should relate to the team's faculty advisor was murkier.

Franklin Jesup Jr., one of the students Kay had recruited for the mock trial program, stumbled out of bed and shuffled downstairs to the kitchen for a late-morning snack. He rarely slept more than a few hours at a time. Nightmares populated by grotesque beings waged war in his mind between midnight and 6 A.M. When he was awake and on-line, he controlled the actions of the surreal cyberspace warriors to the most minute detail. At night, they had the upper hand and made sleep an enemy rather than a friend. Morning light lessened the onslaught.

Frank's father wasn't at home. He had a standing golf date every third Saturday with two of the sales reps who worked for him. When he was in middle school, Frank had unsuccessfully begged his father to let him tag along and ride in the golf cart. Now, he had no interest in watching someone hit a white ball across the grass with a metal stick.

Just turned eighteen, dark-haired Frank had his father's strong features and his mother's slightly dreamy brown eyes. His good looks, the unlimited supply of twenty-dollar bills in his wallet, and the silver sports car that he drove to school could have translated into popularity, but Frank didn't let anyone, male or female, get too close.

"Frank!" he heard his mother call out from upstairs.

He didn't respond.

"Frank!" she called louder. "Are you in the kitchen?"

"Yeah!" he responded. "I'm busy!"

"Jodie's leotard is on the table in the atrium. Bring it upstairs. We're late for ballet practice."

The huge white cockatoo that his mother kept on an open-air perch in the atrium connected to the kitchen squawked when it saw Frank. The bird preened its feathers and moved back and forth along its perch. Frank picked up the leotard and held it up to the bird's beak. It leaned forward and pulled at the elastic fabric until a small hole opened.

Satisfied, Frank walked upstairs with a bowl of cereal in one hand and the leotard in the other. His mother came out of the huge walk-in closet in his sister's bedroom with a frustrated look on her face. In her left hand was a pink ballet slipper. He could hear the sounds of his eight-year-old sister in the adjacent bathroom.

"Have you seen Jodie's other ballet slipper?"

"I think the bird ate it," he said.

"Here, give me that." His mother snatched the leotard from his hand. "We'll be back after lunch."

Returning to his bedroom, Frank turned on his computer. The machine was his only steady companion. He slipped on a pair of head-phones connected to a powerful music system in the corner of the room. Frank's taste went beyond the list of groups familiar to his classmates. Many of the CDs in his storage case came from an underground move-ment that pushed the message and the music beyond any recognizable category. Some of the screams on the tracks were real.

The sounds in his ears energized him as did the battle with the face-less combatants who joined him in an invisible world where the ability to weave a web of skillfully orchestrated spells, incantations, and deceptions was considered as pure an art form as a meticulously choreographed demonstration of oriental martial arts. Currently, only Frank and four other members of the group were free. Everyone else was held in chains of darkness until the game was complete.

6

The web of our life is of a mingled yarn, good and ill together.
ALL'S WELL THAT ENDS WELL, ACT 4, SCENE 3

Scott stopped by Dixon's Body Shop late Saturday afternoon. On weekends he exercised on the arm bike, a device that allowed him to pump his arms rapidly in circles and generate enough physical activity to elevate his heart rate for aerobic benefit. Perry came out of his office and walked over to the machine as Scott finished a hard forty-five minutes.

"You're the Lance Armstrong of the arm bike," Perry said.

Still breathing hard, Scott gasped, "I don't know about that, but I feel like I've climbed a mountain in the Alps." He wiped his face with a towel. "Guess who I had breakfast with this morning at the Eagle?"

Perry sat down on a bench beside him. "Give me a clue. Male or female?"

"Female."

"That cuts it down considerably. There aren't that many single females in Blanchard County. Does she live in Catawba?"

"Yes, but she's married."

Perry gave Scott a sober look. "Don't be going down that road."

Scott laughed. "I'll be careful. I'm not interested in a load of buckshot. She's the teacher at the school who is going to be the sponsor of the mock trial team I told you about. Her last name begins with *W.*"

"Mrs. Willston!" Perry exploded. "I can't believe it! You had breakfast with her?"

"I ordered a full meal, but she only wanted a piece of cantaloupe. You know, it's easier for her to eat something soft. Her teeth are not in good shape."

Perry's jaw dropped. "I can't believe this is happening to you."

"It's going to be a character-building experience, but I'm sure I can handle it."

"What did she look like?"

"Better than ever. She's aged well."

"And her voice?"

"Just like I remembered, especially her laugh."

"Mrs. Willston never laughed," Perry said.

"This teacher does."

"Huh?"

"It wasn't Mrs. Willston," Scott said. "I had breakfast with Kay Wilson. You'd probably remember her as Kay Laramie."

"Kay Laramie? Didn't you date her when we were seniors?"

"Yes. Now she's teaching English at the high school."

"Did she marry someone from around here?"

"No. A guy she met in California. But they've been separated for months, and her husband has filed for divorce. He's living in Virginia Beach with his girlfriend."

"What's she like now?" Perry asked. "All I remember is a skinny blond who made good grades."

"Like I said, she's aged well."

"Which means?"

"She looks great, but she's had a rough time over the past year. I didn't cross-examine her about the details."

Scott selected a pair of dumbbells from a rack. Lying on a bench he began working on his triceps.

"How did you feel being with her?" Perry asked.

Scott paused after completing the next repetition. "I don't know. That's a tougher question than the one I asked you."

———

The first thing Monday morning, Scott stopped by Mr. Humphrey's office. The older lawyer looked up.

"Come in. Did you talk to Dr. Lassiter at the high school?"

"Yes, sir. We ate lunch together, and I've also met with the faculty advisor. We have our first meeting with the students tomorrow night."

Scott didn't summarize his past relationship with Kay Laramie Wilson. Mr. Humphrey was too busy to listen to a story about Scott's high-school dating history.

"You volunteered in the nick of time," the senior partner said. "It would have been a shame not to have a lawyer helping from the beginning."

Mr. Humphrey picked up a phone message and prepared to dial a number. Scott didn't move.

"I didn't come in to talk about the mock trial program," he said. "I need to ask you about something else."

The older lawyer put down the slip of paper. "What is it? I've got a full plate of phone duty left over from last week."

Scott quickly outlined the Garrison situation and concluded by saying, "I can file a motion to keep it in juvenile court, but if the judge lets the D.A. prosecute Lester as an adult, my time will eat up the $2,500 fee long before it goes to trial."

"Have you talked to the boy's father?"

"Not yet. He's a truckdriver, and it may take a couple of days to track him down. Even then, I'm not sure he can pay any more money."

Leland Humphrey ran his thumb down the inside of his right suspender. "What do you want to do?"

Scott didn't hesitate. "I want to stay in the case."

Mr. Humphrey rocked back and forth in his chair a couple of times then sat up straight. "All right. If the boy's father won't pay any more money, the experience will be compensation enough. Keep track of your time and turn it in to me. I'll explain it to the other partners."

"And my lack of experience?"

"You'll learn quickly, but if it becomes a felony charge in superior court, I'll help you out."

———

During the initial interview at the youth detention center, Lester had resolutely maintained his innocence; however, Scott had no illusions about the truthfulness of his client. In law school he'd heard that few lawyers handled criminal cases, fewer still did a good job, and even fewer enjoyed it. There was far more grind than glamour. But for Scott the

Garrison case had the bloom of a fresh opportunity, and no matter what he thought about Harold and Lester Garrison personally, his client deserved due process of law.

In the law-firm library Scott found a thick treatise on criminal law in North Carolina. He buzzed the receptionist and told her to hold his calls. After several hours of research, he closed the volume with a much clearer picture of the possibilities facing his client. Lester was definitely on the bubble. He was young enough to enjoy the limited punishment provisions available in juvenile court but old enough that the judge had the discretion to allow him to be prosecuted as an adult. A delinquency conviction in juvenile court would probably mean a year in a youth detention center. A felony conviction in superior court could result in up to ten years of jail time, but such a stiff sentence was unlikely for a sixteen-year-old boy. Scott didn't need a lawbook to tell him that Lester's preference for racial segregation was a prescription for trouble no matter where he went.

Upstairs in his office Scott found Thelma Garrison's phone number. The old woman answered on the fifth ring.

After introducing himself, Scott said, "I need to talk with Lester's father. How can I contact him?"

"He's somewheres between here and Michigan. He don't never phone here to check on me or the boy. I don't know what he thinks I can do . . ." The old woman's voice trailed off, and Scott couldn't understand what she said.

He waited a second before continuing. "Something has come up on Lester's case, and it's important that I talk to his father as soon as possible."

"I don't see how if he don't call."

"But if you hear from him, please tell him to call me."

"I doubt I will. What's your name again?"

"Scott Ellis."

"I'll try to remember. Is Lester all right? I've been a-worryin' about him. He's been fretful recently, always banging around in that shed of his out back of the house."

"Uh, yes, ma'am. He's fine." Scott decided it would be better not to tell her about the fight at the detention center. "I'm working hard on his case."

"Help him if you can. God knows I can't do anything. Bye."

The phone clicked off.

Scott couldn't count on Thelma. He dialed the phone number for the trucking company where Harold Garrison worked and spoke to a dispatcher. The man promised to leave a message for Harold at his next scheduled stop.

As the last act of the day for his new client, Scott called the district attorney's office. It was after 5 P.M., and he doubted any government employees were still at work, but it was worth a try. To his surprise, a receptionist answered the phone.

"I'll see who is handling the file," the woman said. After a moment, she added, "That would be Lynn Davenport, one of the assistant district attorneys."

"Is she available?"

"I'll check."

He stayed on hold until a woman with an accent that was more New York than North Carolina answered the phone. "Lynn Davenport, here."

"Ms. Davenport, this is Scott Ellis with Humphrey, Balcomb and Jackson. I'm representing a juvenile named Lester Garrison. The receptionist said you were handling the case."

"Yes."

"Have you had a chance to look over his file?"

"Yes."

Scott paused. It didn't appear that Ms. Davenport was going to engage in friendly banter with him about Lester's tattoos.

"I'd like you to consider handling the case as a juvenile court matter."

"No."

"But he's only sixteen, and no one was injured."

"No." The lawyer's clipped accent made her brief answer seem even more abrupt.

"What are your intentions?"

"To prosecute the defendant as an adult for assault with a deadly weapon with intent to inflict serious injury and criminal destruction of property."

Scott's face flushed. "I understand that, but I'd hoped we could cooperate."

"Not unless your client pleads guilty to a felony charge and agrees to a significant prison sentence."

"To a felony with prison time? You're kidding."

"No, Mr. Ellis. I'm very serious. If you don't have any more questions, I have things to do before I leave the office."

Scott couldn't think of anything to say that wouldn't sound petty. "No. I'll be filing my notice of representation in the morning."

"Arraignment will be on Thursday morning at nine o'clock in the old courtroom."

———

Supper was being served when Deputy Hicks pushed open the heavy metal door and stepped aside to let Scott enter. Lester sat alone at a round table. His swollen right eye had turned slightly purple, and the cut on his right temple was healing with the rapidity reserved for young people. Scott sat down beside him.

"Assigned seating?" he asked.

"Yeah. I can't sit with anyone else. In class I'm in the front row under the teacher's nose."

"No more trouble?"

"I'm keeping to myself like you told me to do."

"Good."

"Did you come to get me out? I want to go home."

The young man's mood was subdued. He looked down at his plate of barely eaten food.

"No, I didn't come to get you out. The whole status of your case has changed."

"What do you mean?"

Scott summarized the district attorney's decision to prosecute Lester as an adult. When he finished, Lester put his head in his hands. Scott waited. He couldn't tell if Lester was crying or not, but several other boys looked in their direction, poked one another, and laughed. Scott thought about reaching over to put a hand on Lester's shoulder but hesitated. There had not yet been an invitation to that type of personal touch.

47

Lester raised his head and blew his nose on a paper napkin. "I'd rather be dead than locked up. I'd never make it in a prison where I had to share space with blacks."

Scott recoiled from the sympathy that had welled up inside him seconds before. Instead of reaching over to place a comforting hand on Lester's shoulder, he suddenly had a strong urge to knock him out of his chair.

"Lester, look at me," he commanded.

The young man glanced up through watery eyes.

Scott spoke slowly. "Before I became a lawyer, I served in the U.S. Army. My best friend was a black man from Syracuse, New York, named Steve Robinson. We were as close as brothers. We met in basic training and served together in the same unit for almost three years."

Lester's bleary-eyed look became a dull glare. Scott wasn't going to be stopped by a hostile look from a sixteen-year-old.

"I visited with my friend's family when I was on leave. I slept in their house, ate their food, held his baby girl, and kissed his wife on the cheek when I left. Later, when we were in a very dangerous situation overseas, Steve saved my life. Get one thing straight: I don't agree with you about blacks, browns, yellows, or any combination of colors you can imagine."

Lester grunted. "I can't talk like you, but I've got my reasons."

"Maybe you do, but unless they have something to do with your case, I'm not interested in hearing about them. Is that clear?"

Lester didn't reply.

Scott had intended on discussing pretrial strategy, but insuring due process for Lester Garrison would have to wait for another day.

"I'll be back later," he said and left Lester with his hate and a cold piece of corn bread.

7

Know thyself.
PLUTARCH

The following morning there was a message in Scott's voice mail from Harold Garrison. He immediately dialed the number. It was a freight depot in Michigan.

"Yeah, he's still here. He's in the drivers' lounge waiting for his trailer to be loaded."

Harold answered the phone. "What's happened? Have you taken care of everything?"

"Not exactly."

Scott outlined the status of the case.

Harold swore. "Are you tellin' me they're gonna send a sixteen-year-old kid to prison?"

"Probably not immediately. He'd be sent to a long-term youth detention center until he reached eighteen, then transferred to a facility for younger offenders; however, my focus is not where he might go to jail but defending him from the charges. This is a much bigger problem than a juvenile court proceeding, and the initial fee will not cover the cost of his defense."

"You want more money?"

"Yes."

"I gave you $2,500 a few days ago, and now you want more?"

"That's the way it works in criminal cases. The entire fee is paid up front."

"How much more are you going to charge?"

Scott kept his voice steady. "Another $7,500."

Harold swore again. "What! I don't have that kind of money! You don't even want to know where the $2,500 I paid you came from."

Scott had not considered that possibility.

Harold continued, "How many cases have you won anyway? I'm not paying you to take target practice on my son."

"I'll be prepared," he answered. "I've already met twice with Lester, and I'll be filing several motions with the court before arraignment on Thursday."

Harold grunted. "You'd better get this case moving. I'm tired of you backin' up."

For a moment, Scott had second thoughts about continuing to handle the case. It would be easier to withdraw, refund the fee, and try to forget Lester and Harold Garrison. But Scott wasn't a quitter. Ever since he was a little boy, he'd always tried to finish what he started.

"Okay," he said confidently. "When you come home, call me."

"That won't be anytime soon. I'm on my way to Oregon, and next time we talk, I want some good news. Until that happens, don't ask me for more money."

———

Scott had set aside part of the afternoon to prepare the motions he wanted to file before Lester's arraignment on Thursday. However, the criminal-law books in the firm law library didn't have up-to-date forms, and what he'd learned in law school prepared him more to argue a case before the United States Supreme Court than represent a sixteen-year-old boy in Blanchard County Superior Court.

He took a short walk to the courthouse and copied the standard motions filed by a local lawyer with the best reputation as a criminal defense attorney. Returning to the office, he modified the other lawyer's forms, then drafted a motion asking the judge to send Lester's case back to juvenile court. Finally, he prepared a request that the judge set bond so Lester could be released pending disposition of the charges against him. Scott wasn't sure his client could keep his rage bottled up indefinitely at the youth detention center, and a new set of charges for assault and battery would only make resolution of the entire situation more difficult.

Tonight was the first meeting of the mock trial team. Scott went home to check on Nicky, then drove to the high school. The first meeting would be important. It would set the tone for everything that followed.

Several cars were lined up alongside one of the modular units behind the gym. Scott parked beside a silver sports car. A young man was sitting in the vehicle talking on a cell phone. When he entered the trailer, everyone glanced in Scott's direction. Kay was standing beside her desk talking to a group of four girls.

"Good evening, Mrs. Wilson," Scott said.

Kay adopted his formal tone. "Thank you for coming, Mr. Ellis. We'll start in a few minutes."

Kay introduced the girls to Scott. He caught a whiff of perfume but couldn't tell if it was coming from the teacher or one of the teenagers. He doubted Kay dumped massive amounts of perfume on her neck before leaving home to spend six hours teaching English grammar to high-school students in a trailer. The girls all looked young to Scott, probably ninth or tenth graders.

"What year are you?" he asked.

"We're juniors," Janie answered.

Kay glanced around the room. "I think everyone is here. Take a seat in one of the desks toward the front of the classroom."

While the students found seats, Kay continued, "I have nametags. Most of you know each other, but we need to make it as easy as possible for Mr. Ellis, our volunteer attorney."

She handed a white sticker to a tall, broad-shouldered young man with startling blue eyes. "Print legibly, Dustin."

Kay nodded to Scott. It was his cue to begin.

"Each of you is going to come to the front of the class and introduce yourself as if you were beginning a court case."

He took a couple of steps to the wooden stand beside Kay's desk and made sure his voice carried clearly to the back wall of the trailer. "May it please the court, my name is Scott Ellis, counsel for the plaintiff."

One by one they came to the front. A few giggles greeted the first two or three speakers, but the novelty quickly wore off. Scott made them repeat the sentence slowly and distinctly until he was satisfied with the inflection and pacing of their delivery. One student adopted an exaggerated Southern drawl.

Scott read Dustin's nametag. "Colonel Rawlings," he said, "that sounded a bit fake. Do you intend to maintain that accent until the end of the competition?"

"He's a phony, all right," Frank Jesup called out.

Dustin ignored Frank. "No, sir, I was kidding. Why did you call me colonel?"

Scott saw an opportunity to make a point. "In the nineteenth century, colonel was an honorary title granted to prominent lawyers. They weren't military colonels; it was a term of respect for the position they held and gave them a new identity. That's what I want you to imagine when you introduce yourself to the judges."

"That I'm a colonel?" the young man asked.

"No, that you're no longer Dustin Rawlings, high-school student. You're Dustin Rawlings, advocate for your client and member of the Catawba Mock Trial Team."

"Yes, colonel."

Scott smiled. "Do you play on a school sports team?"

"Yes, I came from football practice to this meeting. After I took a shower, of course." Dustin raised his arms over his head and stuck his nose in his shirt.

"Good. For those who don't play football, tell us what happens on Friday night in the locker room before a game."

"Huh?"

Scott continued, "It's game day. You're going to play a team that beat you by twenty points the previous year then talked bad about you all over the area. When you get to school on Friday, there are paper banners in the hallways and a big pep rally during sixth period. Everyone on the team is wearing their jersey and sits in chairs on the gym floor while the students in the stands scream and stomp their feet. Now, it's a few minutes before the kickoff, and the only people in the locker room are the players and coaches. What do you do?"

"We get ready."

"How do you get ready?"

"We put on our uniforms and listen to a pep talk from Coach Butler."

"That's not all. Put yourself in the situation and give us more details."

Dustin thought a moment. "We become football players. We tape our ankles, strap on our pads, and gather together in a circle around the coach. Everybody takes a knee and puts his hand on his helmet."

"That's it. What's going through your head at that moment? Are you thinking about what you're going to do after the game? Where you're going to eat? Who you're going to run into?"

"No. It gets quiet. Everybody puts on his game face. You know, we all get that look. We're different."

"A different identity?"

Dustin nodded. From the look in his blue eyes it was clear he was in a circle of gridiron warriors in the locker room under the home stands of the football stadium.

"What do you think about during those times?" Scott asked quietly.

"Hitting somebody. Making a play. Helping the team. Winning."

"It's not about you as an individual player, is it?"

Dustin shook his head. "No, it's all team."

Scott paused. The room was silent. "Before we're finished, all of you are going to get that look. Male and female. No matter the role you play. You're all going to be focused. You're all going to take on a new identity. You're going to become a team."

Scott turned to Kay and broke the spell. "Please distribute the materials, so we can give them an overview."

An hour later, Scott and Kay finished going over the preliminary information. Each teenager had a packet of papers similar to the one Scott had received from Dr. Lassiter.

"That's enough for tonight," Kay said. "The next meeting will be at the same time on Thursday. Read the fact summaries for all the witnesses. If there is a particular witness role that interests you, let me know as soon as possible. If you want to be a lawyer, you need to begin studying the rules of evidence on pages eight through sixteen. Mr. Ellis will explain that part of the materials at a later meeting."

While most of the students filed out of the trailer, Kay turned to Scott. "Good speech. I don't know whether to call you 'colonel' or 'coach.'"

"Did it make you want to put on a helmet and hit somebody?" Scott asked.

"No, but I may tape my ankles before I come in to teach in the morning."

Dustin came up to them.

"You were right about what happens in the locker room before a big game," he said. "Did you play football in high school?"

"Three years as a linebacker here at Catawba," Scott answered. "What's your position?"

"Wide receiver. I'll ask my father if he remembers you. He played linebacker, too."

"I'm not that old," Scott responded. "You could be my little brother."

"That's not what I meant. My dad has been coming to the games for years and knows tons of trivia about Catawba football."

Scott smiled. "All the facts about my football career would qualify as trivia."

"We have a game Friday night. You ought to come."

"I might do that," Scott answered.

Dustin left, and Kay gathered the papers strewn across the top of her desk.

"What did you think of the young faces in the room tonight?"

"It was a good first meeting. I only see one problem."

"What?"

"It's going to be hard to decide which students should play the most important roles. Most of them seemed bright and able to communicate."

"Did any of them remind you of yourself at this age?" Kay asked.

Scott scratched his head. "Maybe Dustin, except that he's more extroverted than I was in high school."

"That's true. When we first met, I doubted whether you'd ever put three sentences together in a row."

Scott didn't disagree.

Kay continued, "Also, Dustin may pretend that he's a dumb jock when it suits him, but inside he's a smart young man."

"Like me?" Scott asked.

"Know thyself."

"A philosophical answer. What about you? Are any of the girls similar to you?"

"I'm not sure. Do you have one in mind?"

The names and faces were a blur to Scott. "No, I haven't been around them enough to appreciate the nuances. Women are more complex than men."

Kay smiled. "You're more advanced than Dustin. An eighteen-year-old male would never have said that."

Kay stayed behind after Scott left. It was dark outside, but she wasn't in a hurry to go back to her apartment. Loneliness before marriage is bad; loneliness after marriage is worse. Her only faithful companion was her pen and a piece of paper.

Writing was Kay's lifeline—connecting her heart to the day-to-day world. Since she was a little girl, she'd filled notebooks with thoughts and moods that chronicled her inner journey. She especially loved it when the words took on a life of their own and created a synergy in combination they couldn't express in isolation. She wrote by hand. Sometimes random, sometimes structured. Always seeking to find the key that released a piece of herself through her literary voice, the unique means of expression that set her apart from everyone else on earth.

If writing had color, Kay's favorites were pale blues and rich greens. Recently, she'd been using more grays and browns. But no matter the color, when after the passage of time she read her words and they enabled her to revisit the emotion or feeling she'd described at the time of creation, she was satisfied.

Since seeing Scott's name on his business card, Kay had also browsed through the archives of her high-school memories. She could recall many details about the few months they dated, but her copy of the poem she gave him before he left for the army was gone. It hadn't survived multiple moves back and forth across the country, and all that remained were snippets in her mind. However, she'd never forgotten the desire in her heart when she wrote it. It was an expression of vulnerability and tenderness that unveiled the heart of a sixteen-year-old girl who wondered if there was something more in their future than a senior prom in their past. It was one of the first birth pangs of true creativity within her soul because in revealing her feelings to Scott, she drew water from a deeper well. All she received in response was silence. It had hurt deeply for a few months. But with the resilience of adolescence she'd gone on, and Scott Ellis became a distant memory with no reason to return.

After Jake left, her thoughts didn't revisit a high-school romance with Scott Ellis. He remained buried under several layers of relationships. Kay wanted Jake, not as he was, but as he had been when they fell in love, and a glimmer of hope still burned in her heart that her marriage could be restored. Seeing Scott didn't change the focus of her heart.

Kay took a notebook from a side drawer of her desk. She kept paper close at hand so she could record her thoughts before they escaped like fidgety students at the end of class. Opening to a clean page, she closed her eyes and turned back the clock to a beautiful beach on the California coast. Details of the scene floated to the surface; the sounds of the waves crashing against the rocks returned. Kay saw herself. She saw Jake. She began to write.

8

The humblest citizen of all the land, when clad in the armor of
a righteous cause, is stronger than all the hosts of Error.
WILLIAM JENNINGS BRYAN

Thursday arrived with a crisp snap of fall in the morning air. Up early, Scott pulled on a sweatshirt and walked around in the backyard drinking a cup of coffee while Nicky ran in circles on the wet grass. The sun was casting its first clear rays on the edge of the fishpond when he went inside and dressed for work.

He arrived at the office before anyone else and checked for the third time all the papers he would file in Lester's case. The clerk's office would open at 8:30 A.M., and he wanted to have his motions filed and stamped, so he could hand them to assistant D.A. Davenport as soon as she entered the courtroom. He carefully put everything in his briefcase and walked to the courthouse.

The front of the white-brick courthouse was crowned by a three-story clock tower that had solemnly struck the hour for over a hundred years. Color photographs of the Blanchard County Courthouse had appeared in several calendars featuring nineteenth-century architecture in North Carolina, and visitors to Catawba often mistook the historic building for a church and the clock tower for a steeple. Three massive oak trees grew on the property. In years past, they had provided welcome shade before air conditioning made the South a tolerable place to live in all seasons.

The old courthouse was still used, but in the 1980s the county built a modern, one-story annex that spread out behind the original structure like a bridal train. The clerk's office was in the annex. After filing his papers, Scott passed through a short hallway that led to the back entrance to the original courthouse. Stepping from the new building into the old courthouse was like stepping back in time with its polished wooden floors, high ceilings, broad hallways, and narrow doors with transoms at the top. There were two courtrooms. The main courtroom was on the ground floor and a smaller courtroom was on the second floor. Only the senior superior court judge had an office in the original building. The other judge was headquartered in the courthouse annex.

The first time Scott entered the main courtroom, he thought about the movie adaptation of *Inherit the Wind*, the story of the gargantuan legal battle between Clarence Darrow and William Jennings Bryan in the Scopes evolution trial of 1925. Eloquent speeches and passionate appeals deserve a courtroom with dignity, and the white plaster walls and elaborate columns behind the judge's bench had heard much worth remembering. Scott wished he could put his ear next to one of the columns and command it to replay a sampling of the oratory from days when lawyers were warriors instead of technicians and trials more like mortal combat than computer programs.

He walked down the middle aisle and through a swinging opening in the bar, a waist-high wooden railing of finely crafted walnut spindles. A handful of people were scattered about the room—defendants out on bond, family and friends of people who were in jail, and a few curious spectators. A clerk from the district attorney's office placed a rack of files on the table used by the prosecutors when trying cases. Scott knew that somewhere in the rack was a thin folder labeled *"State v. Garrison."*

At 8:55 A.M. a short young woman with close-cut black hair, dark eyes, and wearing a navy business suit entered the courtroom from a door used by court personnel and went to the prosecution table. Scott went over to her.

"Are you Lynn Davenport?"

Somehow, the diminutive prosecutor managed to look down her nose at him when she answered, "Yes."

"I'm Scott Ellis. I called you about the Lester Garrison case."

"And?"

Scott abandoned any thought of morning pleasantries and put copies of the motions he'd filed on the prosecution table. "Here are motions I filed this morning in the case."

"Anything else? I have a full calendar this morning."

"No." Scott returned to his seat and watched Ms. Davenport flip through the papers in less than ten seconds before dropping them on the table.

When the big clock in the tower began to strike the hour, the clerk of court came into the courtroom and called out, "All rise! The Superior Court of Blanchard County is now in session, the Honorable Wayman Teasley presiding."

Judge Teasley was a former district attorney elected to the bench ten years before. A tall, thin, balding man, Judge Teasley looked scarecrow-like in his judicial robes. He wore black half-frame glasses that he twirled in the air when a lawyer or witness began to get on his nerves. Veteran attorneys knew that if Judge Teasley's glasses started spinning it was time to get things moving.

"Where are the prisoners?" the judge asked a deputy standing next to the jury box.

"They've not arrived from the jail, your honor. There is also a juvenile coming from the detention center."

The judge took off his glasses and gave them a spin. "Ms. Davenport. Begin with the noncustodial matters."

"Yes, sir. Call *State v. Rogers* . . ."

It was a catchall day. The first two defendants didn't have lawyers, and the judge sent them out the door to the public defender's office for an appointment. Another entered a guilty plea and went to the side to talk with a probation officer. The men from the jail arrived in handcuffs and leg irons. At the end of the line was Lester Garrison. He wasn't wearing any handcuffs and looked pale and small sitting next to an enormous male prisoner with a long brown ponytail and full beard.

"*State v. Garrison,*" Lynn Davenport called out. Scott got to his feet and motioned for Lester to come forward. The D.A. opened her folder. "The accused is charged with assault with a deadly weapon with intent to inflict serious injury, assault by pointing a gun, and criminal damage to property."

The judge peered over his glasses at Scott and Lester.

Scott stepped forward. "Scott Ellis with Humphrey, Balcomb and Jackson representing the defendant. I've filed—"

"How old is your client?" the judge interrupted.

"Sixteen, your honor. One of the motions I've filed is a request that the case be sent back to juvenile court."

The judge took off his glasses but kept them still for the moment. "Ms. Davenport, give me the file."

The judge repositioned his glasses and quickly looked through the papers. He closed the file and handed it back to the D.A.

"Why shouldn't an alleged incident like this involving a sixteen-year-old be handled in juvenile court?"

"Your honor, there is more to this case than the charges outlined in the juvenile court petition and accusation filed by our office. We intend to file additional charges of criminal conspiracy to commit murder."

Scott took a step forward. "Your honor, we've not been notified—"

"Hold on, counsel, I'm not going to spend all morning on this case. Ms. Davenport, I'm setting a hearing on Mr. Ellis's motion to remand this case to juvenile court at ten o'clock in the morning. You'd better show me more than the information in this file if you want to prosecute this young man as an adult. I will postpone arraignment until that time."

Lester followed Scott to a small bench against the wall near the other prisoners. The young man was obviously agitated. "Why didn't you ask him to let me out?"

Scott's jaw dropped. "Didn't you hear what the D.A. said? They're going to charge you with conspiracy to commit murder!"

"I didn't try to kill anyone, and they can't prove anything serious against me." Lester looked suspiciously at Scott and jerked his head toward Lynn Davenport. "Someone told that D.A. about my beliefs."

Scott didn't connect the suspicion in Lester's eyes to himself. "Anything is possible."

"Did you talk to her?" Lester asked through clenched teeth.

"Not about that. Remember, everything you tell me is confidential. All I did was try to convince her to send the case back to juvenile court."

"She's prejudiced," Lester said.

If it hadn't been a serious situation, Scott would have burst out laughing. He glanced quickly at Lester to see if the young man with the swastika tattooed on his arm realized the utter hypocrisy of his statement.

"We'll find out more tomorrow. In the meantime, keep your mouth closed and your hands by your side."

When he returned to the office, Scott stopped by Mr. Humphrey's office and told him the latest developments.

"And that's where we are at this moment. Judge Teasley scheduled the hearing on my motion to remand the case to the juvenile court for ten o'clock in the morning."

The older lawyer finished writing a few notes on a legal pad. "Do you know any facts supporting the conspiracy to commit murder charge?"

Scott shook his head. "No, but the kid is a cauldron of rage and bigotry. He's capable of anything."

"You can probably assume the D.A. is coming from a different angle. She has something unrelated to what you already know."

Scott grunted. "She's not volunteering any information."

"What was the judge's attitude?"

"I'm not sure what he was thinking. All I could tell was that he wanted to move through his calendar."

Mr. Humphrey leaned back in his chair. "When Wayman Teasley was the D.A. he was tough but fair. He would work out a deal on a case if it didn't need to be vigorously prosecuted, but when he thought a defendant needed to go to prison, the accused could forget a plea bargain unless he agreed to substantial jail time. You know that thing he does with his glasses?"

"Yes."

"They used to say each twirl equaled five years in the penitentiary."

Mr. Humphrey looked over at the bookcase beside his desk. "Are you up to date on criminal procedure, including the discovery rules?"

"I'm getting there, but the practical aspects of the case have me worried. I don't want to overlook something basic because of my inexperience."

"Hmm." The older lawyer reached for the daily calendar he kept in a leather binder on his desk and turned the page to the following day. "I was planning on taking a day off tomorrow to go fishing on Lake Norman, but the fish never bite when I play hooky from work. If you want, I'll help you out. You've carried my briefcase during a few trials. Now, it's time for me to carry yours. Copy the file, and I'll review it before court in the morning."

Scott walked upstairs to his office. Leland Humphrey was a wise mentor. He'd let Scott enter dangerous and unknown territory, then reached out and offered a helping hand. At 11 A.M. Scott's stomach growled. He'd skipped breakfast in order to get to the office earlier. His stomach rumbled again, and his phone buzzed.

"Kay Wilson on line six."

Scott picked up the receiver. "How are you?"

"Okay. I'm calling between classes. Do you have any time to get together and talk before we meet with the team tonight?"

Scott looked at his calendar. "I'm busy all afternoon."

"Me, too, but on Thursdays I can take a full hour for lunch because it includes my planning period. If you come by the school at noon, we can eat in the faculty dining room."

Scott swallowed. Another meal at the school. "Could we go off campus?"

"I don't have time for that. I'm sorry, if you can't—"

"No," Scott said. "I can make it. Do you want me to come to your trailer?"

"No, I'll meet you at the office. You'll need to sign in when you get here."

———

Thursday's menu featured tacos with applesauce and carrot cake. Scott hadn't eaten applesauce in years. He considered it an appropriate food only for those too young to have teeth or too old to keep them.

"They normally give two tacos," Kay said as they stood in line, "but I can ask them to give you an extra one."

"No, I'm not too hungry today. But an extra scoop of applesauce sounds nice."

Kay didn't catch the irony in Scott's voice and spoke to the kitchen worker behind the counter. "Please give him extra applesauce."

Scott followed Kay to the same dining room where he'd eaten with

Dr. Lassiter. The applesauce was runny. It had spilled over the divider in his plate and come to rest against the shell of one of his tacos. If he didn't eat the taco soon, it would start to get soggy and fall apart.

They ate at a table for two. Several teachers glanced up when he entered the room.

Scott leaned forward and whispered, "Where's Mrs. Willston?"

Kay smiled. "She doesn't come in here very often. I think she brings fruit from home and eats it in her classroom."

"This applesauce would be perfect for her."

"There's Mr. Fletchall." Kay motioned toward a short, heavyset man with only a few strands of hair clinging to the sides of his head. "Were you in his trigonometry class?"

Scott turned his head slightly to get a better look. "For one semester. What happened to his hair?"

"It's been subtracted. Do you want to go over and say something to him?"

"He wouldn't recognize me with my eyes open. I slept through most of his classes."

Scott rescued his taco from the onslaught of the runaway applesauce and took a bite. It wasn't too bad.

"I've talked with the students who came to the meeting," Kay began. "All but two said they were coming back."

"Good."

"What's your plan for tonight?" she asked.

Scott didn't have one. He'd been too busy at the office to think about the meeting but quickly improvised: "Do you think the students have read the facts of the case and looked over the witnesses' statements?"

"Yes. I've heard them discussing it among themselves."

"Okay. I'll talk to them for a few minutes and then assign them different roles. Everyone will be a witness, and I'll do the questioning. I should be able to tell who would be good in a role by their responses to my questioning."

"Would it help if I told you some of my thoughts about the kids before you hold tryouts?"

"Sure."

"Of course, you remember Dustin." Kay opened a folder and started with additional information about the football player. She continued summarizing what she knew about the strengths and weaknesses of each student. While she talked, Scott finished his tacos and chased down as much of his applesauce as he could capture with his spoon. He couldn't put faces with all the names.

"Is Yvette Fisher the one with dark hair and big, innocent eyes?" he asked.

"No, that's probably Janie Collins. She's a country girl who needs a double dose of confidence. She is one of my best students but doesn't realize how bright she is. Next is Alisha Mason."

"Yes," Scott nodded. "The tall, black girl."

"That's right. Her mother is assistant principal of the middle school. Alisha turned me down when I first talked with her, but I guess she's changed her mind. She always has a lead role in school plays and would be great in an important witness role. She and Janie are good friends, so it would be good for them to work together." Checking her list, Kay said, "One more student. Franklin Jesup."

"That's one I remember. He must be a speed-reader. He had questions about the materials by the end of the first meeting."

"Frank probably has one of the highest IQs in the school. His father is a business executive, and they live in a big house on the golf course. Frank is a little moody, but he's probably bored and unchallenged. I'm hoping he will respond to you since you're a lawyer."

Without a weather report, a gathering storm isn't seen until dark clouds billow on the horizon. The plans of darkness for Catawba High School were not yet visible, and no one was available to forecast the future. The clear lines of demarcation that characterize spiritual conflict in the heavens are often blurred and fuzzy by the time they reach the earth. No one knew about the darkness beyond the horizon. No one knew how soon or how quickly it would grow and take shape. No one knew that random relationships held the potential for extraordinary significance. No one knew that choices made in the present would have exponential importance in the future.

9

They have no lawyers among them.

Sir Thomas More, "Of Law and Magistrates"

The second meeting of the Catawba Mock Trial Team began that evening at 7 P.M. Janie Collins, Dustin Rawlings, and Alisha Mason were present. The first time Kay passed around an attendance sheet, Frank Jesup wasn't in the room, but two minutes later his tires squealed outside as he parked beside the modular unit.

Scott pointed to a slender, brown-haired girl with high eyebrows who was sitting very straight and attentive in her chair. "Your name, please?"

"Yvette Fisher."

"Please stand up."

Yvette slid out of her seat.

"Have you read the materials?" Scott asked.

"Yes, sir."

"Including the witness statements?"

"Yes."

"Okay. You are no longer Yvette. You are now Betty Moonbeam."

Yvette looked puzzled. "The passenger in the car? I thought it was Barry Moonbeam?"

"The rules of the competition do not dictate the gender of the witnesses. We may use Barry; we may use Betty."

Yvette stood up a little straighter and said, "Okay, I'm Betty Moonbeam."

"You've got that right," Frank Jesup said as he slid into his seat.

"No comments," Scott said. "You'll regret it when it's your turn." He turned back to Yvette.

"Betty, you are now under oath. Did you go to an end-of-the-year cookout and picnic at Sarah Rich's house?"

"Uh, yes. I was there."

"How did you get to the party?"

"I think I went with Ralph Risky."

"How do you know Ralph?"

"We go to school together." Yvette hesitated. "But I'm not sure how we know one another."

"Make something up," Scott said.

Yvette thought for a moment. "Okay. He plays football, and I'm on the flag corps that performs at halftime."

"Good," Scott said. "You added facts about the witnesses not on your sheet. That's fine if it doesn't affect the important points of the problem. The judges like creative witnesses so long as they don't cross the line into creating facts that affect the legal issues in the case."

"Are you dating Ralph?" Scott asked.

"No, we're just friends. I needed a ride to the party because my parents took away my driving privileges."

Scott acted surprised. "Why did they do that?"

"I've had a few wrecks recently."

"How many is a few?"

Yvette looked around as if embarrassed and answered in a quiet voice, "Five."

"I'm sorry. I didn't quite hear you."

"Five—since January," she said a little louder. A few students laughed.

"Were they all your fault?"

Yvette nodded. "Yes," then she added quickly, "but no one was hurt, and I promised my dad that I would be careful. I cried and begged, but he told me I couldn't drive again until I went to the Fender Bender Driving School and passed their safe driver test."

"Have you taken the course?"

"I was supposed to start during summer vacation, but I was in no shape to drive after the night of the party. I think I was still in the hospital." Yvette stopped. "Can I look at my sheet? I can't remember that part."

"I'll give you a break while I talk to Ralph for a minute."

Scott scanned the room. Most of the boys slid a little lower in their seats. Scott decided it was time to give Frank the spotlight he seemed to crave. "Frank Jesup, you're Ralph. Please stand up. I remind you that you are under oath."

Frank slid out of his chair and stood. "Which do you want? The truth, the whole truth, or nothing but the truth?"

"All of the above, within the guidelines of the problem."

Frank continued. "Why are the names in the case so corny? Betty Moonbeam, Sarah Rich, Ralph Risky?"

"It's often that way," Scott replied. "Even in law-school competitions the professors who write the case histories do the same thing."

"I don't want to look like an idiot spouting these names."

Scott resisted an urge to tell Frank to sit down until he could cooperate.

"Don't worry, Ralph. You'll get used to it. Now, tell me, how did you and Betty decide to go to the party together?"

Frank stroked his chin. "I'd been wanting to spend some time with her. A lot of time if you know what I mean."

"Did you phone her and invite her to ride with you?"

"No, she called me. Not that I was too surprised. She told me about the problems with her father and the car, but I think it was all an excuse to spend some time alone with me."

"Over my dead body," Yvette said.

"No comments," Scott said. "I told Frank to be quiet while you were on the witness stand."

Frank cut his eyes toward Yvette and said, "You should have seen the dress she was wearing. When she sat down in my car—"

"Don't go there," Kay interrupted.

"Okay. I picked her up about eleven-thirty in the morning for the cookout at Sarah's house."

"Had you had anything to drink before you got there?"

"*Moi?*" Frank asked. "I don't drink anything but bottled water and Cheerwine."

"Does Cheerwine contain any alcohol?"

"You're from North Carolina, aren't you? Cheerwine is like a Cherry Coke. It's bottled in Salisbury."

"I know that," Scott answered. "I used to ride my bike to Barnett's Grocery in the summer to buy a cold Cheerwine. But in a competition you might be in front of judges from someplace who've never heard of Cheerwine. The lawyer questioning the witness needs to make sure any uncertainties are cleared up."

"Okay."

"Are you sure you didn't have any alcohol in your system when you and Betty started for the party?"

"Positive."

"Any drugs?"

"Not even a Tylenol."

"How far is it from Betty's house to Sarah's place?"

"About five miles. Sarah's house overlooks a pond and the seventeenth green of the, uh"—Frank thought for a second—"the Maurice Mulligan Memorial Golf Course."

Scott smiled. "Now that's corny."

"Yeah, can I change that?"

"No. Let's have a different Betty take up the story." Scott spoke to the group. "We're jumping around tonight so as many of you as possible can see what it's like to be a witness. In a minute, I may ask one of you to be an attorney." He pointed to Alisha Mason who stood up. "Alisha, right?"

The tall, dark-skinned girl nodded.

"Have you read the materials?"

"Yes, sir."

"Okay. You're in the car with Ralph. Were you concerned about Ralph's driving on the way to the party?"

Alisha looked at Frank. "He drove too fast and had his music turned up loud. I think he was trying to show off, but he didn't do anything crazy or wild."

"Were you worried about your safety?"

"No. I was looking forward to the party."

"When did you arrive?"

"It's about ten minutes from my house to Sarah's place so we got there about eleven forty-five."

"Had the party started?"

"Not really. I wanted to be early so I could help Sarah with the last-minute preparations."

"What did you do?"

Alisha counted on her fingers. "Cut up some fruit. Heated some nacho sauce in the microwave. Popped some popcorn. Put some drinks and ice on a table in the downstairs recreation room."

"What kind of drinks?"

"Mostly Cheerwine."

Several students laughed.

Scott smiled. "I haven't had a Cheerwine in years. Was there a punch bowl at the party?"

"Yes. But I didn't help with that."

"Who fixed the punch?"

"Some of the guys. I think Ralph helped." Alisha paused. "I can't remember the other character's name. Bill or Bob?"

"Billy Bob Beerbelly."

"That's right."

"What kind of punch was it?"

"Ginger ale, fruit juice, and scoops of rainbow sherbet floating in it."

"Nonalcoholic?"

"I thought so. But now, I'm not sure."

"Let's ask Joe about it." Scott pointed to a tall, slender young man with a slightly pointed nose and light brown hair. "Your name, please."

"Kenny." The student's ears turned suddenly red, and Scott realized he'd found a shy student in the group.

"Would you like to be Joe Joker for a few minutes?"

"I guess so." The lanky boy stood up. "But I'm not very good at telling jokes."

"Can you tell me about the punch served at the party?" Scott asked.

"Yes, sir."

"Was there anything in it besides ginger ale, fruit juice, and rainbow sherbet?"

"Yes, sir." The ears turned red again.

"What else?"

"Uh, we spiked it with vodka."

"Who did it?"

"Ralph and me."

"Who brought the vodka to the party?"

"Ralph brought it. It was in the trunk of his car. I went with him to get it after he and Betty got there."

"Were you present when it was poured into the punch?"

"Yes, sir."

Scott again addressed the group as a whole. "What kind of question did I just ask?"

Dustin Rawlings raised his hand. "The kind that's supposed to make the witness look guilty."

"An incriminating question," Scott replied. "Possibly. But I was thinking of something more basic."

"A leading question," Frank said.

"That's right," Scott said. "A question that contains the answer. The witness either says 'yes' or 'no.' If Joe Joker was one of my witnesses in the case, the lawyer on the other side will object if I ask too many leading questions. How could I change my question about Joe's presence at the punch bowl so that it would no longer be a leading question?"

Janie Collins, who had been sitting on the edge of her chair, raised her hand. "You could ask, 'Who was at the punch bowl when the liquor was poured into it?'"

"Exactly," Scott said. "You only have five to seven minutes to question a witness in a mock trial competition and every question needs to bring out as much information as possible."

Scott motioned to Janie. "It's Janie, isn't it?"

"Yes, sir."

"Janie, you are now the lawyer questioning Joe Joker. Take over."

Janie's face flushed slightly. "What am I supposed to ask?"

"Are you familiar with the facts?"

"Mostly."

"Try to get Joe to reveal important information based on the materials you've been given. You can use the sheet to help you remember."

Janie turned toward Kenny. "Who was at the punch bowl when the liquor was poured in?"

"Ralph and me."

Janie paused. "What happened next?"

"No," Scott interrupted. "Too general. Ask a specific question."

"Uh, how much vodka did you put in the punch?"

"Two quarts."

"How big was the punch bowl? How many quarts or gallons could it hold?"

"It was this big," Kenny answered, holding his arms out in front of him. "How much would that hold?"

"I'm asking the questions," Janie said.

Scott smiled. "Good. Keep control of the witness. If Joe keeps that up, you could ask the judge to instruct the witness to answer the questions."

Janie continued, "How strong was the taste of vodka in the punch?"

"Not much with all that fruit juice and sherbet floating around in it. I don't think some of the girls knew what we'd done to it."

"Who drank the punch after it had been spiked?"

"A bunch of people. Me, Ralph, Sarah, and Betty."

"Who showed the effects of the alcohol by the way they acted?"

"I don't know about anyone else. I had a pretty good buzz. I'd never had anything to drink so early in the day."

Scott held up his hand. "Good job, Kenny. You sounded very genuine. Janie, your questions were well phrased. Anyone want to volunteer?"

The next hour and a half passed quickly. Scott asked most of the questions, but he let a couple of students play the lawyer role. They made it through the case to the sad part at the end when Betty Moonbeam ends up in the hospital after a wreck with a vehicle driven by a congenial redneck named Pete Pigpickin. Also on the scene at the time of the collision was a controversial witness named Billy Bob Beerbelly. The last girl to play the part of Betty Moonbeam squeezed out a fake tear as she described her pain and suffering following the injuries she received in the car wreck following the party.

"How do girls do that?" Dustin asked when she finished.

"She thought about something sad," Yvette answered. "Like going out with you."

"That's it for tonight," Scott interjected before Dustin could counterattack. "Here's your homework assignment. Look over the problem and give me your first three preferences. Do you want to be Betty, Joe, Billy, Ralph, Sarah, Pete, one of the lawyers, and so on? I can't guarantee a specific role and everyone will practice different parts in preparation for the competition. The witness roles can be switched between male and female. For example, we can experiment with Barry Moonbeam, Ruth Risky, and Bonita Beerbelly."

"When do we turn in our choices?" Yvette asked.

"Give them to Mrs. Wilson by the end of the day tomorrow."

Most of the students began filing out. Janie came forward to Kay's desk.

"Can you still give me a ride home?" she asked Kay. "My mother had to use the car tonight."

"Of course," Kay responded. "Wait outside, and I'll be there in a minute."

After all the students left, Scott asked, "How do you think it went tonight?"

Kay picked up the brown satchel she used to transport papers to and from school. "They enjoyed it. The boys will be calling each other Ralph Risky and Billy Bob Beerbelly in the hallways tomorrow."

"Do you have ideas about the students who should play the different parts?"

Kay showed Scott a page of notes. "I took notes, but let's see what the kids want to do and plug our comments into their requests."

"Should I call you?" Scott asked.

Kay hesitated. "No, I'll call you."

———

Franklin Jesup Jr. had a reason for his tardiness to the mock trial meeting. It started after supper with a routine household problem—a leaking hose in the washing machine. Frank's mother rarely washed clothes, but their housekeeper had been out sick, and Jodie's favorite pants were dirty and had to be cleaned before school the next day. Vivian Jesup put the pants in the machine and turned it on. She was in the kitchen arguing with Frank Jr. about a nasty scratch she'd discovered on the door of her new car after she'd parked next to his vehicle when Jodie came running upstairs.

"Water is all over the floor downstairs!"

Vivian rushed down the steps, and Frank followed at a more casual pace. Jodie was right. Water was everywhere. It had seeped out of the laundry room and soaked the carpet in the downstairs den. Worst of all, water had also flowed into the patio room his mother used as an art studio. A recently finished watercolor of Jodie was facedown on the floor when the water invaded the room. Frank heard his mother give a piercing scream.

He hurried into the room as she held up the picture. The colors were running down the surface of the canvas.

"It's ruined!" she cried.

Frank stared at the picture for a moment and burst out laughing. The painting wasn't a good likeness of his sister before the water blurred the image and gave the face a grotesque smile that drooped down at the corners of the mouth. Now, it looked totally ridiculous.

"It's better," he said. "It's, uh, Post-Impressionist. No, it's post-diluvian. Get it? After the Flood."

Vivian Jesup took a step forward, raised the canvas in the air, and slammed it down over Frank's head.

Stunned, Frank didn't move. He and his mother stared hard at one another for several seconds.

Frank spoke first. In a low, calm voice, he said, "You shouldn't have done that. I will make you very, very sorry."

"Get out of my sight!" she screamed.

He went upstairs and took a shower to wash the paint from his hair and forehead. His dark hair was still wet when he arrived at the high school.

Later that night after he and Jodie were supposed to be asleep, Frank heard his parents arguing downstairs. He quietly opened the door of his bedroom and walked to the top of the stairs.

"He's going to a boarding school as soon as we can get him admitted," his mother said, her voice rising in volume. "I've had enough of his smart mouth and rotten attitude! He needs to be someplace where people can deal with him."

"No," his father said. "He's not going anywhere."

"I'm dead serious. He's leaving, or I'm taking Jodie and moving to the lake house!"

"Don't get emotional."

"Emotional! You haven't had to put up with him every day for seventeen years!"

His parents moved toward the master suite that occupied the east wing of the main floor, and their voices faded. Frank sat at the top of the stairs for a few seconds, debating what to do.

He crept quietly down the stairs and moved along the wall toward his parents' bedroom. He could hear both their voices getting louder but couldn't make out the conversation. Drawing closer, he hid behind a bookcase in a small alcove outside the bedroom. The door was cracked open, and he heard a loud crash.

"I suspected this!" his mother screamed. "You and your weekend business trips! I'm going to take you for everything you have!"

"Do your worst, Vivian," his father said coldly. "I'm ready for you." There was another loud crash. "Go ahead. Break everything. It's already broken."

10

All the causes which conspire to blind man's erring judgment.
ALEXANDER POPE

Scott knocked on the door of Leland Humphrey's office and stuck his head inside.

"Ready?" he asked.

"Yes. Let's go," the older lawyer replied. He lifted himself out of his chair and slipped on a camel's-hair blazer.

In the reception area they walked past several clients waiting to see other lawyers in the firm. One of them was an expensively dressed woman. Vivian Jesup twisted a tissue in her hands as she waited for her initial appointment with Ann Gammons, the firm's most experienced divorce lawyer.

Lynn Davenport was sitting alone at the prosecution table when Leland Humphrey and Scott entered the empty courtroom. She glanced back at the sound of their footsteps and continued writing on a legal pad until they passed through the bar and set their briefcases beside the defense table.

Turning in her chair, she said, "The deputy who is bringing the prisoner from the youth detention center is a few minutes late. The judge is in his chambers waiting for everyone to get here."

Mr. Humphrey stepped forward and shook her hand. "I'm Leland Humphrey. Mr. Ellis is attorney of record, but I may help out since he is part of our firm. I think we met when you were sworn in a couple of years ago."

The D.A. nodded. "Yes, sir. You hosted a reception for the new lawyers in town at your firm."

The door at the front of the courtroom opened, and Deputy Hicks from the youth detention center entered with Lester in tow. The young man's hair was beginning to grow back and cover his head with a dense, black fuzz.

"Deputy, please inform the judge we're ready," the D.A. said.

Lester sat at the defense table next to Scott and whispered, "Who's the old guy?"

"My boss," Scott answered.

Everyone except Lester stood when the judge strode into the courtroom. Scott tapped his client on the shoulder and motioned for him to stand up.

The judge nodded when he saw Leland Humphrey. "Good morning, Mr. Humphrey. Mr. Ellis."

Leland cleared his throat and in his sonorous courtroom voice replied, "Good morning, Judge."

"Proceed, Ms. Davenport," the judge said.

Ms. Davenport stood with a legal pad in her hand. "Your honor, eleven days ago the accused was arrested following an incident at the Hall's Chapel Church on the banks of Montgomery Creek."

"I know where the church is located," the judge said.

"The church members were having a picnic after their service on Sunday. The minister"—Lynn consulted her notes—"a man named Alfred Moore, and five other individuals waded into the creek for a baptismal ceremony. Approximately one hundred other persons, including a number of young children, were standing on the bank. At that point, the state's evidence will show that the defendant fired four or five shots with a gun. No one was injured, but the people in attendance were placed in fear and apprehension of bodily harm from a dangerous weapon. The windshield of a vehicle parked near the church was shattered and a bullet lodged in the wall of the building above the front door. There is sufficient evidence to support a finding of assault with a deadly weapon with intent to inflict serious injury, assault by pointing a gun, and criminal damage to property."

Scott had given Lester a sheet of paper to record any notes or questions. Scott glanced down. His client had written the same word three times: "Lies, lies, lies."

Davenport continued, "Sheriff's deputies were called to the scene, and a pickup truck owned by Harold Garrison, the defendant's father, was located a half-mile down the road near a bridge that crosses the creek. The defendant was seen in the vicinity of the truck."

"Did the defendant make any incriminating statements?" the judge asked.

"No, sir."

"Did he have a weapon?"

"The arresting officers saw him throw his weapon in the creek and try to run away. He was captured by two deputies coming from the opposite direction. The gun was recovered several hours later. There was only one bullet left in a six-shot chamber."

"Any eyewitnesses who identified the defendant at the scene?" the judge asked.

"Not yet, but we want to schedule some lineups, your honor."

Scott was quickly on his feet. "Judge, we would like the opportunity to file objections to any efforts to force our client to incriminate himself."

Lynn Davenport immediately responded. "The law clearly provides—"

"Not now," the judge said, taking off his glasses in warning. "We'll argue this later if I keep this case in my court. If it goes back to juvenile court, it will be subject to a different standard." He turned toward the D.A. "Ms. Davenport, you mentioned a conspiracy to commit murder charge. Is it related to this incident?"

"No, it has a broader scope."

"Explain."

Lynn looked at Lester. "We have evidence that the defendant has been in communication with members of a white supremacy group that is planning to kill several prominent African-American leaders in North and South Carolina on Martin Luther King Jr.'s birthday."

"What type of evidence?"

"Admissions, your honor. Direct admissions from the defendant."

"Words are not enough, Ms. Davenport."

"Yes, sir, but there is evidence of preparatory acts sufficient to satisfy the legal requirements for a criminal conspiracy. The need to protect the safety of witnesses prevents disclosure of more specific information."

"Have there been other arrests?"

"Not yet, but the evidence we've uncovered has been forwarded to appropriate law enforcement agencies in South Carolina where the other co-conspirators reside."

Scott stood. "Your honor, the state has to identify the witnesses who will testify. Mr. Garrison has a constitutional right to face his accusers."

The judge turned to the D.A. "Ms. Davenport, can you prove extraordinary circumstances?"

"Yes, your honor."

The judge motioned to Deputy Hicks. "Take Mr. Garrison back to the holding cell while I review this issue with the attorneys."

"May I have a minute with my client?" Scott asked.

"All right," the judge said. "We'll take a ten-minute break."

Scott and Leland followed the deputy and Lester to the holding cell, a small jail cell behind the courtroom. Deputy Hicks closed the door with a clang and walked down the hall out of earshot.

"What's she talking about?" Scott asked.

"I bet it came from the school," Lester said. "I met a guy on the Internet."

"You use the Internet?" Scott asked.

"In the computer lab at school during my free period. I told you I'm not stupid. I know how to go on-line and find out stuff."

"Go ahead."

"I did some research on groups that stand up for the white race. I connected in a chat room with a guy in Greenville who knows the names of the politicians who have taken away our rights. We got to talking on-line for a few weeks. I've never met him in person."

"Did you send e-mails back and forth?"

"Yes."

"Were there threats?"

"He listed some people who needed to be removed."

"Removed? What did that mean?"

Lester looked down at his feet. "It could mean a lot of things."

"Including murder?"

"I never said that."

"What did you write?"

"I can't remember everything but nothing that should be against the law."

"What's the man's name?"

"Bossman."

"What's his first name?"

"I don't know his real name. Bossman is his screen name. For all I know, he could be a kid."

"You heard what Davenport said about doing something to carry out a plan. What was she talking about?"

"I don't know. I've told you everything. I'd swear it on my grandmother's Bible. But I'm sure that D.A. could get someone to come in and lie."

Scott looked at Mr. Humphrey to see his reaction. The older lawyer turned to Lester and said, "Okay. You have to stay here while we meet with the judge."

As they walked down the hall toward the courtroom, Scott asked, "What do we do?"

"Find out as much as we can. I doubt Lester told us everything, so we have to convince the judge to help us pry information from Ms. Davenport."

An hour later, Scott and Leland left the courtroom with copies of twelve, hate-filled e-mails that were far more specific about threats of political assassination than Lester had indicated. However, even a quick reading of the communications revealed that their client was the re-sponder, not the initiator, in the discussions. Lester agreed with Bossman that violence was justified, but there wasn't obvious evidence of acts that warranted a criminal conspiracy charge. Freedom of speech allows the expression of hate, even if the reasons for bigotry seemed more appro-priate for a crude leaflet from the Reconstruction South than a printout from a twenty-first-century computer file. The judge also ruled that Lynn Davenport had to reveal the identities of all witnesses.

But Scott and Mr. Humphrey weren't happy. They'd lost the most important issue. The judge ordered Lester Garrison to stand trial as an adult on all charges pending against him. The kinder, gentler juvenile court system would not be the venue for the case. Bond was set at

$75,000. Until that was met, their fuzzy-headed young client would remain in custody at the youth detention center.

When he returned to his office, Scott listened to his voice-mail messages. Number three was from Thelma Garrison.

"I still ain't heard nothing from Harold. Is Lester all right? I have a relative who can carry me to town on Sunday to that place where they're keepin' him. Call me back."

Scott phoned Mrs. Garrison. He didn't try to explain the complexities of her grandson's legal situation but promised to notify the youth detention center that she might visit on Sunday afternoon.

———

After Scott's call Thelma put the old-fashioned, black rotary phone in its cradle and rubbed her hand across her wrinkled forehead. The days since Lester's arrest had been among the loneliest of her life. Not that she and Lester talked very much, but his total absence created a new void in her already empty existence. Thelma's niece came by every day on her way home from work to check on her, but the young woman had two young children of her own and couldn't stay very long.

Thelma's home was a "shotgun house," so named because a man with a shotgun could stand at the front door and get a clear shot across the living room, down the hall, through the kitchen, and out the back door without hitting a wall or doorframe. The old house had two bedrooms and a single bathroom. On the few nights a month when Harold slept there, he camped out with a pillow and a blanket on the sofa.

Lester's absence was especially bad on Saturday—shopping day. The trips to the grocery store were the high point of her week. She didn't go into the store to buy anything, but on shopping day she felt part of the human race. She'd sit in the truck with the window down and listen to the sounds of life passing by—a child crying, a woman laughing, a man calling a greeting to a friend across the parking lot. She imagined the faces behind the sounds.

Thelma told Lester what to buy, but he always spent more than necessary for the simple items she requested. She didn't know whether he purchased something else or simply put some of the money in his pocket before counting it out in her hand. Either way, she didn't have the will or energy to confront him. A few times she'd smelled the familiar odors of beer and cigarettes on his breath and remembered the days when his father and her other sons started down the same path.

Since her sight faded away, Thelma didn't walk anywhere except in the house. Her feet hurt. The doctor had a fancy term for it, but all she knew was that the diabetes was slowly destroying the feeling in her legs. It was six shuffling steps to the nightstand in her bedroom, fourteen steps into the kitchen, eight steps to the bathroom, ten steps to the black phone in the hall, sixteen steps to the front door, and twelve steps to Lester's bedroom door. Thelma got up from her chair and slowly crossed the hallway, going into her room to the nightstand beside her bed.

She turned the knob on her radio. She alternated between two country music stations. Songs of others' sorrow were her favorites, women vocalists her preference. Lyrics that expressed the futility of life in the face of suffering rang true to her soul, and she responded to melodies featuring the high, lonesome sounds of steel guitars—a wailing cry that echoed the whine of bagpipes played by the Scottish ancestors of the Appalachian mountain people. But today she stopped before reaching the signal for one of her usual stations. She paused when a clear voice spoke into the small room, "Please stop and listen for a minute. I have a message for you from Jesus Christ."

Thelma Garrison sat on the edge of her bed. It wasn't a complicated program. A minister from a neighboring town interviewed a woman who shared the testimony of her conversion. Like Thelma, the woman came from a hardworking, hard-drinking family and spent most of her life in the ruts and ditches of life.

Thelma had been to church and listened to preachers who yelled so loud they could have been heard by a crowd of a thousand when the congregation before them numbered less than a hundred. She'd been scared of hell a few times but never overcame her greater fear of being noticed by others to slip out of the pew and walk forward at the end of a church meeting and give her heart to Jesus. She finally decided religion wasn't for her. God was somewhere on the other side of the universe and didn't have an interest in a poor, uneducated girl who dropped out of school in the seventh grade. Her life then proved her point: teenage pregnancy, alcoholic husband, long hours of work for little pay, and one hard experience after another.

The woman described the way in which the Holy Spirit had drawn her to Jesus: "I was listening to a program on the radio one afternoon. It seemed like the person speaking was talking directly to me. I could barely breathe, and then the love of God came into my living room. It wasn't just that God loved everyone; he loved me."

Thelma sat very still with her hands in her lap.

The voice from the radio continued, "I began to cry. I wasn't sad. They were good tears. They washed away the sorrows that had built up around my heart. It was like I took a shower that cleaned me on the inside."

Thelma blinked back tears from her own sightless eyes. Most of her tears during the past sixty years had been ones of anger and frustration. These were different. They rolled off her cheeks, making small dark spots when they landed on her cotton dress.

"I got down on my knees beside my bed and talked to the Lord just like I'm talking to you. That's when it happened. I said, 'Jesus, save me.' And he did."

Thelma listened to the end of the program. When the woman finished talking, the preacher asked the people tuned in to the station to pray a simple prayer if they wanted to know Jesus Christ. Thelma hesitated, unconvinced that it would work for her. There was no hope of sight left for her in this world, and she couldn't believe there was the possibility of new vision in the world to come.

With a deep sigh, she reached over and turned the dial to one of her familiar stations.

11

*In life, as in a football game, the
principle to follow is: Hit the line hard.*
THEODORE ROOSEVELT

The following morning Scott drove south to Charlotte for a hearing in an uncontested breach-of-contract case. The long, watery fingers of Lake Norman on the Catawba River forced drivers traveling south from Blanchard County to select between the interstate highway that crossed the lake on several long bridges and a more scenic course that followed two-lane roads on the west side of the reservoir. Because he wasn't in a hurry, Scott opted for the scenic route. He left early enough to stop in Denver, a small town with no resemblance to its famous Colorado counterpart; however, the cluster of bait-and-tackle shops and mobile-home manufacturing plants was home to a small roadside diner that served the best ham biscuits in the area.

The drive-up restaurant was in a small concrete-block structure with a flimsy aluminum awning. Scott gave his order to a woman with a cigarette hanging out of the corner of her mouth. In less than a minute, she handed him two biscuits wrapped in thin white paper and a large cup of strong coffee. Scott parked his vehicle in the nearest parking spot, unwrapped a biscuit, and took a bite. He was not disappointed. It was hot and fluffy, and the country ham had the perfect mixture of salt and sweet. He washed it down with sips of coffee.

At the outskirts of Charlotte, he stopped at a red light and flipped open the mirror on his sun visor to make sure there wasn't any ham stuck between his teeth. He didn't want to provide a visual replay of his breakfast to the judge assigned to his case.

The courthouse in Charlotte was a series of haphazard buildings linked by skywalks and underground tunnels. Scott had to park a couple of blocks away from the courthouse, and there was a long line backed up at the security checkpoint. As he waited to pass through the metal detector, he examined the contents of a large glass case where the security officers displayed some of the weapons and contraband seized from people who, for inexplicable reasons, attempted to bring switchblades, guns, and drugs into the heart of the justice system.

Unlike the main courtroom in Catawba, the utilitarian courtrooms in Charlotte had as much distinct personality as a row of metal fence posts. Scott slipped into the back door. There were about twenty lawyers spread out on the light-colored benches behind the bar. A woman judge came through a door behind the bench and began transacting the business of the day. Scott had to wait an hour before his case was called. No one appeared for the defendant, and the judge quickly scribbled her name across the bottom of the paper Scott placed in front of her. At times, practicing law was so simple a first grader could do it.

It was a clear day, and on the drive back to Catawba he took a five-minute detour to a place where the State Department of Natural Resources had placed four concrete picnic tables near the edge of the lake. He'd saved half a biscuit from his morning snack, and sitting at one of the tables, he nibbled the cold biscuit while he looked out over the water.

During the time he dated Kay, they spent a chilly Saturday afternoon on Lake Norman. One of Scott's friends had a boat, and they spent an afternoon skiing in early April. The temperature of the water was a shock when Scott jumped in, but he pretended it was as tepid as the end of August.

Scott had been skiing on a slalom since he was ten years old. When his friend gave the boat full throttle, Scott plowed through the water, patiently waiting for the boat to lift him to the surface. The shock of the wind against his wet body made him grit his teeth for several seconds, but after shaking his head a couple of times, he was able to concentrate on skiing and made the slalom come alive. There were only a few boats on the lake, and the water was smooth as glass. He cut sharply back and forth, sending sprays of water twenty feet skyward as he pulled himself to a point almost perpendicular to the back of the boat. Twice, he approached the edge of the wake at high speed and launched himself in the air, clearing the bubbling turbulence caused by the motor and landing on the smooth water on the other side. The third time he jumped, his rubbery legs didn't give him enough thrust and he wiped out.

Scott's friend and his date skied, but it took several minutes of coaxing to convince Kay to give it a try. She sat on the edge of the boat as they drifted in a quiet cove, stuck her toes in the water, and refused to budge. But peer pressure prevailed. Donning a yellow ski vest, she held her nose, jumped in the water, and came up screaming.

Sitting at the picnic table, Scott remembered the scene and smiled. Kay had long legs, and she awkwardly wrestled with the skis as she struggled to slip her feet into the rubber bindings. Her lips were turning blue by the time she was ready. Scott tried to give her last-minute instructions, but she told him to be quiet and get the boat moving before she turned into an icicle. The boat accelerated, and she popped quickly up out of the water. Keeping her legs bent, she stayed directly behind the boat, her wet hair streaming behind her and her mouth wide open. Scott wasn't sure if the sounds coming across the water were screams or laughter. Amazingly, she didn't fall. When she grew tired, she waved once and let go of the rope, sinking down until only her head and shoulders were bobbing above the surface. Praising her profusely, Scott helped Kay into the boat and wrapped her tightly in a large towel. She shivered for several minutes, then refused to let go of the towel until the boat was back on dry ground. Scott chuckled; it had been a day to remember.

He stood up and walked back to his vehicle.

Back at the office, Scott listened to his voice-mail messages. Number six was from a woman he'd dated a couple of times after they met while Scott was walking Nicky.

"Scott, this is Ashley Warren. I know it's late notice, but I'd love to have you over for supper this evening. I've spent a week in Cancún and want to tell you all about it. Seven o'clock would be great. Please call."

Scott hadn't talked to Ashley in a month. She would be tanned from her week in Mexico, but listening to her chatter about the tourist traps she visited didn't sound very interesting. He glanced at his calendar and saw a note he'd written about the home football game for the Catawba Catamounts.

Scott debated his options for several seconds before deciding on a plan of action. Taking out a quarter, he tossed it in the air. Heads he went to the football game, tails he accepted the dinner invitation. He caught the coin and opened his hand. It was tails. He paused before dialing Ashley's phone number. She was attractive but talked nonstop. It would be a noisy evening whether he went to dinner or the game. The issue was so close that his first result required corroboration. Repeating the coin toss, it came up heads. That meant one final throw. Winner takes all. He flipped the coin almost to the ceiling and let it land on the carpet beside his desk so there would be no chance he could influence the outcome. It was heads.

The football game started at 7:30 P.M. Scott arrived fifteen minutes early but still had to park at the far end of the school parking lot. Football Friday night in a town like Catawba was a community-wide event and attendance at the five home games was a top priority on the social calendar. Even if residents of the community didn't have a son or grandson wearing a blue-and-gold uniform, they came anyway. The team represented the town, not just the high school.

Scott walked through the shoulder-to-shoulder crowd toward the main concession stand. Several men wearing blue T-shirts that identified them as members of the Catawba High football booster club had set up grills and were cooking hamburgers as fast as the white-hot charcoal would allow. Scott liked his hamburgers crispy with melted cheese on top, and in a few minutes he had three burgers topped with ketchup, pickles, and onions safely nestled in a paper sack next to a bag of barbeque-flavored potato chips and a soft drink.

He passed by a long row of men who were leaning against a rusty chain-link fence that encircled the playing field. In every sporting venue there is an area devoted to the most loyal fans: the bleachers at Wrigley Field, the west stands at Ohio State, the student section in Cameron Coliseum at Duke. The die-hard fans of the Catawba Catamounts were a no-nonsense group of middle-aged and older men who stood shoulder to shoulder along the rusty fence. Some of them had played football when the team still followed the Confederate battle flag onto the grid-iron; others dropped out and never graduated. But they all took football seriously. Dressed in blue jeans and wearing caps, some chewed tobacco, some chewed gum, and some chewed one of the long blades of fescue grass that grew up into the fence. They didn't cheer. A touchdown by the home team caused nothing more emotional than a nod of the head in approval. They didn't boo. A bad play by a Catawba player caused a chain reaction of spitting down the line. Cursing was reserved exclusively for the referees.

Scott was wearing blue jeans, but the chain-link fence crowd was not in his plans for the evening. He climbed the metal steps of the bleachers. A female voice called his name.

"Scott!"

He looked down the row of bleachers to his left. It was Kay. She was in the middle of the row, standing up and waving her arm.

"Are you with some friends?" she yelled.

"No."

"There's a seat here." She pointed beside her.

Scott gingerly made his way past a dozen spectators. He was almost to the vacant place beside Kay when an overweight man hit him in the leg. Scott lurched forward and watched in slow motion as his drink tipped over and slipped out of his hand. At the last instant, Kay reached up and grabbed the cup before it turned upside down and the lid popped off.

"Good reflexes," Scott said with relief. "I didn't want to give you a soft-drink shower."

Her hair in a ponytail, Kay was wearing tan slacks and a long-sleeve, green, knit shirt. She moved a lightweight coat so that Scott could sit down. It was warm now, but the air would cool quickly once the sun set.

"Have you come to other games?" she asked.

"First one since I moved back. Dustin Rawlings mentioned it the other night."

Kay picked up her game program and ran her finger down the list of players. "He's number 81. Senior. Wide receiver. 6'1" and 185 pounds."

Scott opened his sack, took out a hamburger, unwrapped it, and took a big bite.

"That smells good," Kay said.

Still chewing, Scott mumbled, "It is."

"What's on it?"

He swallowed. "Cheese, ketchup, pickles, and plenty of onions."

"Sounds good," Kay answered.

Scott took another bite and turned his attention toward the field. The opposing team, dressed in white jerseys, red pants, and white helmets, was assembling in the end zone before running onto the field.

"Could I borrow your program?" he asked.

Kay handed him the booklet, and Scott flipped it open to the team roster. Dustin's picture and bio were printed on the right side of the two pages devoted to Catawba's seniors.

"Do you want me to help myself?" Kay asked.

"To what?" Scott turned toward her.

"A hamburger."

"You want one?"

Kay smiled. "Is that a possibility?"

Scott reached into the bag. "Are you sure you like onions? They're pretty strong."

Kay took off the wrapper. "I eat more than cantaloupe. Besides, I'd better eat a few onions in self-defense if we're going to be sitting next to one another."

"I can exhale in the opposite direction," Scott offered.

Kay took a bite. "No, this is a better solution."

Scott opened his small bag of potato chips and reluctantly held it toward Kay. If the quarter had landed tails on the third try in his office, someone would be feeding him right now. "Potato chips?"

"No, thanks," she said. "I don't like barbeque chips."

Scott finished the second burger and the chips at the same time Kay put the last bite of hamburger in her mouth.

"Onions make you thirsty, don't they?" she asked.

Scott didn't wait for further hints. He handed her his drink. "I only have one straw."

"I can avoid that." Kay took off the lid and took a long swallow directly from the cup, waited, and took another drink. "That should hold me until halftime, then I'll treat you to a bag of peanuts and buy a drink of my own."

Scott put the lid back on the cup, sucked on the straw, and drew air.

He tilted the cup and found just enough liquid for one good sip. He took off the lid and shook some ice into his mouth.

The coaches were already along the sideline. The Catawba players were massed behind the goalpost in one end zone preparing to run through a huge paper banner held by several members of the cheerleading squad. The crowd rose to its feet as the team burst through the paper barricade and ran full speed toward the home field bleachers.

After the crowd quieted down, Kay said, "I know you played football but don't remember the position. You were on defense, weren't you?"

"Right side linebacker. It was a lot of fun." Scott remembered days wearing heavy pads in the blazing heat of August and added, "At least the games were fun. Practice was terrible. Nobody likes football practice."

The game quickly settled down to a defensive struggle. Neither team seemed capable of getting a first down, much less a touchdown. Dustin caught one pass for eight yards before being pushed out of bounds. On running plays, he usually had to block the opposing team's cornerback, a muscular young man who hit Dustin so hard on two plays that Scott winced in sympathy. But the Catawba player also got in some licks, including a flying block that freed the home team's running back for a fifteen-yard run. It was the Catamounts' longest play of a first half that ended in a scoreless tie.

"Ready for peanuts?" Kay asked.

"And a drink. Chewing ice makes me thirsty."

"Two drinks and peanuts. Do you want to go with me?"

"Sure."

Scott followed Kay down the steps. They passed Yvette Fisher who saw them together and quickly reported to her friends that Mrs. Wilson was getting a divorce and had a date with Mr. Ellis to the game.

"Do you want another hamburger to replace the one I ate?" Kay asked.

"No. Peanuts are fine."

There was a long line at the concession stand. When they returned to their seats, the second half was about to begin. Catawba had the ball on offense. Kay held the bag toward Scott who took out a few peanuts and cracked one open.

"I stopped for a few minutes at Lake Norman on my way back from Charlotte today," he said. "Do you remember the time we went skiing?"

Kay nodded. "It was freezing. I had goose bumps the size of marbles."

"Was that your first time on water skis? I couldn't remember."

"Second. But it was the first time under arctic conditions."

Kay broke open a shell and put a fat peanut in Scott's right hand. "Here, this is a good one." The peanut rolled into the indention created by a long scar that stretched across Scott's palm from his thumb to his little finger. Kay stared hard for a full two seconds. "Scott, what in the world happened to your hand?"

Scott glanced down and put the peanut in his mouth. "It happened in the army." He pointed to the field. "Look, the quarterback is going to throw it to Dustin."

The Catawba receiver left his feet and stretched out prone in the air in an effort to reach a ball that sailed a few inches beyond his fingertips.

"That was close," Scott said.

With less than a minute to play, the visiting team recovered a fumble on the Catawba twenty-five-yard line. The offense was unable to move the ball, and on fourth down with three seconds left, their coach decided to attempt the least likely to succeed play in high-school football—a field goal. The kicker, a defensive tackle, lumbered onto the field in a uniform covered with dirt from the trench warfare of the previous four quarters. He lined up straight behind the ball and kicked a low line drive that barely cleared the lower bar of the goalpost. The final score was 3-0.

"Tough game," Scott said, as they watched the other team celebrate along the sidelines. The Catawba fans were silent. "Let's find Dustin."

They made their way through the departing crowd. Several of the battered Catawba players were gathering up their gear. Kay stopped to talk to a student in one of her classes. Scott saw Dustin near the Catamount bench beside an older man with the same blond hair streaked with gray.

Dustin's face was streaked with dirt, and he had a small cut on the bridge of his nose. He saw Scott and motioned for him to come over.

"Dad, this is Mr. Ellis, the lawyer who is coaching the mock trial team."

Mr. Rawlings shook Scott's hand. "Number 51, wasn't it? Right side linebacker."

"Uh, yeah," Scott replied with surprise. "That was a long time ago. How did you remember my number and position?"

"I told you he knows everything about Catawba football," Dustin said.

"Not exactly," Mr. Rawlings smiled. "Dustin mentioned you, and I looked you up in a file I have at home."

"He probably knew anyway," Dustin added. "Ask him a question."

Scott thought a moment. "Okay. There was a defensive end who graduated with me. He still lives in Catawba. Do you know—"

"Perry Dixon," Mr. Rawlings answered. "He was a tough competitor. I remember a game in which he sacked the quarterback five or six times."

"That's right. We gave him the game ball. He has it on a shelf at his gym."

Most of the Catawba players were moving across the field.

"I'd better get to the locker room," Dustin said. "Thanks for coming down to see me."

Scott watched him trudge toward the locker room. "I dreaded the locker room after we lost a game. It was bad enough losing, but we had a head coach that would yell and throw helmets through the air."

"I was on the booster club when he was fired," Mr. Rawlings said. "Things are much better with Coach Butler. He knows how to motivate the boys without degrading them."

"That's good. I promise not to yell or throw legal pads if we don't win the mock trial competition."

Mr. Rawlings chuckled. "You've inspired Dustin by coming to this game. The best motivation is based on personal relationship."

Scott found Kay and they walked together toward the exit.

"Is next week a home game?" he asked.

"No. It's at Lincolnton."

"Are you going?"

Kay nodded. "Probably."

"Would you like to ride together?" he asked. "You still owe me a hamburger."

"Maybe."

12

The eternal God is your dwelling place,
and underneath are the everlasting arms.
DEUTERONOMY 33:27 (RSV)

Sunday morning Kay rolled over and turned off the alarm buzzing loudly beside her left ear. The alarm clock was the only thing on her nightstand. The picture of Jake and herself on their honeymoon in St. Thomas was now in the bottom drawer of her dresser. She'd put it under a purple sweater she never wore.

The sun was shining outside the bedroom window of her apartment, and she prepared to force herself out of bed and get ready for school. Then, realizing she had a day of rest, she fell back against her pillow with a sigh of relief and didn't open her eyes for another hour and a half.

When she awoke the second time, she put on a T-shirt and shorts and walked downstairs to the workout room in the basement of her building. Exercising had been one of the bright spots in her marriage to Jake. They had spent many pleasant mornings jogging along the beaches of California and the wooded trails of Virginia, but in the end, Jake had not been willing to go the distance with her. After forty-five minutes going up and down simulated hills on a treadmill, she turned off the machine and sat on a stool in front of a small fan. She was hot and sweaty and lonely. The treadmill was the perfect machine for her. It reflected her marriage— running up and down without going anywhere, sweating without anything enduring to show for it.

Upstairs in her apartment, she poured a glass of water. On her kitchen counter was a stack of papers she'd brought home from her school mailbox. Most of the sheets were administrative announcements and notices about faculty meetings that didn't affect her. She tossed page after page into the trash. In the midst of the stack was a neon orange flyer:

Catawba Community Church is meeting in the gym at the middle school on Sunday mornings at 10:30 A.M. All are welcome. Casual attire.

There was something familiar about the name of the church. Laying the sheet aside, she put her right foot on a wooden stool and leaned forward until she could touch her toes. She didn't want to tighten up. She looked at the notice again while she stretched her other leg. Then she remembered. Janie Collins had invited her to come to one of the meetings.

Kay looked at the clock and made a decision. It wasn't quite 9:45 A.M. She had time to take a shower and get dressed. The only other demands on her day were some papers in her brown satchel that needed to be graded by Monday. Kay made up her mind. She had to get out of the lonely apartment for a few hours. A church that met in a gym might be interesting.

———

At 10:28 A.M. she pulled into a parking space in front of the old, red-brick gymnasium. The long, narrow structure was crowned with high, opaque-glass windows that slid open on levers and had served as the main source of ventilation before the introduction of air conditioning. There were about fifteen cars in the parking lot. Opening a heavy, gray metal door, Kay walked through the foyer that formerly housed the trophy case before it was moved to the new high school. Inside the gym a group of forty-five men, women, and children sat in folding chairs set up at one end of the gym floor.

A young man with a guitar stood in front of the congregation tuning his instrument. Janie Collins sat beside him sorting through a red plastic box containing transparencies. A portable screen was set up behind a black music stand. When Janie saw Kay, her face lit up, and she almost ran to the back of the room.

"Mrs. Wilson! Thanks for coming. Do you want to sit with my mom and brothers?"

"Sure."

After introducing Kay to her mother, Janie returned to her seat by the box of transparencies. Kay sat by the smaller of the two boys. He had a dimple in the same spot as his sister.

A few people were talking, but everyone grew quiet when Janie turned on the overhead projector and displayed the words to a song on the white screen. Without any introduction or comment, the guitarist began to vigorously strum his instrument. Everyone stood and started clapping. Janie's brother began clapping and looked questioningly at Kay until she joined in. After finishing his musical introduction, the leader started to sing and even though the gym was a large room, the group's voices made a valiant effort to fill the void.

One song led to another in a seamless flow. It reminded Kay of a camp for teenagers she attended one summer after moving to California. She closed her eyes and could almost smell the woods that surrounded the open-air pavilion where they held their twilight meetings. Most of the speakers at the camp shared from personal experience, and Kay had listened. She'd liked it better than the dry sermons she heard when her family occasionally went to church.

The words to the last song faded, and Kay felt more refreshed than after her morning shower. A chubby, older man with a thin rim of white hair surrounding his bald head came forward from his seat in the front row. He was wearing a short-sleeve shirt, khaki pants, and brown cowboy boots.

"Good morning," he said. "Welcome to Catawba Community Church. I'm Ben Whitmire. If this is your first time, please raise your hand so that we can give you some information about the church."

Kay was the only newcomer, and the guitar player handed her a brochure. On the back was a picture of Reverend Whitmire and a brief bio. He was a retired minister who had served several churches in North Carolina for more than forty years. He'd grown up in west Texas and attended Howard Payne University in Brownwood. That explained the presence of the boots.

Reverend Whitmire opened a big, black Bible that rested on the music stand and began speaking. The minister had an open-hearted style of speaking and self-deprecating sense of humor that surfaced in the stories he told as illustrations to his sermon. By the end of the message, Kay felt as though she was beginning to know him as a person, not just watching him perform as a preacher.

After the benediction, Janie introduced Kay to Linda Whitmire, a slender, white-haired lady with deep wrinkles around the kindest eyes Kay had ever seen. They were eyes you could talk to. Eyes you could trust. But eyes that saw beneath the surface.

"Come meet Ben," Mrs. Whitmire said.

Kay followed her to the front.

"Ben, this is Kay Wilson. She's a teacher at the high school."

The minister turned and greeted her. "Thanks for coming."

"I enjoyed the service, especially the singing," Kay said. Then suddenly realizing that she'd elevated the worship over the minister's preaching, she added, "I mean, the sermon was good, too."

Ben laughed. "Don't apologize. I like the worship better myself."

"Could you join us for lunch?" Linda asked. "We're going to the Eagle."

Kay glanced over her shoulder. She'd thought about inviting Janie and her family out to eat, but they had already left the building.

"Okay, that sounds great."

"Meet us there," Ben said. "We'll be finished here in a few minutes."

The biggest meal of the week at the Eagle was the Sunday buffet dinner. The congregations of the two large downtown churches converged on the restaurant immediately after the eleven o'clock church service. The Methodists arrived first. Their minister said the benediction precisely at 11:59 A.M., and everyone's wristwatches chirped the top of the hour as they stood to leave the service and move down the street to the restaurant. The Methodists had time to make it once through the buffet line before the Baptists rolled in at 12:30 P.M. The Baptist service usually ran past noon either because the preacher waxed eloquent on point three of his sermon or gave an extra altar call. But there was no anxiety about a lack of food among the Baptist rank and file. Bea Dempsey planned for the flow of traffic as skillfully as a military mess sergeant.

As soon as the Baptists started trickling through the door, Bea pushed back a flimsy brown sliding partition and opened up the overflow room. It was a good system and kept the peace between the two main branches of Christendom in town. After a couple of trips down the buffet line, the two groups met in sweet harmony around the dessert table.

Kay and the Whitmires arrived after the main wave of Methodists but before the Baptists crested through the door.

Bea bustled by to take care of the cash register. "Hello, Kay," she called out. "Hope you all enjoy the buffet today."

"Do you eat here often?" Linda asked.

"Only one time. I'm surprised she remembered my name."

"Bea's great with names," Ben said. "It's good for business. Makes you feel like family."

"I don't have the gift," Kay said. "It took me weeks to learn my students' names."

The buffet line was set up at the back of the main dining room so that the food could be brought out fresh and hot from the kitchen. Kay and the Whitmires zigzagged through the tables and each picked up a heavy, white china plate. Sunday dinner featured every vegetable grown in the local area by the small farmers who sold fresh produce to Bea from June to November. Corn on the cob, green beans, sliced tomatoes, fried okra, mashed potatoes, beets, boiled cabbage, turnip greens, lima beans, and peas with onions sat in stainless-steel serving pans. Everyone ate at least one piece of fried chicken, but for variety there was spiral sliced ham glazed with brown sugar. Rolls and corn bread rested on two large pans.

"This looks especially good today," Ben said three times as they made their way down the serving line.

By the end, his plate was piled high, and he carefully crowned it with a thin slice of ham. A waitress put three glasses of tea on the table without asking what they wanted to drink and hurried back to the kitchen. The Baptists were beginning to come through the door and that meant more of everything.

Ben prayed a blessing on the food and took a bite of fried chicken. "Preacher food," he said. "In forty years of ministry I've eaten enough fried chicken to feed a small city."

"Enjoy yourself, but remember you're not a one-man city," Linda said. Turning to Kay, she asked, "What brought you to Catawba?"

Kay told her story in between bites. Linda's interest was genuine, and Kay was at ease. When Linda asked about her husband, Kay's eyes watered before she could stop them. She needed a surrogate mother and white-haired Linda Whitmire filled the bill. It took three borrowed tissues, but she told the story of her relationship with Jake. Neither woman ate very much. Ben slowed down and listened.

Kay sniffled and glanced around the room. "This is embarrassing."

"That's okay," Linda reached forward and squeezed Kay's hand.

"Unless something happens, the divorce will be final in a few weeks," Kay continued. "For the past year I've been in limbo, bouncing back and forth between anger and sadness."

"What do you want?" Linda asked.

"It depends on when you ask me. I meant what I said on my wedding day, and right now I would like to see a miracle. Tomorrow, I might feel differently. My world has been turned upside down, and I haven't found a place where I feel safe and secure."

Ben leaned back in his chair. "The need for safety and security reminds me of a verse I memorized when I was a little boy in Vacation Bible School. 'The eternal God is your dwelling place, and underneath are the everlasting arms.'"

Kay dabbed her eye with a tissue. "That's a beautiful image, but I don't know where God lives on earth, and I can't say that his arms are underneath me."

"I understand. Are you up for a true story to illustrate my point?" Ben asked.

Kay nodded. "Yes."

Ben pushed away his empty plate. "Try to eat while I talk. Many years ago, Linda and I served a church in Hendersonville, North Carolina. One spring weekend we took a group of young people camping in the Smoky Mountains near the Virginia border. We arrived Friday evening and spent the night huddled in our tents because it rained and rained and rained. In the morning the clouds began to break up, and after breakfast, we took the kids for a walk through the woods above a waterfall.

Linda and I had a new beagle puppy, and I was carrying the little fellow to keep him out of mischief. We came to a spot where a large log spanned the stream and decided to cross to the other side.

"Because it had rained all night, the water was rushing along at a rapid clip, and I decided to make sure the log was stable before letting anyone else try to walk across. Holding the puppy, I stepped out on the log. It was broad, but after taking a few steps, I realized it was too slippery to be safe. When I turned around toward the bank, my right foot slipped off the log. Crazy as it sounds, my first thought was about the puppy, and I threw him toward Linda who was standing at the edge of the bank. He landed safely at her feet about the time I hit the water.

"The water was freezing cold, and although it wasn't over my head, the power of the current began pushing me downstream. I tried to stand up, but the rocks on the bottom were slick, and I couldn't get my footing. I kept falling down. It was like a log flume, and I was a log rushing toward the sawmill."

Kay's sniffles had stopped.

"I remembered from previous trips to the area that there was a bend in the stream ahead of me, and I decided to position myself in the current so that the force of the water would push me toward the bank as the stream swept around to the right. Linda and the kids were running along the path yelling and asking me what they should do. It was all I could do to keep my head above water. I kept trying to stand up, but the water knocked me down and spun me around several times. When the bend came into view, I was able to turn myself in the water so that the force of the stream pushed me into the bank. I reached out and grabbed some limbs that extended over the water, but everything broke off in my hand. The current swept me around the bend, and I twisted sideways. My face hit a rock that was jutting out of the water, and I broke my nose."

Ben rubbed his nose. "I still have a dip caused by the break—it helps keep my glasses from falling onto the floor. But anyway, at the time I was getting more and more desperate. I tried to grab onto anything I could. I tore off several fingernails as I clawed at rocks." He held up his right hand. "Several of them have never grown back straight since that day."

Kay looked at the slightly misshapen fingernails on the minister's right hand and winced.

Linda spoke. "I was running down the path trying to help, but after Ben went around the bend in the stream, he was out of sight. The kids were screaming. I was screaming. It was chaos."

Ben continued, "I was now moving so fast in the water that nothing was slowing me down. All of a sudden, I became very calm, and everything began to happen in slow motion. I began to think in a deliberate, logical manner. I remembered that at the top of the waterfall there was a rock shelf that extended three or four feet out from the cliff. Beyond this shelf was a clear drop of sixty or seventy feet to some more rocks and a deep pool at the bottom of the falls. I realized what I needed to do."

Kay had taken a few bites while Ben talked, but she now held her fork without moving it.

"You stopped eating," Ben said.

Kay glanced at the fork and put it down beside her plate. "I'm not too hungry. Don't leave me at the top of the waterfall."

Ben smiled and shifted in his chair. "Okay. I was able to turn my body so that my legs were straight out in front of me with my feet facing downstream. I came around a bend and saw that the stream disappeared from view about a hundred feet ahead of me. It was the top of the falls. I reached the edge of the cliff and pushed off with my hands, hoping to clear the shelf at the top and the rocks below. As I flew out into the air, the verse I memorized as a little boy in west Texas flashed through my mind as if written with flames of fire. 'The eternal God is your dwelling place, and underneath are the everlasting arms.' Then I blacked out.

"When I came to, I was floating in the water at the base of the falls. The sound of the water crashing down behind my head was deafening. I moved my legs and arms, and everything seemed to be working. I'd cleared the rocks and landed in the deep pool. My face was covered with blood from the broken nose and my hands were bleeding and banged up. But I was alive."

"That is incredible," Kay said.

Ben nodded. "At the base of the falls there was a young couple sitting on a blanket having a picnic. The young man was more interested in the girl than the food, and he was giving her a big kiss when I called out for help. They looked around in surprise and came running to the edge of the pool. I paddled over to them, and they helped me out of the water. I sat on their blanket, shivering with cold and shock, until Linda and the kids came running down the trail. In a few minutes I was able to walk up to the campground. I was taking a hot shower in a cabin when the local rescue squad arrived to search for the body."

"The body?"

"Yes. Someone had called the sheriff's department and reported the accident. They assumed I was dead. One of the rescue workers told me seven people had gone over the falls: five died, one suffered serious, paralyzing injuries, and me—kept safe by the everlasting arms."

Ben held up his right hand. "The strength of this hand wasn't able to save me that day. It took a hand from heaven to take over where flesh and blood failed."

The minister leaned forward. "Kay, no matter the ferocity of the river of life's troubles you find yourself in, no matter how helpless and hurt you feel, no matter what lies behind or lurks ahead, 'The eternal God is your dwelling place, and underneath are the everlasting arms.' That's who he is, and that's where he is."

Kay sighed. "I think I'm somewhere between the top of the falls and the pool at the bottom."

"Then underneath are the everlasting arms," Ben added.

"I hope so," Kay said.

"Maybe that's why you visited the church this morning," Linda said. "To be reminded that the Lord is with you in a time of trouble."

"Yep." Ben looked over at the dessert table. "Telling stories makes me hungry. I'd like dessert."

Ben picked out a generous piece of coconut pie. Linda and Kay each chose a small bowl of fresh strawberries topped with whipped cream.

As they were finishing dessert, Kay said, "I have a question. The beagle puppy in the story. What happened to him?"

Ben laughed. "Oh, Buster lived a long life. And he always loved the water."

At home, Kay closed the door of her apartment and leaned against it for a few seconds. She was still not in the mood to grade papers. She went into her bedroom. On the floor of her closet were several boxes she hadn't unpacked since moving from Virginia Beach. She searched through them until she found what she was looking for—a pink Bible she'd received in a fifth-grade Sunday school class. Inside, she'd carefully written the date and her name in her best, elementary-school handwriting.

She found chapter 33 of Deuteronomy and sitting on the floor read the entire passage. She'd never considered the beauty and power of the Bible's imagery. Moses' blessing of the twelve tribes was not a dusty litany. As she read, it became a rich, vibrant declaration. She took the Bible into the living room and curled up on the couch with her notebook and pen. At the top of a blank page, she wrote, "The Everlasting Arms."

13

Rebellion lay in his way, and he found it.
KING HENRY IV, PART I, SCENE 5

Thelma Garrison sat down in the reception area of the youth detention center. The room was full of strange voices as parents and relatives talked while waiting their turns to visit a wayward teen in the lockup area. Thelma's niece, Bonnie, had driven the blind woman to the YDC for the Sunday-afternoon visit.

They waited an hour before a female officer called out, "Mrs. Garrison?"

"I'm over here," Mrs. Garrison responded anxiously.

"She's blind," Bonnie said, standing to her feet. "Can I help guide her?"

Thelma held on to Bonnie's elbow as they followed the officer down the hallway to the dining room. Lester was sitting alone at one of the round tables.

"Hi, Lester," Bonnie said.

"Hi," Lester responded.

Bonnie guided Thelma to a chair. "I'm going to leave you two alone."

After she was settled, Thelma asked, "Where are you, Son?"

"I'm here, Granny."

Thelma reached out her hand. It was gnarled and wrinkled and shook slightly. Lester leaned sideways and avoided her reach.

"Are you okay?" Thelma asked.

Lester felt the cut over his eye. It was healing quickly. "Yeah."

"Has anybody bothered you? Are you getting enough to eat?"

Questions started pouring out of the old woman. All the ruminations of her long hours alone with anxiety spilled over. "Do you have a good bed? Is there anybody from your school in this place? What are they going to do with you?"

Lester grunted in reply. Finally, he broke the string of his grandmother's inquiries by asking about Jack, a shorthaired brown mutt that he'd raised from a little pup.

"How's Jack?"

Thelma shook her head. "He's pitiful. I don't think he comes out from under the porch except at suppertime. He misses you sore."

"Are you feeding him?"

"Yeah. But he needs you. When are you going to come home?"

Lester scowled. "If it was up to the district attorney, I'd never get out. I don't know when I'm going to get out of this place. My lawyer doesn't tell me anything."

Thelma reached out her hand again. "Move your chair over here."

This time Lester didn't try to avoid her. He picked up his chair and put it beside his grandmother's right hand. "Okay. I'm here."

Thelma groped into the darkness until she felt his shoulder. She ran her hand down his arm, unaware of the swastika tattoo that passed under her fingers.

"It's good to be with you, Lester," she said. "I've missed you more than Jack has."

Lester bit his lower lip. "I've missed you, too, Granny. I'm ready to come home."

The following morning Scott had a dentist appointment and didn't arrive at the office until after 10 A.M. He only had one message on his voice mail—a call from Harold Garrison.

"I'm in Omaha. What's going on with Lester? When is he getting out? I just called my mother, and she said he was in more trouble now than when you took the case. I told you I wanted some good news." Click.

"Have a nice day in Omaha," Scott said to the silent receiver.

He spent the rest of the morning preparing for the bond reduction hearing he'd scheduled that afternoon in Lester's case. He called Thelma Garrison, and she immediately agreed to pledge her house as security on a bond. He then drove to the county tax office and determined that the house and land had an appraised value of $42,000. He obtained certified copies of the documents he would need.

Lester was in the courtroom with a female correctional officer from the YDC when Scott arrived for the hearing. Apparently, Lester wasn't considered a sufficient security risk to require a male guard. No one else was in the courtroom. Scott sat down on the bench next to his client.

"What am I doing here?" Lester asked. "Is the D.A. making up more charges against me for things I didn't do?"

"No, I filed a motion to reduce your bond. The judge will come out in a few minutes and let me argue my request. I talked with your grandmother. She's willing to put up her house as security for your release."

"Does that mean I'm going home today?"

"Maybe. If the judge sets a bond less than the value of your grandmother's house, we may be able to get the paperwork signed by five o'clock."

"She told me she wanted me at home when she came to see me at the YDC."

Scott glanced at Lester and tried to imagine how the young man would look through a grandmother's uncritical eyes. Then he remembered. The old woman was blind.

"We need to get ready," Scott said. "I'm going to ask you a few questions in front of the judge: 'Do you have a place to live?'; 'Are you going to school?'; 'Do you realize that you'll have to come back to court?' Be respectful. This is the judge's first chance to hear from you."

"I'm not stupid."

In a few minutes Lynn Davenport and Judge Teasley entered the courtroom.

The judge sat down and looked at Scott. "Proceed, counsel."

"Your honor, I've filed a Motion for Reduction of Bond, and in support of the motion I call Lester Garrison."

Lester ambled over to the witness stand and raised his thin white arm. He was wearing a long-sleeve shirt and his tattoos remained incognito.

Scott asked a few preliminary questions, then said, "Tell the judge where you will live if you are released on bond."

Lester turned in the chair toward Judge Teasley. "I live with my blind grandma. She needs me around the house and to take her to the grocery store. My father is a truckdriver, and he's gone all the time, so I'm all she's got."

"Are you in school?" Scott asked.

"Yes, sir. I'm a junior at Catawba."

"Will you return to school?"

"I want to go to school. The longer I stay at the YDC the more behind I'm getting in my schoolwork, and I really want to graduate next year."

"Will you be in court when scheduled to appear in your case?"

"Yes, sir. I have my own truck. I bought it after working at a mill last summer."

"That's all."

Lester was an admirable actor. A much better witness than Scott would have guessed.

"Ms. Davenport," the judge said. "You may question the witness."

To Scott's surprise and relief, the D.A. stood and said, "No questions, your honor. My only concern is that if the defendant is released, he will seek to harass and intimidate potential witnesses."

"When do you intend to call the case for trial?" the judge asked.

"As soon as possible. We have the Anderson murder case pending for trial in two weeks, but there is ongoing discussion in that case with counsel for the defendant, and it may be resolved by plea agreement. Everything else on the calendar can be shuffled around."

The judge looked down at Lester and twirled his glasses once.

"I'm going to set bond at $40,000. If the defendant is able to satisfy the bond, I instruct him not to have any contact with the state's witnesses once he leaves the youth detention center. He is further ordered to attend school regularly and spend the remainder of his time at his grandmother's residence, only leaving to assist with her care, go to school, meet with his attorney, or appear in court. Of course, any illegal activity on his part will result in revocation of his bond and an immediate return to custody. Any questions?"

"No, sir," Scott said.

Lester looked up at the judge from the witness chair and with the respect of a summer law clerk said, "Thank you, your honor."

At five-thirty that evening, Lester Garrison walked out of the YDC and got into Bonnie's car. She took him to Bojangles for chicken and biscuits, and on the way home he ate three biscuits and four pieces of chicken. When the car approached Thelma's house, Jack heard the sound of the engine, crawled out from underneath the front porch, and gave a few halfhearted barks. Bonnie's car was a familiar sight.

Lester rolled down the window and called out, "Jack! Jack!"

At the sound of his master's voice, the dog bolted down the driveway in a brown flash. Bonnie stopped the car, and Lester got out to greet his four-legged friend. Jack ran excitedly in circles and jumped up to lick Lester's face when his master knelt down to pat his head. Lester laughed. Jack was the only creature on earth who could make Lester smile.

Lester's dented, white Ford pickup truck with the green tailgate was parked under a huge oak tree in the front yard. He'd bought the truck for $1,800 after working double shifts during the summer at a local textile mill. While Lester was at the YDC, a junk dealer had knocked on Thelma's front door and asked if she wanted him to haul the truck away for no charge.

Thelma was standing on the porch and started crying when she heard the sound of Lester climbing the steps.

"Welcome home, boy," she said and hugged him for at least ten seconds before he pulled away.

Jack ran excitedly back and forth around their legs until they went inside. Like most rural families, the Garrisons didn't allow dogs inside human dwellings. When the screen door slammed in his face, Jack began moaning, and Thelma said, "Go ahead and let him in the house for a few minutes."

The dog lay close to his master's feet. While Bonnie and Thelma talked, Lester leaned over and scratched Jack's favorite spot behind his left ear.

"Does Jack need any food and water?" Lester asked.

"I don't know."

Lester went into the kitchen and put some fresh water in Jack's dish. The dog followed close by his heels. Lester watched him drink.

"Grandma!" Lester called out. "I'm going out to the shed for a few minutes. I need to check on some things."

A previous owner of the property had built a tiny, windowless storage building from scrap pieces of lumber and plywood. The shed had been painted white at one time, but now only a few flecks of paint stubbornly clung to the aging wood. Lester had claimed the little structure as his own. He kept it locked. No one else had a key.

Inside the shed Lester reached up and pulled a metal chain that turned on a bare overhead light. He had put two sheets of new plywood on sawhorses to provide workspace for his projects. An orange extension cord hung down from an outlet built into the light fixture and provided a power source for several tools. Everything was exactly as he had left it. He locked the door and went back into the house. Bonnie had left.

"Lester!" his grandmother called out from her bedroom. "Come in here, boy."

Thelma was sitting in a brown vinyl recliner she'd covered with an old sheet to keep the plastic from sticking to her skin. A square fan was sitting on the floor near her feet doing its best to stir the air in the bedroom. Lester noticed that a sore on his grandmother's leg that wouldn't heal was getting larger.

"Get yourself something cold to drink and come talk to me," she said.

"I'm just here for a few minutes. I have some things to do."

"But you just got home," she protested.

"I've been cooped up for over a week and want to ride around without anyone telling me what I can do and where to go."

"'Fore you go, I need you to check my blood sugar. I've been feelin' like it ain't right all day. I can't even remember if I took my shot this morning."

"You always do it first thing."

"Please, don't go yet," the old woman said pitifully. "I really need to check my sugar."

Lester hated it when she talked in that whiny voice. He walked out of the room and down the short hall past his bedroom to the kitchen. There was a plastic jug of iced tea in the refrigerator and he filled a large glass.

"Lester? Are you comin' back in here?"

He didn't answer. He drank his tea, put the empty glass on the counter, and walked back to the bedroom. "Yeah, I'm here."

"Is the tester thing on the nightstand?"

The apparatus used to draw a tiny sample of blood and determine the glucose content of Thelma's blood was always in the same place. Lester was sure his grandmother touched it twenty times a day to make sure it hadn't grown legs and walked off. Beside it was a packet of disposable lancets.

Lester picked up the hand-held device and handed Thelma a lancet. She pricked her finger and held it out so he could collect a small drop of blood onto a strip of testing paper that he put in the glucose meter. Anything over 109 was outside the normal range. He watched until the digital readout flashed a number. It was 215.

"How is it?" she asked.

"It's okay," Lester said. "It's 95. I've gotta go."

Thelma sighed. "I guess that's good to know. I thought it was high. When will you be home?"

"Not too late."

Lester walked out to the front porch. Jack immediately hopped up to greet him.

"Not this time, boy."

Jack raced to the truck and wagged his tail excitedly, but Lester didn't change his mind. He often took Jack on short trips but not when he was going outside the Catawba area. Lester rolled down both windows before putting the key into the ignition. It was a pleasant evening, and he wanted to feel the wind on his cheeks. Before turning around in the yard, he reached under the front seat and felt the cool metal barrel of one of the pistols he'd purchased a couple of weeks after buying the truck. Its mate was in an evidence locker at the Blanchard County sheriff's department. The pawnshop owner on the east side of Charlotte had taken the cash Lester carefully counted out in front of him, put the bills directly in his pocket, and slid the two guns across the counter. He had never even asked to see Lester's driver's license. The serial numbers had been filed off both weapons.

The truck's engine coughed and sputtered to life. Lester turned on the radio and listened to the scratchy sounds that came through the one working speaker. One thing he shared in common with his grand-mother—they both listened to the same radio stations. He turned right out of the driveway. By the time the sun went down, he would be on the outskirts of Charlotte. There were other things besides stolen guns that were difficult to buy in a small town like Catawba.

14

*The eye is the lamp of the body. If your eyes are
good, your whole body will be full of light.*
MATTHEW 6:22

The following morning, Lester sat in his truck in the school parking lot until he heard the bell sound for first period. He didn't want to go back to school, but the prospect of returning to the YDC eliminated other options. He walked through the front door and turned left down the hallway toward his locker as the last students were entering their classrooms. Frank Jesup glanced over his shoulder and saw Lester. Frank hesitated but knew he couldn't stay and watch the fun.

Lester popped open the door of his locker to grab his history book. Inside was a foot-long piece of shiny metal chain with a lock at one end and a note taped to the other. He pulled off the note:

HERE'S THE PERFECT GIFT FOR YOU. PUT THIS CHAIN AROUND YOUR LEG AND LOCK IT! GET USED TO IT BECAUSE YOU'RE GOING TO THE REAL CHAIN GANG!! SEE YOU ON THE SIDE OF THE ROAD WITH THE OTHER PIECES OF TRASH!!!!

Lester looked up and down the hall to see if anyone was watching. He wadded up the note and put the chain in his backpack. If he found out who put the "gift" in his locker, he had an idea of how he would use it to teach them a lesson they wouldn't forget.

———

Jim Schroder, the superintendent of personnel for the Blanchard County school system, swiveled in his chair and picked up the phone. Behind him on a small credenza was a photograph with a handwritten inscription in the lower right-hand corner: "Da Nang, July 4, 1969." In the grainy picture, Marine Corps Captain James A. Schroder stood in front of a green helicopter surrounded by his crew and several of the mechanics on the base. Of the ten men in the picture, three did not live to see New Year's Day 1970. One more did not live to see New Year's Day 1971. Six survived the war. Of those, one committed suicide in 1975 after spending years in and out of VA hospitals receiving treatment for posttraumatic stress disorder. The other five returned to civilian life, raised families, and tried to forget what they saw from the air and experienced on the ground in Vietnam. Jim punched in the pager number for Larry Sellers, the supervisor responsible for the janitorial and maintenance workers in the school system. In a few minutes there was a knock on his door.

"Come in," he said.

Larry, a husky man in his midthirties, came in. "You called?"

"Yes. I've hired a replacement for Duane Mitchell on the janitorial staff at the high school," Jim said. "He can start immediately. He's already been processed through personnel."

Larry sat down across from Jim's desk. "Good. Any experience?"

"No. In fact, he doesn't speak English. He's a recent immigrant, a Hmong."

"A what?" Larry asked.

"*H-m-o-n-g.* The *H* is silent. It means 'free' in their language, and the name fits. I came in contact with them in Vietnam." Jim pointed at the photograph on the credenza. "My most important job in the war was to rescue American pilots whose planes were shot down by surface-to-air missiles. If North Vietnamese soldiers or Vietcong guerrillas captured a pilot, he would be killed or sent to a prison camp in the northern part of the country. Our best help came from Hmong militia who lived in the mountains of Laos, northern Cambodia, and western Vietnam. They knew the area and were superb fighters: brave, tough, and unselfish."

"Was this man a soldier?"

"I couldn't get a clear story through the interpreter, but I know he had contact with Americans during the war. He saw my photograph, pointed to his chest, and gave me a thumbs-up. He could have been on a rescue team himself. His name is Tao Pang. He's not young, probably about my age. He came in with a relative who speaks a little English. You should have seen his face when I said, *'Nyob zoo,'* which means 'Hello' in his dialect."

"Do you speak the language?"

"Just a few words. Not enough to do any good."

"How will I tell him what to do?"

"We can show and tell until he learns to communicate. Ask the guys at the high school to work with him. If anyone has a problem with him, send him to me." Jim leaned forward, and a glint of the steel that had burned in his eyes when he was a marine returned. "Hmong soldiers died saving American lives. The least we can do is let this man clean our toilets."

———

A few hours later, Tao Pang walked through the front doors of Catawba High School for the first time. He was five-foot-four with short black hair streaked with gray, deep brown skin, and dark eyes. No one but God knew that he was fifty-two years old.

A remnant of the Pang family had settled in North Carolina after entering the country in California. Like countless immigrants before them, the newcomers looked for a place in America that resembled the land of their birth, and the mountains of North Carolina resembled the hills of the Hmong homeland in Southeast Asia.

As a young man, Tao had been a warrior, and when the U.S. government broke its promises and abandoned the Hmong people after the fall of South Vietnam, he wanted to continue the fight. The village leaders disagreed.

"Many of our people have died. Many more will die if we stay. The land has vomited us out, and we must go."

They left that day and began the difficult journey to Thailand. Tao's wife was pregnant, and the journey was difficult for the young couple. After they crossed the Mekong River and reached the first refugee camp in Thailand, she gave birth to a baby girl they named Mai. She was the most beautiful creature in Tao's universe. The tiny infant lived six months before contracting dysentery. Without medical care, she lingered for eight days, growing weaker and weaker. She died at sundown. Part of Tao died with her.

Two years later, Tao's wife became ill with a fever that climbed higher and higher. Tao sat on the dirt floor beside her mat, rocking back and forth, praying to the gods of his ancestors. Exhausted, he finally fell asleep, and when he awoke, she was dead.

It was the end. Tao had no more reason to live. He went outside, looked up at the starry sky, and asked to die. He considered swimming toward the middle of the nearby river until he sank from exhaustion and the waters buried his sorrow forever. But as he walked along the creek-bank, he could not make his feet enter the water. He didn't die. Instead, he entered a zone of numbness where he became a walking dead man.

Several months later a man arrived at the camp. It was in the evening and the heat of the day had been replaced by a southerly breeze that cooled the air. The men of the camp invited the stranger to sit with them on logs in a circle.

"Why have you come to this place?" one asked.

"I am here to tell you about Jesus Christ, God's Son," the man said. "It tells about him in a book I received in Bangkok. It's called the Holy Bible."

"Jesus Christ. We have heard that name from the American soldiers," one of the men answered. "They used it as a curse. I do not want any more American curses falling on my head." Several men nodded in agreement and stood up to leave.

"Wait," the newcomer said. "The soldiers were wrong to use the name as a curse. Jesus came to remove all curses from us."

"How could he do that? Does he know our names or where we live?" another man asked.

"He took the curses upon himself and died for us."

"A dead man can't help me," the first speaker said.

"But he didn't stay dead. He came back to life. The curses couldn't hold on to him."

"Did an American tell you this?" one asked.

"No, it was a Vietnamese man—"

"Hah!" one of the men exclaimed. "We want no part of an American god served by a Vietnamese who hates and kills our people."

All the men walked away. All except Tao.

"Have you seen him alive?" Tao asked quietly. "This Jesus Christ."

"Not with my eyes, but I have met him in here." The man pointed to his chest. "The Bible calls it being born again."

"How can a man be born a second time when he's fully grown?"

"That is a good question. A holy man asked Jesus the same thing."

The stranger told Tao the story of Nicodemus. He concluded by reading from his Bible. "Jesus answered, 'I tell you the truth, no one can enter the kingdom of God unless he is born of water and the Spirit. Flesh gives birth to flesh, but the Spirit gives birth to spirit. You should not be surprised at my saying, "You must be born again." The wind blows wherever it pleases. You hear its sound, but you cannot tell where it comes from or where it is going. So it is with everyone born of the Spirit.'"

As he listened, Tao felt nervous, yet excited.

"Is this Holy Spirit, the one who blows like the wind, a brother to Jesus?" Tao asked.

"Closer than that, I think. They are different, yet one. Who can understand all things about God? But I know that Jesus has broken the power of evil spirits in my life and made me a new man. I'm free from the darkness that threatened to destroy me."

"I know this darkness," Tao nodded. "I hear the voices of hate in my head."

The man bowed his head for a second then looked up. "Would you like to be free?"

Tao rarely made face-to-face contact with anyone except his family and closest friends. Hmong culture did not encourage casual eye contact, and Tao had much to hide in the darkness of his soul. But there was a light and life in the stranger's eyes that Tao had never seen in another person. He invited him to stay with him, and on the third day Tao entered the kingdom of God. He became truly *Hmong,* truly "free."

———

Lunch was served at Catawba High from 11:30 A.M. to 1:30 P.M. One day a week, members of the Tuesday group occupied a small round table in the back corner of the cafeteria. Each student was given thirty minutes to eat, so the identities of the students sitting at the table shifted during the two-hour period.

The prayer group had started years before. The original members had graduated, and the current participants were second, third, and fourth generation, but the simplicity of the founders' mission had been maintained without significant change. When they sat down at the table, the students knew what to expect. They prayed simply, personally, and from the heart. They didn't try to act spiritual; they *were* spiritual.

Janie Collins had been part of the Tuesday group since she was in the ninth grade. Alisha Mason participated on a regular basis. Kenny Bost, shy in class or social situations, felt comfortable and safe in the group. The bond created during their times in the cafeteria spilled over into their contacts throughout the school day. When members passed each other in the hall, they greeted one another with an unqualified acceptance rare in high school.

When someone was praying, the others would listen and agree. Sometimes, a student would write a request on a card and put it in the middle of the table so the topic or person would receive prayer throughout the whole time period. There was one rule about written requests—they had to be suitable to broadcast over the school intercom without causing embarrassment to another person. No gossip prayers allowed. Most members prayed with their eyes open.

And that is what attracted the attention of Tao.

The janitor's first assignment was to stem the tide of trash and fallen food from covering the floor during lunch period. Larry Sellers took his newest employee into the cafeteria, handed him a broom and a dustpan, and pointed at a napkin and piece of bread on the floor. Tao got the message. He began at one end of the room and went from table to table cleaning up behind the messy American teenagers. It was easy labor, and he diligently worked his way to the back of the room.

When he reached the area near the round table where the students were praying, Tao leaned over to pick up a paper cup. He glanced up and saw Janie Collins's face. Her lips were moving; her eyes were open. To a casual observer, she appeared to be carrying on a conversation with the other students around the table. But Tao saw something different.

Radiating from her eyes was the same light that shone from the eyes of the evangelist who came to the refugee camp many years before. He stood up and quickly looked at the other students. The same light was in the eyes of the other four teenagers seated around the table. Tao knew the reason. The only explanation for eternal life in the eyes was the presence of Jesus in the heart.

Tao smiled as he continued picking up bits of garbage. He'd found family in the midst of strangers.

15

My true and honorable wife.
JULIUS CAESAR, ACT 2, SCENE 1

Scott left work a few minutes early so he could lift weights before going to the high school. He moved from position to position on the Nautilus machines, then switched to free weights. He was sitting on a bench panting when Perry came over.

"This is early for you, isn't it?" the owner of the gym asked.

"Yeah. It's mock trial night at the high school. I have to be there by seven o'clock."

Perry helped guide the heavy bar from its resting place, and Scott lowered it to his chest and pushed upward. After ten repetitions, Perry asked, "Trying to get pumped up before you see Kay tonight? You've already got great definition on your pecs. They're about to pop off your chest."

Scott gritted his teeth. "Don't talk to me."

Perry waited until Scott pushed the bar up ten more times, then let it fall into the brackets on the weight stand. Scott lay on the bench and let out his pent-up laughter.

"You know better than to say something like that while I'm under a bunch of weight," he said. "I could have hurt myself."

"I was here all the time. Besides, you're my lawyer. If you get hurt, you'll have to defend me against yourself."

Scott sat up. "That would be an easy case. I'd roll over on you and give me what I wanted."

Perry tossed Scott a towel. "So, what's happening with Kay?"

"Nothing. Why are you so interested?"

"It's not me; it's Linda. I told her what you were doing at the high school, and when I mentioned Kay Laramie, she started cross-examining me. She remembered all about you and Kay dating when we were seniors. Remember, we ate together with a big group at a fancy restaurant in Charlotte."

"Yeah, that's right."

"She also says you made a big mistake dumping Kay when you went into the army."

"I didn't dump her. I tried to call her when I was home on leave. Her father told me that she was going out with Bill Corbin, so I let it die a natural death. A long-range relationship between a guy in boot camp and a junior in high school wasn't in the cards."

"That's not what Linda says."

Scott wiped his forehead. "Really? What else does Linda say?"

"She said you were a 'cute couple.' Kay was good-looking, but as far as I can see, there has never been anything cute about you."

"That's reassuring from your perspective," Scott said wryly. "But remind Linda that Kay is still married and going through a breakup with her husband. I'm not sure she's in the market for another car so soon after wrecking the one she had."

"When is her divorce final?"

"She mentioned a hearing in a few weeks. I could check the file at the courthouse and find out."

Perry nodded thoughtfully. "I'm sure Linda thinks that's what you should do."

Scott twisted the towel and snapped it toward Perry's leg. "Tell Linda to mind her own business. Taking care of you is a full-time job."

That evening the mock trial session progressed better than Scott had anticipated. Young minds grasp facts quickly, and Kay had recruited motivated students. However, the prohibition against asking leading questions on direct examination was constantly violated, and the more aggressive students and witnesses were too quick to let the questioning degenerate into an argument.

"Didn't you know Ralph Risky had been drinking when you got in the car to leave Sarah Rich's house?" one student asked the girl playing Betty Moonbeam.

"No, I didn't."

"Yes, you did."

"No, I didn't."

"You're lying under oath."

Scott jumped in. "Time-out. What's happening here? Any objections? What can the lawyer do?"

Frank Jesup raised his hand. "Two things. The defense lawyer is being argumentative, and the question has been asked and answered. Either objection would be proper. If Betty won't directly admit that she knew Ralph was drinking, it would be better to ask questions showing she had the opportunity to know the punch had been spiked and that Ralph was around the punch bowl with his buddies with a glass in his hand."

Impressed, Scott said, "That's right."

Another problem came up because the students knew the facts too well and neglected important background information. The temptation to bypass the basics and go directly to the controversial parts of the case proved to be a pitfall.

"Testimony is telling a story," Scott said. "Even though the time allotted for each witness in the competition is short, you need to ask questions that create visual images so the judge or jury can see the events happening in their minds as they listen. Don't try to jump too quickly to the end of the story. The judges in the competition know something important is coming, and if you create a sense of anticipation, it will increase the impact of the information you bring out.

"By telling a story, you can also help a favorable witness get into character and increase their credibility. If Betty Moonbeam is your client, make sure everyone in the courtroom can feel her pain and suffering and the devastating effects of the accident on her life. If you're cross-examining Pete Pigpickin, don't let him avoid the embarrassing details about the night he spent in jail after driving a quarter-mile the wrong way down a one-way road. You want to convince the judges that Pete couldn't be trusted to ride a bicycle in public, much less drive a truckload of barbeque."

While Scott talked, Kay sat at her desk and reviewed the preference sheets turned in by the students. She made a list of her recommendations, and when Scott gave the students a five-minute break, she motioned for him to come over. She slid her notes over to him.

"What do you think?" she asked in a low voice.

Scott pulled a chair up beside the desk and read the paper. "I agree that Janie should be encouraged to step out of her comfort zone and take one of the lawyer roles even though she didn't ask for it, but I don't think she and Alisha should be co-counsel. Alisha plays the best Betty."

"I have Dustin and Frank together as lawyers. Who would be with Janie? Yvette?"

"Mix it up a little bit," Scott suggested. "Dustin and Yvette would complement one another. She's more aggressive; he's more laid back. He can give the opening statement and she can do the closing argument."

"That puts Frank and Janie together. I guess they would complement one another in the same way."

Scott hesitated. "I don't know about Frank. He may be hard to control."

"I'm not a lawyer, but it's obvious that he has the quickest legal mind in the room, and Frank needs something to sink his teeth into right now. I found out yesterday that his parents are separated. Maybe this program can give him something positive to focus on."

"But he'll run over Janie."

"Not if we do our job, and she's stronger than you think. I think she'll be a good influence on him, too."

When the students reassembled, Kay announced the primary and secondary roles for each member of the team. Everyone would learn two roles—either two witness roles or a lawyer and a witness part. As they broke up for the night, Janie came forward to Kay's desk.

"Frank offered to give me a ride home tonight, Mrs. Wilson. That will save you a trip, and we can begin talking about the case."

"Are you comfortable with Frank as your partner?"

Janie looked over her shoulder at Frank who was laughing with Dustin. "I don't know him very well, but I can get along with almost anybody."

"I'm sure you'll be okay, but if you have any problems, let me know."

Janie enjoyed the fifteen-minute drive to the trailer park where she lived. Frank put down the top of his sports car, and she laughed as the evening wind swished through her hair. She'd never been in a convertible before. It was ten times better than riding in the back of her uncle's pickup truck.

———

Later in the week, Scott was sitting at his desk making notes about an appellate decision that might help him in Lester's case. He finished and looked out his office window. He hadn't been able to shake Perry Dixon's suggestion that he check the status of Kay's divorce. He decided to take a break and walk to the courthouse. There was no harm in doing a quick check of the public records.

Fall and spring were the best seasons in the Piedmont area of North Carolina. Summer was too hot. Winter too wet. Today, a hint of coolness was edging its way into the air, and Scott enjoyed the pleasant stroll down Lipscomb Avenue.

Passing through the labyrinth of halls and offices in the new section of the judicial building, Scott entered a large open room that contained the official records for the Blanchard County District Court. The two district court judges had jurisdiction over several types of cases, but the bulk of their work was domestic disputes. Divorce cases marched in columns down the pages of the district court docket books: *Jones v. Jones, Harris v. Harris, Thomas v. Thomas, Melrose v. Melrose*. On and on the names went until they all ran together, and the individual tragedy each entry represented became lost in the overwhelming tide of marital disintegration.

He found the volume containing the most recent filings and opened it. On the first page was an entry for *Jesup v. Jesup*. Scott suspected that by the time Frank's parents divided up the marital pie, the court's file would be six inches thick. He turned back several pages before finding what he was looking for: *Wilson v. Wilson*. Scott jotted down the case number on a slip of paper and took it to one of the assistant clerks, a young woman seated at a brown metal desk.

"I'd like to see this file," he said.

The clerk took the slip from his hand and disappeared in between tall lateral filing cabinets that filled the back two-thirds of the room. She returned with a thin folder.

"Are you the attorney for one of the parties?" she asked.

"No, I'm just checking the status of the case."

Scott stepped away from the counter. Inside the file was a Complaint for Absolute Divorce filed on behalf of Jackson Kilpatrick Wilson, Plaintiff versus Kay Laramie Wilson, Defendant. It was a garden-variety divorce. The parties had been living as husband and wife in Blanchard County for more than six months, were separated, and had no children. Jake asked for the division of marital property, an absolute divorce, and "such other relief as the Court deems just and proper." The complaint was verified, and Scott inspected Jake's signature, trying to determine from the handwriting something about him as a person. The quick scrawl across the bottom of the page revealed nothing.

The answer filed by Kay's lawyer was brief. She didn't deny anything except the request for divorce. She didn't want the marriage to end. Her denial had forced Jake to jump through another legal hoop, and his lawyer had already filed the necessary pleading—a Motion for Summary Judgment. Attached to the motion was an affidavit from Jake repeating his request for dissolution of the marriage. It takes two people to make a marriage, but only one to end it. Kay could sign a counteraffidavit, but the motion would be granted, and an order of absolute divorce signed by the judge. A brief notation would follow in the docket book. Case closed. Marriage terminated.

Unless Jake changed his mind.

Scott closed the folder and silently handed it back to the clerk. He turned down the hallway that connected the new building to the old courthouse. When he came to the courtroom door, he stopped and looked inside. It was deserted. He sat on a bench and rested his right arm on the back of the smooth wood. The room was as quiet as a church sanctuary, and the walls made no effort to speak. Today, Scott wasn't trying to listen to the sounds of past trials. The voice he wanted to hear was within him.

Scott had walked to the courthouse out of curiosity, but he hadn't been completely honest with Perry Dixon. The possibility of a relationship with Kay Wilson had crossed his mind after their breakfast meeting at the Eagle. The more he was around her, the more his interest increased. When he read the words on the pleadings and saw Kay's clear intention to save her marriage, it caught him off guard. Scott didn't know how he should react. Ann Gammons had recently handled a case in which an estranged couple reconciled the morning of the final divorce hearing. Anything was possible, and Kay was still married until the judge signed the order ending it.

Scott had to be careful. Even if he could sway Kay in his direction, he wasn't sure he could trust her feelings. The instability of a rebound relationship was not mythical. Scott wasn't naive. He'd been burned badly in a similar situation toward the end of law school and didn't want to repeat past mistakes. He tapped his fingers on the back of the bench. Yes, he had to be very careful.

———

On Thursday night at the mock trial practice, Scott and Kay separated the students and spent the evening working with them on their respective parts. Kay took the witnesses to one end of the classroom and worked on acting skills. Scott's group of lawyers sat in a semicircle in front of him and focused on the simplified rules of evidence that applied to the mock trial competition. The time passed quickly. Kay looked at the clock on the back wall and stood up.

"Let's stop for the night," she said. "Some of you probably have some homework to do before tomorrow."

The students grabbed their backpacks and headed for the door. Frank again offered to take Janie home.

After the young people were gone, Scott asked, "How did it go?"

"Good. And you?"

Scott put his materials in his briefcase and snapped it shut. "Frank and Janie are way ahead of Dustin and Yvette. When Frank has something to focus on, he's an impressive young man."

"What about Janie?"

"She'll eat the other lawyer's case like a piece of fried chicken. I've decided her backwoods accent gives her an advantage. It will lull the opposition into thinking she's dull and impress the judges when she drawls out a sharp, insightful question in that high voice of hers. I wouldn't want to face a lawyer like her in front of a jury in a rural county."

Kay counted on her fingers. "You're safe for another eight years. That's when she'll graduate from law school."

"It could happen."

Kay picked up her brown satchel. "Are you going to the football game tomorrow night?" she asked.

"Are you?"

"Yes."

They stepped outside. It was already dark. The days were getting shorter.

"Would you like to ride together?" she asked.

Scott put his hand on the railing for the wooden steps that led up to the modular unit and faced her. He didn't speak for several seconds.

"Let's ride together," he said simply. "But it's not a date. That probably wouldn't be right. I just want to be your friend."

"Of course."

Kay followed Scott's vehicle out of the school parking lot. He'd been so cool toward her when he arrived at the school that she'd considered not mentioning the game. But loneliness is a relentless enemy. It's never satisfied by yesterday's companions. Scott made her smile, and his light-heartedness was a tonic to her soul. So, she brought it up.

She wasn't prepared for the way he looked at her on the steps outside the classroom. It was very different from anything else she'd seen in his eyes, and a wild thought flashed through her mind that he was going to say he didn't want to help with the students because he didn't want to see her again. But it wasn't a look of rejection. It was a look of attraction.

Kay sighed. Scott may have been hiding a renewed romantic interest in her, or he may have simply wanted to set the parameters for the present. Whatever his motivation in avoiding the word *date* and using the word *friend,* she knew things could quickly change. She needed to be careful.

———

The bomber did his best work in the middle of the night. He wasn't limited by adult supervision, and if he slipped out of bed at 2 A.M., no one noticed. He began accumulating what he needed for his first tests and kept the materials well hidden. It wasn't as hard to obtain information and supplies as he first suspected. "A free society is a porous wall against terror."

Even when he wasn't working on the project, he thought about it as he daydreamed in class. Nothing in school had ever captured his attention so completely. Initially, the other problems in his life increased his frustration, but he decided they were the perfect camouflage. People would think he was focused on the obvious negative circumstances and not realize the direction from which the greatest danger would come.

The darkness watched. Its confidence grew.

16

If a man desire the office of a bishop, he desireth a good work.
1 TIMOTHY 3:1 (KJV)

After finishing his morning coffee, Scott opened the Garrison file and found the phone number for Bishop Alfred Moore, the pastor of the church that used Montgomery Creek for baptism services. An African-American man with a slow, deep voice answered the phone.

Scott introduced himself and said, "I'm a lawyer investigating the incident when shots were fired during the baptism service. I would like to talk with you about what happened."

"Are you with the district attorney's office?"

"No, I represent the juvenile who's been charged with the crime. He's being prosecuted as an adult."

"I see." Bishop Moore paused. "The district attorney told me I didn't have to talk to anyone representing the defendant."

"That's true," Scott admitted. "But it's your choice. There is no legal prohibition against answering questions. I'm simply trying to make sure my client has a fair trial."

"Of course, that's all you want to do. It's all about a fair trial. You're not trying to get your client off the hook even if he's guilty."

Scott didn't want to debate his role as a lawyer in the American criminal justice system with an African-American preacher.

"Will you answer a few basic questions?" he repeated. "I'm not trying to trick you."

"Where do you work?"

"Humphrey, Balcomb and Jackson."

"You work with Leland Humphrey?" The minister's tone changed.

"Yes. He's my boss."

"Why didn't you say so? Why don't you come about noon, and we'll eat together?"

Scott had set aside the whole morning to work on Lester's case, but he hadn't planned on spending it exclusively with Bishop Alfred Moore.

"Uh, sure."

"Leland can tell you how to get to the church."

"Yes, sir."

"Good. I'll see you then."

Scott went downstairs to Mr. Humphrey's office. The older lawyer's door was open, and he was talking on the speakerphone to a lawyer in Raleigh and another in Goldsboro. He motioned for Scott to take a seat and held up his right index finger to signify that the call would be over in one minute. Ten minutes later, he hung up the phone.

"What's the latest on our case?"

Scott looked down at his legal pad. "I just talked with Bishop Alfred Moore, the pastor of the church where the shots were fired. He was a little hostile until I mentioned your name."

Leland laughed. "The bishop! Did he invite you for lunch?"

"Yes. I'm going to meet him at the church at noon. What can you tell me about him?"

Leland smiled. "Nothing right now. I'll go with you."

"Do I need to let Reverend Moore know you're coming?"

"No," Leland said. "That won't be necessary. We're practically brothers."

Scott opened his mouth, but Mr. Humphrey cut him off. "No questions."

Scott spent the rest of the morning trying to interview other witnesses. Everyone was unavailable, and he left message after message. Finally, one of the deputies who arrested Lester returned his call.

"I'm in the middle of a training seminar," Deputy Ayers said. "We're on a break, and I only have a few minutes."

"Thanks for calling," Scott said. "May I tape-record our conversation?"

"No, you can't."

"All right," Scott replied slowly. "I'm just trying to collect information."

"Then ask me a question. I never let a defense lawyer record a conversation."

Scott had written down an outline of questions on his legal pad. "How did you become involved in the arrest?"

"It's all in my report. Do you have a copy?"

"Not yet. The D.A. hasn't answered our discovery requests."

"Okay. I was on patrol with Deputy Bradley. We received a radio dispatch that shots had been fired in the vicinity of the church on Hall's Chapel Road. We responded with blue lights and siren. Bradley saw Garrison in the woods along the creek, and I slowed down. When he saw us, Garrison threw something into the creek and started running. I radioed a unit that was coming from the other direction and advised them to be on the lookout for a slender white male wearing a camouflage T-shirt and blue jeans."

"Who was in the other car?"

"Deputies Hinshaw and Dortch."

"Who apprehended Garrison?"

"We did. He saw the other car and stopped. Bradley got out of the car and grabbed him."

"Did he say anything?"

"Some profanity that was directed at Deputy Bradley."

"Why Bradley?"

"Bradley is very black. Garrison is very white. Do you want to know what your client said? I remember it word for word."

Scott looked up at the ceiling. "Yes."

He took verbatim notes. He'd been around Lester enough that the deputy's recollection of the conversation didn't surprise him. It would be hard to put a positive spin on it for the jury unless they were all wearing white hoods.

"Bradley brought him over to the car, and I asked him what he'd thrown in the creek. He said it was a rock, but I wasn't convinced. I read him his rights and told him to get in the back of the patrol car. He refused and tried to kick Bradley, so I handcuffed him. I asked him if he'd been near the church, and he said, 'What church?'"

"Did he ask for a lawyer?"

"No, counselor. If he had, I wouldn't have asked any more questions."

"Were the other officers on the scene?"

"Yes. They heard me read the suspect his rights."

"Did Garrison say anything else?"

"On the way to the station, he calmed down and asked us what he could do to get out of trouble. I told him the best course would be to tell the truth. Then he started talking about being persecuted and accused Bradley of prejudice."

"Do you think Garrison had been drinking or on drugs?"

The deputy spoke to someone away from the receiver. "Maybe. The kid could have been high because of the nonsense he was talking."

"Was a blood test performed before you took him to the youth detention center?"

"No more questions. I've got to get back to the seminar."

"When can I call—"

The phone clicked off. Scott glared at the receiver before placing it into the cradle. He fumed for several seconds then looked at the clock. It was time to leave for their rendezvous with Bishop Moore. Mr. Humphrey was putting on his sport coat when Scott looked in his open door.

"Ready? We'll take my car," the older lawyer said.

Mr. Humphrey could have owned a silver Mercedes, but he drove an older model Buick that was top of the line when it was new ten years before. His car was a miniature reflection of his office. There were papers in boxes in the backseat, and he had to move an extra briefcase from the passenger seat so Scott could sit down. With so much flammable material in the vicinity, it was a good thing Leland Humphrey didn't smoke.

They pulled out of the parking lot behind the office building. Scott said, "You were going to tell me about Bishop Moore."

"Oh, yes. Do you remember my birthday?" Leland asked.

The office had celebrated Leland Humphrey's birthday the Friday before the Fourth of July. There was a huge cake decorated with symbols of the legal profession.

"It's in July."

"Correct, July 3. That's important when I tell you about Bishop Moore."

"Why?"

"Alfred and I were born on the same day, same year. He was born at home early in the morning; I arrived at the hospital later that evening. The same doctor saw us enter the world. His family lived on one side of the railroad tracks and mine lived on the other, but if you go to the courthouse, you'll find that only two babies were born on July 3 that year in Blanchard County—Alfred Moore and me."

"How did you find out about it?" Scott asked.

"My father was part owner of a lumberyard on Forsyth Street, and I worked there during the summers from the time I was twelve until I graduated from high school. It was hard work, but my father thought I should learn to sweat for a paycheck instead of sorting invoices in the office. Alfred worked there, too. We spent months together every summer stacking wood and loading trucks."

Mr. Humphrey accelerated as they left the center of town. "Of course, he went to a different school, Autumn Hill. It was a pitiful place. I never went inside, but you could tell it was run down from the outside. There was grass growing in the sidewalk, broken windows, and the playing fields were more dirt and weeds than anything else. I'm sure the teachers did the best they could, but there was probably a shortage of everything from textbooks to chalk. Separate but equal was never a reality."

"Where was the school?"

"On Central Avenue."

Mr. Humphrey slowed down for the turn onto Hall's Chapel Road. "When we were growing up, Alfred and I were color blind at the lumberyard, but there were limits we didn't think about crossing when we were out in the community. Years later we worked together on a citizen's committee during integration of the schools."

They crossed the creek on a narrow bridge that warned "No trucks over 5 tons allowed."

"Alfred's mother made the best corn bread," Leland continued. "It would fall apart in your hand and melt in your mouth. He'd bring an extra slab for me, and I'd eat it for lunch while we sat on a stack of boards."

Hall's Chapel Road was a winding country road that crossed Montgomery Creek once, then followed the twists and turns of the stream from a safe distance. Sometimes the stream could be glimpsed through the trees that grew to the water's edge. Most of the houses in the area were small with large vegetable gardens. Corn was popular, and at this time of year dead cornstalks stood crookedly in rows or were stacked tepee fashion in the center of the fields.

"Even when he was a teenager, Alfred knew a lot about the Bible. There was a foreman at the lumberyard we called 'Pharaoh.' He was a hard taskmaster, and Alfred would quote verses from Exodus behind his back."

"Do you know what employees at the firm call you behind your back?" Scott asked.

Mr. Humphrey looked across the seat and raised his right eyebrow. "No, tell me."

"Bushy."

Leland smiled. "The eyebrow thing. At least it's better than Pharaoh."

The road turned toward the left and they could see the water of the stream through the breaks in the trees.

"We're close," Mr. Humphrey said.

They came around a corner and slowed down. The Hall's Chapel Church was nestled under a hill. The trees across the road had been cut down so that people standing in front of the church had a clear view of Montgomery Creek in either direction. The white sanctuary was typical of thousands across rural America—a wooden frame building with ten narrow windows down each side and a steeple on top. Eight broad steps painted a deep green led up to the front door. The parking area was paved with black asphalt that sparkled when hit by direct sunlight. An Oldsmobile similar to Mr. Humphrey's car was next to the church.

"New parking lot," Mr. Humphrey noted. "Offerings must be up."

They got out of the car and walked up the steps to the front of the church. The door was locked.

"He may be in the back," Leland said.

There was a single story building connected to the back of the sanctuary. A side door was unlocked, and they went inside a narrow carpeted hallway. They walked past Sunday school rooms equipped for children with low tables and miniature chairs. It was quiet and everything was neat and tidy. At the end of the hall, there was a plain wooden door with the word *Office* on it in gold, stick-on letters. Leland quietly opened the door.

The bishop, a short, stocky man with gray hair, was on his knees with his back to them. He had his head in his hands and was leaning his elbows on a chair where a Bible rested open before him.

Scott stopped in his tracks, but Leland stepped into the room and called out in a booming voice.

"Bishop! It's Gabriel! I've come to take you home!"

Alfred Moore didn't turn around, but looked toward heaven and prayed, "Lord, I'm ready to go, but I have a final request. Please, send another angel to take me. I don't trust one that sounds like Leland Humphrey to get me there in one piece."

Bishop Moore got slowly to his feet. The preacher was dressed in a dark suit, white shirt, and dark tie. He put on a pair of small, silver-rimmed glasses that he'd put on his Bible. He gave Leland a bear hug and shook Scott's hand.

Alfred Moore's eyes twinkled behind his thick glasses. "I'm glad you brought my old friend. Did he tell you we share a birthday?"

"Yes, sir," Scott said. "And also about the lumberyard and your mother's corn bread. There's only one thing I wanted to ask you."

"What?"

"His eyebrow habit. Has he always done that?"

The bishop chuckled. "His mother told me it started the first time he stuck his thumb in his mouth. By the time I met him, it was irreversible, and I couldn't help him."

"You make it sound like a sin," Leland protested.

"No, it's not sin. That's one thing in your life you can leave alone." The bishop walked over to his desk and turned on an answering machine. "Are you hungry? I thought we might have dinner on the grounds."

"Sounds good," Leland replied.

They went down the hall to the wing of the building on the opposite side of the church.

"How long have you been at this church?" Leland asked. "The last time we talked, you were at Welcome Hill."

"About four months. The previous minister moved to Hickory, and I'm filling in until the church calls a new pastor. I've known most of the people here since they were kids."

They came to the end of the hall. The last room on the left was three times the size of a typical Sunday school room. It was set up with long tables and metal chairs. Against one wall were a sink, a refrigerator, and two stoves.

"This is the fellowship hall," Alfred said. "We had a covered-dish supper last night for the older members of the church, and the people brought more than enough. I put some leftovers in the oven about thirty minutes ago. There's plenty for the three of us, plus anyone else that wanders by."

"Any corn bread?" Scott asked.

"There are several pieces wrapped up in aluminum foil. We can eat inside or under the shelter beside the creek."

"I'd like to go outside," Leland said. "It's a nice day."

Bishop Moore got three plates from a cupboard over the sink. Opening the ovens, he took out containers of food and set them on top of the stove. "Let's see," he said. "You have a choice between baked chicken, roast beef and gravy, and meat loaf. Don't shy away from the meat loaf, Scott," he warned. "The woman who made it doesn't do it as an excuse for nothing else to fix. And for vegetables we have corn soufflé, green bean casserole, sweet potatoes with pecans, and brown rice. Here's the corn bread, and there is a pitcher of sweet tea in the refrigerator. I also have some desserts that I can't show you until you clean your plate."

Leland loosened his suspenders. "That's not going to be a problem."

The men piled three plates with their selections and carried the food and drinks across the road. Many years before, the church had built a rectangular, open-air structure along the banks of the creek. Underneath the roof was a long concrete table at the proper height for adults to stand and eat.

The bishop prayed. "Lord, thank you for this food. Bless Leland. Bless Scott. Don't delay. Release your blessing upon these men—today, tomorrow, and all the days of their lives. For Jesus' sake. Amen."

Scott enjoyed the sound of the stream running over the rocks. The water was clear, making it hard to judge the depth of the water. Mr. Humphrey and the bishop reminisced about events that happened many years ago, and Scott listened. It was a history lesson by those who lived it.

At a break in the conversation, he pointed to a pool about ten feet from shore. "Is that where you baptize people?"

Alfred looked toward the stream. "Yes. It's about four and a half feet deep and cold even in August. I used to wear regular pants, but I've gotten soft in my old age and bought waders."

"What happened the day the shots were fired?" Scott asked.

Alfred wiped his mouth with a napkin. "We'd finished a meal under the pavilion and at tables set up in the parking lot. The candidates for baptism went into the church to change, and I put on my waders. We came outside, and the ones who were going to be baptized stood on a flat rock beside the edge of the water and gave their testimonies while I waited in the stream. When each one finished, they waded out to me, and I baptized them. Leland, you know Nancy Knight, don't you?"

"Her husband works for a trucking company."

"That's the one. We'd been praying twenty years for Nancy. She never could forgive her family for things that happened when she was a girl, and it kept her from coming to the Lord. She let go of the bitterness about a month ago during a revival meeting. When it was her turn to speak, she didn't stop after a few sentences. Tears were streaming down her cheeks, and there weren't a lot of dry eyes in the congregation."

The preacher pointed to an area of dense brush on the opposite side of the stream. "Nancy was wading out to me when I heard a couple of loud pops. I didn't see anything, but people on the bank saw one or two bullets hit the water not far from where we were standing.

"Everybody started running toward the church. Other shots followed. One shattered the windshield of Deacon Wade's car. Another hit the wall of the church. Nancy slipped. I caught her and helped her to the bank. When I looked over my shoulder, I saw someone running through the trees, heading downstream. Somebody called the sheriff's department on a cell phone, and the deputies were here in a few minutes."

"How clearly did you see the person who was running away?" Scott asked.

"It happened fast, but I'm sure he was wearing a blue shirt and had dark hair."

Scott stared at the underbrush on the other side of the stream. "Are you sure he had dark hair?"

Bishop Moore nodded. "Positive."

"Were you wearing your glasses?" Leland asked.

"Yes. I have to wear them. Otherwise, I wouldn't know which end to baptize."

"Did anyone else see this person?" Scott asked.

"I'm not sure. After the first shots were fired, everyone was running away from the water, and he didn't come out from behind the trees until he was downstream. Everyone gathered in the church until the police arrived. It took a while for the people to calm down. Nobody wanted to go outside, and we kept the children away from the windows."

"How long did you stay in the church?"

"Not long. About thirty minutes later a detective told us there had already been an arrest. That made a big difference. He asked questions and several people remembered different things, but I think I was the only one who saw the one who fired the shots."

"Did you see a gun?" Scott asked.

"No, but those bullets didn't fall out of the sky. Someone was aiming in our direction, and I didn't see anyone else on the side of the stream. I'm just thankful no one was hurt or killed."

"We are, too," Leland said.

"Did you tell the detective what you told us?" Scott asked.

"Yes. He was taking notes."

"Anything else?"

"No, that's it."

"Okay, I have one more question," Leland said.

Alfred waited.

The older lawyer picked up his empty plate. "What are our choices for dessert?"

———

On the way back to the office, Scott told Leland about his interview with Deputy Ayers.

"The deputy told me Lester was wearing a camouflage T-shirt and blue jeans at the time of his arrest."

"He could have taken off his shirt as he ran down the stream."

"Possibly. But what about the dark hair? You've seen Lester. He is bald as an egg."

"Yeah," Leland nodded. "That was interesting. Very interesting."

17

Weeping may endure for a night,
but joy comes in the morning.

PSALM 30:5 (NKJV)

On Friday afternoons, the number of lawyers at Humphrey, Balcomb and Jackson quickly thinned out after three o'clock. Following the bounteous lunch with Bishop Moore, Leland Humphrey went home for a midafternoon nap on the couch in his den. Scott stayed until all the partners left the office. He didn't work very hard after three o'clock, but the perception of activity was sufficient for Friday afternoons. His basic goal was to avoid the receptionist broadcasting his name over the general phone system—a sure sign that a lawyer had sneaked out of the building. When the coast was clear, he went down the back stairs and drove to the gym.

The small parking lot was more crowded than usual. He finished his second series of leg exercises performed while lying on his stomach when Perry joined him.

"How's school?" Perry asked.

Scott rolled over onto his back and sat up. "I'm still learning."

"Is English your favorite subject?"

Scott smiled. "You're really on this thing, aren't you?"

Perry shook his head. "It's not me; it's Linda. She asks me every couple of days if I've talked to Scott about Kay Laramie. She has a bad case of matchmaker fever."

"Buy her some flowers. Maybe she'll focus on you instead of me."

"That won't work. I'm already caught. Now, she's working on the rest of the world. If I could charge money for the couples she's put together,

I could give you a free membership. She claims direct responsibility for three marriages in our church last year."

"I'm a hard sell," Scott said.

He moved to the station set up for leg presses and sat down. He selected a large amount of weight and did a set of twenty-five.

"Make sure you push equally," Perry observed. "You're using your right leg more than your left."

"My left knee aches at full extension," he replied.

Scott rubbed an indention that creased his left leg above his knee. It was twice as large as the scar on his right hand.

"Back off the amount of weight until you can do it evenly."

Scott moved the pin to a lower level and did another set of twenty-five.

"That's better," Perry said. "So, what do I tell Linda? She's going to be after me as soon as she finds out you were in the gym today."

"Don't tell her that you saw me," Scott suggested.

"That won't work," Perry responded. "She'll know it immediately if I lie to her."

"Not saying anything isn't lying."

"It is to Linda."

Scott smiled. "For such a strong guy, you're a wimp." He pushed through one final set with the leg press. "Okay," he said when the weights clanged down for the last time. "Tell her I'm taking Kay to the football game in Lincolnton tonight. We're riding together and will probably get something to eat after the game. But it's not a date. I've already told her I just want to be friends."

Perry stood up and patted Scott on the shoulder. "Thanks."

"Oh, one other thing," Scott said. "I went to the courthouse and checked on her divorce."

"And?"

"She didn't want it, but it looks like her husband is going to push it through anyway."

"When will it be over?"

"I didn't see a notice of final hearing in the file. Until then, remind Linda that Kay's last name is Wilson, not Laramie."

By the time he drove home, cleaned up, and took care of Nicky, Scott was ten minutes late getting to the high school. He hated being late and sped across the parking lot to Kay's classroom. Her car wasn't there. The football team and the band had left for the game in buses, and the students' vehicles were scattered across the parking lot. He drove up and down the rows of cars. No sign of Kay or her vehicle.

He glanced toward the lower exit for the lot and saw a blue car going over the hill away from town. He stepped down hard on the gas and shot out of the parking lot, barely missing a minivan coming in the opposite direction. He accelerated up the hill, then had to slam on the brakes to avoid plowing into the rear of a slow-moving logging truck.

The truck was chugging slowly up the hill belching of diesel smoke that enveloped Scott in a pungent cloud. He held his breath and gripped the steering wheel tightly for several seconds. The truck was laboring along, and there was no place to pass on the winding road for at least five miles. Under normal conditions it was a thirty-minute drive from Catawba to Lincolnton. This evening it took Scott an extra fifteen minutes. By the time he arrived at the football field, the parking lot was full, and a policeman directed Scott and other latecomers to a Baptist church down the street.

A few fans were straggling across the parking lot to the entrance for the football field. The red and white of the home team predominated, but there was a respectable showing for the blue and gold of Catawba. Scott was buying his ticket when the Lincolnton fans stood to their feet and cheered as the home team ran onto the field.

Scott walked around the track to the Catawba stands. The seating provided for the supporters of the visiting team was completely inadequate for the number of people who had made the trip. There wasn't a vacant seat in sight, and many spectators were standing in small clusters behind the Catawba team bench. Scott scanned the crowd for Kay. No one waved to him, and he wasn't able to distinguish her face in the crowd. Still looking toward the stands, he turned around and knocked a box of popcorn out of a woman's hand. White kernels flew everywhere.

"Excuse me," he said.

It was Kay.

"First, you stand me up, then you assault me," she sputtered. "I stood in line for ten minutes to buy that popcorn."

Scott started to bend down and pick up the scattered pieces but realized it would not help the situation.

"I'm sorry," he said. "I'll buy you another one."

"Why didn't you come to the school?" she asked. "Did you forget?"

"No, I was late, and you'd already left. I think I saw your car leaving the parking lot, but I ended up behind a logging truck and couldn't catch up."

Kay looked past Scott, and he saw that her eyes were slightly red. There was something bothering her beyond a missed connection or a few pieces of popcorn on the ground.

"What's happened?" he asked.

Kay bit her lip. "I'm not mad at you. Jake called me on my cell phone while I was driving over here. I'm making it hard for him to get the divorce, and we got into an argument. He said some cruel things and hung up on me." She wiped her right eye with her hand. "Sorry. I'll get control of myself."

"That's okay."

Kay sighed. "Let's walk. I lost my seat when I went to the concession stand."

The game started. Scott looked toward the field to see who received the opening kickoff but didn't watch the rest of the play. They walked slowly around the track. Once they reached the area behind the end zone the crowd thinned out, and they were alone.

"I know men don't like it when a woman is emotional," Kay said. "It infuriated Jake when I became upset about something."

Scott didn't respond. A woman's emotions made him uncomfortable, too.

"Do you remember what I said last night on the steps outside your classroom?" he asked.

"About friendship?"

"Yes. I don't have any advice about your divorce, but I want you to know that I care."

It didn't take much kindness to touch Kay's heart. She quickly wiped her eyes with the back of her hand and walked away from the field into the shadows. Scott could tell she was crying. He followed a couple of feet behind her and positioned himself so that her willowy form was hidden from view behind his broad one.

The crowd yelled loudly as the pendulum of football fortunes swung wildly back and forth under the bright lights. But at the edge of the game, real life was lived in the shadows. When the waves of sadness grew less intense, Kay turned around.

"I wasn't sure you'd still be there," she said hoarsely.

"Of course, I am," Scott said.

Kay's lip trembled again, but there was nothing left. She reached in her pocket, took out a tissue, and wiped her eyes. "What's happening in the game?"

"I don't know. Would you like to leave? We could go somewhere else."

"No, I want to stay. I needed to cry, but I don't want to wallow in my sorrows. The game will help me take my mind off myself."

Scott was silent for a moment. "Would a fresh bag of hot popcorn help?"

A tiny smile appeared. "Yes."

"And your own Cheerwine?"

"Only if it lives up to its name." Kay retreated back into the shadows. "I'm sure I look terrible. I'd rather not get in the middle of the crowd at the concession stand."

"I'll get it," Scott offered. "You wait here."

"Okay."

Scott walked around to the home side of the field. He glanced back once and saw Kay standing where he left her. He walked further, and when he looked again, the glare of the lights didn't reach the place where she stood.

Although he'd been stoic while standing guard over Kay's sorrow, Scott was in turmoil. Part of him wanted to drive to Virginia Beach, track down Jake Wilson, and beat him to a bloody pulp. Kay didn't deserve what Jake was dishing out. Another part of Scott wanted to wrap a soft blanket around Kay and make her forget about rejection and pain, but he reminded himself of his conclusion while sitting alone in the courtroom after reading the divorce file. The wrong type of kindness from him would create its own confusion and problems. She didn't need it; he didn't want it.

Scott was jostled in the crowd as he stood in line for popcorn but didn't notice. He reached the front of the line where a frazzled female volunteer intruded into his thinking and asked, "What do you want?"

"Huh?" he responded.

The woman gave him an exasperated look.

"Oh, a large, buttered popcorn and two Cheerwines."

The woman put the food in a flimsy cardboard tray. Scott held his elbows out to protect it as he pushed through the crowd. Retracing his steps, he saw Kay standing on the track behind the goalpost area. The Catawba team was driving toward that end of the field and had the ball on the Lincolnton fifteen-yard line. Scott stopped to watch. The home crowd was on its feet yelling as loudly as it could in an effort to disrupt the play. The young quarterback faked a run up the middle then dropped back for a pass. He looked to the right side of the field, but the receiver was double-covered. He ran to the left. The wide-out on that side of the line had drifted toward the end zone after helping block the defensive end. The quarterback tossed a wobbly pass that the player caught at the eight-yard line. The Lincolnton safety charged forward to tackle him, but the receiver deftly sidestepped the defender and scampered into the end zone for a touchdown. Scott couldn't clap or jump without having to buy another popcorn, but he cheered as loud as he could. Then he saw the number of the Catawba player. It was Dustin Rawlings.

Scott came up to Kay as Catawba was lining up for the extra point attempt.

"Dustin caught that touchdown pass," he said.

"I know. I had a great view of the play."

"Here's your popcorn and drink," he said. "They guarantee that every kernel in the bag is popped and buttered."

"Thanks. Where are we going to sit?"

Scott looked toward the visitor section. The stands were full, and there was less chance of a seat now than when he had arrived. "We'll have a picnic." He set his drink on the ground and took off the black Windbreaker he was wearing. "You can sit on my jacket."

Kay sat down, and Scott stretched out his legs on the damp grass. They shared the popcorn. Several times Scott's thick hand brushed against Kay's slender one as they both reached into the bag. The first quarter ended. They got up and Scott shook out his jacket.

"Let's walk back to our side of the field," he said.

When they reached the edge of the stands, a female voice called out, "Mrs. Wilson!"

It was Yvette Fisher.

"Do you and Mr. Ellis want to sit down?" she asked.

"There's not enough room," Scott said.

"It's okay. We're going to walk around for a while."

The students left, and Scott and Kay sat down to watch the action on the field. The tempo was opposite to the game the previous week. Both teams seemed able to score at will, and by halftime the score was 28-21 in favor of Catawba. While the bands were on the field, Yvette returned and squeezed in next to Kay. Scott left to find the rest room.

"Are you enjoying the game?" the dark-haired student asked.

"Yes. I like it when they pass the ball and score a lot of points," Kay answered. "If there isn't much offense, I lose interest."

"Me, too. Scoring is my favorite part." Yvette shifted in her seat. "May I ask you a personal question?"

Kay glanced at Yvette's slightly upturned nose. "That depends on how personal it is."

"Someone told me that you dated Mr. Ellis when you were in high school."

"That's a statement, not a question."

Yvette frowned. "Okay. I'll try again. Did you date Mr. Ellis when you were in high school?"

Kay stood up. "I'm not going to answer. It's too personal."

The teacher left for the rest room. While she was gone, Scott returned and sat down next to Yvette. He opened a bag of peanuts and offered her one.

"Thanks," she said. "Are you enjoying the game?"

"Yeah, but I really enjoyed the game last week; it was hard-nosed football. I played linebacker in high school and appreciate good defense."

"I like a defensive struggle, too," Yvette said. "Too much scoring is one-dimensional."

Scott glanced sideways to see if the student was teasing him, but her face revealed nothing. "That's an interesting way to put it," he said.

Yvette gave him her best smile. "Didn't you graduate from Catawba High?"

"Yes."

"Is it different now?"

"Not really."

Everyone stood up to cheer as a Catawba running back broke into the clear and ran seventy yards for a touchdown.

After everyone calmed down, Yvette asked, "May I ask you a personal question?"

"Sure."

"Did you date Mrs. Wilson when you were in high school together?"

Scott leaned forward for the extra point attempt that was tipped at the line of scrimmage and sailed wide.

"Off to the left," he said. "Yeah, we dated for a few months when I was a senior and she was a sophomore."

"So, she's younger than you are."

Scott smiled. "Yeah, but she's always been mature for her age."

"Where would you go on dates back then?"

"We didn't have cars so I'd ride my horse over to her family's log cabin. We'd sit on the front porch in rocking chairs and talk."

Yvette frowned, and Scott decided to give her a few tidbits of information she could share with her friends. "We went water skiing once on Lake Norman when the water was freezing cold. I took her to the junior-senior prom. Do you know Perry and Linda Dixon?"

"The man who owns the gym?"

"Yes. We ate dinner with them at a fancy restaurant in Charlotte before going to the dance."

"You must have really liked her a lot."

"Yes, if I hadn't gone into the army after graduation—" Scott stopped. It was time to divert Yvette's curiosity. "How is she as a teacher?"

"She's popular with most kids. What were you saying about the army?"

"Yvette, you're doing a fine job cross-examining me, but this is not mock trial practice. That's all I have to say about dating Kay Wilson in high school or beyond. Would you like another peanut?"

"Uh-huh."

Scott handed her a few more peanuts.

Yvette cracked one open. "Here comes Mrs. Wilson. I'll let her sit down."

Yvette walked over to her friends and engaged in an animated conversation. Scott chuckled.

"What's funny?" Kay asked as she slid in next to him.

"Yvette was grilling me about our relationship in high school."

"She tried that with me but didn't get anywhere. What did you tell her?"

"Not much. I mentioned water skiing and that I took you to the prom."

Kay shook her head. "That's plenty. By Monday morning the school gossip line will have us taking a romantic boat ride on the lake then breaking up after a horrible fight after the dance."

The Lincolnton side of the field erupted in cheers as their cornerback intercepted a pass and ran it back for a touchdown. The touchdown barrage continued into the fourth quarter. With two minutes left in the game, Catawba was behind by four points and had the ball on their own thirty-yard line. The visiting team drove down the field on a combination of runs and short passes. On fourth and four, Dustin caught a crucial pass for a first down and ran out of bounds to stop the clock. With fifteen seconds left, the Catawba fullback ran into the end zone for a touchdown. The game ended with Catawba on top 52-49.

Scott and Kay joined the crowd squeezing through the exit gate.

"Would you like something to eat?" he asked.

Kay hesitated. "Is this a sympathy offer?"

"No, I'm hungry. I remember a local pizza place not far from the field."

"All right."

"My car is down the street. That will help us beat the crowd out of the school parking lot."

Fifteen minutes later, they were facing one another in a tiny booth for two at the local pizza restaurant. The small table was covered with a red plastic tablecloth and a candle in a red-colored glass container was burning in the middle. The place hadn't changed décor since it was built in the '70s.

"What do you like on your pizza?" Scott asked.

"I'm flexible."

"How about zucchini, spinach, and goat cheese?"

"If that's what you want," Kay said. "I would have guessed you were a pepperoni fan."

"I am, but I eat pepperoni pizzas all the time at home. When I eat out, I like variety. Why don't we each pick two toppings and make it a joint effort?"

"Okay."

They placed their order for a pepperoni, mushroom, green pepper, and extra-cheese pizza. The restaurant quickly filled up with students from Lincolnton. A few from Catawba also slipped in the door. The manager dimmed the lights.

"There's Alisha." Kay pointed to the tall young woman who was with a taller young man. "She's with Devon Harris, a basketball player."

The waitress set two small, white plates on the table. "Your pizza will be out in a few minutes," she said.

Scott handed one of the plates to Kay with his right hand. In the flickering light of the candle, the scar across his palm looked inflamed.

"Scott, what happened to your hand?"

He glanced down at the deep indention and touched it with the tips of his fingers.

"It happened in the army."

"You already told me that. It's not classified information, is it?"

"No, just very hard for me to speak about. I haven't talked to anybody in Catawba about it except Perry Dixon."

"Oh, then don't—"

"No. I'll tell you. We're friends."

Kay waited.

Scott took a deep breath. "I was part of a peacekeeping force sent to a small African country. It was not a public mission. We were trying to keep three ethnic groups from committing mass genocide against each other. Nobody really wanted us there because each little army thought they could win if we were out of the picture. One evening there was a bomb threat involving our camp. Bomb threats were common; it was a way for the locals to hassle us. We'd never found anything, but we had to follow procedure and do a sweep of the compound. Three of us were sent to a communications room to check for anything unusual. One of the men saw something suspicious behind a computer in one corner of the room and asked me to take a look. I'd had some training in explosives at Fort Benning.

"On the floor behind the CPU was a small black box about the size of a disposable camera. There were wires leading from the box to the computer and along the wall. There was a bomb specialist in the unit, but I decided to make sure this was not a false alarm and asked one of my buddies, a soldier named Steve Robinson, to help me. He traced the wires around the corner to an area where we stacked large metal trunks that served as supply storage. I decided to check it out. Everything looked normal, and I opened one of the trunks. It was fine, and I asked Steve to check another one. When he did, there was a loud click. I don't know what he saw, but he fell down on top of the trunk, slamming shut the lid."

Scott rubbed his palm again before continuing. "The explosion killed him instantly. I was knocked several feet in the air. The metal trunk was blown to bits, and I had injuries from the metal casing to my hand, left shoulder, and left leg. I could have been killed or lost my sight, so I guess I was lucky. The other man in the room wasn't hurt."

Kay's eyes were big. "I never imagined."

Scott shook his head. "Steve was my best friend."

He reached in his back pocket and took out his wallet. He flipped it open and handed it to Kay. There was a tiny photo of an African-American man in military uniform, a smiling woman in a yellow dress, and a baby in a pink outfit.

"That's Steve, his wife, Amy, and his little girl, Francie. It was taken about six months before he was killed. They shipped his body home. He's buried in upstate New York."

Kay handed the wallet back to Scott.

"I went to see Amy when I returned to the States—" Scott stopped and squeezed his eyes tightly shut for a few seconds. "I've opened a bank account as a college fund for Francie. I put a little bit in it each month."

"Scott, that's wonderful."

"No!" he said sharply. "You don't understand."

"I only meant it was kind of you to do something for your friend's baby."

"I know, but I don't deserve any credit. I didn't follow proper procedure, and a man was killed. I made a mistake, and it cost someone his life."

Kay stayed silent.

After a few moments, Scott continued, "Amy forgave me and told me to go on with my life, but in some ways it hasn't been possible. Deep down inside, I'm always wondering why I'm alive and he's dead. Even if nobody else knows what happened that day, I have to prove to myself that I deserve to be alive."

"How do you do that?"

"By trying to be the best person I can be. I didn't mention it to my boss or Dr. Lassiter, but it's one reason I agreed to help at the high school. I know that volunteering to help kids is a good thing."

Kay shook her head. "I don't know, Scott. I believe we need to be good people, but the pressure you've put on yourself—" She paused. "I'm not sure you can live your whole life like this. I heard what you said about the bomb, and I'm not even sure it's your fault."

"Don't say that! I know the truth. The experts who investigated the incident told us the bomb was designed to explode the next time the computer was turned on or the trunk was opened. There were three wires running along the wall. If I'd cut the right one before opening the trunk, there wouldn't have been any danger, but I didn't think the situation through and acted outside my training."

"Okay, okay."

"And Steve sacrificed himself for me."

They sat quietly for a moment.

"Did you leave the army because this happened?" Kay asked.

"Yes. When my initial term of enlistment ended a few months later,

I came home and went to college. I'd lost my desire to stay in the military, yet I didn't fit in with eighteen-year-old freshman who'd never been away from home. So, I studied a lot, made good grades, and went to law school."

The waitress brought their pizza. All around them, young people were laughing and talking, but Scott and Kay were no longer carefree teenagers. They were an island unto themselves. They ate in silence, each in a world of thoughts far removed from a small town in North Carolina.

———

Sunday morning Kay rolled over in bed and hit the snooze button on her alarm clock before it could jar her to full consciousness. It wasn't set to go off, but she didn't realize her mistake until she woke up abruptly at 7:45 A.M. and thought she had to be at school in ten minutes. Sunday-morning panic attacks were taking their toll on her. She lay in bed for another half-hour but couldn't go back to sleep. She went into the living room, pulled back the curtains, and looked outside. Her apartment was on the second floor of the building, and she had a view of a narrow stretch of grass, a corner of the parking lot, and the wooded area that provided a buffer between the apartment complex and the highway. She opened a sliding glass door and took a breath of the morning air. It was going to be a clear day.

She brewed a cup of coffee and sat on the secluded deck outside her bedroom with her knees under her chin. She opened her notebook. Before going to sleep on Friday night, she'd captured in words some of the tears that fell on the grass of the football field in Lincolnton. The contents of a broken heart are easily poured out, and it didn't take long to write two pages. Reading the words again there wasn't much to change. She sighed deeply, but no tears rose to the surface. She thought about the death of Scott's army friend and wondered if she should try to capture with pen and ink the essence of his self-sacrifice. No. She didn't comprehend raw courage enough to put it on paper. Chronicling Scott's journey was beyond her understanding as well.

She flipped back a few pages and saw the poem she'd written after hearing about Ben Whitmire's unexpected trip over the waterfall. Her verbal images of the everlasting arms were more questioning than confident. Ben Whitmire had survived. She wasn't so sure about herself.

Kay drained the last drops of coffee from her cup and decided to go back for another installment of church.

The crowd hadn't grown in a week's time. When Kay walked into the back of the old gym, she felt a tug on her sleeve and looked down. It was one of Janie's brothers.

"Come sit next to me," he demanded.

Kay followed the little boy to a row of seats. Janie saw her and waved from her place next to the overhead projector. The song leader picked up his guitar and began with one of the same upbeat songs Kay had heard the previous week. She stood and sang along. Less self-conscious than the week before, she thought about the words of triumph that were repeated in each verse. This group of Christians believed that God was on their side in the struggle of life. Another fast song followed, and then two new songs slowed the pace.

Many people closed their eyes during a final ballad that incorporated the word *Alleluia* as part of the chorus. Kay wasn't sure of the precise meaning of the ancient expression of worship, but repeating it over and over with slightly different inflections and pitches enhanced the beauty of its sound to her ears. *Alleluia.* She loved all kinds of words, but she'd never met one quite like this. Surrounded by more common terms, it stood out like a gem set in a ring. *Alleluia.* Each repetition was fresh in its own way. When the leader softly strummed his guitar for the last time and let the chord disappear into the still air, Kay felt a pang of regret. She wanted to visit the place where the music took her one more time. She felt cleansed.

Ben Whitmire, dressed again in khaki pants, a casual shirt, and cowboy boots, ambled to the front of the room and greeted the people. He caught Kay's eye and smiled at her in personal welcome. The sermon was about God as a loving Father who wants to adopt us as his very own. It was the first time Kay had heard the Supreme Being described as a heavenly daddy—Abba, Father.

She listened to every word.

And the longing to know God's love began stirring in Kay's heart so strongly that it made her chest hurt. She wondered how the other people in the room could stand the pressure of the moment. She swallowed, but her mouth was dry.

The minister looked across the congregation. "When I see your faces this morning, I see people of all ages and backgrounds who share a common need to be adopted into the family of God. He is your Abba, Father. He chose you as his very own before the foundation of the world. No matter what has happened in your life up to now, each of you has a destiny in his love. If you hear his voice calling to you today, how will you respond? Will you hold up your arms to him?"

Ben asked everyone in the congregation to close their eyes, and Kay squeezed hers shut. The minister's kind voice penetrated the darkness behind her eyelids.

"Some of you need to reach up to God this morning. If that is you, lift your hands as a physical sign of the inward desire of your heart."

Kay didn't have to debate. Her fists, which had been tightly clenched by her side, opened, and she gracefully lifted her hands to heaven. She whispered, "Abba, Father."

The ends of her fingertips tingled, but she didn't notice. The greater touch was in her heart.

18

And I blessed them unaware.

SAMUEL COLERIDGE

Scott's phone buzzed and the receptionist said, "Lynn Davenport from the district attorney's office on line five."

He pushed the blinking light.

"We've reached a plea bargain in the Anderson murder case," the D.A. said in her clipped voice. "I'm moving Garrison to the next trial calendar. We're going to try the assault case involving the church first and the conspiracy case later."

That was good. Scott wanted the trials separate to avoid the taint of one charge creating a bias against Lester on the other. The D.A.'s decision eliminated the need to file a motion to sever the cases with the judge.

"When?"

"Two weeks."

"Two weeks! I've got a lot of preparation to finish. I'm not sure I'll be ready by—"

"We're giving your client his constitutional right to a speedy trial. Our calendar has fallen apart, and we need cases to try. If you want a continuance, take it up with the judge."

Scott set his jaw. "I'll consider my options."

"Oh, one more thing," the D.A. added, "if your client wants to plead guilty, we can talk about a reduced sentence."

"How reduced?"

"I'd say five to seven years."

"On probation?"

Scott heard Lynn Davenport laugh for the first time. It wasn't a pleasant sound.

"Jail time. Maybe five in and two out. Something like that. We'd have to work out a plea on the conspiracy charge, but if I know he's going to be in jail for a while, we could consider something to run concurrent with additional probation time after he gets out."

Scott grunted, "I'll tell him but won't recommend it."

"Suit yourself. It's the only offer I'm making."

Scott called Thelma Garrison and left word for Lester to contact him as soon as he got home from school. Then he went downstairs to Mr. Humphrey's office. The senior partner's door was closed, so Scott stuck his head around the corner and asked the older lawyer's secretary if he was with a client.

"No. He just walked in a few minutes ago."

Scott knocked lightly on the door, and the familiar deep voice called, "Come in!"

Leland Humphrey had his feet propped on the corner of his desk and was reading the local newspaper.

He looked over the top of the page at Scott and said, "Did you see this article? One of the new commissioners is going to make a motion that the county build a minor-league ballpark next to the fairgrounds. What would we call our team? The Catawba Crayfish?"

Scott sat down without responding to the serious ramifications of a rookie-league baseball team in Blanchard County. He had his own challenges.

"I talked with Lynn Davenport from the D.A.'s office this morning. They're going to put the Garrison case on the trial calendar in two weeks."

Mr. Humphrey closed the paper. "We need to file a motion to sever the two cases."

"Not necessary. She told me they were going to try the church case by itself. She also offered a plea bargain: five years in jail followed by two on probation."

"For both cases?"

"Just the church case, but she said she would take a plea on the conspiracy case and run it concurrent with the assault charges. There wouldn't be any additional jail time."

Mr. Humphrey ran his thumb down the inside of his right suspender. "The conspiracy case is weak. She must not have much beside the e-mails she gave us."

"I haven't done any investigation on it, but it's a ridiculous offer on the assault charge. Bishop Moore's testimony is enough to create a reasonable doubt."

"Don't get overconfident. All the chickens in the henhouse haven't been counted. You have other witnesses to interview."

"I know, but the call irritated me. Davenport is so arrogant. I can't wait to get into court and knock her back on her heels."

"Have you interviewed all the officers involved in the arrest?"

"Only Ayers. He was with Officer Bradley, a black man whom Lester insulted and tried to kick when they were putting him in the patrol car. I can't remember the names of the other two deputies."

"See if they will tell you anything. There may be minor inconsistencies in their stories that can be brought out at trial. Who else is on the state's list of witnesses?"

"A few people who are probably members of the church. I should have asked Bishop Moore about the names the other day, but I was enjoying lunch so much I forgot."

"That's correctable. Alfred will tell you how to contact anyone in his flock."

"Should you call him?" Scott asked. "He trusts you."

"No, now that he knows you, he'll talk to you." Mr. Humphrey tapped his fingers on the edge of his desk. "One of the best ways to prepare for a case is to look at it through your opponent's eyes. Pretend you're the D.A. and tell me what you're thinking."

Scott tried to mimic Lynn Davenport's accent. "Okay. I grew up in New York, and I've been a bully all my life."

"Drop the accent and don't assume facts. What are the strongest parts of your case?"

Scott counted on his fingers. "Lester was caught running away from the scene. He threw the gun that may have fired the shots into the stream. He yelled racial slurs at one of the deputies who arrested him. He couldn't look more like a redneck racist if you hung a sign around his neck and put a Klan hat on his head. It's all circumstantial, but it makes Lester the most likely perpetrator of the crime—opportunity, motivation, presence at the scene."

Mr. Humphrey nodded. "You've convinced me. He's guilty. Let's hear your defense."

"The only eyewitness describes someone else. It's not a crime to be walking on the creekbank. There's no confession—"

"Wait," Mr. Humphrey interrupted. "Could Bishop Moore be right and Lester still be the person he saw?"

Scott thought a minute. "A hat or a toupee?"

The older lawyer smiled. "Let's go with a hat. Isn't it possible that Lester was wearing a dark cap that fell off his head as he ran through the bushes or that he tossed it aside before the deputies caught him."

"We don't know," Scott admitted.

"And need to find out," Mr. Humphrey finished.

Scott prepared a motion to continue the conspiracy case to another term of court as a precaution so he wouldn't have to try the cases back to back. He also hoped that once Davenport lost the first case, the second one would evaporate.

Shortly before lunch, the receptionist buzzed him. "Lester Garrison on line three."

Scott picked up the phone. "Did you get my message?"

"Yeah. My grandmother phoned the school and got me out of class. What happened?"

"We need to talk in person. Can you come to my office this afternoon?"

"Where is it?"

"Downtown near the courthouse. It's a two-story building on the corner of Lipscomb Avenue and Trade Street."

"Okay. I can be there by four o'clock."

Scott had an appointment at four, but he could reschedule it. "That will work. See you then."

Four o'clock came without any sign of Lester. After waiting fifteen minutes, Scott called downstairs and asked if anyone was waiting for him.

"No, sir," said the high-school student who served as backup receptionist for a few hours in the afternoon.

At four-thirty Scott looked out the window to see if Lester was wandering up and down the street. There were people on the sidewalk but no sign of Lester Garrison. He called Thelma Garrison's number. No one answered.

At five o'clock his phone buzzed. The high-school girl said in a low voice that Scott could barely hear, "Your appointment is here."

"What?"

"Lester Garrison. He goes to my school."

"Okay. I couldn't understand you. Tell him I'll be there in a minute."

Scott was walking down the hall when he met the young girl. Wide-eyed, she asked, "Are you his lawyer? Everyone at school has been talking about what he did at the black church. Or supposedly did," she added quickly.

"Don't mention he was here."

"I won't, Mr. Ellis. I know everything is confidential."

Lester was slumped down in a chair in the corner of the waiting room. Scott offered to shake hands. Lester quickly wiped his right hand on his jeans before reaching out. Scott noticed that the young man's fingernails were full of grease.

"I had trouble with my truck," Lester said. "It wouldn't start when I went out to the parking lot this afternoon. I think someone messed with the carburetor."

Scott's hand felt oily as he showed Lester the way to the conference room. Lester put his hands on the table then picked them up when he saw that his fingerprints would smudge the shiny surface.

"Do you want something to drink?" Scott asked. "We have soft drinks, coffee, and water."

"Uh, sure. Working on the truck made me thirsty, and I didn't have time to stop before coming here. Give me a water."

Scott asked the receptionist for two waters. When she brought them in, she looked at Lester without speaking. He glanced up at her, and

Scott thought he saw the hint of a scowl around the corners of the young man's mouth.

When she left, Lester grunted, "She goes to my school. Does she know anything about my case?"

"No. Your file has been in my office. Everything that happens here is confidential."

Lester shrugged. "It hasn't been confidential at the high school. If the judge hadn't told me to stay in school or go back to jail, I would have dropped out. Everybody is talking behind my back, and there has been some harassment."

He told Scott about finding the chain and note in his locker. "And that's not all. Last Friday I went into the rest room in the gym near the end of the day. Someone came in behind me and turned out the lights. There are no windows in there so I couldn't see a thing. I tried to find the door and two guys knocked me up against the wall. One of them punched me in the arm and told me not to come out until I had counted to twenty. Then they left."

Lester pulled up his sleeve. In the center of the lightning bolts was a deep purple bruise.

"I think the guy had something metal in his hand to cause such a bad bruise."

"Did you recognize the voice?" Scott asked.

"No, but I'm sure it was a black guy. They won't come out into the open and fight one-on-one."

"Did you report it to the office?"

"What good would that do? I'm the only one who is going to look out for me. I have a right of self-defense, don't I?"

"But you don't need any fights," Scott replied. "That will get you back to the YDC faster than anything else that could happen."

"I'll do what I have to do," Lester said flatly. "My chance will come."

"Let me bring you up to date on the case," Scott said.

He began with the phone call with Deputy Ayers.

"That's not the way I remember it," Lester snorted. "They roughed me up before throwing me in the back of the patrol car."

"Okay. And the gun?"

"Like I told you at the YDC. I was scared and tossed it in the creek. It shouldn't be against the law to carry a pistol along the creekbank, but when they came roaring down the road with the siren on and the blue lights flashing, I panicked. What would you do if the police surprised you like that?"

It was a good question, and Scott made a note on his legal pad. His client was barely seventeen and his conduct could be explained as an immature reaction caused by the stress of the moment.

Lester listened closely to Scott's summary of the conversation with Bishop Moore. Scott watched his client's eyes when he reached the part about the person with the dark hair. Lester's gaze shifted, and Scott couldn't follow where the young man's memory traveled.

"Do you have a black hat?" Scott asked.

"Uh, I have a black baseball cap, but I wasn't wearing it when I was arrested. I'd shaved my head a couple of days before and didn't have any hair at all. That means the preacher's testimony will help my case, won't it?"

Scott nodded. "I think so, but there are other things you have to consider."

He outlined some of the strengths of the state's case. Lester didn't like what he heard.

"You sound like you're giving up."

"No. Just being realistic. If I ignore the other side, we are more likely to get blindsided. I have to get ready to try this case and want to give it our best shot."

"I'm not guilty. My father said it's your job to prove it."

Scott decided not to mention that the state had the burden of proof. As a practical matter, juries often expected the defense to present a plausible alternative to the prosecution's case in order to gain an acquittal.

"Mr. Humphrey, the senior partner in the firm, is going to help at trial. He's one of the best lawyers in this part of the state."

"Okay."

Scott hesitated. He'd intended to mention the plea bargain, but decided it would be better to end the conversation and bring it up when Lester's father was present.

"When is your father going to be back in town?"

"I'm not sure. We never know until he shows up on the front porch."

"When he comes in, I'd like to meet with both of you. In the meantime, stay out of trouble."

———

Outside the office, Lester's truck refused to start. He cursed, got out, and raised the hood. He didn't want to run down the battery by turning the engine over again and again without effect. He unscrewed the wing nut that secured the cover for the air cleaner and set the round metal piece on the pavement. The carburetor was stained a deep brown but there wasn't any obvious obstruction blocking the flow of fuel.

"Need some help?" a voice behind him said.

Lester turned around. It was a tall, African-American man with graying hair. He was dressed in clean blue overalls and brown work boots. He looked at Lester through rimless glasses.

"No, I got it running a few minutes ago." Lester went around to the cab of the truck and retrieved a screwdriver.

The man took a step back but didn't leave. Lester leaned over the engine and adjusted the idle screw. He checked again to make sure the carburetor wasn't locked in the choke position and climbed behind the wheel. He turned the key. The engine rolled over and tried to come to life but couldn't catch. When Lester got out of the truck, the black man was peering at the left side of the carburetor. He had Lester's screwdriver in his right hand.

"I don't need any help," Lester repeated.

Ignoring him, the man pointed with the screwdriver. "Something is wrong with this spring. When you turned the key, it couldn't bring the butterfly valve to the right position." He reached around the front of the carburetor, unhooked the spring, and held it between his dark fingers. He rolled it back and forth. "See, it's been twisted and doesn't have the tension it needs to work."

Lester swore. "That's what they did. When I find out—" He grabbed the spring out of the man's hand. It flew from his grasp and rolled under the truck. Lester got down on his hands and knees and peered under the vehicle. The man joined him and in a few seconds said, "Here it is. It's hard to see in the shadows."

The man handed the spring to Lester. "I'm sure you could get another one from Hill's junkyard for a buck or two. They have several older model cars and trucks with the same engine."

"Yeah, I've bought some parts from them, but that's four or five miles from town."

"I could give you a ride," the man offered. "I don't have anything else to do."

Lester hesitated. "Don't you work?"

The man smiled, revealing a shiny gold tooth in the front of his mouth. "I've worked plenty, but now I'm retired and loving every minute of it."

Lester had never voluntarily been in a car with a person of another race. "What are you driving?"

"My truck. It's parked down the street."

Lester was out of options. "Okay."

The man stuck out his hand. "I'm Thomas Greenway."

Lester shook the man's hand. "Lester Garrison."

Lester lowered the hood of his truck and followed Mr. Greenway to the sidewalk. Mr. Greenway stopped in front of a dark blue Ford pickup that was the same year as Lester's. It had been beautifully restored. Lester's mouth dropped open.

"Is that your truck?" he asked.

"Yep. That's why I thought maybe I could help you out. I know most everything about this model."

Lester ran his hand across the smooth paint on the hood. There was a narrow white stripe down the side and fog lamps beneath the front bumper. Mr. Greenway had replaced the standard wheels with chrome ones and put on larger tires than when the vehicle came off the showroom floor many years before.

"How long have you had it?" Lester asked.

"About five years. It wasn't in as good a shape as yours when I bought it, but the frame was solid and the body wasn't rusted. I've spent hundreds of hours on it, and more money than I could get back if I tried to sell it."

Lester pressed the button on the shiny door handle. The door opened without a hint of a squeak. He sat down in the passenger seat. The vinyl was cleaner than a new plastic tablecloth. When the African-American man turned the ignition, the engine gave a deep-throated rumble.

"What kind of pipes do you have on it?"

"I changed it to dual exhausts and modified mufflers. I didn't want it to sound like a Harley, but I don't mind if people know I'm coming down the road."

He backed out into the street. Lester rolled down the window so he could hear the sound that escaped through the baffles of the mufflers. They drove north away from the center of town. Riding in the truck, Lester forgot to focus on the color of Mr. Greenway's skin.

The junkyard was on a two-lane road that wound past small farms and a subdivision that contained ten or twelve modest houses. The owner of the junkyard lived in a rambling, red-brick home. He had fenced off a large field behind his house and filled it with rows of wrecked vehicles in various stages of decay. A small sign on the road read "Hill's Auto Salvage," but the hundreds of cars in plain view made the sign superfluous.

Mr. Greenway pulled into a gravel drive and stopped in front of the small wooden building Mr. Hill used as an office. Behind it was a larger metal building devoted to systematic cannibalism of the most valuable parts from the vehicles destined for the fields. At the sound of the truck, the proprietor came out of the metal building.

"Howdy, Thomas," Mr. Hill said. "What can I do for you?"

"This young man needs a spring for a carburetor on a truck like mine. Do you have something in the shop or do we need to go to the field?"

"Only a spring?"

"I'm thinking that's the problem."

"I don't have that sort of thing inside. Go get one."

Lester and Thomas walked between the rows of automobiles and trucks. The old man walked briskly and took two turns without slowing down.

"Do you know where you're going?" Lester asked.

"Yeah. There's a row of Fords toward the back of the lot."

The trucks were lined up like nursing home residents in wheelchairs enjoying the late-afternoon sun. Thomas raised the hood on one and took off the air cleaner. In a few seconds he held up a spring so Lester could see it.

"What do you think?" he asked. "It looks tight."

Lester nodded. "Okay."

As they walked back to the shop, Thomas asked, "Have you thought about fixing up your truck?"

"Not really."

"Where do you go to school?"

"Catawba High."

"I didn't make it past eighth grade at the old Autumn Hill school. I dropped out and went into the mills."

Mr. Hill charged Lester a dollar for the spring and in ten minutes they were back in town standing in front of Lester's truck.

Lester raised the hood. "I don't want to mess it up trying to put it on."

"I'll show you," Thomas said.

The two leaned over the engine. Lester held the spring between his white fingers stained by engine grime, and Thomas guided him with his weathered black hand to the correct spot.

"Fit it here first, then it connects underneath."

Lester attached it on the second try.

"Okay," Thomas said. "Give it a try while I watch from here."

Lester got behind the wheel and turned the key. The engine turned over once and started running smoothly. Thomas looked around the edge of the hood and smiled. He reattached the air cleaner and handed Lester his screwdriver through the window.

"Thanks," Lester said.

"I love these old trucks," Thomas replied, patting the door. "If you decide you want to do some work on it, give me a call. I know almost everything about them." He got out his wallet and handed Lester a card. "I don't have a business, but my granddaughter made these for me on her computer. It has my name and phone number on it. Call me anytime."

"Okay." Lester looked at the card. It had a row of tiny red hearts around the edge. He laid it on the seat beside him.

Lester's truck didn't miss a beat as he drove out of town. When he turned down the road to his grandmother's house, he glanced at Thomas Greenway's card. Picking it up, he read it again, then tossed it out the window.

19

*Are not all angels ministering spirits sent
to serve those who will inherit salvation?*

Hebrews 1:14

Tao Pang learned quickly. He couldn't read the labels on the different containers of cleaning solutions, but it didn't take him more than two or three times of show and tell to remember how and where to use each substance. Larry Sellers was pleased with his work. He valued someone who came to work on time and did his job carefully more than an employee who put on a good show when the boss was in view but spent the rest of the day finding secluded spots in the building to hide from work.

Tao's favorite job was buffing the floors. After the students left for home, he would sweep a hallway with a long-handled dust catcher to pick up bits of paper and loose trash, then use the buffer and a spray bottle of polishing compound to make the floor shine. Back and forth, he would let the buffer work its way naturally down the hall. The rhythm of the machine formed the backdrop for melodies that Tao sang softly under his breath.

The songs would have sounded odd to Western ears; they weren't based on an eight-note octave. But the singsong style was perfect for the looping cadence of the buffer. Often Tao improvised, creating musical pictures from childhood memories of mountains and streams. At other times, spontaneous praise to Jesus flowed from his heart. People who walked by might catch a hint of his song, but they wouldn't be able to decipher its message.

During lunch period, Tao often assisted in the cafeteria: cleaning the floor, wiping off tables, and taking bags of garbage to the Dumpster.

Whenever he worked in the dining hall, he looked for the holy assembly he'd spotted on his first day at work. One Tuesday, after the students began streaming into the room and the noise reached a high decibel level, Tao checked the table in the back corner. Several students were seated around the circle, but this time it wasn't the students who arrested his attention; it was the attentive figures standing behind them.

Tao had seen heavenly messengers in Thailand. After his conversion, he took a journey from the refugee camp to Bangkok. On the return trip he was accompanied one afternoon by a spry old man who listened to Tao's many questions, answered a few of them, and shared a meal with the pilgrim from his brown food bag. At first Tao thought he was a holy man, but his fellow traveler didn't have a pious look. He laughed too quickly and enjoyed the sights and sounds of the surrounding forest more than a person who held himself aloof from association with this world.

After they finished their evening meal and Tao asked his last question, they lay down under the stars for the night. Tao was almost asleep when he briefly opened his eyes and saw the old man disappear from view. Tao was gripped with a sudden fear. He thought he'd seen a ghost, and all the superstitions sown into his mind from childhood swept over him. But the night air wasn't filled with fear, and Tao knew the being was good, not evil. So he banished anxiety and slept peacefully, undisturbed by troubling dreams. In the morning, he rose up refreshed and continued on his way. Later at the refugee camp, Tao read about the activities of God's holy angels in the Bible, and in the years that followed he occasionally discerned their unseen presence.

Today, the angels stood around the table. They were clearly visible, and Tao counted eight of them. Their dominant characteristic wasn't their appearance but their unrelenting focus. They were interested in nothing in the room except obedience to their assignment on behalf of the young people seated at the table. Tao picked up the soapy cloth he was using to wipe off the tables and tentatively came closer. One of the angels became aware that Tao had entered the edge of their realm and glanced toward him. Tao stopped. He didn't want to intrude or disrupt what was happening with the students. The angel looked away, and Tao's quick prayer for guidance didn't yield a negative response. He came closer. Two students who had been sitting at another table walked past him on their way to the drop-off window for dirty dishes and silverware.

As Tao watched, one of the angels spoke to a tall girl with dark skin. The words out of the messenger's mouth were like tiny flames of fire, and Tao saw the girl's lips move in immediate response to the unseen prompting. Tao felt the brush of a gentle wind on his cheeks. Fire in one realm, cool refreshing in another.

"Father," Alisha Mason said. "We ask you to send your holy angels to our school to watch over and protect every student and teacher. We need your help. We want your help."

Janie Collins continued, "We pray for the students at this school who are confused and lost. We believe that Jesus is the way, the truth, and the life for them. Please reveal yourself to them in ways they can understand and draw them to you. We ask you to do this for Frank Jesup and Leila Farner."

After swallowing a bite of his sandwich, another student continued, "We pray the same thing for Larry Bingham, Kimberly Griffin, and Lester Garrison."

On they prayed. Unaware of the guardians who stood watch over them. Oblivious to the helpers sent to guide them.

Tao put his cleaning cloth on the edge of a table and picked up a paper napkin that had fallen on the floor. When he stood up, the angels were gone. Disappointed, he began wiping off the table. He finished and looked again in the direction of the table. Nothing. A couple of students left, and another one sat down. Then a cool breeze brushed Tao's cheek. He smiled.

———

Scott spent two hours Tuesday afternoon working on the mock trial materials. He couldn't tell the students specific questions to ask on direct or cross-examination, but he could identify the most important issues and keep them in mind when critiquing the students' performances. Likewise, he couldn't provide a detailed outline for an opening statement or closing argument, but he could ask questions designed to guide the students in selecting the most persuasive points to emphasize.

He worked late and drove straight to the high school. He was a few minutes early, and Kay's car was parked beside the modular unit. The door to the classroom was propped open to let in the cool evening air. Kay was sitting at her desk intently writing on a piece of paper. As he walked up the steps, Scott determined not to revisit the conversation they'd had after the football game. He'd opened the door to her, but he wanted to keep it by invitation only. He knocked on the doorframe.

"Hello!" he said.

Kay looked up without putting down her pen.

"Come in. I'm finishing up a thought."

Scott walked in and sat down in front of her desk. Kay immediately returned to her paper and scribbled a few more lines. A few strands of her hair escaped and hung down on the edge of the page. She blew them out of the way and kept writing.

"Done," she said in a few minutes.

"Grading papers?" Scott asked.

"No, writing one."

"What about?"

"Adoption. Do you handle adoptions?"

"I represented a couple last year who brought a little girl to the U.S. from the Philippines. She was supposed to be six, but I think she was closer to nine; it's hard to tell because she was so small. She'd been living on the streets before an agency took her in and gave her a place to stay. It was a great experience for everyone, including me."

"I've had a great experience of my own," Kay said. "That's what I was writing about."

"With a student who's adopted?"

Kay pointed to herself. "No, me."

Puzzled, Scott said, "You're not adopted. You look more like your mama every day."

Kay smiled. "I'm not sure how well you remember my mother, but that's not what I'm talking about. I've been adopted by God."

Scott gave the teacher a closer inspection. She looked happy, not crazy.

"What are you talking about?"

"I've been going to church services in the gym at the middle school on Sunday mornings. Janie Collins invited me." Kay picked up the papers from her desk and handed them to Scott. "Here, read this. It describes everything better than I can tell you."

Scott read the first few lines quickly then slowed down and carefully worked his way through the pages. He didn't comment until he turned over the final sheet.

"Interesting," he said.

Kay waited. Scott handed the sheets back to her.

"I'm not looking for compliments, but do you have any other reaction besides 'interesting'?"

"You're a good writer," Scott said, laying the pages on the corner of the desk. "Very descriptive, almost passionate. I guess you could call it spiritual." He paused. "How am I doing?"

Kay pushed her hair behind her ears. "Okay, I guess. You still sound detached, like a newspaper book reviewer. I mean, did it affect you emotionally?"

"Do you want an honest answer?" Scott asked.

"Of course."

Scott's eyes met hers. "What you've heard and felt about God's love struck a chord in you. Other readers may hear the same notes. I didn't."

"That's better. Will you give me another honest answer?"

"I'd rather hear the question first."

"Do you think this is just an emotional response by a woman who's been rejected by her husband?"

"It's not what I think that's important but what you believe yourself. Because religion is such a personal issue, I usually consider it off limits. I was baptized as a kid and believe in the Ten Commandments. Whatever anyone wants to believe is up to them."

The students started trickling in. Yvette Fisher gave Scott a knowing smile, appreciative of the information she'd purloined at the football game. She'd not exaggerated the relationship between Scott and Kay to the extent the teacher predicted, but several female students now viewed the tall, blond teacher as more human because she'd eaten bittersweet fruit in a high-school romance.

Dustin Rawlings limped in and sat down in a desk so he could extend his right leg straight out in front of him. Scott came over to him.

"What's wrong? I was at the game Friday night and didn't see anything happen to you."

"I hurt it in practice this afternoon. A guy fell on me in a pileup."

"I hope it's not serious. Do you want to go home?"

"No, I've had it on ice for an hour."

Scott slid an extra chair over to the desk. "Use this if you want to elevate it."

Janie, Frank, Alisha, and several others came in as a group. By 7:05 only one of the regular students was missing, a young man at home battling the flu.

"We're going to break up into groups," Scott said, "but first I want one of the lawyers to practice an opening statement in front of everyone. If you're a witness, remember what the lawyer says because you need to support it with your testimony if it's consistent with the written facts you've been provided."

"And if it's different?" one student asked.

"That's your lawyer's problem. The other side will know as much about the facts as you do and will pick up on anything that seems incorrect."

Scott turned to Yvette and Dustin.

"Which one of you is going to do the opening statement?"

Dustin raised his hand. "I am."

"You get a bye tonight," Scott said.

Janie and Frank were sitting beside one another on the other side of the room.

"What about you?" Scott asked.

Janie raised her hand. "We thought Frank should do the closing argument, and I'll do the opening statement."

"Why?" Scott asked.

Frank spoke up. "Janie is more organized, and I'm more of a—"

"Jerk," someone said in a stage whisper from across the room.

Scott knocked on the wooden podium with his knuckle. "We'll hear from Janie. Who is the bailiff?"

"Veronica Jones," Kay said.

A cute, red-headed girl with green eyes and freckles raised her hand.

"Have you studied the materials?" Scott asked.

Veronica stood up. "Yes, your honor," she replied in a clear voice.

Scott smiled. "Good start. Please call the court to order."

"All rise!" Veronica called out and waited until everyone stood up. "Oyez, oyez, the Superior Court of Russell County is now in session, the Honorable Scott W. Ellis presiding."

"Why did she say 'hey you, hey you'?" Dustin asked.

"Tell him, bailiff," Scott said.

"It's from French. It means, 'hear ye, hear ye.'"

"That's right," Scott said. "Not long ago I heard a bailiff pronounce it, 'ow yez, ow yez!' It sounded like he had a tack in his shoe." Several students rolled their eyes, and Scott knew his attempt at high-school humor had failed. He looked to Kay who shook her head.

"Thank you, bailiff," he said. "Please be available if I need your assistance."

"Yes, your honor."

"You may be seated," Scott said to the students. Turning to Janie, he said, "Counsel, you may proceed with your opening statement. Will you be representing the plaintiff or the defendant?"

"The plaintiff. I've written something down but haven't had anyone check it. Is that okay?"

Scott gave the student a stern look. "Counselor, the word *okay* is inappropriate in this courtroom. I instruct you to avoid it in the future."

Janie's cheeks turned slightly red. "Okay, uh—"

Scott interrupted. "I remind all attorneys to use words appropriate for a court of law. You don't have to be too formal, but when asking the court's permission, don't use casual slang. Okay?"

Janie smiled slightly. "Yes, your honor."

"You may proceed for the plaintiff. Please come to the front of the room."

Janie came to the podium with several sheets of paper. The pages were visibly shaking in her right hand. Kay stepped to the side of the classroom and leaned against the wall.

"May it please the court," Janie said with a slight tremor in her voice. "My name is Janie Collins. My co-counsel is Frank Jesup, and we represent Betty Moonbeam, the plaintiff in this case. Betty was injured in a car wreck. We think it was Pete Pigpickin's fault because he ran a stop sign without looking where he was going and plowed into the side of a car driven by Ralph Risky, who was not negligent and hadn't been drinking enough from the punch bowl at the party at Sarah Rich's house to affect his driving according to the blood test taken at the hospital an hour after the wreck." Janie paused to catch her breath.

"Oh yeah, Pete was driving a truck loaded with barbeque, and it went everywhere after he ran into Ralph's car. There will be several witnesses who will testify: Betty, Ralph, Joe Joker, Billy Bob Beerbelly, Dr. Feelgood, and Archie Expert. Betty doesn't remember much about the wreck because she was thrown from the vehicle, but she thinks Ralph is an okay, I mean, good driver. Ralph will testify about what happened before and after the wreck. He is a pretty good witness. Billy Bob was at the intersection in another truck and saw what happened. Joe Joker is a friend of Betty and Ralph. He doesn't know a lot of new information, but he can corroborate Ralph's testimony."

She looked at Scott before continuing. *"Corroborate* means he will say the same thing so that you can believe what they both say. And then, Dr. Feelgood will tell about Betty's injuries, which is important because we are asking for a lot of money for her pain and suffering. He has seen a lot of people in pain. Betty's injures were—"

Janie looked down at her papers, trying to find the data she needed. "Uh, multiple contusions, a concussion, and a communist fracture of her left leg. If you've ever broken a bone, like I did a couple of years ago when I fell on the ice and broke my left arm, you know how painful it can be.

"Mr. Expert knows a lot about what happens when there is a wreck and will explain how the pattern of the barbeque on the road proves that Pete should have gotten a ticket from the police, and it was wrong for Ralph to get a ticket or be charged with contributory negligence, which is a bad law anyway. In North Carolina if Ralph, who was driving Betty, was a tiny bit negligent, Betty won't get anything against Pete Pigpickin's insurance company unless Pete had the last clear chance to avoid the wreck." She looked at Scott again. "Or at least that's what I think the law is, and it doesn't seem right. After you hear all the evidence, we believe your decision will be easy. My co-counsel, Mr. Frank Jesup, will tell you what to do in the closing argument. Thank you very much."

Still breathing twice as fast as normal, Janie looked at Scott, whose mouth had dropped slightly open the deeper Janie went into her opening statement. This was going to be harder than he'd thought.

"Thank you, Janie," he said. "It takes a lot of courage to go first. Let's break up into groups for lawyers and witnesses."

When the last student left, Scott looked at Kay and burst out laughing. "I've been holding that in for over an hour," he said. "I was doing all right until Janie called the injury to Betty's leg a 'communist' fracture. It made it sound like she broke it before the Berlin Wall came down."

"What's the correct medical term?"

"*Comminuted.* It means the leg was shattered at the site of the break. In our small group, I told Janie to say 'severe fracture.' An opening statement is not the place to try out fancy new medical words."

Kay sniffed. "Of course, I'm sure you never commit a courtroom faux pas and everything goes according to plan."

"I'm a beginner myself. I walk downstairs to Mr. Humphrey's office all the time for advice."

"You didn't humiliate Janie in the small group?"

"Of course not and, to his credit, neither did Frank. Janie is a bright girl. She was just nervous. By the time of the competition, she'll have an opening statement that is a lot smoother and less rambling." Scott chuckled again.

"Now, what's funny?"

"The part when she criticized the North Carolina rules about contributory negligence. I agree with her, but a sixteen-year-old girl judging principles that have been around for 250 years—"

"Shows that she's analytical enough to be in the courtroom."

———

It was too cold for Frank and Janie to ride with the top down. As they were leaving the school parking lot, Janie said, "I think Mr. Ellis was holding back his criticism to avoid hurting my feelings."

"Who knows what Ellis was thinking? I doubt he has a lot of courtroom experience, and I think he volunteered to help because he's after Mrs. Wilson. I heard she's getting a divorce, and they dated in high school."

The breakup of Kay's marriage was news to Janie and explained why the teacher had come to church alone.

"Are you sure about the divorce?"

"Yeah, someone heard it from one of the other teachers."

After a few moments of silence, Janie said, "My parents are divorced. My father left when my youngest brother was about six months old. Now he's living in Louisiana, and I only see him for a couple of weeks in the summer."

"My parents are splitting up," Frank replied matter-of-factly. "My mother moved out a few weeks ago and took my little sister with her. I'm glad about it."

"You say that now, but you'll change your mind. I miss my dad, and I'm praying he'll come back."

Frank grunted. "Don't pray for my mom. I'm happier the way things are."

He dropped off Janie and drove home. His father was in the downstairs study drinking an expensive whiskey. Frank joined him in the dimly lit room and sat in a high-backed leather chair.

"Where have you been?" his father asked.

"I told you. I'm on a mock trial team that meets on Tuesday and Thursday evenings."

"Oh, yeah. Don't get any ideas about being a lawyer. Every lawyer I've dealt with has been a shyster who overcharged me and didn't produce. They're all parasites."

"Don't worry," Frank replied. "I want to grow up to be just like you."

His father took another drink and didn't catch the cynicism in his son's voice. Frank looked at his father with disgust. There were dark circles under the older Jesup's eyes, and he'd missed a button on his shirt when he changed clothes after work.

20

Sing to the LORD a new song.
PSALM 96:1

Harold and Lester Garrison arrived at Humphrey, Balcomb and Jackson without an appointment. Scott told the receptionist to have them wait in the small conference room. When Scott joined them, Harold was sitting at the glass-topped table, and Lester was touching General Hoke's nose.

He turned and asked Scott, "Is this an original painting?"

"Uh, it's an oil painting of a Confederate general from North Carolina. His name is on the little plate at the bottom."

"I know he's a Confederate general from North Carolina," Lester said with exasperation. "He's wearing a major general's uniform for Lee's Army of Northern Virginia. I know a bunch of stuff about the Civil War."

"Okay, but the general is long gone, and you have more immediate problems we need to discuss. The D.A.'s office is pushing your case harder than Grant did the Confederates at Vicksburg."

Scott summarized his findings for Harold. When he mentioned Bishop Moore's recollection about the man on the other side of the creek with black hair, Lester quickly looked at his father who didn't say anything. Harold Garrison had a head full of thick, black hair.

"I think the D.A. should drop the case," Harold said when Scott finished. "And I want to sue her for violating our constitutional rights."

"Were you listening to me?" Scott asked. "We've got some strong arguments, but nothing is certain in court."

"That's lawyer talk." Harold snorted. "Anybody could win this case."

An image of Harold arguing to the jury in a stained white T-shirt flashed through Scott's mind. No class in law school had prepared him for the Garrison family.

"I have a legal duty to mention one other thing," he said. "The D.A. brought up the possibility of a plea agreement when she called the other day. She didn't make a formal offer, but mentioned five years in prison followed by two on probation for the charges on the church case."

Lester jumped up from his chair. "But I'm not guilty!"

"I'm not recommending it," Scott said calmly. "But I have an obligation to communicate the offer to you. What do you want me to tell her?"

"That's easy," Harold said and swore.

"Lester?" Scott asked.

The young man shook his head. "Yeah. No way."

"Any counteroffer?"

Lester narrowed his eyes. "I'm not guilty. Are you trying to get me to plead guilty so you don't have to represent me?"

"No, just doing my job. I'll tell Davenport that we're not interested in any plea bargain because you're not guilty."

"And tell her like you mean it!" Harold added.

After Lester and Harold left the office, Scott stayed for a minute to reorganize the file. He looked up at General Hoke's portrait.

"General, how would you have handled Harold and Lester Garrison?"

The general stared down with eyes that had seen much death and borne the weight of great responsibility but didn't reveal any nineteenth-century wisdom applicable to present-day attorney-client relationships.

Mr. Humphrey, a more immediate source of advice, was meeting with a client and not available for a debriefing, so Scott went up to his office. An hour later his phone buzzed.

"Kay Wilson, on line 4."

"Hey," she said. "I'm between classes, so I have to be quick. Do you have plans for lunch?"

"No."

"Would you like to eat it with a friend?"

Scott smiled. "At the school?"

"Of course. We're having tacos and applesauce again, and it made me think about you. Lunch is at 12:20."

"I'll be there."

Kay's call was brief, but it drove away the lingering darkness from his earlier encounter with the Garrisons. There was a lightness in her voice that made him notice that the sun was shining outside his window.

Scott looked down at the street below. A woman and her small child were holding hands as they walked happily down the sidewalk. No matter what happened in *State v. Garrison* during the next few weeks people would still hold hands and eat tacos and applesauce. He opened Lester's file and called the sheriff's department. Maybe Officers Hinshaw and Dortch were on duty.

———

After the phone call to Scott, Kay returned to her classroom. Her next group of students arrived and began working on an assignment that involved reading excerpts from a technical journal and answering detailed questions about the subject matter of the article. It was a new method of developing reading comprehension in the computer age.

While the students labored in silence trying to decipher the convoluted language, Kay secretly basked in the outer court of the realm where heavenly creatures surround the throne of God in unceasing worship. All morning she'd lived in the midst of a song—a first fruit of the new life taking shape within her.

It had been a morning unlike any other. It began at daybreak.

Before her eyes were fully open, the song came to her. She lay in bed, listening, amazed, afraid to move lest it leave. Then, when the demands of the day made her get up, she threw back the covers, and to her delight, the song didn't disappear. It was stronger, more alive, more enduring than the mundane activities of her morning routine. Over and over a refrain of thanksgiving, joy, adoration, and praise rippled through her. She hummed softly as she walked through her apartment.

Music has the capacity to bypass the mind, speak to the heart, and communicate a thought with a richness of feeling beyond the ability of words. It is one of the many doors that lead to the deep places of the human spirit. Every door has its own key. Each key is unique.

A mountain vista.

A beach on an unclouded day.

A painting that captures the mood of a moment.

A poem or phrase.

A smell, a taste, a touch.

And there is a door to the heart that only opens to the sound of a song.

The circumstances of Kay's life had never been more bleak. The night before her attorney had left a message on her answering machine that the final hearing in her divorce case was scheduled in two weeks. Jake had signed an affidavit stating that the marriage was irretrievably broken, and there was nothing Kay could do to stop him. Her marriage had failed, and although Jake had abandoned her, Kay couldn't shake the nagging accusation that somehow it was probably her fault. If she'd written a poem that expressed her mood before she turned out the lights, it would have been a melancholy ballad, not an ode to joy. She'd gone to bed sad, only to awaken surprised by the glory of a new day and a new song.

Driving to school, she didn't listen to the radio for the morning news or weather report. Better news echoed within her. She didn't stop by the teachers' lounge to drink a cup of coffee or chat for a few minutes, but went straight to her classroom to be alone. She wanted to safeguard her newfound treasure from intrusion by unknowing outsiders. Fortunately, it was a test day for most of her classes, and once she handed out the questions, she sat at her desk and continued to listen to the sounds of heaven that had been released in her heart. She decided to share her joy with someone familiar with her pain. During a break, she had called Scott.

———

At lunchtime Scott stopped by the school office to sign in. Dr. Lassiter came out and greeted him.

"How is the mock trial team doing?"

"Fine. We're meeting two days a week in the evenings."

"Is Mrs. Wilson providing the assistance that you need?"

Scott hadn't considered evaluating Kay's role in the process and quickly decided to put in a good word for her.

"She's outstanding. I couldn't ask for anyone better. We're meeting today in the cafeteria."

"Excellent." The principal patted him on the shoulder. "It's a Mexican menu today. I hope you like tacos."

"Tacos and applesauce," Scott responded. "Two of my favorites."

He walked down the crowded hallway to the cafeteria. Kay was not in sight, and he waited inside the door. In a minute, she came into the room from the opposite side. He watched her make her way toward him. She was as beautiful as ever, but the thing that immediately grabbed Scott's attention as she came closer was the expression on her face. She looked very happy.

"What's happened?" he asked. "I put in a good word for you with Dr. Lassiter, but it's too quick for it to translate into a pay raise."

Kay smiled. "We'll talk in the faculty dining room."

They made their way down the food line. Scott received the normal ration of applesauce and two tacos. Dessert was listed as rice pudding. He inspected the granular pellets inside the congealed substance. They were not moving, which he took to be a good sign.

As soon as they sat down, Kay burst out, "Scott, I have had the most wonderful morning. Ever since I woke up, I've had a song inside my head."

Scott nodded and swallowed his first bite of taco. "I've done that. When I get a new CD, I'll hum my favorite cut over and over for days. What's the name of the song?"

"No, this is different from what you're talking about. It's not a song I've heard before. It's spontaneous."

Scott chewed another bite as he listened. "What kind of song?"

"Simple words—thank you, praise you, bless you."

"Oh, is it something you learned at church?"

Kay shook her head. "No. At first I thought it could be a memory coming to the surface, but it's not. I'm sure it has something to do with what has happened to me at the church, but the minister didn't talk about God putting a song in your heart."

So far, Kay hadn't made a bit of sense.

Still clueless, Scott asked, "Did you write it down?"

Kay didn't answer. She put her hand over her mouth. "There it is again." She closed her eyes.

This was getting a bit weird. Scott watched for a second, then glanced around the room to see if anyone else noticed that Kay Wilson was sitting in front of a full plate of food with her eyes closed and her hand over her mouth. The rest of the teachers and staff were munching their tacos, unaware of the newborn mystic in their presence. Scott swallowed a couple of bites before Kay opened her eyes and looked at him. She was beaming.

"I'm sorry. You must think I'm crazy," she said.

"I'm not sure what to think," Scott answered truthfully. "You seem happy."

"*Happy* is not the right word; it doesn't describe what's happening. I mean, my lawyer called last night and left a message that the final hearing in my divorce case is in a couple of weeks. My circumstances are as bad as ever, but something has changed in my outlook."

"Coping is important," Scott replied, hoping the new word fit.

Kay leaned forward. "The song in here," she said, pointing to her heart, "is more powerful than my troubles. Everything around me looks more vibrant and alive. Even your tie looks different. I've seen it before, but today the colors are more bright."

Scott glanced down at the blue-and-gold tie that hung from his neck. It was his favorite. A tiny spot of sauce from the taco had landed on one edge, and he carefully wiped it off with his thumb. Kay's sorrow at the football field he understood. This new song and its effects on her attitude were outside his universe.

"I know you are a very creative person," he said slowly, "but the words you're using don't compute in my legal brain. At least you're not down in the dumps. I hated it when you were so sad."

Kay sat back in her chair and relaxed. "I know. Thanks for caring."

"And you were a good person before this morning," Scott continued. "If this is better, then go for it."

"So, do you think I'm crazy?" she asked.

Scott captured the last mouthful of applesauce with his spoon.

"Maybe. But it seems like a good crazy."

———

By the end of the day, Scott had made little progress in further investigating the Garrison case. None of the police officers had returned his calls. He tried to reach Bishop Moore, but the preacher was out of town for the afternoon and would not be home until the following day. At

5:30 P.M. he left the office. A few minutes later he pushed open the door to Dixon's Body Shop.

Perry was not in sight and the gym was more crowded than usual. After changing clothes, Scott decided to take a spin on the arm bike and was whirling away when Perry walked through the front door of the building with a short, stocky, older man with a bushy head of gray hair and a thick neck. Scott continued on the arm bike and watched as the older man strapped on a well-worn weightlifting belt and proceeded to warm up by easily lifting heavy barbells that would have been the personal best for many of the patrons of the gym. Perry stood ready to assist, but it was soon obvious to Scott that the stranger was not going to need any help.

The man began performing a procedure known in weightlifting as a *snatch.* Squatting down low to the floor, he put his hands far out on the barbell. After getting a firm grip, he pulled up the weight, quickly locked his arms overhead, then stood up with the weight in the air. After a few minutes everyone else in the gym stopped to watch. Scott let the arm bike slowly rotate until it came to a halt. Additional weights were put on the end of the bar. Scott tried to calculate the total and had to start over when he lost track of the combination of large black discs.

This was a serious lift, and the gray-haired man circled the barbell, staring at it and breathing slowly. He didn't look at anyone else in the room. Taking a couple of deep breaths, he approached the barbell, squatted down, and positioned his hands. The room was completely silent. Perry stepped back.

Then, with a yell that began deep in his chest, the man pulled up on the barbell and, with a movement so rapid that it was hard to follow, locked his arms overhead. He was still in a deep squat, and Scott stared at the man's knees, wondering how they could stand the strain. The weightlifter's thighs began to quiver as he tried to straighten his legs. He pushed upward and with a supreme effort slowly stood to his feet. He held the weight over his head for a couple of seconds then stepped out from under it, letting it fall to the mat in front of him. Scott wondered if the foundation under the floor might crack.

Several people clapped and yelled. The man gave a slight bow and walked over to the water cooler. The show over, the other men returned to their own activities. Perry walked up to Scott.

"What did you think of that?" Perry asked.

"Awesome. Who is he?"

"I can't pronounce his name. He's a fifty-nine-year-old Bulgarian. He was on their Olympic team about thirty years ago and came to the U.S. when things opened up."

"What's he doing here?"

"He heard about you and wanted to get some pointers about the arm bike. He'll be over to ask you some questions after he rests for a minute."

"No, tell me."

Perry sat down on a stool. "He has a job with a company that makes door locks. They advertise their locks as the strongest and most durable in the industry. He's their poster boy. One of the owners of the company has a house on Lake Norman and brought him up for the day. He wanted to work out before he puts on an exhibition at a trade show in Charlotte tomorrow."

"That was poetry in motion. I couldn't believe how quick he was."

"It's a lot more speed and technique than most people think."

"Is he going to do anything else?"

"I don't think so. He wanted to do some regular lifting and offered to put on a brief exhibition. I like to provide extras to my customers."

Scott watched as the Bulgarian began doing bench presses, his arms moving up and down like pistons.

"What should I tell Linda?" Perry asked.

"Linda? About what?" Scott asked.

"When you mentioned poetry, it made me think of English teachers. When I think of English teachers, I think of Kay Laramie."

Scott opened a bottle of water and took a drink. "Tell Linda that Kay Wilson and I are friends—period. Her divorce is final in a couple of weeks, and she has been bouncing all over the chart. The other night at the football game she was crying her eyes out. Today at lunch she was talking about God putting a song in her heart and couldn't wipe the smile from her face."

Perry shrugged. "What's unusual about that? She's a woman."

Scott chuckled. "Be careful, or I'll report you to the chauvinist thought police."

"Is she going to go back to Kay Laramie after the divorce is final?"

"I didn't ask her because it wasn't my business."

"Was it your business when you read her file at the courthouse?"

"Don't badger the witness," Scott answered. "Just tell Linda that Kay's name will not be Ellis anytime in the foreseeable future. I know better than to consider anything beyond friendship while she's going through a divorce. A lot has changed in the years since high school."

"And a lot hasn't." Perry motioned toward the weightlifter. "Some things have enduring strength."

———

Sometimes, the sound and appearance of a word reflect its function. Not so with *bomb*. There is a softness to the word that hides its meaning. Spoken in a normal tone of voice, it does not convey a sense of explosive devastation. In a crowded room, it could be confused with a word of healing like *balm*.

Bomb. He'd muttered and written the word over and over and over until it lost any sinister connotations and became a familiar friend. He wrote it on the margins of test papers in silent, hidden warning, but he was always careful to obliterate it before a teacher might see it. He was not a voice secretly crying for help. He was a volcano waiting to erupt.

He revisited the image of the fire-filled hallway until it became a familiar fantasy. When he didn't want to go to school, the mild rush he felt when he walked down the main hallway and imagined the moment of explosion drew him back. He often placed people he hated at the center of the maelstrom. He knew he couldn't control everything about the moment of destruction, but he allowed himself to hope that particular individuals would be in the wrong place at the right time, or from his perspective, the right place at the right time.

The number grew. It never shrank.

21

My sheep hear My voice.
JOHN 10:27 (NKJV)

Tao Pang was learning more English words. Most of them related to his work—*trash*, *bathroom*, *mop*, even *disinfectant*. Names were another matter. He was amazed at the length and complexity of Western names. It wouldn't have been much more difficult for him if he'd landed in Russia.

One afternoon he found a school yearbook in a trash can in the school office. The binding had been damaged and the book discarded. Tao recognized the outline of the school building imprinted on the cover and picked it up. He began to look at the pictures. The hundreds of faces on the pages were unfamiliar until he came to a group photograph of the janitorial staff. There were most of his coworkers, standing stiffly at attention in white shirts and dark-colored pants in front of the school trophy case. He continued turning pages, studying photos of the marching band, the chorus, the basketball team, the football team, the girls' softball team. He could tell the yearbook was a record of the people and events at the school, but the significance of many of the pictures could not be understood without the ability to read the captions. Toward the back of the volume, he saw pages of advertisements for local businesses. When he finished, Tao put the book in the large, plastic barrel he was using to collect the garbage.

"Take the book."

Tao stopped and turned around. The voice was so clear that he thought someone had spoken to him from one of the offices. Then he realized the message was in his own language. No one in Blanchard

County other than his family members knew those words. He picked up the yearbook from the trash container and looked at it again.

This time he turned the pages more slowly, searching for the reason behind the command. The first section was devoted to seniors whose formal pictures were twice the size of the rest of the student classes. Tao could tell these were the older students. Nothing he saw on the pages caused him to pause. A third of the way through the junior-class pictures, he stopped. He recognized a young woman's face. She looked like one of the girls who sat at the cafeteria table where the angels had assembled.

"Does this have to do with her?" he asked.

He studied the picture more closely. The girl had short, dark hair and a gentle smile. She had good eyes—clear eyes that had lost the need to hide what lay behind them. Yes, the girl with the good eyes was one of the students at the table.

"Pray for her."

Tao didn't look around this time. This was a command he understood. He'd heard the Voice directing him to pray for a specific individual before. The identity of the person was the first step. Knowing what to pray was the second.

"What do I pray?"

Not for her salvation. The girl was a Christian who attracted the attention of heaven—a fact proven by the angelic messengers surrounding the table. But there was a role for him to play as well. He waited.

"Hold her close to your heart."

Tao put his hand on his chest. How could he do that? When he touched his shirt, he felt the outline of his empty pocket.

On the receptionist's desk was a cup containing an assortment of pencils, pens, and a small pair of scissors. Tao picked up the scissors, carefully cut out the girl's picture, and put it in his pocket—close to his heart. The rest would come as he needed to know it.

He placed the yearbook on top of his cleaning cart. Later, he put it on the shelf in the closet where he kept cleaning supplies.

———

Scott had a voice mail from Bishop Moore. He returned the call, and the preacher answered the phone.

"I need your help," Scott said. "The Garrison case is going to trial in a couple of weeks, and I'd like to talk to some of the people who were outside at the time the shots were fired."

"I could give you a list of church members with their phone numbers."

"How many are there?" Scott asked.

"Oh, about seventy-five families. Some of the families are pretty large."

"How many of the church members were at the baptism?"

"I don't know for sure, but I'd guess at least three-fourths of them plus visitors."

Scott thought about the prospect of trying to interview over a hundred strangers who would be suspicious of his reason for calling. He hadn't gained the confidence of Bishop Moore until he mentioned Leland Humphrey's name, and it would be ten times more difficult with the members of the church. But somewhere in the haystack of names and numbers might be another witness who would testify that the shooter on the other side of the stream was a man with black hair. Someone might know more.

"Okay, send them over," Scott said. "May I tell them you gave me permission to contact them?"

"Well," the bishop hesitated. "I'm not sure."

"I wouldn't try to coerce anyone."

"I know, but whether they want to talk to you is their business. Many of the church folks are at their jobs during the week, so it will be hard to reach them. You'd have to call after five o'clock in the afternoon."

"Whatever it takes."

Scott hadn't spent his evenings calling a long list of names since he sold kitchen knives one summer during college.

"I have a better idea," Bishop Moore continued. "Why don't you come when they're all going to be together in one place?"

Surprised, Scott asked, "You would set up a meeting so they could talk to me?"

"Not exactly. We already have a meeting scheduled. You would just show up. I'm thinking about the regular Sunday-morning service. We're having dinner on the grounds this Sunday, and if anyone is willing to talk to you, it would be your best chance."

Giving up a Sunday morning with the newspaper to avoid the drudg-ery of countless hours on the telephone over the next week would be a small sacrifice. And the food would be good.

"That sounds like a great idea. What time should I be there?"

"'bout ten o'clock."

"I might ask Mr. Humphrey to come, too."

Bishop Moore laughed. "Yes. Leland can tell me if I know more about the Bible than when we were stacking lumber together."

Both of Mr. Humphrey's eyebrows shot up when Scott told him about his plans for Sunday morning, but the older lawyer wouldn't be able to join him. He and his wife were going to be out of town all week-end. Scott would be the only white face in the crowd.

———

Scott heated leftover spaghetti in the microwave and ate supper standing up at the kitchen counter. He was sitting in the backyard drinking a beer in front of the fishpond when the cordless phone on the bench beside him rang.

"Where are you?" Kay asked.

"Uh-oh," Scott said.

He had forgotten about mock trial practice. He looked at his watch. It was 7:15 P.M. All the students would be sitting at their desks waiting for him to arrive and give instructions for the evening.

"I'm on my way," he said.

"Did you forget?"

Scott ignored the question. "Tell the lawyers to work on their direct and cross-examination of Pete Pigpickin, and ask the witnesses to write out more questions for the attorneys to consider. I'll be there in ten minutes."

Still wearing blue jeans and a Wake Forest T-shirt, Scott threw his mock trial materials into the front seat of his SUV and drove at high speed to the high school. He dashed up the steps, then walked more nor-mally into the classroom. The students were sitting in groups as he'd instructed. Every eye turned toward him.

"Sorry I'm late," he said casually. "Busy day at the office. Keep work-ing in your groups while I discuss some things with Mrs. Wilson."

Kay looked at him and said under her breath, "Were you working on a lawsuit against a spaghetti manufacturer? You have some sauce on the corner of your mouth."

Scott licked the corner of his mouth and tasted tomato with a hint of oregano.

"I'm busted again," he said. "With all that's happening at work, I forgot about the meeting."

"Don't worry. I'm not going to send you to Dr. Lassiter for a paddling."

An hour later Scott was testing the knowledge of a fast-talking young man playing the role of Ralph Risky.

"I made a perfect score on the written test in driver's education," Ralph said proudly. "My instructor taught me to always come to a complete stop and look both ways before entering an intersection. If a student in our class didn't stop, he had to get out of the car and apologize to the stop sign."

"Did you ever have to apologize?" Scott asked.

"No, sir," Ralph said forthrightly.

"You don't know anything about Mr. Pigpickin's driving history, do you?"

"No, but I bet it's bad. He should have apologized a dozen times to the stop sign he ran when he hit Betty and me."

Scott reviewed his notes. "Would it surprise you to learn that Mr. Pigpickin has a commercial driver's license?"

"He should be in a commercial all right. He'd be the one driving like a maniac in a TV ad for lawyers who promise a lot of money to anyone injured in a car wreck."

Scott smiled. "Ralph, that's going too far. You have to stick closer to the facts given on the handout sheets."

"Okay," the student replied. "We'd talked about that answer the other night and wondered if it would be okay."

Scott looked at his watch and spoke to the group. "You're making great progress. I can tell that you've been studying the roles. That's what it takes. Whether you are a witness or a lawyer, it has to become second nature to you. If you know the facts, it frees you to get into character as a witness."

Kay dismissed the students. Janie and Frank, their heads close together as they talked, stayed at the back of the room for a few minutes.

"Do you need any help?" Scott asked.

"No, thanks," Janie replied. "Frank is helping me with my opening statement."

Scott went to the front of the room.

"You were right," he said to Kay in a low voice. "Those two are getting along better than I thought they would."

"I've seen them walking together in the hall recently."

Scott glanced back at the two young people. Janie was intent on writing something, and Frank was almost touching her as he leaned close to her shoulder. Janie finished writing and smiled at Frank. They left together.

When he was alone with Kay, Scott asked, "Have you heard any good songs lately?"

She looked at him suspiciously. "Are you teasing me?"

"Maybe. You'll have to admit that what you told me at lunch yesterday was unusual."

"I think you described it as a 'good crazy.' But no, there haven't been any songs today. However, I read a poetic chapter in the Psalms last night and starting writing down my own thoughts. It was random as it came out, but in reading it over I saw a progression from my thoughts toward God and then back again from him to me. It was like a cosmic dance."

Scott felt the conversation slipping again into the twilight zone of Kay's imagination. He had an idea to bring it back to earth.

"Would you like to go to church with me on Sunday?" he asked.

Surprised, Kay said, "I didn't know you went to church."

"I don't go regularly, but I'm visiting a black congregation out in the country this Sunday. I've met the pastor, and he invited me to come."

It was Kay's turn to try and keep up with Scott's thoughts. "Wait. Why were you invited?"

"It's because of a case. I'm representing a young man charged with a crime involving the church, and this is a way to talk to potential witnesses."

"A church member committed a crime?"

"No, only my client is charged. I can't talk about the details of the case, but he's a student here at the school."

Kay's mouth dropped open. "Lester Garrison?"

Scott nodded. "Tattoos and all."

When he returned home from mock trial practice, Frank Jesup had an unnerving experience while talking with his father. He suddenly felt detached from his surroundings and watched his own movements and words as if they were being performed by someone else. He slowly drifted to the corner of the kitchen and looked down on himself and his father as they stood across from each other near the refrigerator. He closed his eyes tightly for a couple of seconds, and when he opened them, everything was normal.

"What is it?" his father asked. "Are you okay?"

"Uh, sure," Frank answered. "Just a little tired."

"Don't stay up all night on the computer. I'm going out for a few hours, and I don't want to see your light on when I come back."

"Rena's condominium?" Frank asked, even though he knew the answer. His father grunted.

"Why doesn't she move in with us?" Frank continued. "It seems stupid to have to run over to her place every night."

"I can't move her to Catawba while the divorce is pending. Your mother is trying to crucify me, and I don't need to help her."

After his father left, Frank tried to watch TV, but nothing held his interest. He surfed through eighty channels without scoring a hit. The computer was drawing him, and he wandered upstairs to his room. He turned on the machine and quickly negotiated the labyrinth of controls his group had constructed to protect the privacy of their warfare. Within fifteen minutes he was in another world. No one detected his entrance through a doorway he'd created the previous week. Frank's mind cleared, and he entered a zone of heightened consciousness and razor-sharp insight. Creativity came easily, and he saw what to do with precision. He could have pounced on the other warriors quickly, but he settled back and began to slowly weave a web of deception that further masked his presence so that when the blows fell his victims wouldn't be able to identify their assassin. That's the way he wanted to do it. Patient, anonymous, deadly.

Frank's father didn't come home.

22

Abraham believed God, and it was
credited to him as righteousness.
JAMES 2:23

When he woke up Sunday morning, Scott opened the door of his closet and surveyed his wardrobe. It's always better to be over-dressed than too casual, and he didn't want to offend the people at Hall's Chapel before attempting to interview them. He selected a gray suit, white shirt, and a blue-and-red-striped tie. After he straightened his tie, he looked in the full-length mirror attached to the back of his bathroom door. He looked more like a prep-school graduate than a soul-food lover. Immutable things can't change.

Kay's apartment was on the other side of town. He drove down Lipscomb Avenue past the courthouse and into an area where develop-ers had built a few modern apartment complexes. Scott had thought about living in the same apartments that Kay and Jake chose. It would have been less work than maintaining his house, but he would have for-feited the backyard and couldn't have taken in Nicky.

He climbed the steps and knocked on the door. He waited, then knocked again. Kay opened the door. She was barefoot and wearing a long violet dress. Her hair was still slightly damp and on her shoulders.

"Come in," she said. "I had a late start, but I'll be ready in a minute."

Kay disappeared down the hall, and Scott sat in one of two chairs at a glass-topped table next to the kitchen. He looked at the other chair and wondered if it was Jake's seat. There was an arrangement of silk flowers in the center of the table. Kay had a few blown-up photographs of beach scenes on the walls. The only personal photo in sight was a small picture on the kitchen counter beside the table. It was Kay at about age eight wearing a pair of shorts and a skimpy top. She was standing outdoors in front of an easel and laughing at the watercolors she'd splashed on the piece of paper.

Scott tapped his fingers on the table. He suspected Kay's minute might be longer than a literal sixty seconds. He walked into the living room area. On the low table in front of the couch were a notebook, a Bible, and a cup of coffee that looked more like the night before than this morning. He glanced over his shoulder and raised the cover of the notebook. It was filled with Kay's handwriting. He let the cover fall closed without reading anything and picked up the Bible. He opened it to the book of Psalms. Kay had marked verses on page after page with a hot pink highlighter. Scott read a few of them without fathoming why they were selected.

Kay came around the corner and saw him. "Getting in the mood for church?" she asked.

Scott put the Bible on the table. "Are you sure it's not sacrilegious to use a pink highlighter in a Bible?"

"You already think I'm crazy because of the song I heard the other day. Using a pink highlighter shouldn't be too hard to accept."

"I got into trouble once in Sunday school for using a crayon to decorate the margins of a Bible."

"I don't think there is anything wrong with artwork in the Bible. I've seen pictures of medieval Bibles in which every first letter of a book is very ornate."

"My scribbling didn't qualify as art. Are most of your highlights in Psalms?"

"Yeah, I've been hanging out with David. He's become my favorite songwriter of the week."

Scott had heard enough. He checked his watch. "Ready to go?"

"Yes. Bring the Bible. It may come in handy."

Scott picked up the Bible, and Kay turned toward the door. She looked refreshingly beautiful. As Scott walked past the two chairs at the table, he wondered again why Jake Wilson bailed out of a relationship with this woman.

Carrying the Bible and feeling like a boy going to Sunday school,

Scott opened the door for Kay, and she slid into the front seat. Before leaving home he'd tidied up his SUV in preparation for his passenger. His brown briefcase was in the backseat. Inside was a legal pad with a series of questions written on it and a small tape recorder in case he wanted to take a verbatim statement from a witness.

There were swirls of late-morning fog at the edges of the highway, and Scott missed the turn for Hall's Chapel Road. He saw the sign as they passed by and turned around in a driveway. The fog increased as they drew closer to the creek.

"On a clear day you can see the water from the road," Scott said. "This fog won't last long, and it will be sunny by the time we get out of church."

They were a couple of minutes late. A family in a minivan pulled into the parking lot in front of them and the mother, father, and three little girls got out. The family was dressed in their Sunday best. The girls had matching blue-and-white dresses, the father was wearing a black suit, and the mother was draped in a flowing white dress and high heels. Scott was glad he'd decided not to come casual. When the oldest of the girls saw Scott and Kay, she tugged on her mother's sleeve and pointed in their direction.

Scott leaned over to Kay. "We're about to find out what it's like to be in the minority."

Sounds of singing could be heard from within the white building. They walked up the steps, and two teenage boys, also dressed in dark suits, opened the doors to let them in. There was a narrow foyer that led into the sanctuary.

A middle-aged man with a badge pinned to his jacket that said "Usher" came up to Scott and Kay.

"The bishop said you'd be coming," he said. "We've reserved seats for you. Follow me."

Scott and Kay walked down the aisle together. It was covered with a deep red carpet that matched the color of the cushions on the pews. There were about 150 adults and children in the room. Everyone was standing as they sang. The floors underneath the pews were polished wood, the walls were white, and the ceiling was painted with billowy white cloud shapes softly brushed onto a sky-blue background. Several ceiling fans stirred the air. At the front of the room on the left was the piano, and on the right was a modern electric organ. Bishop Moore stood on a raised platform beside a white, wooden pulpit. The choir members were dressed in red-and-gold robes. Virtually every man in the sanctuary was wearing a dark suit. Many of the women were dressed in white, but there were plenty of other colors represented.

Scott and Kay followed the usher all the way to the front pew of the church. He picked up two "Reserved" signs that had been placed on the red cushions, and Scott and Kay took their places.

The sound of the instruments and the singing reverberated from the wooden walls and ceiling. A heavyset woman was playing the piano on the left, but Scott's attention was drawn to a slender man in his thirties who was playing the organ. Apparently, he was also the choir director because he would play the keyboard furiously for several seconds, then leap to his feet and wave his arms in front of the choir. When he would point in their direction, the singers would increase their already significant volume. The leader would then sit down and let his fingers fly over the keys for several moments before he jumped up again. Everyone in the sanctuary was clapping their hands. It was a triumphant song that talked about God's deliverance of his people. Bishop Moore, who had his eyes closed with his head slightly tilted up as he sang, occasionally stopped to listen, then joined in again.

Scott and Kay didn't know the song, but someone down the pew handed them a hymnbook opened to the appropriate page. They held the book between them and mouthed the verse in an effort to catch up, but it was no use. Trying to follow the printed words while stiffly holding a hymnbook didn't have the ability to communicate what was happening in the room. Kay looked at Scott and shook her head.

"Forget the book," she said. "I'm just going to clap."

The first song ended, and the leader moved seamlessly to the second, an antiphonal interaction between congregation and choir. No hymnbook was necessary. It was all about Jesus. The congregation took the lead.

"Who is he?" the congregation sang loudly.

"He's my Savior," the choir responded.

"Who is he?" the people asked again.

"He's my Rock," came the reply.

"Who is he?"

"He's my Healer."

On it went—an African-American catechism. Since the congregational part was the same, Scott and Kay joined in. Sometimes the choir sang a phrase in response. At other times, a member would break forth in a spontaneous song that gave further expression to the particular aspect of Jesus' nature or ministry that had been identified. When the choir sang, "He's my Shepherd," a woman on the front row of the choir closed her eyes and delivered a solo about Jesus, the Good Shepherd who always watches over his sheep no matter where they are or the problems they face. Her voice rose and fell with a depth of emotion and passion that made the hair on the back of Scott's neck stand up. It was as good as anything he'd heard while scanning the radio dial and listening for a few minutes to a soul music station.

At Hall's Chapel, the truth was known. Soul music didn't originate in the ghetto; it was birthed in the church. Only among the people of God did it have its fullest expression.

Scott glanced at Kay, whose eyes were closed. Her hair was blond and her skin white, but Scott sensed that Kay was able to travel with the soloist as she soared into the heavens and then came back to earth. Apparently, the poetic heart knew no boundaries of color or culture.

"Who is he?" the congregation asked again.

"He's my Lord."

A third song followed. It was a slower melody, and the choir and congregation began swaying back and forth. The movement was contagious, and Scott joined in. After a few sways, he bumped into Kay.

"Sorry."

Kay smiled at him and whispered. "Scott, you're going left when everybody else is going right."

More songs followed. When the music ended, Scott looked at his watch—almost an hour had passed. The man beside Bishop Moore stepped to the pulpit. He went through a list of announcements that included the birth of a baby, three people in the hospital, a prayer meeting on Wednesday night, and the dinner that would follow the morning service. Bishop Moore joined him.

Looking down at Scott, he said, "I invited Scott Ellis to join us this morning. Scott, come on up."

Scott climbed the three steps that stretched across the front of the sanctuary and stood beside the bishop, who put his hand on Scott's shoulder.

"Scott is an attorney who works with Leland Humphrey, an old friend of mine. I'd also invited Leland to come this morning, but Scott decided to bring someone else."

"Amen!" a woman sitting next to Kay said in a loud voice. Several people laughed.

Scott looked at the sea of friendly, yet curious, black faces.

"Thank you," he said. "This is my friend Kay Wilson. She's a teacher at Catawba High."

The bishop continued, "They are going to join us for dinner. Please make them feel welcome."

Scott returned to his seat. The man assisting in the pulpit stepped forward.

"Ushers, please come forward," he said. "We'll receive the morning offering."

Four men wearing the usher badges walked to the front of the sanctuary carrying small baskets and stood across the front, facing the people.

"Brother Samuels, please pray," the assistant said.

One of the ushers prayed, then the man in the pulpit called out, "Tithers, come forth!"

As soon as he spoke, the choir began singing. It was a song of thanksgiving and the congregation immediately joined in. Instead of passing the plates down the pews, the ushers waited at the front for the people to come to them. Men and women streamed down the aisles, joyously singing as they came.

After the last one returned to his seat, the man in the pulpit called out, "Those with offerings, come forth!"

Scott watched as the scene was repeated. The choir struck up a different song, and the congregation joined in. Some of the same people returned. Others who did not respond to the first invitation, including a number of children, joined them. A few people waved their gifts in the air as they walked forward.

Kay reached in her purse and took out her wallet. She took a few steps forward and deposited an offering in the basket held by the usher who had led them to their seats.

Scott leaned over and asked, "What's the difference between a tithe and an offering?"

"I'm not sure, but when I saw the children, I decided it was safe for me."

Scott didn't carry a lot of cash in his wallet. He received frequent flyer miles from his credit card and used it for even routine purchases. He stuck his hand in his pants pocket and felt a bill. It was five dollars left over from a forgotten purchase. Folding it over to hide the smallness of the amount, he put it in the offering plate. It was only the second time he'd given to a church since he started practicing law.

After the offering was collected, the organist played a riff down the keyboard that served as the introduction for a solo by one of the male members of the choir. The congregation remained seated but nevertheless began to sway back and forth. Scott intentionally bumped into Kay who responded with a gentle elbow to his ribs. When the last hum died down, Bishop Moore took his place behind the pulpit. His first words sounded like the end of a sermon rather than the beginning.

"To the glory of Jesus Christ, Amen."

Putting both hands on the pulpit, the minister began to pray.

"Thank you, Lord! You are good! You are all the things we've sung about this morning. You are greater than we can think or imagine. You are the Alpha and the Omega, the beginning and the end. Please, share more of yourself with us this day through the preaching of your Word. Hear the cry of your people for fresh manna. Say something to us and do something in us that will make a difference when we walk out of this sanctuary into the world you created. In Jesus' name, Amen and amen."

Scott hadn't thought much about the possible content of Bishop Moore's sermon, but he anticipated a first-rate lesson in public speaking. The oratorical skills of black preachers were legendary for a reason. Whether by conscious knowledge or cultural influence, they utilized the tools that communicated best with an audience: parallel thought progression, repetition, and rhetorical questions.

"Now, I've got someplace to go this morning," Bishop Moore began.

"It's going to be a journey to a faraway place in an ancient time, but I promise that if you go with me you'll be glad for every step of the way because the road back will pass through the center of your heart."

"Where are you going, Preacher?" asked a man seated on the front pew to the left of the platform.

"I'm going back, way back. All the way back to Abraham, a man who walked alone with God before there was anyone else listening to what the Lord was saying."

Bishop Moore began by telling the story of Abram, a boy living in Ur of the Chaldees. It was a story simple enough for a child to follow, yet told with such ample description that Scott could almost taste the fruit from the street vendors in the city bazaar where Abram and his friends spent their days playing. By the time the boy became a man, Scott could appreciate the courage required to obey the command from the unknown Voice to "*leave your father's house and go to a land I will show you.*"

"Can you imagine what the world was like in Abraham's day?" the bishop asked. "He is on the road to an unknown place, following the voice of a God he could not see. There were no friends who shared his beliefs to tell him he was on the right path, no church family to comfort him and lift him up when the problems of life knocked him down, no support from brothers in the faith who would come by to encourage and pray with him. Can anyone appreciate the faith of this man?"

"I can," several voices responded.

The bishop continued, "Time after time, the Bible repeats the same statement about Abraham. One of those times is in James 2:23 where it says, 'Abraham believed God, and it was credited to him as righteousness.' Abraham was alone. He was isolated. He was a minority of one. He was a stranger in a strange land. Was it easy for him to believe?"

"No," came the response from the congregation.

"You're right, it wasn't easy, but he did it anyway. He believed God. In the face of a world that worshiped idols made of silver and gold, he believed in the invisible God whom the heavens and earth could not contain. He was a good man who tried to live a righteous life in the midst of a wicked people. He believed that God existed. But was that enough to credit him with righteousness in Jehovah's sight?"

"No," came a louder response.

"James agrees with you. In chapter 2, verse 19 it says that 'even the demons believe . . . and shudder.' So, what was the reason for Abraham's righteousness? What did he believe that pleased God so greatly?"

Scott didn't have a clue.

"Do you think it's important to know the answer?" the preacher asked. "Is there anyone in this room who wants to know?"

"Tell it!" a man sitting near Scott shouted.

Speaking slowly for emphasis, Bishop Moore answered, "He believed in the promise of God, and his belief became faith."

Scott had never considered the relationship between belief and faith. He regarded the two terms as synonymous, but as he listened to Bishop Moore, he realized that unless belief produced day-to-day trust in God, it could not be considered faith.

"God's voice spoke a command and a promise to a man in Ur of the Chaldees," the bishop said. "Abraham's part was to hear and obey. It's the same with each of us in this room. The voice of the Lord is going out over the whole earth looking for an ear that will hear and a heart that will obey."

The preacher scanned the congregation for several seconds, then pointed to a person sitting someplace behind Scott and Kay. "The voice of the Lord is calling out to Neal Gillis in Blanchard County, North Carolina. Will you hear and obey?"

"Yes, Lord!" a man responded.

The preacher's finger made a leisurely journey to a spot closer to where Scott sat. "The voice of the Lord is calling out to Larinda Evanston in Blanchard County, North Carolina. Will you hear and obey?"

"Yes, Lord! Every day!" the woman answered.

The bishop's finger moved again. It started at the far end of the pew where Scott sat and moved slowly toward him. Scott suddenly felt a drop of perspiration drip down inside his shirt. God was about to cross-examine his soul. He believed in God, but he wasn't sure he had faith. The finger moved closer. Scott didn't want to make eye contact with Bishop Moore, but almost against his will, he looked up. The bishop's eyes met his, and in an instant, Scott realized that any masks he placed over his face could not hide the condition of his heart. The finger paused over him for a second that seemed like a year, then quickly reversed course to encompass the entire sanctuary in a sweeping motion.

The preacher cried out, "The voice of the Lord is calling out to each and every one of you in Hall's Chapel Church! Will you hear and obey?"

A resounding, "Yes, Lord!" echoed from the congregation and rolled off the walls.

Relieved, Scott remained silent.

The preacher continued to talk for another ten minutes. At the end of the service, several people came forward and knelt in front of the carpeted steps that led to the platform. Bishop Moore and a few church leaders prayed with them. There was not a lot of emotion except for a woman who cried softly. Scott grew fidgety. Kay sat motionless beside him with her eyes closed.

Finally, the bishop resumed his place behind the pulpit and pronounced a benediction. Conversations broke out as people stood up and moved toward the aisles. A woman came over to Kay and introduced herself. She had a niece who was in one of Kay's classes at the high school.

Bishop Moore walked down the steps toward Scott and shook his hand. Nothing in the preacher's expression revealed what he'd seen in their moment of unspoken conversation.

"I hope you enjoyed the service," the preacher said. "I know it was different from what you're used to."

"I enjoyed it," Scott said, not sure if he'd given the correct response. "I don't go to church very often."

"You're welcome here anytime," the bishop said. "It's good for our people to worship together. Usually, we're the ones who cross the color line that divides the church, so it's nice when it works the other way."

Kay rejoined them.

"Bishop Moore, why were several of the ladies in white sitting on the front pew together?" she asked.

The bishop smiled. "Oh, that's the Mother Board, the older women in the church who pray and intercede for the meeting. Without their prayers, we wouldn't get very far."

A small, robust woman dressed in a peach-colored dress with a large hat on her head and a bright smile came up to them.

"This is my wife, Rachel," the preacher said.

Scott shook her hand. "Pleased to meet you."

Mrs. Moore gave Kay a hug.

"We're glad you're here," she said. "You picked a good Sunday to visit because we're going to eat. Alfred says you liked the leftovers he gave you and Leland Humphrey the other day."

"Yes, ma'am. They were great."

"This will be twice as good and three times as much."

23

In the heat of summer, every man walking out of Hall's Chapel would strip off his jacket and loosen his tie by the time he took two steps across the parking lot. Today, the remnants of the morning fog had burned off in the noontime heat, but the temperature was still cool enough to be comfortable. Most of the women disappeared into the section of the church where Scott and Leland Humphrey first talked with Bishop Moore. In a few minutes casserole dishes covered in aluminum foil and plastic cake carriers began pouring forth from the fellowship hall.

"That was a different kind of church service," Kay said. "But I liked it, especially the music."

"I had trouble with the choreography," Scott said.

Kay laughed. "It's a rare white male who has any rhythm."

"Toward the end of the sermon, I thought Bishop Moore was about to single me out. It made me nervous, but the bishop had mercy on me."

Alisha Mason came up and greeted them.

"Mrs. Wilson, come meet my family. I've told my mother a lot about you."

Kay left with Alisha, and the man who sang the solo before the sermon introduced himself to Scott. After some small talk, Scott decided to gather information in an informal way.

"Were you here on the day of the shooting?" he asked.

"Yes."

"What happened?"

"Well, the bishop was baptizing some folks and shots were fired. I grabbed my little boy and ran back to the church."

"Did you see anybody on the other side of the stream?"

The singer shook his head. "No."

"Is there anyone else that knows more about what happened?"

"I'm not sure. I think the bishop is the one who saw the most."

"Yeah, I've already talked to him, and he seemed to remember more details. Was he wearing his glasses when he was in the water baptizing the people?"

The man paused. "I can't remember. He always wears glasses because his eyesight is so poor, but I can't be certain that he had them on during the baptism service." The man pointed to the stream. "Preachers have been known to baptize themselves over there if they step on a slick rock."

"Do you think he had them on?"

"I really can't say. Sorry."

The man left and another walked up. Scott went through a similar series of questions without learning anything new. It seemed that the incident happened so fast and the underbrush on the other side of the stream was so dense that it would have been hard to tell who or what was there. Neither man could remember whether Bishop Moore was wearing his glasses.

Two long tables positioned end-to-end were heavy-laden with a cross-section of favorite recipes. Bishop Moore found Scott and Kay and brought them to the head of the serving line.

"You're our guests, so you have to go first."

"What about the children?" Kay asked.

"They can follow you," the bishop said. "In my day, the youngsters had to wait until the adults finished. There were times when the only parts of the chicken left for us were the necks and the backs."

Scott looked at the platters of golden brown chicken. "I don't see many necks."

The bishop smiled. "You'd have to special-order them. The last time I saw a chicken neck was on the end of a string when I was trying to catch crabs at the coast."

It was self-serve, buffet style. Scott moved deliberately down one side of the table, carefully placing everything on his plate so that the right foods would be in contact with one another. The outdoor feast was organized. It began with congealed salads, pasta salads, and macaroni salads. Next came the meats: fried chicken, roast beef, ham, and some meat pies thrown in for variety. The vegetables followed with everything from homegrown asparagus to zucchini pie. Scott loved zucchini pie if it was thin and slightly crispy. He carefully wedged a large piece between a scoop of sweet potato casserole and green beans seasoned with bits of bacon. The desserts followed. Fortunately, there were extra plates at the beginning of the dessert area. Scott put his food plate on the edge of the table and loaded his dessert plate with banana pudding from a huge pottery bowl with a blue ring around the top.

The bishop led them to a table in the shade. Before Scott could get up to walk to the drink table, Rachel Moore came over to them.

"What would you like to drink?" she asked. "We have tea, lemonade, and water."

"Lemonade sounds good," Kay answered.

"Sweet tea for me, please," Scott said.

Mrs. Moore returned and placed a large Styrofoam cup of tea in front of Scott.

"This is from my pitcher," she said. "I've already squeezed some lemon in it."

Scott was thirsty after the long church service and took a long drink.

"Aah," he said. "Perfect. Where's your pitcher? I'm sure I'll want a refill."

Mrs. Moore pointed to the drink table. "It's the green-colored glass one on the end."

Soon, Scott and Kay were surrounded by other people. On one end of their table was a family of five. The youngest child, a little boy, was pouting and sat in his seat with his arms over his chest, refusing to eat anything. Directly across the table from Scott and Kay was an older couple. The man had obviously lost weight. His shirt collar was too big for his neck, and the only hair he had left was a white fringe around his dark head. He nodded to Scott and mumbled a greeting when he sat down. His wife was an opposite personality. Rotund and jolly, she was dressed in white with a large, multicolored hat on her head. After she breathlessly put down her plate, she reached across the table and vigorously shook their hands.

"I'm Bernice Kilgore and this is my husband, Benny," she said. "I rushed through the line so fast I'm not even sure what I put on my plate. I didn't want anyone to get to you first."

Scott looked at Mrs. Kilgore's plate. What it lacked in organization, it made up in quantity. It was the work of someone who knew that all food ended up in the same place.

Mrs. Kilgore smiled at Kay. "It's Kay, isn't it?"

"Yes, ma'am."

"It was wonderful having you with us this morning. I was in the choir on the second row."

Scott recalled the face. Mrs. Kilgore didn't sing a solo but her exuberance was obvious.

The black woman ate a few quick bites before continuing. "Did you get some of this corn soufflé? Margie Duckett brought it. She's standing near the bishop."

She pointed, and Scott looked over his shoulder. There was a crowd that included several women in the vicinity of Bishop Moore.

"I have some," Kay responded. "It's delicious."

Mrs. Kilgore leaned across the table and whispered, "I gave Margie the recipe, but mine doesn't taste as good as hers. How does she make it so fluffy? It's like eating corn-flavored air."

Scott held his fork toward Kay's plate. "May I try some of yours?"

Kay balanced a small bite of the yellow confection on the end of his fork and he put it in his mouth. He chewed for a few seconds, then said, "Very tasty. Do you think it's all gone?"

Before anyone answered, Mrs. Kilgore was out of her seat. She returned with a generous portion of soufflé and set it down beside Scott's banana pudding.

"This is all that was left," she said. "I had to rescue it from some hungry-looking folks that were coming down the line."

"I didn't want you to do that," Scott protested. "That's not right. Someone might get upset."

Mrs. Kilgore laughed. "Look at that table. Nobody is going hungry today. If they do, it's their own fault."

Mrs. Kilgore knew a great deal of information about everyone in the church. In between quick bites of food, she told several stories about members of the congregation and mentioned names so fast it was impossible to keep them straight. Scott listened while he worked steadily through his meal. He shared his extra plate of corn soufflé with Kay who also sampled a few bites of banana pudding.

When Mrs. Kilgore took a break from storytelling, Scott asked, "Were you here on the day the shots were fired?"

"No, Benny and I were out of town visiting my old auntie in Kannapolis. She is 102 years old and still gets around without using a walker."

Scott didn't have any follow-up questions about Mrs. Kilgore's aunt and returned to his banana pudding.

Mrs. Kilgore leaned across the table and patted Kay's hand. "When I saw you come in the sanctuary, I asked the Lord to give me a word of encouragement for you, and I think he showed me something. Do you want me to share it with you?"

"Okay," Kay said.

"While I was sitting in the choir, I believe the Lord showed me that you have been going through a time of great sorrow, yet in the midst of it, you're experiencing a new joy. I know that doesn't seem to go together, but I think that's right."

Kay's eyes widened. "Mrs. Kilgore, that's—"

The black woman held up her hand. "Just listen. You can ask questions when I finish."

"I also want to reassure you that God loves you," Mrs. Kilgore said. "I can see that you've started opening your heart up to Jesus and taken some big steps in your journey with him. Don't stop. Go on. He's been with you in the lonely hours and has a record of every tear you've cried. It says in the Psalms that he puts our tears in a bottle of remembering. Even when it seems that the nearest person to you was a thousand miles away, you've never been alone."

Kay's eyes now watered, and she quickly brushed away a fresh tear that pooled in the corner of her right eye. It was another drop for the bottle stored in heaven.

The black lady continued, "Your sorrow is real, but the joy is going to win in the end. It's a powerful joy—the joy of the Lord, one of the fruits of the Holy Spirit. David wrote about it in the Psalms and Paul wrote about it in Galatians. This world can't give it, and this world can't take it away because it comes from another place. I believe you'll face a great test in the future, so I'd encourage you to spend time reading in Psalms and the Holy Spirit will speak to you in a very personal way. If you open yourself fully to the Lord, he will put a new song in your heart that will drive out the sadness when it threatens to return."

Kay's mouth had dropped open. The last two bites of Scott's banana pudding sat untouched on his plate.

"Finally, you're something of a poet yourself," Mrs. Kilgore said, "and the Holy Spirit will speak to you in the dark hours of the night. Put your thoughts down on paper; don't trust your memory, because it may be gone in the morning. In the future, the Lord may use your writings to encourage other people by touching their hearts in the same deep way that he touches yours."

Kay waited a few seconds, then asked, "Is that all?"

Mrs. Kilgore smiled. "Yes, I guess that's about it. It's your job to ask the Lord if any of these things are true and how they affect your life."

Kay spoke rapidly, "I don't know where to start. I've been going through a painful divorce, but over the past week or so I've had a lot of joy. I opened my heart to the Lord in a church service recently, and a few days later I heard a new song in my mind that stayed with me most of the day. I told Scott about it at lunch. He thought I was out of my mind—"

"I didn't say that," Scott interrupted.

"Don't lie," Kay shot back. "Mrs. Kilgore will know it if you do."

The black woman laughed. "It's not like that. I don't know everything, just what the Holy Spirit shows me to encourage someone in their walk with the Lord. It's a great comfort for most folks to know that God hasn't forgotten them. He'll send someone like me to tell them a few things so they'll know they're on the right path or help them see where it lies."

"It's like the call-in psychics on TV," Kay started, then quickly added, "no, I'm sorry, I'm not suggesting—"

The smile didn't leave Mrs. Kilgore's face. "I know what you mean. I explain it this way. The gifts of the Holy Spirit are like money in the Kingdom of God. God's children use the gifts to help people come to the Lord Jesus or grow as Christians. But wherever there is real money, criminals will come along and produce something counterfeit. That's the work of the enemy. He wants to deceive people. Even when his servants say something that's true, it's counterfeit. It's supernatural, but it doesn't bring people closer to the Lord. That's the test."

"Where did you learn about all this?" Kay asked.

"Mostly from my granny. Now she was a sight to behold. When I was a little girl, we would sit together in the evenings on an old porch swing at her house. She would put her hand on my head and pray and pray and pray as we rocked back and forth. After a while I would go into the house to drink a glass of water or go to the bathroom. When I'd come back, she'd put her hand on my head and keep on going like nothing had happened. Sometimes we'd sit there until the stars came out. People were all the time coming by to ask her to pray for them. She'd pray and tell them what the Lord showed her. I heard some amazing things on her front porch."

"How did you know what to say to me?"

"Oh, it came a little bit at a time during the service. Then when I started talking with you, more followed behind. It takes faith to talk to someone like this, but you are so sweet that it wasn't hard at all. You were willing to listen. Some folks are too afraid to come out from where they're hiding to let the Lord tell them how much he loves them. Do you want some carrot cake? Gladys Hornsby brought it, and it's almost as good as my sister's recipe."

After they finished eating, Scott talked to five or six other people about the shots fired during the baptism. Their comments were so similar that it all ran together. He never got the tape recorder out of his vehicle. It was midafternoon before he and Kay said good-bye to Bishop Moore and drove out of the church parking lot.

"Well, that was a bust," Scott sighed as they rounded a curve and the church disappeared from view. "I didn't find out anything new. I'd hoped someone at the church would give me a new angle to use in Lester's case. I couldn't even corroborate what I already know."

Kay spun toward him in her seat. "What! This has been one of the most incredible days of my life! I wouldn't have traded the time at the table with Mrs. Kilgore for ten thousand dollars. And the church service was good, too. Just because you didn't find out anything about your case doesn't mean there weren't plenty of opportunities to find out about other important things."

Scott started to reply but nothing appropriate came to mind. They rode in silence for several minutes.

When they reached the main highway and turned left, Kay spoke. "Why didn't you ask Mrs. Kilgore if she had anything from God to tell you?"

Scott had considered it. But after dodging a bullet from Bishop Moore, he didn't want to get winged by a word from the dessert-loving prophetess.

"If she'd had something, she would have brought it up."

"When did you become an expert about these things?"

Scott kept his mouth shut. Lawyers can pretend to become experts about a lot of things, but it was time to invoke his Fifth Amendment right not to incriminate himself.

24

Did tremble like a guilty thing surprised.
WILLIAM WORDSWORTH

On his way to the office Monday morning, Scott passed the court-house and wondered what his feelings would be in one week. If Lynn Davenport stayed true to her word, *State v. Garrison* would be the first case called for trial, and Scott would have the responsibility of choosing twelve people to decide Lester's fate. On his desk at the office was a thick stack of questionnaires completed by prospective jurors. For some of them, jury service would be a twenty-dollar-a-day opportunity to be someone important. Others viewed the civic duty as a major disruption and called the clerk's office with creative reasons to avoid serving.

Shortly before lunch, he made a final note on his legal pad about the questionnaires and stood up to stretch. Scott wouldn't be able to flip a coin in the courtroom; he had to use a better system. He'd eliminated a few jurors from consideration because they'd been victims of a crime or had relatives who worked in law enforcement. There also might be people in the jury pool whose racial views ran parallel to Lester Garrison's. As personally distasteful as that might be, Scott needed a subtle way to ferret out those persons and try to keep them in the jury box.

One of the people summoned for jury duty was the wife of Officer Bradley, the deputy whom Lester cursed and tried to kick at the time of his arrest. Mrs. Bradley would be excused for cause, and Scott wouldn't have to use one of his strikes to remove her from the case. Many others remained in limbo. There were individuals who might not be favorably disposed toward a teenager like Lester, and the brief questionnaires didn't provide enough information to make that decision. Mr. Humphrey was Scott's most valuable resource. With his vast experience and personal knowledge of the people in Blanchard County, the older lawyer had promised to check the list and go over it with Scott later in the week.

Before he left for lunch, Scott stopped by Mr. Humphrey's office to give him an update on the case. Leland Humphrey, his feet propped on the corner of his desk, was reading a deposition and dictating a summary of the testimony.

"How did it go at the church on Sunday?" the older lawyer asked. "I thought about you at twelve o'clock when I was walking out of church with my brother and his wife in New Bern."

"We were at the midway point of Bishop Moore's sermon at twelve o'clock."

"Did you learn anything?"

"I learned a lot. Nothing about the case."

Mr. Humphrey chuckled. "I'm sorry you had to go by yourself."

"I didn't go alone. I invited the teacher who is helping coach the mock trial team at the high school. She loved it."

Mr. Humphrey's left eyebrow shot up. "Who is the teacher?"

"An old classmate named Kay Wilson. She was Kay Laramie when we were in high school together."

"Does she know Lester Garrison?"

"Yes, he's one of her students, but I haven't talked to her about the case."

"Why not?"

"If she knew anything, she would have mentioned it. She has two hundred students a day."

Mr. Humphrey ran his right thumb down the outside of his suspender. "I'd ask the teacher a few questions. Maybe check some of his papers to see if he wrote anything that would be relevant."

"Is that wise? The e-mails Davenport showed us were enough to prove a conspiracy to commit murder, and I don't want to uncover evidence that helps prove either one of the state's cases against Lester."

"I'm not talking about evidence that hurts us. The first rule of litigation is never do anything that will hurt you more than it helps you, but there may be some favorable evidence hidden out there." Mr. Humphrey looked at his watch. "Are you on your way to lunch?"

"Yes, sir. I'm walking down to the Eagle."

"I'll join you."

It was an overcast day, and the clouds held the threat of an afternoon rain. The Eagle was three blocks from the office, and the lunchtime business crowd was flowing through the front door by the time they arrived. Many business deals in Blanchard County were hatched over a plate of meat loaf, green beans, mashed potatoes, and corn bread. Some deals succeeded; others failed. A few ended up as lawsuits in the courthouse around the corner. But the food was never a point of contention.

In the back of the restaurant there were two long tables for ten. One was reserved for the Democrats, the other for the Republicans. There had been an upswing of Republicans in Blanchard County since the 1960s, and there was often a spirited debate between the two evenly matched camps. It wasn't unusual for the men at the tables to argue back and forth on a specific issue, and each group had members whose voices carried over the din of the restaurant.

Several people in the restaurant recognized Leland Humphrey, and he and Scott worked their way through the crowd to a table near the Democrats. Mr. Humphrey didn't alienate his clientele by becoming too closely identified with a single political party. He limited his political activity to influencing the selection of judicial candidates. His goal was to win in the courtroom, not at the ballot box.

They ordered their food, and Mr. Humphrey sipped his tea.

"Have I ever told you about my first jury trial?" he asked.

"No, sir, and considering what's ahead for me, it's probably the right time to tell the story. But I have one question."

"What?"

"Is this going to help me or hurt me?"

Mr. Humphrey smiled. "You'll have to be the judge of that."

The older lawyer settled back in his chair.

"When I started practice in Catawba, there were only eight lawyers in the whole circuit. I went to work for Harvey Kilpatrick, a friend of my grandfather who did real estate and business work. I don't think he'd been out of the deed room in years and never took a case if there was a chance it would end up in court. A baby duck mimics its mother, so when I started working for Mr. Kilpatrick, I began doing the same type of work. If you go back far enough in the records, you'll see my signature as the notary on a lot of deeds.

"After about a year in practice, I was sitting at my desk one day when our secretary told me a man had walked in off the street and wanted to talk to a lawyer. Mr. Kilpatrick was out of the office, so I decided to talk to the prospective client. It turned out the fellow was new to the area. He worked at a cotton mill, grew a big garden, and raised cows on a few acres he leased along the railroad. One of his cows had been hit by the train on the way to Raleigh, and he wanted to sue the railroad. After I interviewed him, I agreed to take the case and filed suit against the Norfolk and Southern Railroad."

Scott chuckled. "A big case. How much was the cow worth?"

Mr. Humphrey didn't change his expression. "I don't remember the exact figure, but it was the best cow he had, practically a member of the family. I think the original complaint contained over thirty paragraphs because I wanted to make sure I wouldn't lose on a technicality. I had no idea how much dust my little lawsuit would stir up. Apparently, a lot of farmers were suing the railroad over dead cows that lined the tracks from here to Richmond. Rumor had it dishonest cattlemen were dragging carcasses of cattle who died from natural causes to the railroad tracks so they could be hit by the next train, then filing claims with the railroad. The railroad would pay instead of trying to fight, and the situation got under the skin of a corporate big shot who told his lawyers enough was enough and decided to make an example of the next dead cow case that came into the home office. That was my little lawsuit. The fact that I was a new attorney probably made the decision easier."

The waitress brought their food while Mr. Humphrey was talking. Scott buttered a corn-bread stick.

"Who represented the railroad?"

"No one locally. A firm from Raleigh sent three lawyers who set up shop in the Palmer Hotel. One of the first things they did was file a motion to have the cow's carcass exhumed for examination."

"An autopsy on a cow?"

"Yes." Mr. Humphrey cut off a piece of meat loaf with his fork and looked it over before putting it into his mouth. "The judge granted their request, and I went to the farm on the day they dug it up. Nothing was secret in Catawba, and the case was a big topic of conversation. There must have been thirty men in overalls standing by when they hauled the cow back into the light. A veterinarian hired by the railroad examined the remains and made a bunch of notes in a notebook. There wasn't pre-trial discovery in those days, so I didn't know what the vet was going to say until he was on the witness stand."

"Trial by ambush," Scott said.

Mr. Humphrey's right eyebrow shot up. "That was the accepted way. After digging up the cow, the three railroad lawyers filed motions asking the judge to dismiss the complaint. There were a couple of close calls, but the judge left me hanging on by my fingernails, and the case was put on the fall trial calendar. I talked to the two trial lawyers here in town, and they told me the key would be getting men on the jury who owned cows. Everyone knew the railroad had a lot of money, and even though my client was new to the area, the farmers would look out for one of their own. I asked around and found out all I could about the potential jurors and had a star by the names of everyone who owned at least one cow. If the juror also lived near the railroad, I put two stars by his name. When it came time to pick the jury, I was able to sneak two single stars and one double star onto the panel.

"My opening statement was stiff, but the facts were simple and it would have been hard to confuse anyone with half a brain. My client owned a cow. The railroad owned a train. The train hit the cow on my client's land. The railroad owed my client the value of the cow."

Mr. Humphrey paused to eat a few bites. "The defense lawyer's opening statement didn't reveal anything about his trial strategy. All he said was that after hearing the evidence the jury would rule against the farmer."

"Nothing about his veterinarian expert?"

"Not a peep. My first witness was the farmer. He had the bill of sale from his purchase of the cow and gave graphic testimony of the cow's condition after it was hit by the train. It was enough to make a grown man cry. Most of the jurors gave the chief defense lawyer a cold stare when he began questioning my client. He began by asking the farmer where he was born and went through a painstaking, detailed line of questioning that revealed every place the man had lived from infancy to the present. Everyone in the courtroom but me was about to fall asleep. Then he asked my client why he didn't butcher the cow after it had been hit by the train."

"A mitigation of damages argument?" Scott asked.

"So I thought—for about three minutes. My client got a little red in the face and said that the cow was too mangled to salvage. Then the railroad lawyer went over to one of his associates who gave him a piece of paper. It was a claim filed by my client for the value of a cow. The only problem was that it was dated the previous year in another county where my client had admitted living. Another sheet followed. Then another. After six cows had been slaughtered by the railroad, the defense lawyer asked my client how many times he'd filed claims against the railroad for killing his cows.

"He sputtered around for a few seconds, then admitted he'd had a lot of bad luck with cows and trains. I was so relieved when the lawyer finally finished that I didn't ask any follow-up questions. The defense then called the veterinarian who said that the cow in my case was so badly diseased that it was probably dead before the train left Richmond for Atlanta. The meat was contaminated and unsafe to eat. That's why it wasn't butchered. Finally, the lawyer called a private investigator who had documents proving that my client would buy diseased cattle, create a fictitious bill of sale, and drag the stricken animals, dead or alive, to the train tracks for a date with the next locomotive. I made a feeble effort at cross-examination of the investigator, but it was pointless. My closing argument lasted five minutes. The jury stayed out thirty minutes, just long enough for everyone to smoke a cigarette."

"I'm surprised you didn't go back to work in the deed room after the trial," Scott said. "That case would have discouraged anyone who had any desire to be a trial lawyer."

Mr. Humphrey smiled. "My young pride took a beating, but to their credit, the railroad lawyers didn't smirk or rub it in; they packed up and returned to the city. I told my client to expect a visit from the sheriff, and he was out of the courthouse in less than a minute. I was about to slink after him when the judge asked me to come into his chambers. I knew I was about to get chewed out, but there was nothing to do but take my medicine. Judge Taylor was about a hundred years old and was the boniest man I've ever seen. I knew he was going to point his eight-inch index finger at my chest and tell me not to darken his courtroom again. He told me to sit down and stared at me for at least a minute without saying a word. I could sense that the volcano was building up pressure before a massive eruption. Then he started chuckling. The chuckle became roaring laughter. My face got red, and I went from embarrassment to anger in a matter of seconds. He held up his hand and stopped me before I blurted something out I'd later regret."

"Mr. Humphrey," he said, "I hope you'll return many times to my courtroom. You have the potential to be a fine trial lawyer, and you must not let this experience keep you from taking cases in the future. But there are some lessons you can learn from what happened today."

Scott interjected, "Don't take any dead cow cases against the railroad unless you know the cow and the owner personally."

Mr. Humphrey smiled. "That's the specific application. Judge Taylor wanted me to learn the general principles."

"First," he said, "know your client better than he knows himself. Spend plenty of time investigating and analyzing the weaknesses in your own position. Hope for the best; prepare for the worst. That way you'll be ready for anything. If you don't ferret out the truth about your case in the privacy of your office, the other side will embarrass you by dragging it into the open before the judge and jury. Second, facts are durable things. Attorneys who claim irrefutable evidence can disappear by legal sleight of hand are deceiving themselves and doing a disservice to the people they represent. No matter how you describe it, the sun still rises in the east and sets in the west. Third, don't let your emotions or pride keep you from settling a case prior to trial. Always ask yourself what is in the best interests of the client. A fair settlement is always better than an adverse verdict."

Mr. Humphrey ate a bite of cold meat loaf. "I appeared in front of Judge Taylor several times before he died a few years later. In one of those cases, the other side refused a reasonable offer of settlement, and the jury returned a large verdict for my client. It was small by today's standards, but it helped make my reputation in the community."

Scott put his fork and knife on his empty plate. "Okay. I'll keep digging in Lester's case. I don't want any dead cows turning up in the courtroom."

25

And I will do whatever you ask in my name, so that
the Son may bring glory to the Father. You may ask
me for anything in my name, and I will do it.
JOHN 14:13-14

It was dark outside when Lester finished his sandwich and ate the last
potato chip. His father had been on the road since the day after their
meeting with Scott. Without Harold around to tell him that no jury
would convict him without any eyewitnesses, Lester's fears had increased
on a daily basis. His appetite was down, and he would wake up at 4 A.M.
unable to go back to sleep. The youth detention center had been bad; a
prison work camp would be a thousand times worse.

Thelma called from her bedroom, "Lester! Are you still in the kitchen?"

Lester walked down the hallway and stuck his head into the room.
"What is it?"

"Will you put the medicine on my leg? I think the sore is draining."

Sometimes Lester walked out the front door when Thelma asked him
for help, but his looming date with judgment made him more willing to
serve than normal. The tube of antibiotic ointment was on his grandmother's nightstand. He put a disposable plastic glove on his right hand
and squeezed a thick line of the white substance on the end of his finger.
He rubbed it lightly on the two-inch ulcer. It was gross, but everything
about his grandmother was repulsive. The spot hadn't changed in over a
week, and he knew that for a diabetic anything was hard to heal.

"Okay," he said. "It's looking better."

Outside, he could hear Jack barking in the field behind the shed.

"Thanks," Thelma said. "I'm going to lie down and prop up my leg
on a pillow so that I don't rub off the medicine until I go to sleep."

"I'll be outside. I want to see what Jack is doing."

Lester stepped onto the front porch. There were no streetlights in the country, and the glimmer from the neighbor's house down the road didn't penetrate the darkness more than ten feet from their windows. Without the city glare to hide their presence, the stars were on display from one end of the fall sky to the other. Lester took a deep breath. There were always bright lights on at the youth detention center, and it was probably the same in a work camp where some of the men in the barracks didn't want to face what might be in the darkness.

Lester leaned against the side of the house. The paint was peeling badly, and he picked off a big piece and dropped it on the ground. He could get in his truck and leave before the sun came up and brought him another day closer to his court date. He had $534 hidden in a white sock in the toe of a smelly old boot in his closet. In four hours, he could be in Georgia, Tennessee, South Carolina, or Virginia. He doubted the police would mount a serious search for a seventeen-year-old boy who should have been tried in juvenile court. His grandmother had put up her house for his bond, but no sheriff with a compassionate cell in his body would dump a blind woman out on the side of the road if he ran. He swore and kicked the ground.

Jack came running. The dog didn't know a curse from a blessing, but he recognized his master's voice. He stopped and wagged his tail. Lester sat down on the ground and leaned against the house. Jack came over and quickly licked Lester's chin before lying down beside him and leaning against his leg.

"What should I do?" Lester asked. "Go or stay?"

Jack put his head on Lester's thigh and closed his eyes in contentment. The dog didn't know anything except the immediacy of each moment. To be with Lester was all he desired.

"Would you go with me?" he continued. "We might end up out West. I've heard you can see more stars there than anyplace else."

Jack's eyes remained closed.

"I could leave all my problems behind. Use a different name and find a job in a place that doesn't ask questions. There's nothing here except trouble."

They sat on the ground in silence for several minutes. Lester fantasized about a new life in another place.

It was getting cool, and Lester rubbed his hands together. He had a small heater in the shed. He walked back to the little building with Jack at his heels. The key was in its usual hiding place. He opened the door, turned on the light, and began working. There were other reasons to stay in Catawba. The last sound Thelma heard in the distance before she fell asleep was Lester banging on metal.

———

The front doors of the school were unlocked each morning at 6 A.M. Carrying a paper sack containing a piece of fruit and leftover rice, Tao arrived a few minutes later. He walked down the hall and admired the clean floors that softly reflected the fluorescent lights overhead. He went to his storage closet and took out several dust rags to clean the lockers. Beginning at the far end of the hallway, he wiped the top of the metal lockers with a rag and deposited larger pieces of trash in a blue plastic bucket. One identical locker for each student, each student a different number, each person a unique individual.

Tao started with a quiet cadence of prayer for the young people who in an hour and a half would rush up to one of the lockers, jerk open the door, grab a book, leave a book, and hurry down the hall. He patiently made his way along the hallway. When he touched certain lockers, his heart rejoiced. In front of others, he experienced sadness. Usually, he didn't feel anything. But regardless of his feelings, he prayed. For each locker, for each student.

Tao believed in God's omnipresence. He'd been confused at first by the idea that God was everywhere at once. It had seemed too similar to the worship of rocks, trees, and streams that he knew were not gods at all. Then he learned that although God created all things, he was not confined to any of them. All things were not god, but God was Lord of all things. Thus, the blessing of the Holy Spirit's presence could be manifest throughout creation. Tao's prayers weren't a ritual; they were based on a broad view of the influence of the heavenly realm.

In Tao's culture supernatural revelation was accepted, not analyzed. This perspective had led to great spiritual darkness for the Hmong people through the negative influences of animistic religion, but it also proved to be fertile soil for the promises of Jesus. Tao read Jesus' words in John 14:13–14: "And I will do whatever you ask in my name, so that the Son may bring glory to the Father. You may ask me for anything in my name, and I will do it." These verses opened an enormous new vista for Tao—the potential impact of prayer as the invitation to God's glory. He realized that prayer was not an effort to appease an angry God poised to kill him, but a family privilege granted those who entered into relationship with the Father, Son, and Holy Spirit.

Thus began Tao's daily habit of talking to Jesus. When alone, he often spoke out loud. He would speak, then listen. When other people were present, he stepped back into the secret place of his heart and continued the divine communication. Whether out loud or in his heart, the process was the same. He would speak, then listen. And over the years he learned to recognize the voice of the Good Shepherd who said, "My sheep hear my voice."

Tao also read in the New Testament about Jesus and the apostles demonstrating the power of God through natural objects. Jesus made mud with his saliva that had the power to open the eyes of a blind man. A few loaves of bread became more than enough to feed a multitude. Pieces of cloth touched by the apostles were laid on sick people who were healed.

So, Tao prayed for school lockers. They were made of thin metal painted a light tan. But to those lockers would come many young people who needed God. He asked the Lord to touch each one, to awaken them to the knowledge of Jesus Christ, to protect them from the evil one.

It took almost an hour to go up and down the hallways. When he finished, no paper or broken pencils remained on top of the lockers, and by faith, there was a deposit of blessing for those who would soon arrive for the school day.

———

Scott left a message on Kay's voice mail at school asking her to meet with him before the mock trial team session. He was preparing for the Garrison trial in earnest and wanted to find out if anything from Lester's schoolwork would help with the defense. He then spent most of the morning working on an outline for his young client's testimony.

The defendant in a criminal case does not have to take the witness stand, and Scott wasn't sure if testimony from Lester would help more than it hurt, so he wanted to evaluate Lester's performance during a couple of dry runs. One of the keys to a successful defense would be to portray Lester as an innocent victim of unwarranted suspicion—a Tom Sawyer on the riverbank who was mistakenly swept up in an overzealous criminal investigation by well-meaning police officers trying to find someone to blame. Scott would spend a lot of time developing Lester's background, revealing his care for his blind grandmother, and portraying him as a hardworking young man who had saved enough money over the summer to buy his own truck. He hoped there were a lot of male truck owners in the jury pool.

Lester was scheduled to come to the office the following afternoon for the first of three preparation sessions. Scott would ask direct examination questions and see how his young client responded. Mr. Humphrey had agreed to serve as a surrogate prosecutor. To assist the older lawyer, Scott prepared questions to be used in cross-examination. Mr. Humphrey could probably do a better job on the spur of the moment than Scott could by preparation, but it was good practice for Scott to anticipate the lines of attack Lynn Davenport might follow. Through repetition of questions and answers, Scott hoped Lester would develop an automatic response to the D.A.'s likely assaults and turn her questions to his advantage by using them as the springboard for further explanation of his innocence. At least that was the theory.

Shortly before lunch, Kay called.

"Can we talk before the meeting?" Scott asked. "I wanted to ask you some questions about Lester Garrison."

"Me?"

"Yes. I'd like to look over his schoolwork and see if there is anything helpful in it."

"I doubt you'll find anything. Lester is a fair student who could do a lot better. Do I need to ask his permission?"

"No, I'm his lawyer."

"He's not here today anyway. I didn't check with the office to see if he called in sick."

"I hope he's sick," Scott replied. "One of the conditions of his release

pending trial is that he attend class. No exceptions except illness or
death. If he lays out of school, the judge will throw him back in the
youth detention center."

"Do you want me to find out?"

Scott thought for a second. "I'm sure Dr. Lassiter received a copy of
the judge's order, so I'd rather not stir it up. We only have a few days until
we find out what's going to happen with the whole situation."

"Of course, I'll have to report him absent from class."

"I understand. Is six o'clock this evening okay?"

"I guess, but I won't have a chance to eat supper."

Scott was ready. "Do you like Chinese?"

"Yes."

"Supper will be delivered to modular unit three."

Scott hung up, then realized he hadn't asked what she wanted him to
order. It didn't matter. After ten minutes in one of those little white cardboard boxes, all Chinese food tasted the same.

———

The Tuesday group sat at their usual table. Tao came into the cafeteria as
soon as he finished cleaning the boys' locker room in the gym. The lunch
hour was in full swing. Five young people were seated at the table. One
of them was the dark-skinned girl whose picture he had carried in his
pocket for the past week. The angels were nowhere in sight.

"I've got to make a decision, and I don't know what to do," Alisha said.

"What about?" Janie asked.

Alisha looked over her shoulder. There was a long line at the food
service area. She couldn't tell if there was a threatening face in the room
or not.

"I know we're not supposed to talk about things mentioned at the
table to other people, but this is so serious I'm not sure I want to risk it."

"Then don't," Janie said matter-of-factly. "We can pray without knowing any details."

They sat quietly for a few seconds, then Kenny Bost prayed. "Father,
you know even more about this situation than Alisha. Show her what
you want her to do. Protect her and take away all fear."

Another student continued, "Give her the strength to do the right thing no matter what others might tell her. Show her what you want her to do in a way that is so clear she won't worry anymore."

Janie had her Bible on the table. She opened it and turned several pages. "Isaiah 30:21 says, 'Whether you turn to the right or to the left, your ears will hear a voice behind you, saying, "This is the way; walk in it."' Lord, please do this for Alisha. Let her know which way to turn and what to do."

Tao's heart began beating faster. Something was happening at the table. He moved closer. He was using a broom to sweep up food that had dropped on the floor. He could hear the students' voices. Tao could understand more and more simple English words beyond what he needed to perform his job, and if he was listening to one person in a quiet place, he could often get the gist of a conversation. But the roar of sounds in the cafeteria made distinguishing a specific voice as difficult as identifying a single drop of water in a rainstorm. The girl with dark skin was speaking. She closed her eyes, and he knew it was a prayer.

Tao leaned on the broom, bowed his head, and began praying softly in his local dialect. Two girls walked by, overheard him, and gave him a strange look. He kept his head lowered for almost a minute until the burden lifted. He looked up. The dark-skinned girl opened her eyes and nodded to the other students.

"I know what I need to do," she said. "Thanks."

Tao couldn't hear what she said, but he knew what she meant. "*Va tsang*—thank you," he said.

The bomber didn't want a metal pipe filled with nails. A few people cut or maimed or killed was inconsistent with his vision of fire engulfing the main hallway. However, the practical preparation of a bomb with the capacity to damage or destroy a large building presented a challenge. There weren't any books in the school library by nineteenth-century anarchists. No chemistry textbooks contained an appendix explaining how to build an explosive device.

His salvation came through the Internet. The information available at the click of a mouse would have amazed Lenin and the Bolsheviks. Ultimately, the student could have dedicated his project to Timothy

McVeigh. The Oklahoma City bomber used a truck filled with fertilizer. The student had a different goal. He wanted a bomb within the school, not parked outside. But the Internet links to McVeigh's name led him into the dark places where information was available and resources could be located.

He had begun purchasing supplies as soon as he had conceived the idea. Innocent items standing alone could become deadly in the right combinations. He learned that the major expense of demolition related to safety. If he was willing to sacrifice personal protection, the price of mass destruction was surprisingly cheap.

26

He wished that he, too, had a wound, a red badge of courage.
STEPHEN CRANE

Scott stopped at the Chinese restaurant and looked at the takeout menu. The last time he'd eaten Chinese food with a date, she'd ordered Mongolian beef. He decided to add a chicken dish in case the beef didn't hit the mark. Scott would eat whichever meal Kay rejected. He stepped up to the counter. "Mongolian beef, Hunan chicken, three egg rolls, fried rice, and duck sauce."

"How many egg rolls?" asked the young, oriental girl behind the cash register.

Scott hesitated. He loved egg rolls. "Make that four."

Kay wouldn't want more than one. That would leave three for him. He drove quickly to the high school. The parking lot was deserted except for Kay's car beside her trailer. He carried the food up the wooden steps to the classroom. Kay was at her desk grading papers.

"Dinner is served," he announced, setting the bag on her desk. "Let's eat first. The smell of the food was torturing my stomach all the way over from the restaurant."

"What did you get?" Kay asked.

Scott took out the containers and opened them. "Fried rice, Hunan chicken, Mongolian beef, and egg rolls."

"Mongolian beef is my favorite," she said.

That made Scott's choice easy. "I prefer the chicken."

Kay cleaned off one end of her desk.

"Chopsticks?" he asked, holding up a pair that was in the bag.

"Of course."

They both used chopsticks. Kay was more adept than Scott. She could capture a single grain of rice and transport it safely to her mouth. Scott's technique was more of a crab approach. He chased the rice and chicken around his plate while opening and closing the sticks until some of the food could be scooped up.

He quickly ate two egg rolls. Kay finished one, then asked, "Are there any more egg rolls? I always order two or three if they're not too big."

Scott looked in the box where the remaining egg roll waited. It looked smaller and smaller.

"These were fairly large," he said. "Are you sure you want another one?"

Kay picked up the container. "You've already eaten two, so we can split the last one."

"Okay," Scott agreed reluctantly.

Toward the end of the meal, Scott used a plastic fork to finish eating. More than five minutes with chopsticks raised the possibility of a muscle spasm in his right hand.

"What do you have to show me about Lester?" he asked.

Kay pulled open the lower drawer of her desk and took out a manila folder. "Everything he's turned in is here. He's been in the literature and creative-writing track this semester, so there are several short papers and one longer one. They're not in order."

She opened the folder. The first page was a short essay on *To Kill a Mockingbird*. Scott immediately suspected Lester wouldn't like the book because of Atticus Finch's racial tolerance. He was right. Lester's biting critique reflected their conversations at the youth detention center.

"He didn't like the book," Scott said simply.

"No. He thought I was trying to brainwash him."

"A good idea," Scott replied.

Next came Lester's two-paragraph analysis on the excerpt from Thomas Wolfe's *Look Homeward, Angel*. In the margin beside his small handwriting was a pair of carefully drawn and shaded lightning bolts. Underneath he'd added a dark swastika that had been colored in so completely that it shone.

"Voluntary artwork," Scott noted.

"I see it all the time, but I prefer a smiling face with a caption that says,

'Have a nice day.' I don't know why Lester did that. I guess it's his way of proving that he can do whatever he wants in the margins of his paper."

"Did you say anything to him about it?"

"No. If he'd written a message or threat, I would have notified the office, but drawing a symbol is not something to report. I usually try to ignore them."

Scott rubbed his finger across the swastika. The paper was slightly wrinkled because of the concentration of black ink.

"If the D.A. saw this, she'd try to find a way to blow it up on a poster board and hang it on the wall of the jury room."

Several nondescript pages followed. No artwork, but there were small blocked areas of black ink that could have been words or drawings in the margins of several pages. Nothing unusual about Lester's attempts to answer the questions. His grades fluctuated wildly. He made a ninety-eight on one test, followed by a sixty-seven the following week. One of the first papers of the year was on *The Red Badge of Courage*. Lester had written a two-page report and received a B+ for the paper.

"He liked this one," Scott commented when he saw the grade on the top of the first page.

Kay looked over his shoulder. "Yes. When I graded that paper, I thought he might be a diamond in the rough."

Scott leaned back in his chair. Lester knew the story, and he'd thought about it. His sentences were short and choppy. Scott could almost hear Lester's voice spitting out his opinion.

A bloody bandage is a red badge of courage. Most people don't know anything about courage. They haven't been in danger. You can't know what you will do until you have to do it. The boy in the book ran away. He came back. That is what counts. In a war people die. True courage is to come back and kill your enemies.

The paper continued, but Scott stopped. He slid the paper over to Kay with his finger on the paragraph. "What did you think when you read this?" She read the paragraph again while Scott watched. "Especially the last sentence."

Kay paused. "I didn't think about it. I was grading twenty-eight papers and probably thought it was Lester's opinion about one of Stephen Crane's themes. I don't penalize a student who is trying to analyze literature."

Scott put the paper back in the folder. Lester's words weren't literary analysis. It was his personal creed. He slid the folder across the desk to Kay.

"I don't think there is anything in there that helps me."

"I'm not surprised."

Scott continued, "Mr. Humphrey says that most cases are determined by the facts, not the lawyer's skill, and the public perception that a brilliant lawyer is always the difference between winning and losing is wrong. I'm a rookie, but the facts against Lester are totally circumstantial. Unless a jury believes strolling down the creekbank on a Sunday afternoon is a crime, he should be around for the rest of the school year to write reports and draw pictures in the margins of his tests."

"What do you believe about Lester?" she asked.

Scott shrugged. "My opinion didn't go up after looking at his papers and artwork. There's no doubt he's a racist, but my opinion is not the issue. My role is to defend my client. He says he's not guilty, and I don't have any direct evidence otherwise."

"That's why I'm not a lawyer," Kay said bluntly.

Surprised, Scott asked, "Did you think about going to law school?"

"No, but listening to you is a good reason not to consider it in the future."

"I understand, but due process of law has to apply to everyone to protect all of us. It sounds theoretical until you meet someone like Lester. Then you have to decide if you really believe in the Constitution."

"So, your involvement in the case is about high ideals."

Scott smiled. "Well, defending the Constitution isn't all that's motivating me to work hard. There is also the small matter of my competitive ego and desire to beat the arrogant assistant district attorney who is prosecuting the case."

Kay banged a chopstick on her desk like a gavel. "Mr. Ellis, thank you for your honesty."

The door of the classroom opened and Janie Collins walked through the door.

"I smell Chinese food," she said.

"You just missed the last bite of rice," Kay said.

When the mock trial session started, Scott focused his attention on the four students who would be lawyers. The more Scott was around Dustin Rawlings, the more he liked him. The young man was confident without being cocky, and it was obvious that with his positive people skills he would succeed in the future. Yvette Fisher was a bit scatter-brained and had an argumentative streak that raised its head if a witness refused to cooperate. Janie was developing nicely, and Frank was the source of both admiration and frustration.

The evening's session began with Yvette cross-examining a young man playing the Billy Bob Beerbelly role. The witness stubbornly refused to agree with Yvette's characterization of his past drinking history. It quickly became obvious that someone had been coaching Billy in an effort to protect him from a damaging cross-examination. Yvette was the first lawyer to try to crack the code.

"You must have me mixed up with my twin brother, Bob," the witness said. "He's had a bunch of speeding tickets and a couple of DUIs."

"I think you're the one who is confused," Yvette shot back, shuffling through the papers on her desk and looking for the documents that proved prior convictions.

"If you're looking for papers from the court, it won't do you any good. The police are always confusing me and Bob."

"Really?"

"Yep. Happens all the time. Even our mama can't keep us straight. She gets us confused."

Yvette had found the papers she'd been looking for. Holding up a conviction for DUI, she said, "There's nothing confusing about this DUI conviction in March. Your blood alcohol level was at 1.8."

"Can I see that paper?"

Yvette handed it to him. "Your name is on the top of the ticket."

The witness squinted at the paper for several seconds before answering. "It says here William Robert Beerbelly. Billy is short for William, and Bob is short for Robert. That could be either me or Bob."

Yvette sputtered. Scott had seen this coming about halfway through the questioning and interrupted, "Billy Bob, that's clever, but the judges may not let you get away with creating a new character. Whose idea was it to do this?"

The witness pointed at Frank who had been watching the exchange without comment.

"We were talking at lunch the other day, and Frank suggested it. Otherwise, Billy has to admit to being a big drunk who could have caused the accident."

Scott turned to Frank. "Your theory works if you're on one side of the case. What if you have to argue the other way? How would you cross-examine Billy?"

Frank smiled. "I'm going to use another witness to blow Billy out of the water. It won't matter if he has five brothers who drink and drive."

Scott mentally ran through the testimony of the other witnesses. He didn't see the angle. But then, he hadn't thought about Billy Bob either.

"I'll consider it, but you need to make sure you don't violate the rules against going outside the scope of the facts. The judges won't allow chaos."

"It won't be chaotic," Frank responded. "I understand the rules; I'm just using them to my advantage."

When it was time to break up for the evening, Scott picked up the white sack from the Chinese restaurant. "I'll dispose of the trash properly," he said.

Kay took out her wallet. "How much was my part?"

"No, it's on me."

"Thanks. Next time I'll buy my own egg rolls."

Scott left, wondering if his reluctance to share had been so transparent. He followed Frank and Janie down the steps. The two young people got in Frank's car and sped off into the night.

Alisha Mason lingered near Kay's desk until everyone else was gone.

"Mrs. Wilson," she said, "I know it's late, but can I talk to you for a minute?"

Kay put down her brown satchel. "Sure. What is it?"

Alisha glanced back toward the door. "It's about Lester Garrison. I know one reason you and Mr. Ellis came to the church on Sunday was so he could talk to people about the shooting. He asked my cousin some questions. Is he Lester's lawyer?"

"Yes."

"Has he talked to you about what happened?"

"No, I guess a lot of his information is confidential."

Alisha paused. "I saw something, but I'd rather not get involved."

"Didn't the police talk to you on the day it happened?"

"Yes, but I've realized something since then and need advice from someone I trust. If I tell you something, will you repeat it to Mr. Ellis?"

Kay was Alisha's teacher, not Scott's private investigator.

"Not if you don't want me to."

Ten minutes later, Alisha finished.

"You're positive one of the two people you saw was Lester Garrison?" Kay asked.

"I am, now." Alisha nodded. "When I saw Lester in the hall yesterday, he was wearing the same shirt, and it clicked."

"Have you talked to your parents yet?" Kay asked.

"No, I spent the afternoon with a friend before coming here."

"You need to discuss it with them. I'm not sure what your legal obligation is in this type of situation. You may want advice from a lawyer."

"But not Mr. Ellis?"

Kay paused. "No, not him."

Frank and Janie stopped at a fast-food restaurant for French fries and a drink.

When they sat down with their food, Janie said, "I have some good news. My father called last night. He may come for a visit in a few weeks."

"Has he promised before and not shown up?" Frank asked.

"Yes," Janie admitted. "Last Christmas."

"I rest my case. You're only setting yourself up for disappointment." Janie nibbled a fry. "How do you think I should feel?"

"Why ask me? I don't feel anything."

"But—" Janie stopped. "I mean, you have to feel something when your parents are going through a divorce."

Frank looked straight in Janie's eyes. "No, I don't."

27

Hope deferred makes the heart sick,
but a desire fulfilled is a tree of life.
PROVERBS 13:12 (RSV)

Scott greeted Nicky and plopped down in his chair to watch TV. He flipped through the channels, but the canned jokes on a sitcom couldn't keep his attention or make him smile. At a commercial break, he went into the kitchen and took out Nicky's leash. At the sight of the leash, the little dog shot around the corner to the front door and began jumping up and down with excitement. Scott knelt on the floor, caught Nicky in midhop, and snapped the leash onto the dog's collar.

Scott rarely took Nicky out for a walk after dark. Every shadow was a threat, and Nicky spent most of his time darting into the darkness to bark at unseen monsters, then scampering back to safety at his master's side.

Scott pushed the button on the leash and let Nicky run out to the end of the line. The dog strained for a couple of seconds trying to pry another inch of freedom before yielding to the restraint. Scott set an easy pace; he was walking for contemplation, not exercise. They soon entered one of the pools of blackness that Nicky found both fascinating and terrifying.

In the darkness, Scott thought about Kay. He was trying to be careful, but Perry Dixon's lighthearted encouragement to consider the possibilities of a relationship with the teacher struck close to home. Every time he was around her it was harder to avoid letting his mind wander unhindered into the possibilities. He didn't want to get on a roller coaster of emotions. He didn't want to make a mistake. Whether feelings for him were stirring in her was as hidden as the surrounding darkness.

Scott walked into the glow from a streetlight. A few hardy moths that had not yet succumbed to the cooling fall temperatures flew crazily back and forth. Nicky perked up and marched confidently toward the gray area that separated the light from the night. A rumble rising in his throat, the little dog strained forward to challenge the shadows. All his senses were on high alert. The decision to hold him close or let him go was in Scott's hand. He pressed the button and Nicky bounded forward into the unknown. Scott followed.

When Kay got home, she was still thinking about her conversation with Alisha. The message light on her answering machine was blinking. She pressed it, and Jake's voice came into the room.

"Hey. I'm sorry about the other night. I have something I need to talk to you about. Don't call me; I'll keep trying to get in touch with you. Save your pennies. Bye."

She listened for a few seconds to the silence at the end of the message. Married couples develop familiar sayings that communicate more than the ordinary meaning of the words used. *Save your pennies*. As teachers, Jake and Kay had never had a lot of money, and the phrase about pennies had become their shorthand way of letting each other know that they were living life together. Together, their pennies would be enough to provide what they needed.

The following day, Scott spent the morning working on other files. Until Lester's trial was over, his life would be divided into two parts: *State v. Garrison* and everything else. The tedium of reviewing a lease-purchase agreement for one of Mr. Jackson's business clients made him glad for the prospect of a day in court. He was walking out the back door to lunch when he met Mr. Humphrey coming into the building.

"Are we still on the schedule for this afternoon?" the older lawyer asked.

"Yes, sir. Lester Garrison should be here at four o'clock."

"I was sitting in court all morning waiting for a hearing that took ten minutes," Mr. Humphrey said. "I used the time to write out a few questions. I'm not sure about the facts, but it will give me a place to start."

"I've prepared some cross-examination questions for you, and I know you'll spot things when you listen to him on direct."

"How are you feeling about the case?" the older lawyer asked.

"I think I should win, and I'm afraid that I won't."

Mr. Humphrey nodded. "That's a healthy perspective. I'll see you later this afternoon."

Lester was scheduled to arrive at Scott's office at 3:30 P.M. At 3:45, Mr. Humphrey buzzed Scott.

"Is he here yet?" the older lawyer asked.

"No, sir. I'm sure he knows about the appointment."

"Let me know. I don't have anything else on my calendar for the rest of the day."

When fifteen minutes more passed, Scott called Thelma Garrison to find out if Lester had come home from school before leaving for the appointment. No answer. Then the thought crossed Scott's mind that Lester might have decided to skip town. He hadn't been in school. He had a truck. His father probably had contacts all over the country where the boy could hide out. Scott decided to tell Mr. Humphrey his suspicions and ask him what to do when the phone buzzed. It was the receptionist.

"Lester Garrison is here for his appointment."

"Send him into the small conference room."

Carrying the file that was growing thicker by the day, Scott went downstairs to Mr. Humphrey's office. The older lawyer was writing on a legal pad with his legs propped up on the corner of the desk.

"He's here."

They walked into the conference room. Lester was standing with his back to the door looking at the painting of General Hoke. When he turned around, Scott stopped in his tracks.

"What happened to you?"

Lester grimaced. "I ran into a door."

Lester's face was splotchy with bruises, and he had a long cut over his left eye. The damage was as bad as the harm from the fight at the youth detention center. The young man had either received a thorough beating or taken a quick trip through the windshield of his truck.

"Sit down and tell us," Scott urged.

Lester slouched down. "There's nothing anybody is going to do about it. The police want to send me to jail for something I didn't do, but I doubt they'll prosecute the guys who did this to me."

"Who was it?" Scott asked.

"I had some words in the parking lot on Tuesday morning with a punk who smarted off to me, so we went into the woods behind the football stadium to settle it. I got in a few good licks, then one of his friends showed up and hit me in the head with a tree limb."

"Did you report it to the principal's office?"

"This wasn't a fight on the playground in first grade," Lester sneered. "If the principal had found out, I'm sure I'd be sitting in a cell at the youth detention center."

"Probably," Scott agreed. At least Lester didn't totally ignore the possible consequences of his actions. "What caused the argument?"

"The first guy started telling me what was going to happen to me in jail. I didn't want to listen to it. After the fight I went home and my grandmother called the office and told them I was sick."

"Where is your father?" Mr. Humphrey asked.

"On the road. He'll be back this weekend."

Scott turned to Leland Humphrey. "Can he go to court looking like this?"

"What would be your argument for a continuance?" the older lawyer asked. "He can communicate; he admits starting the fight."

"No, the other guy smarted off to me, first," Lester interrupted.

"Who landed the first blow?" Mr. Humphrey asked.

"I did. And the second, too. If the other guy hadn't showed up, I'd have whipped him."

Mr. Humphrey raised his left eyebrow and looked at Scott.

"Okay," Scott said. "A continuance is unlikely. Let's get started."

Scott explained his basic trial strategy to Lester, who listened closely and asked a few questions. Lester's answers were passable.

"Do you see where I'm going with these questions?" Scott asked.

"Yeah. I like the part about my grandmother. She's sick all the time, and the jury won't find me guilty if it meant she would be left alone. She could die if I wasn't there to take care of her. Are you going to use her as a witness?"

"I've thought about that," Scott said. "Does she know what you were doing on the day of the shooting?"

"I don't remember what I told her. Usually, I just leave. She can hear the door close and knows the sound of my truck."

"Then I'm not sure her testimony would add anything to the case. She can't see anything, so she couldn't describe your clothing. Was your father in town?"

Lester hesitated. "Uh, yeah. He picked me up at the jail."

"What had he been doing that day?"

"I'm not sure. Probably drinking beer at Vernon's Tavern. That's where he hangs out."

"On Sunday?" Scott asked.

Lester shifted in his seat. "Oh, that's right. It's closed on Sunday."

Scott waited. "Go ahead. Where was your father?"

"Uh, you'll have to talk to him."

"You haven't talked about it?"

"Why should I?" Lester asked sharply. "I'm the one who got caught, not him."

"You got caught?" Scott asked. "Caught doing what?"

Lester's face flushed. "Don't try to trick me. I was walking down the creekbank minding my own business when the cops showed up. I was so scared that I said some crazy things, and they threw me in the back of the patrol car."

"Remember, this is trial practice. You have to choose your words carefully or the D.A. will convict you from your own mouth. Let's start from the beginning."

Scott had a long list of questions that brought out Lester's life story in the most sympathetic way possible. He knew his client wasn't the kind of young man the women on the jury would want to take home to meet their daughters, but he hoped to awaken compassion based on his mother's abandonment. They moved to the day of the arrest.

"I'd been walking up the creek looking for some good places to fish," Lester said. "I was going back to the truck to get my fishing rod when I was arrested."

Scott turned to Mr. Humphrey. "Do you want to ask some questions?"

"Not yet, but I'd like to make a comment about how to testify. Lester, think before you answer. You're giving an answer before Scott has stopped talking. There's nothing wrong with waiting a second or two before you respond. That's especially important when you're being cross-examined."

"Okay."

Scott continued. "Did you walk down the creek all the way to the Hall's Chapel Church?"

"I avoid that church. I don't want to be around those people."

Mr. Humphrey held up his hand. "Answer the question; don't use it as a chance to let the jury know how prejudiced you are. This is not a political trial involving your racial ideology!"

"Huh?" Lester's eyes narrowed. "I'm not sure what you mean, but I don't think separation of the races is prejudice. There are black people who believe the same way. It makes sense—"

"Mr. Humphrey is right," Scott interrupted. "Don't look for chances to give speeches. How close did you get to the church?"

"I never saw it."

"Did you hear anyone yelling?"

"No."

"Did you hear any gunshots?"

"No."

"Did you see anyone else on the creekbank?"

"Only the police."

"Why would the deputies say you were running along the creekbank?"

"I wasn't running. I'm a fast walker."

"Were you trying to avoid them?"

"I didn't want them to hassle me. I don't trust the cops. After what's happened, I trust them less."

Mr. Humphrey's right eyebrow shot up and he spoke up. "Leave the argument about the police to Scott. It will sound better coming from him."

"Were you trying to avoid them?" Scott continued.

"No, sir."

"Good. Be sure you say 'yes, ma'am' and 'no, ma'am' to the D.A."

"Yes, sir," Lester said, emphasizing the "sir."

"But not like she's a Marine Corps drill instructor. Did you throw a gun into the stream when you saw the police?"

"No. The only thing I threw in the water was a rock."

"Why would you do that just before the police confronted you?"

"I'd been throwing rocks up and down the stream. I was just messing around."

"Do you own a gun?"

"No, sir."

"Have you ever owned a gun?"

"No. I'm seventeen years old. I couldn't buy a gun if I wanted to."

"Did you see anybody from the church that day?"

"No."

"Did you yell anything at them from the other side of the creekbank?"

"No, sir."

"Did you fire any shots in the water during the baptism?"

"How could I do that if I wasn't anywhere near them?" Lester asked.

"Answer the question," Scott responded. "Take your time because the jury will be paying attention. It's your time to let them know how sincere, honest, and innocent you are."

Lester took a breath and spoke slowly, "I did not fire any shots at anyone. I'm sorry it happened, and whoever did it should be punished because it was wrong. But these charges against me are a mistake. I'm innocent."

Scott looked at Mr. Humphrey who nodded. "Good answer," the older lawyer said. "That's the way to do it."

They continued for another hour. Mr. Humphrey goaded Lester during cross-examination, but instead of blowing up, the young man paused and gave a calm answer.

"We'll get together again Friday afternoon at three-thirty," Scott said. "Here is a list of the people in the jury pool. Read it over and make a note beside the name of anyone you know. I'd like your father to look at it, too."

"He'll be home Saturday."

"Just so we have the information by Monday morning when the jurors arrive."

After Lester left, Scott and Mr. Humphrey went into the older lawyer's office. Leland tore out three pages from his legal pad and handed them to Scott.

"Here are some suggestions I jotted down during your questioning." The older lawyer rubbed his eyebrows. "After he started taking our advice, he didn't do too badly. He's an intelligent young man."

Scott nodded. "I know. How can he be so ignorant?"

28

*There is no witness so dreadful, no accuser so terrible
as the conscience that dwells in the heart of every man.*
POLYBIUS

The receptionist buzzed Scott and told him there was a hand-delivered letter for him from the D.A.'s office. Correspondence from the other side of a case on the eve of trial is never good news. He quickly ripped open the envelope and took out a single sheet of paper. It was a supplemental list of witnesses who might be called by the prosecution in the case: a police officer, a detective, and Alisha Mason. Scott's eyes stopped when he saw the student's name. He had intended to talk to her at the church, but he'd focused on the adults, and she left before Scott finished eating lunch. Fortunately, he could talk to her after mock trial practice that night.

He called Lynn Davenport in the slim hope the D.A. might provide information about the additional police officers. When she answered the phone, Scott didn't make a vain effort at morning pleasantries.

"I received the names of your additional witnesses. What are they going to say?"

"You'll need to ask them," she said curtly.

Scott bit his lower lip. "Did you tell them to cooperate with me?"

"I didn't tell them not to. That's up to them."

Scott gave up. "Okay."

"One other thing," she said before he could hang up. "I have another plea offer for your client."

"I don't think he's interested."

"I don't care if he takes it or not, but we've talked it over with the people from the church, and if he pleads guilty to intent to inflict bodily harm, we'll recommend a six-month boot-camp program and three years probation."

Scott sat up straighter in his chair. "What about the other charges?"

"I'll drop them."

"And the conspiracy charge?"

"It will go away."

"Why the change of heart?"

The D.A. gave a short laugh. "It's not my heart. It's the docket. There is a kidnapping case we'd like to move to the head of the calendar. It will take a full week to try it."

Scott had read about the kidnapping case in the paper. Four defendants were accused of transporting illegal aliens from Mexico and working them without pay on a farm outside of town. The trial proceedings would have to be translated into Spanish, and everything would take at least twice as long.

"I'll talk to Garrison," Scott said.

"Let me know by Friday at three o'clock."

"He's coming in at three-thirty."

"That will be too late. We have a conference call on the other case with Judge Teasley at 3:15. If Garrison doesn't accept, all offers will be withdrawn, and you're number one on the calendar."

Scott put down the receiver. For the first time, he wondered if going to trial in Lester's case was the best course of action. The boot-camp program for young offenders might be good for Lester. There would be no shortage of surrogate father figures yelling orders and forcing the young man to the point of physical exhaustion so that his mind would be receptive to lessons of discipline, self-control, and commitment to a group. Among those ordering him to run faster and work harder would certainly be African-American guards who could command Lester's obedience even if they didn't gain his respect. But boot camp for Lester required something his client couldn't give—an admission of guilt.

By late that afternoon, Scott had talked briefly with the police officer and detective who had been added to the witness list. The officer had transported Lester from the YDC to the courthouse. During the trip,

Lester had talked about the case. Scott cringed. A police officer couldn't question a suspect without informing him of his Miranda rights, but there was no prohibition against listening to a defendant's voluntary ramblings if he chose to open his mouth. However, Lester's story from the backseat of the car was essentially the same thing he'd told Scott and Mr. Humphrey. No harm done.

The other witness, a detective, had conducted follow-up interviews with members of the Hall's Chapel Church. He told Scott the names of the people he'd interviewed but wouldn't reveal the information obtained. Scott recognized two names from his Sunday-morning visit. Included in the list was Alisha Mason.

Finally, he left a message with Thelma Garrison that Lester needed to leave school early the following day, so he could be at Scott's office by 2 P.M.

After a hard workout at the gym, Scott was relaxed when he arrived at the school. Dustin Rawlings looked up and smiled when he saw Scott.

"Are you coming to the game tomorrow night?" he asked.

Scott hadn't thought about high-school football all week. "Who are you playing?"

"Maiden. It should be a good game."

Maiden was a tiny town with a big-time football program. During Scott's high-school career, Catawba had beaten them once in four years.

"No, I'll be getting ready for a trial that starts next week," Scott said.

"I wish I could watch you," Dustin replied. "It would help me prepare for the mock trial competition. Maybe if you wrote a note to Dr. Lassiter, I could get out of school."

"Not this case," Scott answered. "Maybe another time."

Scott looked for Alisha Mason, but she hadn't arrived. He stepped sideways and collided with Frank Jesup.

"Excuse me," he said.

Frank gave him a dark look and grunted, "Watch it."

Scott stifled a comment about showing respect and moved out of the way. Frank sat down next to Janie and smiled. Scott watched the two young people chatting for a few seconds. The young man's dark hair and scowl made him look like a thunderstorm waiting to erupt with a bolt of lightning and a clap of thunder. There was still no sign of Alisha when Kay called the meeting to order.

"Is Alisha Mason going to be here tonight?" Scott asked in a low voice to Kay.

"I haven't heard from her, but I think she'll be here. Why?"

"I need to talk to her."

Scott didn't notice the look of concern that passed across Kay's face.

It was Scott's night to work with the students playing the witness roles. After his run-in with the mutated Billy Bob Beerbelly created by Frank Jesup, he wanted to make sure the witnesses didn't change the characters too much from the information contained in the official materials. It might be fun to let the creative juices run wild, but it could result in serious deductions from the judges if the students went too far.

Toward the end of the session, the door of the classroom opened and Alisha walked in. She was wearing a nice dress and slid into a seat across from Scott.

"Sorry, I'm late. I was with my family at the funeral home."

"Thanks for coming," Scott said. "Do you want to go through the direct testimony of your witness part?"

"Okay."

Scott asked the questions and Alisha answered without a hitch. When she finished, it was time to end for the night.

Scott spoke to the group. "Before next week, I have a couple of suggestions. Witnesses—take time to read over the materials again. Don't assume that because you studied everything several weeks ago that it's still fresh in your mind. Now that you've learned how to express some of the material, you may see something else that you didn't notice the first time. Lawyers—practice in front of a mirror or someone in your family."

"Like my little brother?" Dustin asked.

"How old is he?" Scott replied.

"Uh, I think he's ten."

"Perfect. If he can understand what you're saying, it will be clear to anyone. Try to develop a smooth delivery. Don't be too fast. Slow is better, because you can't assume that your listeners have any idea what you're going to say."

Kay added, "Three more weeks until the regional competition. I've received information about the teams in the competition."

She handed two sheets of paper to Scott who skimmed them while Kay continued. He saw a familiar name as the advisor for one of the teams.

"That's all," Kay said. "From what I heard tonight, we're getting better and better."

As the students got up to leave, Scott spoke to Alisha. "Can you stay for a couple of minutes?"

"I really need to get home."

Scott held up two fingers. "A couple of minutes."

Alisha looked at Kay.

"It's up to you, Alisha," Kay replied.

She hesitated. "Okay."

When the other students were gone, Scott asked Alisha, "Do you want to sit down?"

"No thanks, I need to go soon."

"I'll get to the point. The district attorney's office notified me this morning that you might be a witness in Lester Garrison's case. I'm his lawyer. Do you know why your name has been added?"

Alisha looked again at Kay. Scott noticed the eye contact between them.

"What's going on?"

"Alisha confided in me."

"Can I join the club?" Scott asked sharply.

"That's part of the problem, Mr. Ellis," Alisha said, her voice quivering slightly. "I didn't want to make you mad, and I was scared."

Startled, Scott asked, "Of me? I'm just trying to find out why your name turned up on the state's supplemental witness list. I'm not going to get angry no matter what you say."

Alisha shook her head and looked at the floor of the classroom. "I'm not scared of you. It's Lester."

Scott could have kicked himself. It wasn't about him. Alisha Mason had beautiful dark skin, but in Lester Garrison her color provoked an unreasoning hatred. If she linked him to the shooting, she would become a specific enemy.

"All right," he said. "Before you say anything else, let me tell you a few things. First, you don't have to talk to me."

Scott waited until she looked up and her eyes met his.

"Yes, sir," she said softly.

"Second, whatever you've told the district attorney or the police will come out in court, and Lester will be there."

Alisha's lip quivered again. "I know. But I have to tell the truth."

"So, one way or the other your testimony is not a secret."

"But if I tell you what I know, will Lester find out before the trial?"

Scott nodded. "Yes. I'll have to discuss it with him as part of our trial preparation."

"And you'll try to make me look like a liar when I'm on the witness stand, won't you?"

Looking at Alisha's anxious face, Scott wavered in his constitutional convictions. He glanced at Kay, hoping he wouldn't see contempt for him in her eyes. No contempt—only compassion. For both him and the student.

He spoke slowly. "I don't know what you're going to say under oath. My job is to make sure that the jury considers the evidence in the light most favorable to my client. If I have to challenge your testimony, that's what I will do. It's not unlike what you've been learning in the mock trial program. Only it's real."

Alisha nodded.

"I won't yell at you," Scott continued. "But if there is something you say that doesn't fit with other information, I will point it out."

"But I know what I saw."

Scott waited. Alisha said nothing.

Finally, he asked, "What did you see?"

Alisha sighed. "Okay. I wasn't on the bank with the others during the baptism. I'd wandered off by myself and saw two people on the other side of the stream crawling through the bushes like they were in the army or something. They disappeared for a few seconds, then I heard a loud popping sound. I thought someone had set off some firecrackers. One of the shots went through the bottom of my dress. I didn't see the hole until a few days later."

"Where is the dress?" Scott asked.

"The police have it."

"Could the hole have come from something else?"

"Maybe, but I never wear that dress anywhere but church, and when you lay it down, you can see where the bullet went through the front and out the back. When I saw the hole, I almost passed out. I could have been killed. Anyway, I hid behind a tree and looked across the creek. I saw a baldheaded man wearing a camouflage shirt running through the bushes. I didn't realize it was Lester until I saw him wearing the same shirt the other day at school. He turned sideways, and I suddenly realized he was the person I saw on the creekbank that day."

"Did you see his face?"

"No, sir. But it was Lester. I could tell by the outline of his head."

"There are a lot of people who shave their heads."

Alisha shook her head. "I'm sure it was Lester."

"Even without seeing his face?"

"Yes, sir."

"Did you recognize the other person?" Scott asked.

Alisha shook her head. "No. I never got a clear view of him. Lester was closer to the water, so I could see him better."

"What color hair did the other person have?"

Alisha paused. "Lester shaves his head, so he doesn't have any hair. I think the other person had dark hair, but I never saw his face, either."

"Have you ever seen Lester's father?"

"No. Do you think it could have been his father?"

Scott shrugged. "His father hasn't been charged with any crime, but he has dark hair. He's shorter and heavier than Lester. Do you remember anything else about the clothes the two men were wearing?"

"The woman at the district attorney's office asked me that, too. I don't know. I'm just sure it was Lester in a camouflage shirt."

"And you don't know who fired the shots?"

"No, sir. They were out of sight when that happened."

"Did you see a gun?"

"No."

Scott thought for a moment. "Anything else?"

"No, I've told you everything I can remember."

"Okay. Thanks for talking with me."

Alisha turned and walked toward the door. Scott called after her.

"Alisha!"

"Yes?"

"Don't worry about how I will treat you on the witness stand. You can handle anything I might ask."

When the student was gone, Scott sat down in a chair beside Kay's desk.

"Will her testimony be enough to convict him?" Kay asked.

"Maybe. It's the only eyewitness evidence that Lester was in the vicinity of the church when the shots were fired. But"—Scott tapped the top of the desk with his index finger—"it could help me more than it hurts me."

29

Those oft are stratagems which errors seem.
ALEXANDER POPE

The following morning, Scott was sitting at his desk thinking about his trial strategy. One of the chief skills of a trial lawyer is the ability to present negative facts in a positive way. He buzzed Leland Humphrey's secretary.

"Let me know when Mr. Humphrey arrives."

"He won't be in until late this afternoon."

Scott would be on his own when he met with Lester at 2 P.M.

If Alisha Mason was right, Lester had lied to Scott from his first interview at the youth detention center through their simulated direct examination earlier in the week.

When the receptionist told Scott that Mr. Garrison had arrived for his appointment, Scott delayed ten minutes, hoping that Mr. Humphrey would return to the office. He wanted the benefit of his mentor's wisdom about Scott's new theory of the case, but the time deadline from Lynn Davenport on the plea bargain didn't give him much leeway. After waiting as long as he dared, he went downstairs and opened the door to the reception area. Lester was nowhere in sight. Harold Garrison, dressed in brown pants and a short-sleeve white shirt, sat in a chair by the front door. The older Garrison hadn't shaved, and when Scott approached, it was obvious he hadn't bathed either.

"Where's Lester?" Scott asked.

"He's coming. His truck just went past the front of the office."

The door opened and Lester walked in. The bruises on his face were fading, and the cut over his eye didn't look as raw. Still, he looked more like a redneck brawler than a fun-loving teenager.

"Two things we need to discuss," Scott said, as soon as everyone was seated in the conference room. "I'll get right to the point. The state has an eyewitness who says she saw you across the stream from the church."

"That's a lie!" Lester blasted out.

Scott continued without responding. "She didn't see you holding a gun or firing the shots. She had walked downstream a few feet and noticed you crawling through the bushes along the creekbank. After the shots were fired, she saw you running downstream."

Lester swore. "That's impossible! Nobody at the church even knows who I am."

"I've interviewed the witness. She's a student at the high school."

"Who is it?" Lester asked sharply. "Is she black?"

"Yes," Scott answered the second question and ignored the first.

"She's lying through her teeth. It will be my word against hers, and I don't think a jury will believe a white person over a black."

If it hadn't been a serious moment, Scott would have laughed out loud. The contrast between Lester's angry, beat-up face and the sincere honesty in Alisha Mason's countenance the night before couldn't have been more stark. There was no doubt in Scott's mind who the jury would find more credible.

"That may be a risk you choose to take," Scott said. "But I have another idea. The witness told me something else. She says you weren't alone."

Lester immediately glanced at his father whose jaw was set like a block of concrete. Harold gave a quick shake of his head. That was enough for Scott. As soon as he saw Harold sitting in the reception room, Scott had set up his revelation of Alisha's testimony in order to gauge the interaction between father and son. When he saw the split-second look between them, Scott made up his mind about *State v. Garrison.* Lester might have been present on the creekbank, but the more culpable Garrison hadn't been charged with a crime. Not yet.

Harold asked the next question. "What did the D.A. lady say about this other person?"

"Not much. She didn't see his face but said that he had dark hair. She didn't see anybody but Lester after the shots were fired. Lester was closer to the creekbank while the other figure was hidden by the underbrush."

Harold nodded. "Nobody saw Lester do anything."

"That's right," Scott agreed. "The state's case is still based on circumstantial evidence. However, it places Lester at the scene within seconds of the gunshots. The judge will let the jury decide if that is enough to convict."

Lester swore again. Turning to his father, he said, "You told me they couldn't find me guilty without an eyewitness."

Harold's expression didn't change. "They won't."

"Lester, I can't give you the same guarantee," Scott said. "The law allows a jury to decide guilt or innocence based on circumstantial evidence. It happens in courtrooms every day."

Harold slammed his fist down on the table. "She's lying! And your job is to prove it."

Scott kept his calm. "That's one way to go about it. I can argue that the witness didn't have a clear view and couldn't make a positive identification. However, that will only give her a chance to reassure everyone in the courtroom that she's telling the truth, the whole truth, and nothing but the truth. By the time I'm finished with my cross-examination, the jury will have had two opportunities to listen to her testimony, and they'll remember it much better when they go to the jury room to decide the case."

"Hold on. What are you suggesting?" Harold asked.

Scott answered with a question. "Who's on trial?"

Lester again looked at his father. "I am," he said.

"And my job is to defend you," Scott replied. "I'm not concerned about anybody else. My only goal is to provide Lester Garrison with the best defense possible."

"Get to the point," Harold said.

Scott kept his voice level and looked at Lester.

"All the witness does is place you in the vicinity of the church. She will not testify that you fired any shots."

"Then that's your argument," Harold said. "There aren't eyewitnesses, and Lester ain't guilty."

"That's true, but it has to be set up correctly," Scott responded. "One of the best defenses in a criminal case is to show that someone other than the defendant could have committed the crime."

"What do you mean?" Harold asked.

"The state has to prove beyond a reasonable doubt that Lester committed the crime. The girl will testify that there was someone else on the creekbank." Scott paused and looked straight at Harold. "Someone who is not on trial—an unidentified John Doe. Bishop Moore told me that the only person he saw on the other side of the creek had black hair. His testimony is corroborated by the girl who saw someone with black hair creeping through the bushes. We can line up witnesses all the way to the back of the courtroom and prove that Lester's head was shaved on the day the shots were fired. Whatever the color of your hair, it was still inside your head. After all the testimony is given, my argument to the jury is that both the girl and Bishop Moore are telling the truth. There was someone on the bank with black hair, and it wasn't Lester Garrison. This unknown person had just as much opportunity to commit the crime as Lester Garrison, and without an eyewitness showing a gun in Lester's hand, the state can't prove its case."

"But what if I'm asked who the other person was?" Lester asked tentatively.

"That's easy. You won't testify. No one can make you say a word, and if you decide not to be a witness, the D.A. can't mention it. The Constitution specifically gives you the right not to incriminate yourself. In fact, the judge will tell the jury not to consider whether or not you testified in reaching their decision."

"It sounds kind of risky," Lester replied. "It won't make sense if I don't stand up for myself. Won't the jury think I'm trying to hide something if I don't testify?"

"What would you say if the D.A. asked you who was the dark-haired person on the creekbank with you that day?"

Lester sputtered. "Uh, I'd stick to my story that I wasn't near the church at all. No one was with me."

"That might work. But there will be a lot of witnesses who will say shots were fired, and a very believable young woman who knows you on sight and will place you at the scene."

"What's her name?" Harold asked.

"You may not know her." Scott tried one last dodge.

"I might," Lester interjected. "She claims she knows me. Who is it?"

"Alisha Mason."

Lester nodded. "I know her."

"Where does she live?" asked Harold.

"I don't know. I interviewed her at the high school."

Scott looked at his watch. He only had a few minutes to go over the plea bargain. "One more thing: the D.A. offered a better deal in return for a guilty plea."

Harold's face grew slightly red. "How many times do I have to tell you to fight for my boy—"

Scott cut him off. "I have an obligation to communicate an offer to my client. I'm not making a recommendation. They will modify the assault with a deadly weapon to inflict serious injury charge and omit with intent to murder. There will be no conspiracy charge for the Internet stuff. You plead guilty and receive a six-month sentence in a boot-camp program followed by three years on probation. The offer is on the table until three o'clock today, then it's withdrawn. Any questions?"

"What time is it?" Lester asked.

"You have ten minutes," Scott replied. "Do you want to talk in private?"

Lester nodded.

"Okay. The receptionist will page me when you finish."

Scott stepped into the reception area and exhaled. The atmosphere around the Garrisons was so stale that he didn't want it in his lungs. He left the room and walked down the hallway to Mr. Humphrey's office. The door was cracked open and he could see the older lawyer's feet on the edge of his desk. He quietly pushed open the door. Leland Humphrey's eyes were closed, and his face looked so peaceful that Scott decided not to disturb him. There wasn't anything the older lawyer could do at this point. The immediate decision rested with the two-man jury in the conference room.

Scott was paged by the receptionist. "Mr. Ellis. Your clients are ready for you."

He drained a glass of water in the kitchen and looked at his watch. It was 2:58 P.M. When he saw the Garrisons' faces, he knew their answer.

They were standing in the doorway of the conference room. He came in and shut the door. His question was a formality.

"What do you want to do?" he asked Lester.

Harold answered, "Tell the D.A. that Lester ain't going to plead guilty. I reckon we'll follow your advice. Lester won't testify. We don't think a jury will convict him."

Scott looked directly at Lester. "Is that your decision?"

Lester nodded. "Yes. I didn't do it."

"Okay. I'll make the phone call. Wait here in case something else comes up."

Scott walked up to his office and closed the door. He dialed the D.A.'s office and asked for Lynn Davenport.

"I've met with my client and his father," Scott said.

"Is he going to accept the deal?"

"No, he's not interested."

"Your client is making a mistake."

"That's his choice," Scott said.

"Be ready on Monday. No offer is on the table from this point forward."

Scott set the phone receiver in its cradle. Harold's agreement with Scott's suggestion that Lester avoid the witness stand was not surprising. The older Garrison was savvy enough to realize that if Lester testified there was a risk that he might say something that implicated Harold in the incident at the creek. Lester's silence was Harold's best protection.

Scott went downstairs and told Lester to be at the office at 8 A.M. Monday morning. Now that his client wasn't going to testify, the burden of defense rested completely on Scott's shoulders.

After the Garrisons left the building, Scott checked on Mr. Humphrey. He was still enjoying his siesta.

Scott was quietly closing the door when he heard Mr. Humphrey snort something that sounded like, "Overruled!"

Scott stuck his head back into the office. Mr. Humphrey's eyelids fluttered and he came out of the dream world courtroom back to his comfortable office.

"I'm sorry to bother you," Scott said. "I think you were dreaming."

The older lawyer dropped his feet to the floor and rubbed his eyes.

"Dreaming? It was a nightmare! I couldn't get the judge to reject a clearly inadmissible piece of evidence. No matter what I argued it was overruled."

Scott sat down in one of the burgundy leather chairs in front of Mr. Humphrey's desk.

"Speaking of dreaming, wake me up when *State v. Garrison* is over."

"What's happened?"

Scott summarized his interview with Alisha Mason and his advice to the Garrisons about how to handle it.

Mr. Humphrey nodded. "You did well. Let Lester sit in his chair like a scared kid and keep him off the witness stand. He's smart but not very cuddly. The less the jury hears from him the more likely they'll have sympathy for him, especially if they think the police haven't done their job by arresting the other person on the creekbank."

Scott decided to test his personal conclusions of the identity of John Doe.

"Who do you think is the other person?"

"The father would be my guess," Mr. Humphrey responded. "And he ought to come forward and take full responsibility for the situation. If he did, the boy would be no more than an accessory who would get a slap on the wrist."

"That's what I thought. He's in the running for worst father of the century."

"Did you talk to Lester alone?"

"No."

"That might be in order first thing Monday morning."

"But the plea bargain is withdrawn."

Mr. Humphrey's right eyebrow shot up. "That could change if Lester decides to tell a different tale."

30

You cannot plan the future by the past.
EDMUND BURKE

Nicky greeted Scott with wild excitement. No matter what had happened in the dog's life he was universally consistent in his enthusiasm for Scott's arrival. A bad day for Nicky became a good day as soon as Scott walked through the door. Scott set down his briefcase and gathered up two handfuls of the small stuffed toys that Nicky played with in the house. Nicky didn't share Scott's preference for neatness, and Scott tolerated Nicky's failing to put away his toys. Scott picked up his pet and put him in a tiny storage closet beside the kitchen.

"Count to sixty," Scott commanded, as Nicky yelped and scratched at the door.

Scott took the toys into the backyard and put them under bushes and behind trees. He wedged Nicky's favorite toy, a stuffed hedgehog, in a low limb of an ornamental cherry tree. When he was finished hiding all the animals, he returned to the house. Nicky continued complaining from his darkened prison cell.

"Did you count to sixty?"

Nicky scratched harder. Scott opened the door, and the dog shot into the backyard. Scott followed and sat on the bench by the pond.

Nicky loved hide-and-seek. He would find a toy, retrieve it, and run to Scott who would take it from the dog's mouth and lay it on the bench. There were no good hiding places. Nicky's nose was too sensitive to be fooled by a pile of leaves or a temporary barricade. The backyard was his kingdom, and he knew every nook and cranny. Within a few minutes every item except the hedgehog was on the bench. Nicky made another circuit around the enclosure and returned in triumph.

Scott shook his head. "Where's hedgehog?"

Nicky spun around and made a slower inspection of the yard. He stopped at the cherry tree and looked up. He stretched up to his full height and sniffed, but the hedgehog was barely out of reach. He strained a couple of times and then began jumping up, nipping the stuffed animal with his teeth. After five tries it dislodged and came down at his feet. He proudly picked it up and presented the prize to Scott. His reward was a treat that Scott pulled from his front pocket.

Scott fixed a pizza. It was the third one of the week. While it cooked, he opened his briefcase and organized the papers he'd brought home from the office on the dining room table. He rarely took work home, but the demands of the Garrison case made him live outside the usual boundaries of a world under his control. He made a few notes about his cross-examination of the sheriff deputies who arrested Lester until the kitchen buzzer signaled that the pizza was ready. He was eating a piece gingerly to avoid burning his tongue when the phone rang.

"Hello," he said with a hot bite still between his teeth.

"Scott? Is that you?"

It was Kay.

"Yeah." Scott forced himself to swallow. "You caught me in the middle of a bite of pizza."

"Sorry."

Scott waited for her to explain the reason for her call. When she didn't say anything, he asked, "Why didn't you go to the football game?"

"I didn't want to face the crowd. How about you?"

"I'm working on Lester's case."

"Are you going to be working on the case all weekend?"

Scott looked at the papers on the end of the table and made a decision.

"Not tonight. Would you like to get together? I have four pieces of pizza left. Three for you and one for me. If you come immediately, it will still be hot."

Scott gave her directions. It was less than ten minutes from her apartment to his house. Scott put the pizza back in the oven to stay warm and picked up the rest of Nicky's toys. When the dog heard footsteps on the sidewalk, he ran barking to the front door. Visitors were not common in the lair he shared with his master.

Scott opened the front door. Kay was casually dressed in jeans and a yellow shirt. Nicky jumped up and down until she let him smell her hand. She rubbed his head.

"You must be Nicky."

"The one and only," Scott answered. "Come in. Nicky and I will give you a quick tour."

It didn't take long to see the house. Nicky followed along, his feet clipping against the wood floors. Scott saved the backyard for last. It was still possible to see the whole area in the twilight from the last rays of the sun behind the trees on the west side of the property.

"It's like an English garden," she said. "I can see why you like it here."

They stopped by the fishpond. "Is this where you were sitting when I called the other day?"

"Yes, and forgot to wipe the spaghetti sauce from my mouth."

They went into the kitchen and Scott took the pizza out of the oven.

"No, thanks," she said. "I've already eaten."

Scott took out an extra plate from the cupboard. "If you come to my house, local custom requires that you eat my food."

Kay selected the smallest piece, and they sat at the dining room table. She seemed melancholy.

"I'm glad you called," Scott said. "I didn't want to spend the evening with Lester Garrison."

Kay nibbled her slice of pizza. "Did you tell him about Alisha?"

"Yes, but I've found a way to explain her testimony so that I don't have to impeach her. It makes as much sense as anything Lester has been telling me. If Alisha sticks to the story she told me Thursday night, it may work out to my advantage in the end."

"So, are you ready for the trial?"

"Not yet. Mr. Humphrey says a lawyer is never totally prepared; he just runs out of time to do anything else. It's like life. You can't anticipate everything."

"That's the truth."

They ate in silence for a minute.

"I had two messages on my answering machine when I got home from school," Kay said. "The first was from my lawyer. My divorce hearing has been moved to Monday at nine-thirty. The second call was from Jake. He's getting married next weekend."

Scott was about to take a bite of pizza and stopped in midair. He couldn't believe it. It was like something from an afternoon soap opera.

Kay continued, "I'd been holding out a tiny hope until tonight. Jake left a message the other day apologizing for the way he acted the night of the football game. I'd thought maybe he realized his mistake. Now this."

Scott looked at Kay. There was nothing he'd seen in Kay's personality or conduct since he walked into her classroom that justified this level of rejection and abuse.

"Forget him," Scott said. "He's a fool. If he—"

"No," she interrupted. "I'm not trying to get you to react."

"I'm entitled to my opinion. If he had any sense, he'd crawl on his knees from Virginia and beg you to take him back. You don't deserve getting dumped for someone else. You're beautiful, smart, fun to be with—" He stopped.

Kay's eyes were watering. She wiped them with her napkin.

"I was feeling worthless when I called you," she said. "I was hoping you'd make me laugh."

"Instead, I made you cry."

"That's what I need to do, but it seems like every other time we're together, I'm an emotional mess."

In a few seconds, Kay's napkin was soggy history. Scott went into the bathroom and returned with a box of tissues. He sat still at the table beside her. Untouched, his pizza grew cold.

After a few moments, he spoke slowly. "What I said was the truth. You're beautiful, smart, fun to be with, and"—he paused—"very vulnerable. I don't want to take advantage of that vulnerability."

This caused a fresh torrent of tears, and Scott sat silently. The lack of selfishness he felt toward Kay was a surprise to him.

"Thank you," she said simply. "For now, that's all I can manage."

Nicky ran up to Kay and stood up with his paws on her leg. He had his stuffed hedgehog in his mouth. Kay wiped her eyes one more time and patted his head.

"What's that?"

Scott looked over the corner of the table.

"Before Nicky chewed off one of its legs and both eyes, it was a healthy hedgehog. He wants you to throw it so he can run after it. It's his way of cheering you up."

Kay took the slightly moist animal from Nicky's mouth and threw it out of the dining room and across the foyer. It slid across the floor and under Scott's chair in the living room. Nicky took off at top speed, retrieved it, then trotted back and held it up to Kay. She threw it again. This time, the little dog took the stuffed animal into the foyer where he lay down on the area rug in front of the door and began to chew vigorously on one of the remaining legs.

"Isn't he going to bring it back?" Kay asked.

"Not necessarily. Nicky plays by his own rules. You can't always predict what he's going to do with something when he catches it."

They spent the next hour looking at photographs. Scott pulled out two boxes of pictures that chronicled his life from high-school graduation through the present. Included were shots from army days, summer vacations, scenes from California that were familiar to Kay, life in college, and several girlfriends. Kay asked about the women who had floated through Scott's life. Without feeling awkward, he gave an honest, uncritical assessment and an abbreviated, sanitized version of their relationships. The last woman in line was a girl he met in law school. Her hair was as dark as Kay's was blond.

"She's an attorney in Washington, D.C.," Scott said. "We spent a lot of time together our last year in law school after her fiancé broke off their engagement. She decided to take a job with a big government agency. I didn't want to live in the D.C. area and haven't seen her since graduation."

"That sounds analytical."

"What do you mean?"

"What did you feel for her? You describe the end of your relationship as if you were moving your money from one mutual fund to another."

"Okay, I'll tell you. It hurt then. It hurts now."

Scott didn't reveal how the pain of the breakup had been a restraint on releasing his heart toward Kay. He didn't want another rebound relationship that was quickly discarded when someone else came along.

"Did you ask her to consider living in North Carolina?" Kay asked.

"No, she made her plans before I talked with Mr. Humphrey about a job."

Kay studied the picture for a few seconds. The woman was sitting on a big rock on the Wake Forest campus looking down at Scott.

"If you had," Kay said, "she would have said 'yes.'"

Startled, Scott leaned closer to the picture. "How can you tell that from a photo?"

"The way she's focused on you. It's an 'I'll follow this man to the ends of the earth' look."

"No way."

"I'll prove it to you," Kay challenged. "Did she ever look at you like this?"

Kay met Scott's gaze and held it for a few seconds. It wasn't a come-hither look, but a more serious invitation to commitment. Scott had to admit he'd seen that look in his girlfriend's eyes.

"Uh, yes," he said.

They finished the second box of photos. Nicky was fast asleep on the rug with the hedgehog between his front paws.

"I've kept Nicky up past his bedtime," Kay said. "I'd better be going."

Scott glanced at his pet. "He's had a fun evening."

"Will I see you at the courthouse on Monday?" she asked.

"Probably not. I'll be in the big courtroom in the older part of the building. The domestic hearings are in a smaller courtroom in the new wing. They herd folks through like cattle."

"For the slaughter of marriages." Kay shook her head.

"I'm sorry—," Scott began.

"I'm all right," she said. "I needed tonight. You've helped me more than you know."

"We'll talk on Tuesday," Scott said as he walked her to the front door.

"Call me after the trial is over. And I'll be praying for you and Lester. I've been doing a lot of praying about everything recently."

The words *prayer* and *Lester Garrison* hadn't appeared in the same paragraph in Scott's mind. After Kay left, Scott held the picture of his former girlfriend down so Nicky could see it.

"What do you think?" he asked. "Would you like to meet her?"

The dog sniffed the picture, grabbed his hedgehog, and trotted back to his cage.

———

At the end of the school day that Friday, Janie Collins had stopped Frank in the hallway near the front door of the high school and asked if he was going to the big game against Maiden that night.

"No, I haven't been to a football game since I was a freshman."

"I'm going," she said.

Frank looked at his mock trial partner with a mixture of curiosity and disdain. He'd been around her enough to know that she wasn't a fake, but he considered her kindhearted sincerity a form of weakness.

"Have a good time," he responded.

"Would you like to sit with me and a few of my friends?" Janie persisted.

"Who are they?"

Janie mentioned several students. Frank didn't know any of them except as faces in class. However, sitting with Janie wouldn't be the worst way to spend an evening. A crack opened in his armor.

"Why are you inviting me?" he asked.

"Because it will be fun. You can meet my friends, and maybe some of your friends will be there, too."

Frank didn't have any close friends. His acerbic tongue was a lash that kept him isolated.

"I don't know," he said. "I'm going to be busy."

"Doing what? It's Friday night."

"A project I'm working on."

"Take a break and join us. We'll be sitting in the south bleachers near the twenty-yard line."

"I'll think about it."

"I'll get there about fifteen minutes before the game starts to make sure there are enough seats."

Frank's father wasn't home, and he fixed a sandwich for supper. The atrium near the kitchen was empty. His mother had taken the bird with her before Frank could complete the animal's obscenity training. He thought again about Janie's invitation and made up his mind. He would go to the game and see what happened.

It was a couple of hours before he needed to leave. He went upstairs, put on his headphones, and turned on the computer. When he entered the game, he found an intriguing scenario. Someone new had arrived. Frank quickly saw that the newcomer was a more formidable foe than the other warriors. A glint came into his eye as he gripped the mouse and stared into the screen. When he looked up, it was almost 9 P.M. He'd lost track of time. The football game usually ended around 10 P.M. Frank turned back to the screen as one of his favorite music cuts came through the headphones.

31

*See to it that no one misses the grace of God and that no
bitter root grows up to cause trouble and defile many.*
HEBREWS 12:15

Kay spent the day cleaning her apartment from top to bottom. It kept her busy, and by late afternoon, the kitchen floor shone and there wasn't a stray blond hair anywhere in the bathroom. In the midst of her activity, she accumulated a few items to give Jake on Monday: two books on golf, a white T-shirt, a pair of brown socks, and a garish tie his mother had given him for his birthday. When she finished, the apartment was as cleansed from outward signs of Jake Wilson's presence as the home of an Orthodox Jewish housewife in preparation for Passover.

Pouring a glass of water, she sat in a padded chair on her balcony with a notebook and a pen. Instead of writing, she watched the activity in the parking lot beneath her. Groups of people came and went. A husband and wife with a baby in a stroller crossed the parking lot and drove away in a minivan. Birds darted through the trees. No one looked up. Kay was invisible in her isolation. A person alone is acutely aware of separation from others while the rest of the world passes by without taking notice. She went to bed early.

The following day her disposition stayed dark even though the morning sun shone into her bedroom. She thought about hiding under the covers until noon but decided to go to church instead.

Janie's little brother saw her as soon as she walked through the door of the gym and he waved to her. There were a few more people present in the congregation than the first time Kay had visited. As soon as Kay was in her seat, the guitar-playing song leader stepped to the front, and the words to a song appeared on the screen. Kay didn't watch what other people were doing. She immediately joined in herself. In a few minutes she was in the place of praise, love, and adoration where the music took her. The heaviness resting in her heart rolled away like a hidden stone. She closed her eyes and lifted her hands as her spirit was replenished with living water. She could face tomorrow.

After the last note faded away, Linda Whitmire came forward and welcomed everyone to the church. Ben followed her to the front and silently watched his wife walk back to her seat.

"Isn't she beautiful?" he asked in a voice that left no doubt as to his sincerity.

His wife smiled. Linda's face was wrinkled, her hair snow white, and she carried at least thirty-five pounds more than she should on her small frame, but Kay knew that to Ben Whitmire his wife was beautiful. She was slightly jealous with wonder.

"Do you know why?" Ben continued.

Kay waited.

Ben looked across the congregation. "Linda is so beautiful on the inside that it can't be hidden from the outside. That's what I want to talk about this morning—the beauty of our inner person. This beauty doesn't apply only to women." Ben rubbed his hand across his balding head. "You know, God thinks I'm beautiful, too."

A few people laughed, and for the next thirty minutes Ben explained the process of inner transformation under the loving hand of an almighty God. Kay listened. To her, the events of life seemed haphazard—more like random marks on a page than notes that created a symphony. Ben had another perspective. He believed that everything—including a difficult relationship—was a golden opportunity for change.

"In one of the first churches I served," he said, "there were three women who didn't like me. They'd loved the previous pastor and resented it when I came to serve their church. Of course, I didn't know how they felt at first, but Linda picked up on it and told me I was in for a hard time at their hands. 'Hard' was an understatement.

"They talked about me behind my back in the church and around town. They criticized what I said, accused me of things I'd never thought of doing, and generally made my life miserable. During my sermons, they would take notes, and later repeat what I said out of context and crucify me over the telephones and in kitchens all over the area. The ringleader of the group was the richest member of the church—her father had started the biggest bank in the area—and no one was willing to take up my case against her. After a year, they convinced my secretary to quit, then wrote letters to denominational leaders asking them to kick me out of the ministry because I couldn't administer the staff of the church.

"I didn't respond very well. I asked God to take them to heaven, which was my religious way of asking him to get them out of my life. That didn't happen, so I prayed that they would leave the church, the town, and the state. That didn't happen, either. Week after week, month after month, they came to the services, sat toward the front, and glowered at me. I lost count of the number of ways in which they were able to create problems for me. This went on for two years until I was whipped. They had won, and I began making other plans for the future. I bought a book so I could learn how to sell life insurance when I left the ministry."

The preacher paused. "Then one night I had a dream. In the dream I was sitting in the lap of my Heavenly Father. I couldn't see his face, but I knew who it was because of the love I felt in his presence. There was an open space in front of us containing a large block of beautiful marble.

"'*Do you know what that is?*' he asked me.

"Somehow I knew that a block of marble wasn't the right answer, so I replied, 'No.'

"'*That's you,*' he answered. '*The person I want you to be is hidden inside.*'

"At that point hands appeared out of the air and began to chip away at the marble. It reminded me of an old Walt Disney movie. The hands were moving almost faster than my eyes could follow, but it wasn't fast enough for me. I wanted to see the finished product.

"'Make them go faster,' I said.

"'*Are you sure?*' he asked.

"Not taking my eyes from the scene before me, I cried out, 'Yes! Faster!'

"The hands worked at a furious pace. In no time, I could distinguish a body with a head. Then the arms and legs took shape. The rough outlines were refined, and the facial features were revealed from their secret place within the rock. When it was finished, I couldn't believe the beauty of the new creation. It put Michelangelo to shame.

"'Is that me?' I asked, not fully believing that it could be so.

"'*Yes*,' he answered.

"'Thank you,' I whispered in awe.

"'*You're welcome*,' he answered, then added, '*but don't you want to thank my helpers?*'

"I knew he was referring to the hands. 'Yes! Let me see them!'"

Ben Whitmire smiled. "I'd never seen an angel before and my anticipation was high. Maybe angels had hands as well as wings. Then from behind the magnificent statue appeared the smiling faces of my tormentors—the three women from the church. They waved to me, and I woke up. God wasn't using angels to do the work of changing me; he was relying upon my enemies.

"I didn't sleep the rest of the night. I paced the floor, arguing and debating, until I came to terms with the lesson he wanted me to learn. The difficult people and circumstances in life are often the tools God uses to bring forth the enduring beauty of Christian character. If we want to be transformed, we have to be changed. One of the ways God uses is the challenge of difficult relationships."

The minister continued, "You're probably wondering what happened after I realized the truth. Well, the next Sunday I went up to the women before the service and thanked them for coming. They gave me a strange look and started whispering furiously after I walked away. Nothing changed, the gang of three continued their activities. They gossiped, criticized, and plotted my downfall. But my heart was free. Time after time, I went out of my way to show kindness to them, and when one of them lost a brother to cancer, I drove a hundred miles to attend the funeral. Eventually, she quit the group. The other two never let up and badgered me until I left town for a larger church. But when I packed the moving van and drove down the driveway of our house for the last time, I didn't take any negative baggage of bitterness with me. Instead, I went to my next church with a few sizable chips knocked off the block of marble that was becoming a person who looked more and more like Jesus."

Ben took off his glasses. "Today, I call people like those women 'grace-growers.' When I see one coming, I don't run or fight; I ask God what part of my life is going to be refined and transformed through this person. Do any of you have any grace-growers in your life? They may not be exactly like the ones at my church, but they are God's instruments for your good."

Kay didn't have to think long.

———

From the time he was a little boy, the bomber had never had a normal life. He came from a womb of contention and lived in strife from his earliest years. Environment plays a powerful role in shaping character, and as a product of hate, he bore the imprint of those who molded him. Upon reaching the age of moral accountability, he made the influences of childhood his own. From then on, blame for who he was and what he did could not be shifted entirely to others. It lay at his feet.

The student sporadically intersected with a basic routine of home and school, but none of his classmates would have characterized him as normal. He was different. He had no friends. No one knew his true thoughts, and he kept hidden from everyone the deepest levels of darkness that had inhabited his soul.

Recent upheaval in his circumstances could have diverted him from continuing to plan his attack, but they didn't. His problems reinforced his resolve to go forward. Circumstances caused delays, but he continued to construct a device capable of destroying the main school building.

In the meantime, no one suspected. No one knew about the coming ball of fire.

32

And sheath'd their swords for lack of argument.
KING HENRY V, ACT 3, SCENE 1

Scott spent Sunday at the office finishing his trial preparation and then went home to practice his opening statement in front of the long mirror in his bedroom. He paced back and forth, gesturing with his hands and experimenting with different levels of volume in his voice. Nicky served as the lone juror. Eventually, the little dog went to sleep on the floor.

According to Scott's calculations, the Garrison trial would last two days. Monday morning would be devoted to selecting the jury, followed by opening statements and at least partial presentation of the state's case in the afternoon. The rest of the case would take place on Tuesday. Since Lester wouldn't testify, the defense case would be Scott's closing argument. He'd written an outline of his jury summation, leaving plenty of blank spaces on the pages to add helpful information that came out during the trial. He hoped there would be tidbits. Mr. Humphrey had assured him that the state's witnesses never presented a monolithic wall of consistent testimony. There were always cracks and crevices that an attentive lawyer could use to his client's advantage.

He'd been over every aspect of the case a hundred times, but there was one thing lacking in Scott's preparation. Passion. He'd anticipated his first jury trial since the early days of law school. Now that it was at hand, he was having trouble psyching himself up for the battle. It was more difficult than he'd expected to divorce himself from the hate-filled premise of Lester's beliefs and the unsavory aspects of his client's character. Intellectually, Scott knew that professionalism prohibited his personal feelings from influencing his obligation to defend his client with a zeal that protected those accused of crimes from arbitrary adjudications of guilt. However, the importance of the Constitution seemed faraway when Scott listened to Lester's racist venom and considered what Harold Garrison had done to his son. He needed an emotional boost, and despite what he told Kay, feeding his competitive ego and venting his animosity toward Lynn Davenport weren't the kind of motivating factors he wanted to rely upon.

During a fitful night, Scott dreamed about the Garrison case. The images that flashed through his mind were random and disconnected. It wasn't as if the case began efficiently and moved to an orderly conclusion. It simply spun around like a merry-go-round that never stopped.

Bleary-eyed, Scott awoke thirty minutes before his customary 6:30 A.M. and fixed a pot of strong coffee. Nicky scratched at the door to his cage, and Scott let him out to run across the dewy grass in the backyard. Sipping his coffee, Scott stood on the back step and watched Nicky's morning antics. When the little dog saw him, he ran as fast as he could from the back corner of the yard and greeted his master by shaking his entire body. Life wasn't complicated for Nicky. The only frustrating images in his dreams probably featured fat rabbits who disappeared under fences.

Scott didn't eat any breakfast and arrived at the office before 7 A.M. Dressed in his best dark suit with a striped tie, he'd combed his hair in a way he hoped would make him look a little older. Mr. Humphrey wanted to walk over to the courthouse no later than 8:30 A.M. so that he and Scott would have plenty of time to shake hands and exchange pleasantries with as many jurors as possible. The lawyers couldn't mention the case, but there was no prohibition against being friendly.

Scott had finished putting all his papers in the appropriate folders when Mr. Humphrey came into his office.

"Beautiful morning, isn't it?" he boomed.

Scott hadn't noticed the weather.

Mr. Humphrey continued, "Are you ready? I was thinking about the case at breakfast and told my wife I almost wished I could try it myself. You have a great shot at winning this one."

"Then why am I feeling so flat?" Scott asked.

Mr. Humphrey's right eyebrow shot up. "Ah, pretrial malaise."

The older lawyer sat down across from Scott's desk. "Don't worry. You only have so much emotional energy at your disposal. The fire will come when the battle really begins. If you waste it anticipating the trial, it won't be available when it counts—in the courtroom."

"I hope so."

The receptionist called Scott over the intercom.

"Mr. Garrison is here."

"Father and son?" Scott asked.

"No, sir. Just the son."

"I wonder where Dad is this morning?" Scott asked.

"Maybe he's gone fishing at Montgomery Creek," Mr. Humphrey said.

The two lawyers walked downstairs together. Lester was pacing back and forth in the reception area. As instructed by Scott, he was wearing a white shirt, a tie, and his newest pants. His shirt and pants were wrinkled, but it was the best Scott could hope for under the circumstances. Lester's face had improved, but it still bore signs of its collision with the tree limb. The sight of the young man's obvious nervousness had a calming effect on Scott.

"Good morning, Lester," he said. "Let's go into the conference room for a minute."

They sat down and Lester began popping his knuckles.

"Where's your father?"

"He dropped me off so he could go by his work and pick up his paycheck. He'll be here in a minute."

"That's okay," Scott replied. "Because I want to talk to you about the dark-haired person at the creek."

Lester sat up. "There wasn't nobody else! She's lying! I've been thinking about it all weekend, and I think you ought to let me tell my side of the story to the jury."

Scott didn't debate. He wasn't sure how much time he had before Harold arrived.

"Was your father with you?"

Lester gaped at Scott for several seconds.

"Do they have a witness claiming my father was there?"

Scott glanced at Mr. Humphrey to see if the older lawyer wanted to take over. He shook his head.

"No," Scott said. "But the presence of a dark-haired figure made us suspect that you may have been with your father. Both Bishop Moore and Alisha saw a dark-haired person."

Lester laughed. "That's crazy."

Surprised by his client's response, Scott leaned forward and spoke with intensity. "Lester, this is not a joke. If your father fired the shots, he should be the one on trial, not you. When this was a juvenile court case, the most that could have happened to you was a slap on the wrist. Now it's in superior court, and in a few minutes you're going to trial and can be sentenced as an adult. I don't think the D.A. is going to have an easy time convicting you, but if the jury decides that you're guilty, you could be sent off for a long time."

Before Lester responded, the door opened and Harold Garrison walked in.

"We need to talk to Lester alone for a few minutes," Scott said. "Wait in the reception room."

"He's trying to get me to say that you did it," Lester blurted out.

"Did what?" Harold's eyes flashed.

"Wait a minute," Scott said.

"Fired the shots on the creek," Lester finished.

Harold took a step toward Scott. "You snake! I ought to—"

"Hold it!" Mr. Humphrey commanded. "Mr. Garrison, be quiet and listen."

His face red, Harold stayed put.

Mr. Humphrey continued, "Our job is to defend your son, and if you were involved in this incident, you need to hire your own lawyer."

"I paid you to fight for my son, not turn him against me and force him to lie!"

"Would it be a lie if he said you were with him on the creek?" Scott asked.

Harold looked down at Lester. "Go ahead. Tell him."

Lester shrugged. "The truth?"

"Yeah." Harold nodded.

Lester sighed. "No, he wasn't there."

"Then who was with you?" Scott asked.

Lester stared at the glass-topped table. "It was my cousin Kendall. He lives in South Carolina and came up for the weekend. He has black hair. We took my pistol down to the creek to mess around. We heard the people from the church singing and decided to sneak up on them. Kendall popped a few shots in the water and up in the air to scare them. He wasn't trying to hit anybody. We just wanted to see them run."

Scott sat back in his chair. "Why didn't you tell me this before?"

Lester looked at his father and didn't answer.

"Did you put him up to this?" Scott asked Harold.

"I don't guess it matters."

"How can I get in touch with your cousin?" Scott asked Lester.

Harold answered. "We don't want him dragged into this."

"But he's the one who ought to be on trial!" Scott protested.

"Are you deaf? I don't want him dragged into this," Harold repeated.

"But why?"

"I guess that's our business, ain't it?"

"Lester, do you know—"

"You heard what he said," Lester interrupted. "I don't want Kendall's name mentioned, either."

"Leave him out of it, period," Harold added.

Several thoughts flashed through Scott's mind. None of them made sense.

"Don't we have to be in court in a few minutes?" Harold asked.

Mr. Humphrey nodded. "Let's go. I have a few notes in my office."

"I'll get the rest of my file," Scott said.

Scott followed Mr. Humphrey out of the reception area and through the door that separated the public and private parts of the building. As soon as they were alone, Scott hit his left palm with his right fist.

"This is crazy! All Lester has to do is tell the truth, and he's off the hook. What is going on here?"

Both of Mr. Humphrey's eyebrows stretched toward the top of his head. "That," he said, "is a question I'm not sure we will be able to answer today. Cousin Kendall may be as real as Bishop Moore, or he could be as fictitious as John Doe. Harold knew we suspected him, and creating a convenient relative may be their response to the questions we asked the other day about a dark-haired accomplice."

"What do I do?"

Mr. Humphrey smiled grimly. "Welcome to the enigmatic life of a trial lawyer. Stick to your theory of the case because the Garrisons won't give you anything else to work with. We don't always know the truth or understand the motivations behind what our clients tell us. That's why there will be two sides arguing in the courtroom, and the right to make a final decision will rest not with us or the D.A. but with the jury. That's their job. You do your job."

Mr. Humphrey was right. Scott was back to advocating a position that was possibly more true than he'd suspected—the wrong person was on trial.

The four men walked out the front door of the office and down the sidewalk toward the courthouse. Mr. Humphrey was right. It was an exquisite morning. Cool air, low humidity, bright sunshine. A great day for a walk along a creekbank.

The streets around the courthouse were clogged with an equal number of cars and trucks. The Ford dealer in Catawba had sold more pickup trucks than cars every year since opening his dealership in 1959. People parked along the street on all four sides of the block where the courthouse complex rested. There wasn't an empty parking space all the way down the street past the Eagle. Bea Dempsey didn't mind if the folks going to the courthouse left their vehicles in front of the restaurant. A trial week provided some of the best lunch crowds of the year.

Several clusters of men and women were talking and smoking cigarettes before walking up the steps to the courthouse. Smoking maintained a strong following on tobacco road. A few people glanced at the entourage that walked silently up the sidewalk. It was obvious that Scott and Mr. Humphrey were attorneys. It was equally apparent that one or both of the Garrisons would therefore be involved in the proceedings scheduled to begin inside at 9 A.M. Several men greeted Mr. Humphrey, who shook hands and slapped a few backs on his way up the sidewalk to the front of the building. Scott was feeling less lighthearted.

The courtroom was beginning to fill up. Lynn Davenport was not in sight. The foursome walked down the aisle and past the bar to the defense table. Scott showed Lester where to sit in the farthest seat from the jury box.

"Don't unpack yet," Mr. Humphrey said to Scott. "Let's meet a few people."

Leaving the Garrisons by themselves, the two lawyers walked past the low wooden railing that divided the courtroom. Mr. Humphrey was as jovial as a good-natured farmer at the county fair and didn't appear to have any more pressing responsibility than deciding whether to buy peanuts or popcorn. He introduced Scott to so many people in such a short period of time that names became a blur.

"I hope they leave me on your jury," one older man said to Mr. Humphrey. "I served on a case you tried where the lady said the light never turned red and plowed into the side of the chicken truck. You did a dandy job."

Mr. Humphrey moved on and whispered to Scott, "I don't remember what he's talking about."

One of Mr. Humphrey's nieces, a secretary for a local CPA, was on the panel. She would be excused for cause. Several former or current clients were in the courtroom. Trying a case against a lawyer like Mr. Humphrey, who had grown up in Catawba and practiced law in Blanchard County for forty years, was a challenge. The D.A. would either have to use most of her strikes to remove jurors who knew Leland Humphrey or try to convince those who did that in this case Mr. Humphrey's client was in the wrong. Scott saw an African-American man who looked familiar.

"Who is that?"

The older lawyer followed Scott's finger. "That's James Dillard. You may have seen him at Bishop Moore's church."

Scott remembered. The tall, thin man was in the Hall's Chapel choir. "He's not on the witness list."

"Then he's in the jury pool. I think I remember seeing his name."

"Would we want to strike him?" Scott asked.

"That's a good question. Since you're arguing that Alisha Mason and

Bishop Moore are telling the truth, he might be a keeper. Let's explore it with him when you question the prospective jurors."

It was almost 9 A.M., and the jurors who had been outside smoking snuffed out their last cigarettes and came into the courtroom. Scott and Mr. Humphrey rejoined their client. Scott leaned over to the Garrisons.

"Do you see any friendly faces?"

"There's one guy I used to work with years ago," Harold said. "We didn't get along. He was a jerk."

Lester looked nervously over his shoulder and shook his head.

Lynn Davenport and another lawyer from the D.A.'s office came in a door beside the judge's bench. They were followed by a deputy sheriff who called out in a loud voice, "All rise! The Superior Court of Blanchard County is now in session, the Honorable Wayman Teasley presiding."

There was a rustle as the room responded to the command. Judge Teasley strode into the courtroom and took his seat behind the bench.

"You may be seated."

The judge welcomed the jurors, then turned to one of the assistant district attorneys.

"Proceed, Mr. Johnson."

There were several uncontested matters to be handled. Two men and one woman pleaded guilty to writing bad checks. A man with a scruffy growth of gray beard pleaded guilty to his fifth DUI while driving without a license. He was sentenced to five years in prison. Two more people entered guilty pleas, but Scott wasn't paying attention. He was organizing all his paperwork on the table so that he could find anything he needed in a matter of seconds.

Assistant D.A. Johnson sat down, and Lynn Davenport stood up.

"Your honor, at this time we call for trial *State of North Carolina v. Diaz, Barrera, and Contraras.*"

Judge Teasley looked at the defense table. His eyes wide, Scott was staring across the room at Lynn Davenport.

Two lawyers in the front row behind the railing stood up.

"Ready for the defendants, your honor."

33

If a man will begin with certainties, he shall end in doubts.
FRANCIS BACON

M r. Humphrey began putting papers in his briefcase.

"What happened?" Lester hissed.

"They called another case for trial," Scott replied. "We need to move out of the way."

"I thought you—"

"Later," Scott cut him off.

Scott joined Mr. Humphrey in quickly cleaning off the table. The lawyers representing the men charged with kidnapping stood waiting with their clients for them to leave.

When he snapped shut his briefcase, Mr. Humphrey spoke up, "Your honor, may we approach the bench?"

The judge nodded. Scott followed Mr. Humphrey. Lynn Davenport joined them.

"Judge, the D.A. told Mr. Ellis that the Garrison case would be number one on the court's calendar."

The judge took off his glasses. "Is that true, Ms. Davenport?"

"Yes, sir. But we learned over the weekend that several key witnesses in the Diaz case may not be in the United States at the next term of court. There was no opportunity to advise Mr. Ellis."

"I see," the judge replied. "Gentlemen, the state has the right to call the cases it chooses for trial."

"Of course, your honor. I was merely seeking clarification," Mr. Humphrey said.

"Ms. Davenport, when do you anticipate reaching the Garrison case?"

"Two weeks, your honor. You have a small jury pool coming in, and we can handle it at that time."

"Very well."

The lawyers left the bench and led Harold and Lester into the hallway. Scott explained what had happened.

"So, we have to come back in two weeks?" Harold asked.

"Yes," Scott answered. "The judge lets the district attorney's office decide which cases to try."

"I want to get this over with," Harold said.

Scott looked at Lester, who didn't say anything. "How about you? Are you disappointed?"

"Uh, yeah."

"The delay will give us more time to prepare"—Scott paused—"and you can think about the situation with your cousin."

"There's no use bringing that up again," Harold said sharply. "I told you to drop it."

Scott's eyes narrowed. "I'll mention anything I think necessary."

Mr. Humphrey stepped in. "That's all for today. You fellows can leave, and we'll be in touch in a few days."

The Garrisons walked down the hallway toward the front door.

"The battle has started," Scott said. "But it didn't begin in the courtroom."

"Let the situation cool down. Lester will be reconsidering his decision now that it's out in the open. I wouldn't be surprised if you get a call from him by the end of the week."

"There's no reason to stay here," Scott said. "I'm going back to the office."

"I need to review a file," Mr. Humphrey said. "I'll see you later."

Outside the courthouse, Scott saw a familiar figure walking away from the annex. She was dressed in black.

"Kay!" he called out.

She turned her head, saw him, and stopped. He walked quickly to where she stood.

"How did it go?" he asked.

It was obvious she had been crying. She was clutching a rumpled tissue in her hand. Her voice revealed her anguish.

"How can a lifetime commitment be obliterated so easily? So quickly!"

Scott had no answer. Divorce was a cold statistic until it touched someone you knew.

She continued, "We waited about fifteen minutes to see the judge. Jake sat with his lawyer; I sat with mine. We didn't talk, but the lawyers seemed to have a good time discussing bass fishing. When they called the case, we went in to see the judge. It took less time than trading in a used car. After it was over, I asked my lawyer a question, and when I turned around, Jake was gone. No good-byes. Nothing."

Scott sensed the rising flood of emotion in her might burst out again into the open. He asked the first question that popped into his mind.

"Where are you going now?"

Kay managed a weak smile. "That's a very big question. It's hard for me to think beyond my next breath. What did they tell you in boot camp? 'When the going gets tough, the tough get going.' In a few minutes, I'm going back to school to teach my classes. Those kids need me even if Jake doesn't. Beyond that, I may go back to California; I may go to Maine. I guess I can go anywhere I want. I'm not sure."

Scott wanted to suggest that she stay in Catawba but didn't. Kay wasn't looking for practical advice; she just needed to vent.

"I'm going back to the office," he said.

"I'd forgotten about Lester's case," Kay replied. "Are you taking a break?"

"For two weeks."

"Two weeks!"

Scott explained what happened.

"Then I guess I'll see Lester in class tomorrow," she said.

"I'll walk you to your car," Scott offered.

Kay had parked several blocks down the street in the opposite direction from the Eagle.

When they reached her car, Scott put his hand on the roof and said,

"I know what we need to do. Let's get in your car and leave. We'll stop by my house, pick up Nicky, a couple of fishing poles, and drive to the mountains. We'll catch our supper in a beautiful mountain stream. You can take off your shoes, sit on a rock, and cool your toes in the water while Nicky barks at the rushing water."

Kay didn't hesitate. "Okay. But you drive. I'm beat."

Scott smiled. "Remind me not to play poker with you. You called my bluff."

Kay opened the door of her car.

"I'll see you tomorrow night," she said.

Scott watched her drive away. There was no doubt about it. Jake Wilson was an idiot.

There was a surrealistic quality to the rest of the day. Scott worked in his office, but he felt he should be standing in the old courtroom with all senses on full alert trying Lester Garrison's case. In midafternoon he glanced at the clock. If the case hadn't been postponed, he would have been cross-examining the state's witnesses and hoping the testimony didn't explode his theory of the case. Instead, he was moving paragraphs from one page to another in a commercial lease agreement.

After work, he drove to Dixon's Body Shop. Perry was sitting in his office doing paperwork. When he saw Scott, he came out to greet him.

"I didn't think I'd see you this week because of your trial."

"The case was postponed for a couple of weeks."

Scott changed clothes and began his workout. Forty-five minutes later, he'd completed a circuit that involved every major muscle group. Hard physical activity released friendly endorphins that produced a natural euphoria, and Scott took a break to enjoy the gentle rush. Perry came over and sat down across from him.

"Kay was at the courthouse today for the final hearing in her divorce case," Scott said. "She and Jake are history."

"Did you see him?"

"No. I was wrapped up in my own business. I ran into her outside, and we talked for a few minutes."

"How did she handle it?"

"She's devastated. I thought she had already worked through a lot of her feelings, but she was ripped up pretty bad by the final blow."

"Did she take back her maiden name? I always thought Laramie was a cool name. Not nearly as boring as Wilson or Ellis."

"Or Dixon," Scott added. "I didn't ask her. Since they didn't have any kids, I'd think she would want to put it all behind her and start fresh."

"What's your plan of action? Once the word is out that she's available, the line of hungry males will stretch down the street and around the corner."

Scott threw his towel at Perry's head.

"There aren't enough single guys in this town who could keep her interested to fill half the seats in her classroom. I'm not worried about competition."

Perry leaned forward. "So you're in the race? Linda will want to know."

Scott was silent for a moment. He didn't even know if there would be a race. In the aftermath of Jake's betrayal, he didn't know when she would be capable of feeling something for another man. Her marriage had been a huge wall between them. He didn't know how to act now that it was gone.

"I don't know what I'm going to do."

Perry shook his head. "Linda won't be happy with that answer. It sounds too passive; she believes in action."

Scott slid some weights on the barbell and tightened the collar that held them in place.

"Linda needs to lift weights," he said. "It would help clear her mental pores of all the romantic daydreams she has about me and Kay Wilson."

At home that evening, Nicky greeted Scott with less enthusiasm than usual. The little dog immediately trotted over to his empty food dish where he began to hit it with his paw until Scott replenished it.

"Sorry, boy," Scott said. "I didn't think about you when I left this morning."

Scott went to the refrigerator. Except for drinks, the main compartment was empty. He looked over his shoulder at Nicky. The dog was happily crunching away at the small nuggets of food.

"Who's going to fill *my* food bowl?" Scott asked him.

Nicky ignored him and continued chewing.

Scott opened the freezer and found a frozen dinner that he'd avoided for months. He put it in the microwave, and six minutes later peeled back the plastic cover. The meal looked better in the picture on the outside of the package than when he set it on the kitchen counter.

Carrying the food into his bedroom, he turned on his computer. Clicking on the weather forecast, he typed in the name of a town near one of his favorite spots in the mountains around Asheville. The projected forecast called for a perfect weekend. The leaves would be beautiful, and there might be an opportunity to hook a few trout in a mountain stream. He debated for a minute. After the events of the day, Kay needed a pleasant diversion to look forward to. He decided to gamble.

Scott picked up the phone and dialed Kay's number. The phone rang several times. No answer. He didn't want to leave a message on the answering machine. Disappointed, he was about to hang up when he heard Kay's breathless voice.

"Hello?" she said.

"It's Scott. How are you doing?"

"I'm out of breath. I'd gone to the laundry room and heard the phone ringing as I walked up the stairs."

Scott spoke before he could change his mind.

"Are you still open to a trip to the mountains? I checked the weather for this weekend. The leaves should be pretty, and I know some great spots to visit along babbling mountain streams. You were ready to go this morning. Now I'm calling *your* bluff."

Several seconds of silence followed. "How far is it?"

"About three hours. We could leave Saturday morning and come back Sunday afternoon."

"Overnight?"

Scott was ready. "I have two tents and all the equipment we'll need to set up separate households. We'll have a steak on a stick for supper, and I make great campfire coffee in the morning. Of course, Nicky wanted you to come, too."

"Oh, Nicky is going to chaperone?"

"Yes. He's an excellent watchdog."

"Who is he going to protect? Me or you?"

"You'll have to ask him."

Kay paused. "I'll let you know tomorrow night."

After he finished eating, Scott went to the garage and sorted through his camping gear. He stored all his camping paraphernalia on large, plastic storage racks against the back wall of the garage. Each rack had a dedicated purpose: sleeping bags, cooking gear, air mattresses, backpacks. He'd been in the woods enough to know what was essential. Too many times he'd been miles from home and realized that he needed an item he didn't have. Those moments made an indelible imprint on his memory, and he never made the same mistake twice.

One of his tents was a very lightweight two-person dome with a green rain fly. The other was an even lighter stargazer model with sides made of an almost invisible screen mesh. It was like sleeping under an open heaven without having to worry about being carried away by mosquitoes. If a midnight rainstorm threatened, he could lower waterproof flaps in a matter of seconds. He decided Kay would prefer the privacy of the dome tent, and he could commune with infinity from the stargazer.

34

Who may ascend the hill of the Lord?
Who may stand in his holy place?
PSALM 24:3

L ester Garrison didn't want to go to school. He rolled over in bed and stared at the faded yellow wall of his bedroom. The dingy room was cramped, and the bare bulb in the ceiling produced an unrelenting glare that attracted moths at night through holes in the screened window. The moth invasion was worse in the summer, but even at this time of year a few large specimens swirled around like tiny bats when he got ready for bed. But for all its faults, the room was home, and it was safe.

"Lester!" his grandmother called. "Are you up yet?"

In her sightless world, Thelma Garrison less and less lived by the sun. She often slept during the day and roamed the house in the night. She might have been awake for hours listening to the radio.

"Yeah," he answered.

He shut his eyes in an effort to lose consciousness, but it was no use. His mind was in gear, and he couldn't go back to sleep. He got up and put on a faded pair of blue jeans and an old T-shirt.

"Did you take a shower?" Thelma called when she heard him in the kitchen. "I didn't hear the water running."

"I took one last night," Lester lied. He poured a glass of orange juice and opened the door to the front porch. Jack was waiting for him.

Lester put on a brown jacket and sat down on the top step. Jack lay down on the step below his master's feet and lay his head on his paws. Harold Garrison had called the truck terminal as soon as they arrived home from the courthouse and caught a load to Louisville before sunset. Lester was working in the shed when his father left without saying good-bye. In the morning light, Lester looked at his old truck and again considered his options. He could be halfway across the country before anyone would miss him. Jack would love it.

He finished his juice and went inside to his bedroom. He opened the door to his closet and took out the old boot where he kept his money. It was gone. He quickly checked the other boot. It was empty. He tore through his closet looking for the dirty sock.

"Grandma!" he yelled. "Has anyone been in here?"

Thelma shuffled down the hall until she stopped at his door. "I think your father was in there yesterday. What happened?"

Lester swore. "He stole my money!"

"He wouldn't do that."

Lester held up the boot. "I kept it in this boot. Did you see—" He stopped and stormed out of the house.

He was still steaming when he arrived at school. He skidded into a parking space and slammed the door of his truck. The bell for the start of the first class of the day sounded, and he went to his locker to get his books. He jerked open the door. A G.I. Joe doll with tiny tattoos drawn on its arms was hanging from a hook with a rope around its neck. A note pinned to the chest read, "Lester Garrison - RIP." He jerked the doll from the hook. When he did, its head popped off.

He stared at the headless figure. There were people at Catawba High School who would regret they'd ever heard the name Lester Garrison. He didn't need any money to make that happen.

———

During his midmorning break, Tao took the yearbook to the break room and fixed a cup of hot tea. Sitting alone at a table, he studied the book that was one of his main windows to America. Flipping the pages, he'd memorized many of the scenes, and even though he couldn't read the captions, the pictures often told a story that was easy to understand.

Tao had immediately recognized the purpose for the floats built for the homecoming parade. They were similar to the ornate objects used in pagan festivals in Southeast Asia. Every float in the yearbook featured various depictions of the local god of the high school—a feline creature somewhat smaller than a lion. Other than in pictures, Tao had never seen the school mascot, a catamount, and he wondered where the animals lived in the midst of the cars and subdivisions of Blanchard County.

There were photographs of students riding on the floats with their bodies painted in the school colors and symbols. Boys decorated their chests with giant cat paws; girls made intricate drawings on their faces that included long whiskers. From the appearance of the leaves on the trees in the photographs, the festival took place in the fall.

Other pictures were more puzzling to him. In several photographs, a group of male students were dressed like the girls who performed tumbling routines at the sporting events. Instead of showing shame at their loss of face and embarrassment for dressing like women, the boys appeared ridiculously happy. Tao could find no cause for joy in what he saw.

Although he used the yearbook to learn about life in an American high school, Tao stayed true to the reason he'd retrieved the volume from the trash can in the first place. God had spoken to him, and the book was a tool the Heavenly Father used to speak to his servant. God loved people, whether they were pagan Hmong who walked in fear of the spirits of rocks, trees, and rivers in the Laotian mountains or American teenagers worshiping a different set of idols in a small town in North Carolina. So as he scanned the pages of the yearbook, Tao kept his heart open for divine direction and cut out the pictures of students and teachers who needed special attention in prayer. He'd carry a couple of the photos in his pocket and glance at them during the day, seeking the Lord's specific direction and influence for each person. He didn't try to remember names—that would have been too difficult, but he would try to connect faces in the crowded hallways with the photographs in the book. Time after time, he would see one of the students whose image was close to his heart and smile. No one ever noticed. Pictures of several members of the Tuesday group that met in the cafeteria spent days riding in Tao's shirt pocket as he performed his job. Others were selected for no other reason than a gentle nudge of the Spirit. Living in the unseen world of God's reality, Tao didn't rely upon what he saw with his eyes or knew with his mind.

Several members of the Tuesday group had noticed a change in their meetings over the past few weeks. It isn't easy to focus attention for prayer in the midst of a crowded high-school cafeteria, and because they ate while they prayed, there was an inherent casualness about the sessions around the table. This wasn't bad. One of the beliefs of those who started the group was that communication with God is not limited to dimly lit sanctuaries on Sunday mornings at 11 A.M. Jesus Christ is Lord of the whole earth, and his children are commanded to pray without ceasing no matter where they are. Nevertheless, a natural result of the group's location was disruption from the surrounding environment. The students at the table tried to concentrate; however, at times they would be distracted by what was happening in other parts of the room.

But not now.

Janie, Alisha, and several others noticed the change. They found themselves staying longer and eating less. The noises of the cafeteria were still present, but an awareness of a Presence greater than the distractions of their world made it easier to remain spiritually focused. It was as if an invisible curtain had been cast around the table, and those who passed through it entered into the inner court of another realm. The students prayed the same words as before, but the faith to believe that God would answer increased. At times Janie felt glued to her chair, held by an unseen hand that firmly let her know that she was on duty before the throne of heaven. Alisha found herself on the verge of tears.

Each Tuesday, Tao stood watch while the students prayed.

Today, he saw the shimmering veil that encircled the table. He opened his eyes wide with amazement. The barrier didn't appear as a solid piece of cloth but glistened like the thinnest of waterfalls—an intentional mist. It looked so wet and real that he glanced down to see if there was moisture collecting on the floor. He stepped closer. The floor was dry. There was no need to get a mop.

"Father, bring every person in this school to yourself," Janie said. "We offer ourselves to you. Use our lives in any way you want to."

A quiet chorus of "Amen's" and "That's right" circled the table.

Alisha thought about a friend who had made some terrible choices in the past few weeks, and the dam behind her eyes threatened to break.

Several others prayed a sentence or two. There were moments of silence that didn't seem awkward.

Then, a young man prayed, "Lord, do whatever it takes to bring a revival to Catawba High"—he paused—"and let it start with us."

He flipped open the Bible resting on the table beside his sandwich and read from the Psalms, "'Who may ascend the hill of the LORD? Who may stand in his holy place? He who has clean hands and a pure heart, who does not lift up his soul to an idol . . . He will receive blessing from the LORD and vindication from God his Savior.'"

He closed the book and continued, "Lord, are my hands clean? Is my heart pure? Change my life so that I can be the kind of person you really want me to be. I don't want to compare myself with others and become proud of the things I don't do. I want to be righteous in your sight because of who I have become on the inside. Break the power of sin in my life and set me free to love you and other people."

Tao saw a tiny ray of light come out of the veil and go through the heart of the young man sitting at the table. God was at work, and the fire of Tao's own desire to pray for the young people received fresh oil. Something was going to happen in this place because the students were praying. Tao didn't know what, but he wanted to be a part of it. He didn't know when, but he was certain it would happen.

35

Do not speak to a fool, for he will scorn the wisdom of your words.
PROVERBS 23:9

Kay was talking with Janie Collins and Alisha Mason while they waited for the other students to arrive for mock trial practice.

"Thanks for telling us what's been happening in your life," Janie said, her brown eyes shining. "When we heard that you were getting a divorce, we started praying for you in the group that meets in the lunchroom on Tuesday."

"To know that you have met the Lord," Alisha said. "It makes me want to laugh and cry at the same time."

Kay gave both girls a hug as Scott came through the back door of the classroom.

"Thank you," she said. "And don't stop praying."

"Thanks, Ms. Wilson, I mean Ms. Laramie," Alisha said. "We won't."

Scott stepped forward. "Where's my hug?"

Kay smiled slightly. "That would give Yvette something to talk about. We probably don't want them to think about anything except mock trial practice."

"Did I hear that you're Kay Laramie again?"

"Yes, an older and hopefully wiser return to my former name."

"It's a good name," Scott said.

"And I intend to keep it for a while."

Scott set down his briefcase.

"Before we get started, I want to mention something to the kids about the team we've drawn in the first round."

"Sure."

Frank Jesup made his entrance into the room and loudly proclaimed, "Order in the court! Did anybody hear about the case of *State v. Garrison?*" Pointing to Scott, he continued, "In this corner, Scott Ellis, Esquire, attorney for the accused, Lester Garrison, our resident redneck racist."

"That's enough, Frank," Kay said. "This is not something to joke about."

"I'm not joking," Frank responded. "It's the truth, isn't it, Mr. Ellis?"

"No comment," Scott said dryly. "I can't discuss the case because of attorney-client privilege. That's one of the first lessons a lawyer learns—to keep his mouth shut. I suggest you put it into practice immediately."

Frank made a fake bow and sat down.

Scott took out his copy of the sheet Kay had given him about the regional competition.

"The first team we'll face is from one of the expensive private schools in Charlotte. Their advisor is a lawyer who works for a big firm in the Bank of America tower. He went to Duke Law School; I went to Wake Forest. We were on opposing teams in a mock trial competition my third year in law school. It was the southeast regionals, and the winning team would advance to the national finals in Washington, D.C."

"Who won?" Yvette asked.

"Duke. But it was a controversial decision. Two of the three judges were Duke graduates and the other went to Chapel Hill. Our team had beaten UNC the previous round and that didn't make their alumni happy."

"Who cares about that stuff?" Frank asked.

Scott ignored Frank's question. "I want us to do well because it's the right thing to do, but I couldn't help thinking about the past when I saw the other lawyer's name. I'd like to beat them."

"We'll do it, coach!" Dustin called out. "Bring 'em on!"

Scott smiled. "Yeah, that's it."

Frank continued the evening in rare form, while Scott seethed about the student's opening salvo of the evening.

"Wouldn't it be better to object to the testimony by Billy Bob on the grounds that it calls for a conclusion not supported by sufficient opportunity to observe what happened?" Frank asked. "It says in the rule book that all opinion testimony must be based on facts in evidence."

"No," Scott replied. "As a lay witness, Billy Bob is not offering an expert opinion about the cause of the wreck. He's just telling what he saw."

"But it would have been impossible for him to see the vehicles before the collision. The facts state that he was getting a pack of chewing tobacco from the glove compartment."

"That goes to the weight of the evidence, not its admissibility. You should certainly cross-examine Billy Bob about his ability or inability to observe what happened. The judge or jury decides what to believe."

"Are you going to let a jury decide whether Lester Garrison should go to the chain gang?" Frank asked, then quickly added before Scott could respond, "I know, I know. Attorney-client privilege. I'll try to keep my mouth shut. Like a real lawyer."

Frank's attitude was affecting the other students, and there was tension in the circle of would-be attorneys. Janie didn't say anything. Yvette wasn't as reticent.

"Why don't you stuff it, Frank?" she said at one point after Frank had monopolized the discussion and cut her off. "This is a mock trial team, not the Frank Jesup show."

"That's a well-phrased objection," he responded. "Why don't you try it out in the competition? 'Stuff it, your honor.'"

Scott didn't interrupt. The kids needed to vent.

"She's right, Frank," Dustin said. "You don't have a clue about teamwork. You may end up being one of the best lawyers in the competition, but if our team doesn't flow together, the judges will notice it and deduct points."

"This isn't a football game," Frank retorted.

"But we still need to look out for each other," Janie added. "You've helped me a lot, and we're not your enemies. You're coming across so angry that it's going to hurt our chances."

Frank glared around the circle. Scott watched him. The young man was seemingly immune from peer influence, but Janie's comment had an effect.

Frank chose to disengage. "Whatever. We're wasting time."

They continued the session, but the situation wasn't resolved. Frank refused to contribute, and Scott decided it was Frank's way of trying to silently manipulate the other students into admitting they were wrong. It didn't work. When they realized Frank had checked out of the meeting, the remaining three members began working together. Frank became invisible.

When it was time to end the meeting, Scott turned to Frank and asked, "Could you stay for a few minutes? I'd like to talk to you."

Frank shook his head. "No, I don't have time for a lecture."

Scott didn't give up. "Not a lecture, a talk."

"It's not necessary."

The young man turned toward the door. On his way out of the room he stopped for a second to say something to Janie, then left the room alone.

Kay came over to Scott and asked, "How did it go?"

"Let's talk after the students leave."

Janie left with Alisha. When the last student filed out, Scott sat down in front of Kay's desk.

"Frank was dominating the meeting by arguing with me and cutting off the others when they tried to say something. I asked him to stay for a few minutes so we could talk. He refused and walked out of the room. His attitude stinks."

"I heard one of his other teachers give it a name the other day in the faculty lounge. She called it the 'Frank Factor.' He causes a different kind of disruption. Usually, the behavior problems in class come from students who don't know what's going on academically and cut up to pass the time. Frank already knows everything, so he harasses the teacher to entertain himself. You're a new challenge because as a lawyer you're smarter than the rest of us."

"Right," Scott said wryly. "Whatever his motivation, he's challenged the wrong person. I'm thinking about kicking him off the team. The kids made a good point. He's not a team player."

Surprised, Kay said, "That's pretty drastic. I'm not sure he's done anything to justify it. What would I tell Dr. Lassiter if Frank's father complains?"

"Tell him to call me. I'll give them an earful."

Kay shook her head. "What he said about Lester's case was wrong, but that's not enough to remove him from the program. This is a public school, and we can't pick and choose our students."

Scott leaned forward. "That's true for a math class he has to take for graduation, but belonging to the mock trial team is a privilege, not a right."

"But the response should be to help him. Have you considered trying to spend time with him after class? Not to chew him out but to say something positive."

"No," Scott admitted.

"But don't try to help him out of guilt," Kay added. "Do it because you want to. Like one of the good coaches who influenced you in school."

"I had some decent coaches and some horrible coaches."

Kay looked straight into Scott's eyes. "You're the only coach in Frank's life. What kind of coach are you going to be?"

Scott tapped his fingers on the desk. Kay was right.

"Do you remember Coach Lockhart?" he asked. "He was the defensive coach for the football team my junior and senior years."

"The bald man with the big nose?"

"Yeah. And forearms like Popeye. If a player didn't demonstrate a commitment to his teammates, he ran wind sprints after practice until he understood the concept."

Kay smiled. "Frank needs to run wind sprints."

"Yeah, something like that."

They walked outside together. It was a clear night, but the security light near the corner of the trailer kept the stars hidden. Scott took a deep breath.

"Great camping weather," he said. "When you get away from streetlights, you can see hundreds of stars."

"Don't the trees block the view?"

"Not where I'm taking you," he responded. "We'll camp in a small open field by the stream. You can count stars until you're drowsy, then go to sleep with the sound of water gurgling over rocks in your ears."

"I haven't accepted your invitation."

"Is there anything else I can say to persuade you?"

Kay smiled. "No, but we have to go as friends."

"I wouldn't want to take an enemy into the woods. That would be dangerous."

"And I'll be safe with you?"

Scott looked in her eyes. "Yes."

———

The following morning, Scott was sitting at his desk thinking about how to reach out to Frank Jesup. Swiveling in his chair, he faced his computer and typed the password for the legal research database used by the firm. The query screen popped up, and he entered the key words he wanted to research. After forty-five minutes of browsing, he'd printed fifty pages of single-spaced information from four separate articles. He stacked the sheets neatly on his desk. They should be sufficient for at least one good workout. Coach Lockhart would be proud. He called and left a message on Kay's voice mail at the school.

"I have an idea about Frank Jesup. Ask him to come thirty minutes early to the meeting tomorrow night."

When Scott arrived, Frank was waiting. The student was coolly congenial. Kay made an excuse to leave the trailer.

"I located some articles from legal journals about serving as lead counsel in complex litigation," Scott said. "When there is more than one lawyer in a case, it takes coordination to take advantage of the differences in skills and aptitudes of the people involved. Our case isn't particularly complex, but I'd like you to look them over and give me your ideas about implementing some of the suggestions for the lawyers on the team."

"Are they going to read the articles, too?" Frank asked.

"No," Scott said simply.

He didn't want to flatter Frank, just inform him.

"Write down your thoughts, so you and I can discuss it."

Frank didn't protest. "Okay."

Scott had thought Frank would put up more of a fight. He was suddenly at a loss for words and looked questioningly at the young man. In the constant activity of the mock trial practices, Scott had never really thought of Frank except as an intelligent student with a sarcastic mouth. He now saw him as a seventeen-year-old boy whose parents were splitting up. For all Scott knew, Frank blamed himself for his family's problems.

"How are you doing?" he asked more softly.

"What do you mean?"

"Uh, in school?"

"I make straight As."

"That's good. If you do well in college, you could go to law school."

The patronizing look returned to Frank's face. "Should that be my goal in life? To be a lawyer?"

Scott bristled. "I'm just letting you know you can be anything you want in life."

"I doubt you'd understand what I think about life. I've taken the next step beyond Darwin. It's not survival of the fittest, but choosing when and how you want to die. That's the next step in human evolution."

Frank was right. Scott didn't understand. He voiced his immediate reaction.

"That's morbid."

"No, it's mortal," Frank replied. "If you're honest about it, life is a game. My goal is to set my own rules and end it on terms of my own choosing."

"The world out there will make that hard to do. Society sets the rules."

Frank smiled, but it wasn't a happy look.

"I accept the challenge, and we'll see who wins."

Scott stood up. "Why don't you look over the articles until the others get here?"

"Okay."

While Frank read, Scott walked outside to get a breath of fresh air. Someone with more skills than he needed to help Frank Jesup.

———

When the other students arrived, they did a simulated trial of the whole case. Scott hadn't worked with the witnesses in several sessions, and he was pleased with their progress. There was a good smattering of humor, and it had the flavor of make-believe that the judges would enjoy without turning a mock trial into a mockery.

Scott looked at the clock on the back wall. The session had zipped by. "Okay," he said. "That's it."

When the room was clear, Kay turned to Scott.

"How was your time with Frank?" she asked.

Scott shook his head. "He's going to read the information I gave him, but our conversation didn't go anywhere. I don't know what's wrong with him."

"I'm sure he's upset about his parents breaking up."

"I guess, but he also has a fixation about controlling his own death."

"His death! Do you think he's suicidal?"

Scott mentally replayed what he could remember of their conversation.

"Possibly. If he were my kid, I'd have him in counseling or on medication."

Kay looked troubled. "It's always hard to decide what to do when a student is depressed. You don't want to be an alarmist, and you don't want to miss a warning that might help avoid a more serious problem."

"I don't know about Frank," Scott replied. "Would it do any good to contact one of his parents?"

"Only if they see a problem, too. If they don't believe there is a problem, they resent the suggestion. A lot of parents know their child needs help, but it takes a confirmation from someone like a teacher to get the ball rolling."

"I'd say Frank is already a loose cannon," Scott said.

"I'll think about it."

They walked outside together. When they reached the bottom of the steps, Scott said, "Before you leave, I have something for you to read."

"Do I need my red pen?" Kay asked.

"No."

Scott returned from his vehicle with a sheet of paper.

"How does this sound? 'I think that I shall never see a poem lovely as a tree.'"

"That's taken."

Scott handed her the paper. "Okay, then something more practical. It's a list of stuff you might want to bring on the camping trip."

She read it over and said, "It's fine as far as it goes."

"What do you mean?"

"There are other things I need to take."

"Remember we're carrying everything on our backs," Scott warned. "It's only one night, and we don't want to take unnecessary stuff."

"I know." She patted his arm. "But you're strong."

36

When you come to a fork in the road, take it.
YOGI BERRA

Scott went downstairs to Mr. Humphrey's office.

"It's Friday, and I haven't heard from Lester or Harold Garrison," he said. "What do you think I should do about cousin Kendall?"

Mr. Humphrey leaned back in his chair.

"Let's talk about your options."

Scott held up one finger. "I could do nothing and try the case on the theory that the wrong person is on trial."

"Were you happy with that approach before you found out about Kendall?"

"Mostly. It fits with the testimony from the other witnesses and keeps Lester from committing perjury." He held up a second finger. "Two, I can try to locate Kendall without the help of my client and find out what I can from him or about him. If he is willing to confess to the crime, Lester is off the hook."

"How would you convince him to do that?"

Scott held up his fist. "Would this work?"

"Let's eliminate coercion as a method of investigation."

Scott continued, "I could uncover something about Kendall that would convince Lester to tell the truth about his cousin's involvement. If this information is corroborated, it might even convince the D.A. to drop the case without going to trial."

"Would you be happy with that result?"

Scott wanted to try the case, but he knew a voluntary dismissal was the best immediate solution for Lester.

"Yes. Lester goes free, and I can come back to the office to work on commercial leases for Mr. Jackson. Everybody is happy except Kendall and me."

"Any other options?"

Scott thought a moment. "I contact Kendall. He calls the Garrisons. They get mad at me for violating their instructions to leave him out of the case."

"Do you have to limit your investigation if that's what your client wants?"

"Yes. My job is to zealously represent my client, but that can be modified if he doesn't want the help. People on death row drop their appeals all the time."

Mr. Humphrey raised his left eyebrow. "Have you considered any other reasons why the Garrisons do not want you to contact Kendall?"

Suddenly, it hit Scott. "They're afraid of him."

Mr. Humphrey nodded. "Harold is an overweight truckdriver, and Lester is a skinny teenager. All we know about Kendall is that he has dark hair. He could be a very dangerous individual."

Scott nodded. "So, I stay with option one."

Mr. Humphrey shook his head. "No, you try to find out everything you can about Kendall without revealing the reason for your interest. Then we'll decide what to do next."

———

Early Saturday morning, Scott laid two backpacks and small piles of other camping paraphernalia on the floor of the living room. A curious Nicky walked around sniffing everything. Scott's hands had touched everything, but there were other scents of unknown origin that the little dog couldn't identify—wild smells more earthy than the occasional whiff of rabbit or squirrel he'd get in the backyard. "We're going camping," Scott said. "With Kay. Do you remember her?" Nicky's tail curled in a natural question mark as he wagged it.

"I'll probably do some fishing, too."

Scott went outside and returned in a few moments with a slender fiberglass rod. He set it down on the floor for Nicky's inspection. The little dog started at the bottom and followed his nose up to the tip of the rod. The smells at the end of the stick were very strong. Nicky barked.

"That's right. Trout. If I could train you to smell rainbow trout in the water and tell me where to fish, we'd become famous. Scott Ellis and his fish-finding dog, Nicky."

It was a foggy morning. Scott loaded everything in the back of his SUV, then phoned Kay to make sure she was awake.

"For minutes and minutes," she answered with a yawn.

"Are you ready?"

"Yes, my steamer trunk is packed."

"Okay, we're leaving now."

Scott opened the door and looked down at Nicky. "Let's go for a ride."

Ride was a word Nicky understood, and he shot out of the house and jumped in the front seat of the vehicle. Panting with excitement, the little dog pressed his wet nose against the glass of the passenger window.

It was a cool morning, and Scott was wearing a lightweight jacket over a T-shirt decorated with a picture of a man fishing in a stream and the words *A Perfect Day*. Anticipating an increase in temperature once they started hiking, he had put on khaki shorts with multiple pockets for odds and ends. He mentally went down his list of items for the trip during the short drive to Kay's apartment. He didn't let Nicky get out at the apartment complex, and the little dog barked at Scott's back as his master walked up the steps to Kay's apartment.

Kay opened the door. She was wearing shorts the same color as Scott's and had slipped on a warm jacket against the chill of the morning. In her right hand she held a yellow pillowcase stuffed with unknown items having odd shapes and corners.

"What's in there?" Scott asked.

"The things I need that weren't on your list. I thought I could empty it at the campsite and stuff it with clothes for a pillow."

"Good idea," Scott said. "How heavy is it?"

She passed it to him, and he weighed it in his hand.

"Not too bad. Do you want me to carry it in my backpack?"

Kay shook her head. "No, I'll carry my fair share."

"Okay, we'll distribute everything once we reach the beginning of the trail."

Nicky's whole body shook with excitement when Scott returned. Kay sat down in the passenger seat, and the dog quickly licked her chin before Scott ordered him to the backseat. Nicky stayed put until they turned onto the main highway, then slowly worked his way into Kay's lap. Scott saw him out of the corner of his eye.

"If he bothers you, let me know."

Kay gently stroked the fur behind Nicky's neck.

"He's fine."

They picked up speed and left the Catawba city limits heading west. The fog wrapped around the trees alongside the road like a white skirt.

Kay ran her finger down Nicky's back.

"You sure are white," she said.

Scott glanced down at his own stocky legs then looked at Kay. Her long legs were shapely, but they hadn't seen the sunlight for over two months and were a couple of shades paler than his own.

"I don't get out in the sun except in the summertime," he said. "You're pretty white yourself. The lights in your classroom don't double as a tanning bed."

Kay laughed. "I was talking about Nicky, not you."

"Oh. Nicky's legs are not only white, they're extremely hairy."

"Furry."

The fog lingered for another thirty minutes. They stopped and bought two coffees at a country store. Kay didn't want anything to eat, but Scott ordered a pair of sausage biscuits. He quickly ate both of them except for a morsel he passed to Nicky.

They stayed on two-lane roads that began to climb upward as they neared the mountains. Along the way, they passed modest farmhouses, fields plowed under for the coming winter, a few scattered cattle, and thickening forests. Nicky fell asleep in Kay's lap as the sound of the wheels on the road droned on and on, and Scott felt the stress and tension drain out of his body as the miles slipped behind them. He loved the mountains. They had always been therapeutic for him, but he'd always gone alone or with male friends. He wondered how the inclusion of Kay would affect the solitude he enjoyed there.

The road began to twist and turn as it ascended higher. They had to slow down as the asphalt switched back and forth. A rain shower had fallen the previous night, and there were still tiny pools of water on the leaves that stretched over the roadway. The slightest breeze caused these pockets of moisture to fall, and several hit the windshield with a plop. Scott turned on the windshield wipers for a few seconds.

"Is it going to rain?" Kay asked.

"That was last night," Scott said confidently. "It will be clear for the next twenty-four hours. Cool in the morning but warming up during the day."

It was 10:30 A.M. when they reached a country crossroads and a small store that advertised live bait and fishing tackle. Scott stopped at the intersection.

"Would you like to fish when we reach the stream? I brought an extra rod and reel, but you'll need a license."

"No, I'd rather relax. Fishing sounds like work."

A few miles beyond the store, Scott turned onto a gravel road that was the last leg of their journey to the trailhead. Nicky raised his head at the change in sound, then dropped it back to Kay's leg when he realized that it didn't mean they were going to stop. Scott flipped the switch that engaged the four-wheel-drive feature of the vehicle. After bounding along for another twenty minutes, he suddenly pulled into a tiny parking area. An old blue pickup and a new Mercedes were parked next to each other. He pulled in beside the truck.

"This is it," he said. "The trail begins on the other side of the big oak tree."

"How do people find places like this?" Kay asked.

Scott pointed to the pickup truck. "I'd guess the man driving the truck has been coming here since he was a little boy." Turning toward the Mercedes, he added, "The fellow with the fancy car probably found out about it on the Internet."

Scott let Nicky run around while he organized their backpacks. He'd left plenty of room in Kay's pack and positioned the pillowcase in a protected place. He could easily pick up her load with one hand, but he knew it would get heavier in a hurry. His own backpack contained all the cooking gear, the tents, and several pieces of equipment that didn't weigh much individually but added considerable weight when put together.

"Ready?" he asked.

Kay had been exploring the edge of the clearing with Nicky. She grabbed Scott's backpack and started to pick it up. It didn't budge.

"I'll pass on this one," she said. "It's full of bricks."

"Only the necessary items to guarantee a pleasant stay in the wilderness."

Scott lifted the other pack and held it until Kay slipped her arms through the straps.

"How does this feel?" he asked.

She took a few steps. "Fine. It may be a little off balance to the right."

Scott made a few adjustments. Kay took a few more steps.

"That's better."

Scott put on a black Appalachian State University cap with a mountaineer's silhouette in the shape of Grandfather Mountain across the front. He took a camera from a pocket on the side of his pack and set it down on a tree stump.

"What are you doing?" Kay asked.

"Tradition. I always take a picture before starting out and when I get back to the parking area. I'll get into my pack and set the timer on the camera. Hold Nicky so he'll be in the picture."

Scott's pack was so heavy that he had to lumber over to the camera, push the button, and walk slowly back to Kay. Nicky was squirming at the confinement in Kay's arms, but she held on to him until the red signal light flashed and the camera clicked.

"Okay," Scott said. "We're off. Get ready for some aerobic exercise."

The trail was three feet wide. Scott had picked it because it offered scenic leaf viewing, a mountaintop vista, and the excellent camping spots beside a clear, rocky stream. The temperature was comfortable when they were standing in the parking lot, and the air was cooler under the trees that covered the trail. However, the weight of the backpacks quickly caused them to get warm once they started walking. After less than half a mile, Kay stopped and took off her jacket.

The path wound gently uphill for the first mile. Because he constantly zigzagged back and forth to investigate the fringes of the trail, Nicky walked twice as far as Scott and Kay. When he began to tire, he stayed closer to Scott's side. The gentle grade was followed by a steeper section that culminated in a sharp ascent with multiple switchbacks that left everyone panting at the top of a ridge line.

"Water break," Scott said, huffing.

They slipped off their backpacks. Scott had brought a tiny dish, and setting it on a level spot, he filled it with water for a grateful Nicky. The little dog stuck his whole nose in it.

Kay wiped her forehead with a blue bandanna. She pressed her fingers to the side of her neck.

"Is something wrong?" Scott asked.

"Checking my pulse. When you said this would be aerobic, you weren't kidding. I think that last climb elevated my heart rate into the red zone. Are you okay? Your pack weighs a ton."

"The first fifteen minutes are the worst. Then I get used to the weight and enjoy the exertion. There is one more steep place, then the rest of the trail is downhill to the stream."

They both took several long drinks of water.

"Are you ready for something beautiful?" Scott asked.

"Yes, let's get going." Kay started to pick up her pack.

"Not yet. We'll leave our stuff here and take a short detour. Bring your water bottle."

"Will everything else be okay?"

"I'm taking the camera. Most thieves aren't willing to hike this far into the woods to carry anything out."

Refreshed by the water, they walked a few feet down a side trail that turned sharply right on a narrow path. They followed this new trail for a couple hundred yards, until it curved around a massive tree. Beyond the tree was a narrow promontory that ended in an overlook and several large boulders whose tops were exposed to the sunlight. As far as they could see, the hills stretched out at their feet. Higher mountains could be seen in the hazy distance. Everywhere, reds, yellows, oranges, browns, and a few stubborn greens were displayed on nature's canvas.

Kay stopped. "You're right. It's beautiful."

In the open air of the overlook, the breeze that perennially brushed the mountaintops quickly cooled their cheeks. Nicky lay down on a rock. Scott sat beside him. Kay moved away and found her own rock. She gazed in silence at the colors, then leaned back and looked at the sky. The clouds were fluffy and didn't harbor the threat of rain.

They stayed for forty-five minutes. Scott had seen people come to the overlook, spit into the valley below, and go on their way. He liked to climb mountains, but he enjoyed the view at the top even more. It was a moment to savor. Today, for the first time in his life he realized it was better when shared with someone else. Nicky fell asleep, and Scott moved gingerly across the boulders to Kay.

"May I share your rock?" he asked.

Kay scooted to the side, and they gazed at the same view for several moments.

"You're doing okay, aren't you?" he asked.

Kay nodded. "Better than okay."

Scott resisted the urge to cross-examine her. He'd thought that one purpose for the trip would be to keep her from getting depressed over the events of the past week, but during the drive to the mountains, he realized that, for whatever reason, Kay was living in a place of peace where depression didn't seem to have a key.

"It has to do with Jesus," she said, "but I don't want to lose what's happening by talking about it."

"Then don't."

Kay sat for a moment, then patted the boulder on which they sat.

"No, it's like this rock. If I can't talk about it, it's not real. Ever since the divorce hearing on Monday, I've been spending time alone at my apartment, thinking, reading, listening, writing."

"Singing?"

"Not this time. But every night the reality of God's love for me and my love for him has been so real. At times I'm overwhelmed. Instead of feeling abandoned and rejected, I've felt accepted and secure. Somehow the empty place in me that Jake could never fill has been satisfied."

"I'm glad you're not hurting. You've been through a lot you didn't deserve."

"I'm not sure what I deserve, but I'm grateful for what I've been given. It has changed my life."

A stronger breeze blew over them, then subsided. Kay turned her face toward his.

"Scott, what are you afraid of?"

Scott looked down into the valley. "Falling off this rock."

"No, I'm serious. I think everyone is afraid of something. As long as I can remember, I've been afraid of being alone. That's why it's been so important for the emptiness inside me to be filled. Otherwise, the thought of being by myself would be more than I could stand."

Scott raised his eyes and looked across to the farthest range of blue hills at the edge of the horizon. He knew Kay would only be satisfied with the truth.

"I like being alone, so we're different in what we fear."

He glanced at the silhouette of her face. They were different in a lot of ways.

"I haven't thought a lot about it, but I guess I'm afraid of making a mistake. That's why the situation with Steve Robinson bothered me so much. Of course, the same thing works in other parts of my life."

"Is that why you never married?"

Scott scooted up on the rock and decided to be totally honest.

"Yes. I've had several relationships, but they only went so far. I've been afraid of making a mistake and ending up—" He stopped.

"Divorced like me?"

Scott didn't respond.

"Go ahead. I know you weren't talking about me. I want to know what you think."

Scott spoke slowly. "I know there is a risk in every relationship, especially in marriage. Someone told me that without risk there is no reward, but I haven't met anyone who seemed worth the risk. Maybe I'm too picky; maybe I'm bound by fear of failure. It just hasn't happened."

Kay let his words soak in.

"Okay, I understand. I've had another fear that's also gone—the fear of death. Jake made fun of me, but I had trouble watching movies where a lot of people died. Sometimes I thought a cold might be lung cancer. It wasn't a constant thing, but every so often I'd struggle with irrational thoughts of death."

"When did it stop?"

"Over the past few weeks, I've changed my thinking about death. It's not something to seek, but it's not something to fear. My future is in God's hands, and whether it's short or long, I'll be okay. I know it sounds crazy, but I can honestly say that I could die tomorrow without regret because I trust so totally in God's love. Nothing else has ever been so real."

Scott immediately thought of Frank Jesup's comments about ending life on his terms and started to challenge her but cut off the words before they escaped his lips. Kay wasn't thinking about self-control over death but confidence in something or someone who controlled her destiny.

"Okay, I can accept that, but don't die now. You haven't seen the stream, and I don't want to carry your backpack."

Kay smiled. Scott held out his hand and helped her stand up.

"There's more to see down the trail. Let's get going before we stiffen up."

No one had disturbed their backpacks, and they were soon on their way along the ridge line. Ridge running was pleasant because of the vistas that occasionally opened up when the trees thinned out on the sides of the trail. Eventually the path veered off the ridge and they began to climb down into a valley.

"Going down is easier than climbing up," Kay said. "Will we have to climb this hill when we hike out tomorrow?"

Scott was walking ahead of her down the trail and looked over his shoulder.

"There is only one way in and one way out, but tomorrow we won't have any food to carry with us."

"Am I hauling the food?"

"Part of it."

"I promise to clean my plate. How much farther to our campsite?"

"We'll come alongside the stream in a few minutes. The trail follows the stream to the spot I'm thinking about. It's about another hour or so."

The air was stuffier as they left the higher elevations, but it became cooler when they made their first contact with the stream. The water flowed rapidly across rocks worn smooth by the constant friction. Nicky ran forward and began lapping the cool water that was inches deep at the bank and no more than three or four feet deep in the middle.

"Nicky's braver than me," Scott said. "We'll drink bottled water until I can purify some later."

"Is it this shallow everywhere?"

"Mostly. It's deeper than it looks because the water is clear, but I doubt there's a place for miles where it's over my head."

The trail hugged the creek bank for another hour of walking. They passed several clearings that looked like good campsites to Kay, but Scott kept on going.

"I was here several times when I was in college. The place ahead is worth the extra walking."

Finally, they came to a larger clearing where the stream took a leisurely turn. In the bend was the deepest pool they'd encountered. Upstream from the deep pool were some crisp rapids, followed by a smaller pool and a ten-foot waterfall.

Kay stopped and surveyed the scene. "This has got to be it."

Scott smiled. "Welcome to Branham's field."

37

To your tents, O Israel!
1 KINGS 12:16

Kay slipped off her backpack and let it drop to the ground with a thud.

"I hope there wasn't anything in there that would break."

"Only my grandmother's china for our supper tonight. Drink some water and relax while I set up our campsite." Scott sat down against a tree and eased out of his backpack so that it remained upright.

"You don't need my help?"

"Nope. You've done all the aerobic activity scheduled for the morning and afternoon sessions."

Scott opened the tops of the backpacks, and in less than fifteen minutes he had pitched both tents so that they faced the stream. Kay sat on a big log, drinking some water and watching.

"Which one do you want?" he asked when he finished.

"The igloo," she answered. "Or whatever you call it."

"The dome. Eskimos don't try to backpack with igloos."

Scott pointed to the stream. "If you're thinking about igloos, you need to cool off."

While Scott continued organizing the campsite, Kay walked over to the water. There were gentle ankle-deep rapids close to the bank. Taking off her shoes and socks, she put one of her aching feet in the water. It was cold. She took a few steps farther into the stream until the water came up to her knees. The rushing flow washed away her fatigue.

Turning toward Scott, she called out, "This is wonderful!"

She took another step, slipped on a rock, and fell, soaking her shorts.

Scott turned when he heard her scream. Nicky barked and came running to the bank. Kay was struggling to her feet.

"Are you all right?"

"Yes. I didn't realize how fast I could lose my footing. Did you see me fall?"

"No, but every fish within a couple of hundred yards is talking about it. Nicky will drag you out if you fall in again."

Kay took a few cautious steps to a large rock that protruded out of the water and sat down. She soaked a red bandanna in white foam that bubbled around the boulder and rubbed it around her neck and against her face.

Finished with his preliminary work at the campsite, Scott walked to the edge of the stream and took off his shoes and socks. He took small steps into the water.

"The rocks with moss are safe," he said. "The ones without any growth on them are the worst." He shifted his weight to avoid losing his balance. "It feels good, doesn't it?"

"Yeah. Except the bruise where I fell."

Scott reached Kay and handed her a granola bar.

"I thought you might want a snack."

Kay ate while Scott continued moving slowly along the stream. Every so often he would stoop down and pick up a rock and inspect it.

"What are you doing?" she asked.

"Looking for gold nuggets."

"Did they pan for gold in this stream?"

"No, but I've always thought they should have."

"If you find one, I get half of the profits," Kay demanded.

He stood up and looked at her. "Why?"

"I carried in one of the backpacks, and I don't make much money as a teacher."

Scott nodded. "Okay. Two good reasons."

In a few minutes Kay's shorts had dried in the warm afternoon sun that shone through the trees. Scott held her hand as she navigated her way back to shore.

"What next?" she asked.

Scott looked at the sky. "We don't have a schedule, except that we eat when we're hungry and sleep when the campfire goes out. I'd like to do some fishing. You can watch or stay here and rest."

"I'll watch."

Scott had brought an ultralight fishing pole that came apart into four pieces. It was so thin that it almost disappeared when he stood in front of the trees along the bank. He decided to try the pool near the camp-site before venturing farther upstream.

Using a small metal lure shaped like the bowl of a baby's spoon with a hook underneath it, he cast across the pool and slowly dragged the lure along the bottom of the stream. On the first cast he had a strike. The pole bent double and a fat ten-inch rainbow trout jumped once into view above the surface of the water before Scott brought it to the bank. Nicky went crazy with excitement. Wetting his hand so that the mucous on the fish's sleek body wouldn't be disturbed by his touch, Scott held it so that Nicky could sniff it from tail to gill, then released it back into the water.

"That would have been good in a skillet," he said. "But we have steak tonight."

He pulled two more fish from the pool before they stopped biting. He moved to a smaller pool that churned and bubbled at the base of the waterfall.

Pointing to the white foam, he said, "Fish will wait for dinner to come over the falls."

On his first cast, Scott's lure was sucked under and caught on a rock. He lost it when he pulled the line free. He tried a different one, but lost it in the same spot. Kay watched him patiently tie on a third lure.

"Aren't you upset?" she asked.

Concentrating on the knot, he didn't look up. "About losing the lures? It's part of the process. I've left a lot of dollars in these streams."

He avoided the fishing lure graveyard and hooked the biggest fish yet, a fourteen-inch rainbow that made a short run away from the pool before Scott reeled it in. It was a magnificent trout. After losing another lure without any more bites, they moved to a different place. The after-noon passed at a leisurely pace as they slowly moved down the stream.

Scott only caught one more fish, a tiny fingerling. He threatened to feed it to Nicky, until Kay told him that the baby's mother would go to her watery grave in grief if he didn't release it.

The sun was behind the tops of the trees when they returned to their campsite. Zipping open one of the side pockets of his backpack, Scott took out a small plastic bottle containing a green liquid. He handed it to Kay.

"If you'd like to clean up in the stream, use this. It's biodegradable. It does a great job on pots and pans and leaves your hair silky and manageable. Don't use too much; it's very concentrated."

Kay looked at the bottle skeptically before handing it back to him. "You use it to scrub pots and pans?"

"And me."

Scott walked to the stream, took off his shirt, and stepped into the deep pool until the water came up to his waist. He poured a few drops of the cleaner in his hand, held it up for Kay to see, and lathered his upper torso. The soap covered the scar on his left shoulder and a few more drops finished off his neck, face, and hair. After dunking himself in the water a few times, he waded out and dried himself with a sport towel.

"Very refreshing," he said. "How does my hair look?"

"Not very silky."

"After you."

"Okay. But if I want to get baptized, I'm going to wait until Bishop Moore can arrange it properly."

She took the soap and went to the edge of the water where she carefully washed her arms, face, and legs without getting in deeper than a few inches.

Scott started a fire with dead limbs and twigs. In a few minutes, the wood was crackling and a narrow column of white smoke was rising from the forest floor. Kay rejoined him.

"How was the bath?" he asked.

"Okay, but it could have been warmer. You don't want to heat a few gallons of water for me, do you?"

Scott smiled. "I forgot the bathtub. It would have made my backpack too heavy. They make special plastic bag containers that can be filled with water and hung from a tree during the day. The sun's rays heat up the water, and someone can take a short shower before going to bed in the evening. I've never used one because I enjoy the stream. It's part of the experience."

Some previous campers had dragged logs to the edge of the fire ring. Kay sat down while Scott built the fire. The sun was below the horizon. The woods across the stream were already dark, but a few diffuse rays of twilight still reached the little clearing. The fire created a circle of light that included the logs and the backs of the tents.

Scott stood up. "Ready for supper?"

"I'm starving."

Scott went to Kay's backpack and retrieved a lunch-size collapsible cooler. Inside were several cubes of steak and four ears of corn that he'd shucked and wrapped in aluminum foil. He positioned the ears around the edges of the fire. After putting a piece of steak on the end of a sharp stick, he handed it to Kay.

"This is like the fancy restaurants where you cook your own food at the table. Be careful to cook the steak and not your stick. There's nothing worse than the end of the stick falling in the fire just before the meat is done."

Kay held the meat high over the top of the flame.

"Not that high," Scott corrected. "Here, I'll show you."

He sat next to her on the log and, putting his hand over hers, held the stick the proper distance from the hot coals located a few inches away from the center of the fire. Nicky was sniffing the air at the smell of the meat. Scott let his hand stay over Kay's a few seconds longer than necessary.

"I've got it," she said.

Scott withdrew his hand and stuck a slightly larger piece of steak on another stick and sat across from her on another log. In a few minutes the meat was sizzling.

"Is it ready?" Kay asked.

"How rare do you like it?"

"With the moo still in it. Light brown on the outside with a cold, red center."

Scott was surprised. He let his meat drop too close to the fire and his stick began to smolder.

"Are you serious?"

"No, but it sounded like the thing to say out here in the middle of the woods. I'm trying to be rough and tough. Medium would be nice."

After experimenting with their first two pieces of meat, they perfected the art of cooking cubes of New York strip over an open fire. They ate the corn when it was properly roasted and the melted butter had soaked into the kernels and turned slightly brown. Nicky feasted on tidbits of steak from both of them. They drank purified stream water that matched the best Chablis.

For dessert, Scott pulled out a few marshmallows. Kay carefully roasted hers; Scott set his on fire and ate the charred remains. A slight wind picked up and blew the smoke from the fire into his eyes, so he shifted to the log beside Kay for his last three marshmallows.

Scott was feeling mellow and debated eliminating the distance between them on the log. Kay's marriage was officially over, and her availability was having a greater effect on him than he'd suspected. Their honest discussion at the overlook emboldened him to consider something more for their relationship. Friendship was fine, but the way Kay had adapted to the rigors of the camping trip made her even more attractive to his eyes. The light from the fire reflected off her hair and made her head seem ablaze with gold. Scott shifted his weight to move closer. Kay stood up and dropped her stick in the fire.

"It's done, I guess," she said. "Jake has a new wife."

The mention of Jake's name was a jolt. Scott had forgotten that Kay's ex-husband was going to remarry on Saturday.

She continued. "I thought about it a lot during the hike after we left the overlook. I know I have to go on because of the choices he made. That's hard to accept, but it's the truth, and there is nothing I can do about it."

The fact that their minds had been on such diverse tracks threw Scott off balance. If Kay was thinking about her ex-husband, she wasn't thinking about him. He'd been thinking about her and assumed that if he could read her mind, her thoughts would be written in similar language. Not so.

Kay stretched. "I'm tired. Is it okay if I go to sleep?"

"Sure, your sleeping bag is in the tent. Your pillowcase is still in your backpack."

"I'll put everything in the tent."

"Is there any food in your pack?"

"No."

"Good. A raccoon might want to join you in your tent if it smelled food."

"Anything bigger than raccoons?" Kay asked.

"No. I don't think so."

Kay picked up her almost empty backpack and put it inside the door of the tent.

"Good night," she said as she zipped up the screen door flap.

"Good night."

Scott stayed by the campfire for over an hour after the sounds of Kay trying to get comfortable gave way to silence. Nicky was asleep at his feet. The formerly white dog was a dingy brown after his day in the woods.

The sound of the water rushing over and around the rocks of the stream was joined by the scratchy calls of a few hearty katydids that slowly rubbed their legs together like a chorus of miniature chain saws. In a few weeks the frosts of early winter would still all sounds in the forest except the swirling noise caused by the never-tiring movement of the stream. If he could have blocked out the music of the water and the insects, Scott could have heard the rustle in the leaves that signaled the journey of a raccoon along the woodland floor to the far side of the stream where it discovered the remains of the apple that was Scott's afternoon snack. It was a rare find, and the raccoon happily held the core with its front paws and nibbled it down to the stem before sticking his face in the water for a wash and cold drink.

Scott stared at the few remaining red-and-orange embers of their campfire. On the other side of the fire was the dark silhouette of Kay's tent. He couldn't tell if she'd zipped up the front flap over the screen mesh or not. Probably did. A closed tent gave a false sense of security— a black bear looking for food wouldn't knock and ask permission before trying to stick his nose inside. But then, Kay's greatest enemy was not the unseen adolescent black bear prowling on the ridge a half-mile north of their campsite—the thoughts inside Scott's head were a more immediate threat.

He sat motionless, struggling with how to respond. An increasing part of him wanted to see if he could share her tent for the night. His attraction to her was already stronger than any he'd had for a woman in years, and his fear of making a mistake in love was not the uppermost thought in his mind. He listened again to the calls of the katydids, each one making as raucous a sound as possible. Scott knew their motivation. Katydids didn't sing out of vanity or the love of music. They raised their cry in the night because they desperately wanted to attract a suitor from across the clearing. But the longings of the human heart are not as simple to define as a katydid's call, and Scott didn't know what response to expect from the other side of the dying campfire.

Ever since Kay had reentered his life he'd tried not to push too far past the barrier of friendship. Intellectually, he knew that what he told Perry Dixon in the male-only atmosphere of the gym was right, and even though the legal "wall" of her marriage was down, Kay needed time to process the final ending of her relationship with Jake. However, like the katydids in the dark night, Scott saw the passage of time as an enemy. Tonight was a lost opportunity. A small piece of unburned wood on the edge of the fire flared up. Scott was a man; Kay was a beautiful woman. The close contact they'd had all day had caused desire to flame up within him. He stood up, startling Nicky who jumped awake.

But Scott didn't take a step toward Kay's tent. His code of honor reared its head and reminded him that he'd promised her safety. He didn't know whether to resent the code or be thankful for it. Maybe someday they would share a tent, but not yet. Kay's heart and his hormones were not in sync. He took a deep breath of cool night air, leaned over, and patted Nicky on the head.

"Remind me not to bring a girl dog on a camping trip," he said. "I wouldn't want to put you through the torture."

Nicky stretched out and yawned.

"Let's get in our tent."

The little dog followed his master to the tent and fell asleep with his back against Scott's feet.

Scott was up and had a small fire crackling when Kay stuck her head out into the cool morning air. Her hair was disheveled, and she blinked her eyes against the smoke that suddenly shifted in her direction. Scott was squatting beside the fire, carefully laying larger twigs into the center of the flames. He turned toward her.

"Good morning," he said. "You look beautiful."

"Right." Kay ran her hand through her hair until it got stuck in an unyielding tangle. "I'd stick my tongue out at you, but I'm afraid what might be on it."

"Some fresh coffee will take care of that. I'll have some ready in a few minutes."

Kay looked toward the stream. Mist was rising along the edge of the water.

"What time is it?"

Scott glanced toward the sky. "Daytime. Night is over. Remember, we're using a camping clock without numbers."

She yawned without covering her mouth. Her head disappeared inside the tent and the zipper went back up. Scott heard various unidentifiable sounds coming from the tent for the next few minutes and had the coffeepot close to boiling when a more orderly Kay Laramie, her hair in a ponytail, opened the door of her tent and stuck her feet outside while she put on her shoes.

"Is the hot water ready?" she asked.

"Almost."

Kay stood up and stretched her arms. "That's not enough for my bath."

"Splash your face in the stream a few times. It's so refreshing you'll forget about hot water. How do you want your coffee?"

"With lots of cream and sugar."

By the time she returned, Scott had the coffee ready. He'd lined a backpacking skillet with pieces of thick bacon and mixed a half-dozen eggs together in a large plastic cup. Kay's cheeks were pink and drops of water were dripping from the edges of her hair.

"How was it?" he asked.

"You lied. It was so cold all I could think about was hot water."

He handed her a Styrofoam cup of light brown liquid. He'd made it weak with lots of creamer from a baggie and a packet of sugar.

"Here's your coffee. Maybe that will help. Breakfast happens fast over an open fire."

He fried the bacon and wrapped it in aluminum foil to keep it warm while he scrambled the eggs. It was all done in a few minutes, and he handed a plate to Kay.

"Can I pray?" she asked.

"Sure."

Kay closed her eyes. "Father, thank you for this day and this place you've created. Thank you for Scott and the friend and protector he has been to me. And thanks for this breakfast. Amen."

Scott took a bite of egg and bacon together. It was perfect.

He swallowed and asked, "Why did you call me a protector in your prayer?"

Kay sipped her coffee. "You've been a safe man for me to be around the past few months when I could have gotten into trouble with someone else. You protected me from myself and any predatory males."

"Oh," Scott said, sheepishly remembering his internal debate of the previous night. He was a less noble knight than Kay suspected.

"I feel great this morning," she said.

Scott kept eating his eggs and bacon. He wasn't sure what he felt, but the breakfast was very good.

When they finished eating, Scott used his miracle green soap to clean the pots and pans. While he was crouching down at the edge of the water, two fishermen walked into the clearing. Nicky barked until Scott told him to be quiet. Kay was inside her tent. The men nodded to Scott and went upstream to the large pool. They cast lines across the pool and in a few minutes deposited three fish in their creels. They moved up to the smaller pool beneath the waterfall, and after each losing a lure, they left the clearing. Scott's best fish was safe for another day.

Nicky ran over to the door of Kay's tent and scratched until she zipped it open, and he hopped inside. Scott's frustration was past, and he laughed at the little dog's success. In a few minutes, they emerged. Kay was wearing a sky-blue T-shirt with a picture of a hummingbird on the front and a pair of old gray shorts.

"When will it warm up?" she asked, rubbing her arms.

Scott looked up at the sky. The sun was gaining momentum in its upward journey.

"Soon. It's going to be a clear day. Can you get those clothes wet?"

"Why? Are you going to throw me in the water?"

"No, I'm thinking ahead to the day's activities."

"Should I put on a bathing suit?"

"Yes, underneath your clothes."

Kay disappeared for a minute before reemerging. "Okay, I'm ready for anything."

"Let's go."

The top flap of Scott's backpack could be detached and used as a fanny pack. Carrying a couple of bottles of water, a few granola bars, and the camera, they took a trail that climbed steeply away from the stream, crossed a ridge, then descended back down to a place where the water rushed thirty feet down a rockface into a deep pool.

"Behold sliding rock," Scott announced grandly.

"How deep is the water at the bottom?"

"Deep enough. The danger is at the top. I've come here with friends after we've had too many beers and had problems getting off to a good start. It's not much fun going down backwards when you can't position yourself to miss that boulder on the side." He pointed to a large rock on the far side of the smooth surface.

"Ouch."

"Don't worry, I'll show you how to do it without danger."

Scott was wearing an old pair of cutoff jeans. He took off his shoes, socks, and shirt. He carefully walked into the stream until he was almost to the middle. Sitting down he scooted forward.

"This is the ideal beginning point!" he shouted.

He pushed himself forward then slid rapidly down the face of the rock into the pool. He disappeared for a second, then stood to his feet. The water came up to the middle of his chest. He shook the water from his hair and smiled. Nicky barked excitedly from the bank.

"It's brisk!"

"Are you going to do it again?" Kay asked.

Scott looked puzzled. "Anyone who takes the trouble to find this place stays until they wear a hole in their blue jeans."

He walked to the bank. There were some moss-covered rocks that made getting out less treacherous than expected. He walked up the trail to the top and repeated his slide to the bottom.

"Ready?" he asked when he reached the bank the second time.

"I guess."

Kay followed him up the path. He held her hand and guided her to the takeoff spot. It appeared higher getting ready to go down than looking up. She nervously got in position, and he gave her a gentle push. The ride was a blur, but the shock of the water at the bottom was unforgettable.

She came up screaming.

"It's freezing!"

"Only for a second!" Scott called out. "Move over, I'm coming down."

Scott lay down on his stomach and went down face first into the water.

"Don't expect me to do that," Kay said when they were standing on the bank.

"No pressure. But I bet you're hooked."

"Maybe a few more times."

They didn't stay until Scott wore a hole in his shorts, but Kay lost track of the times she zipped down the rockface and splashed into the pool. They took half a roll of pictures. When they finished, they sat on a sunny rock eating granola bars.

They returned over the hill to their campsite. Scott looked at the sky.

"It's time to start back."

Kay cleared out her tent, and Scott efficiently broke camp. He was intent on his task and didn't notice the way Kay watched him. When he finished, they put on their backpacks and retraced their steps up the trail.

Scott took the lead when the trail was narrow. They walked side by side when it broadened. Nicky, now used to the exotic smells, plodded along without bothering to use his energy exploring. The last leg of the hike was downhill, and they covered it in half the time it took them to hike up the previous day.

"Downhill is better," Kay remarked.

"I always like a trip where the last stretch is the easiest."

They returned to the parking lot where Scott took another photograph.

"I take a posthike shot to make sure I didn't lose anyone."

On the ride back to Catawba, Kay talked and talked for the first hour. She had a lot of questions about other places Scott had visited in the mountains. After they left the winding roads, her eyelids grew heavy, and she fell asleep. They were nearing Catawba when she woke up.

"Are we almost home?" she asked.

"Yes. It won't be long."

Kay closed her eyes in contentment. "Hot water!"

38

You know my methods, Watson.

SHERLOCK HOLMES

Monday morning Scott wrote the available background information about cousin Kendall on two lines at the top of a legal pad: "Kendall - cousin of Lester Garrison - from South Carolina - in Blanchard County on the date of the incident at Hall's Chapel Church - dark hair."

Scott assumed Kendall's last name might be Garrison. He did an Internet search for any Kendall Garrisons in South Carolina and came up empty. He then wondered if the name was spelled differently. He typed in Kendell Garrison and scored two hits, both in the Orangeburg, South Carolina, area. Locating the phone number for one of them, he dialed it. A lady with a distinct African-American accent answered the phone.

"I'm trying to locate Kendell Garrison," Scott said.

"Both junior and senior are at work. Do you want to leave a message?"

"No, ma'am. Thank you."

Scott hung up. The Kendell Garrisons of Orangeburg, South Carolina, didn't fit the profile. Lester's cousin had dark hair, not a dark face.

Scott tried other more unusual spellings without success. He was about to give up when he had an idea. He looked at the clock. Lester was still at school. Hopefully, Harold was out on the road. Scott dialed the Garrison's phone number. Thelma answered on the fifth ring.

"Hello," the old woman said.

In the enthusiastic voice he used when selling kitchen knives, Scott asked, "May I speak to Kendall?"

"Kendall? He don't live here."

"I'm sorry to bother you. How can I reach him?"

"At his house in Gaffney."

"Do you happen to have that number?"

"It's here someplace, but I can't see anymore. My grandson will be home later. Do you want him to call you?"

"Don't go to any trouble. That's Kendall Garrison in Gaffney?"

"Garrison? No Kendall is a Kidd."

Scott was thrown off guard. "How old is he?"

"In his early thirties, I reckon."

Scott realized his mistake. "Oh, Kendall Kidd. I'm sorry."

"Who's a-calling? I can have my—"

"Thanks."

Scott put down the receiver. He typed in Kendall Kidd in Gaffney, South Carolina, the peach capital of South Carolina. The name and address popped up. Cousin Kendall was not a figment of the Garrisons' imaginations. Scott pressed the print button.

———

During the final week of preparation for the mock trial program, the students showed Scott how serious they could be. The sessions bore no resemblance to Scott's concern in Mr. Humphrey's office that he would be stuck in a room of bored teenagers, and the young lawyer began to harbor a secret hope for something better than a mediocre result in the competition on Saturday.

Frank had read the articles Scott assigned and made an effort on Tuesday to be a leader, not a dictator, but it didn't last. Toward the end of a productive practice, Scott told the lawyers to work together while he and Kay coached the witnesses on some final points. Unsupervised, Frank ridiculed Yvette so severely that she began to cry. She tried to fight off the tears, but they squeezed their way to the surface anyway, and she ran out of the room. Scott looked up and saw her go past and suspected what had happened. Kay quickly followed Yvette out the door.

Scott jumped up and went to the corner where the four students had been sitting. Janie was also about to cry. Dustin was glaring at Frank, who was making notes on a sheet of paper as if nothing had occurred. The room was totally silent and every eye was on Scott and Frank.

"Tell me what happened," Scott said in a low, firm voice.

"She can't handle the pressure," Frank responded. "She needs to toughen up if she expects to do well on Saturday."

"No!" Dustin said, his face turning red. "You little jerk. If you do that again I'll—"

"Wait," Scott interrupted. "Janie and Dustin, go over there with the others and get back to work."

Janie got up and Dustin followed more slowly. Scott sat down next to Frank.

"What are you trying to prove?" he asked. "The competition is on Saturday, and you're trying to blow up the team."

Frank scoffed. "She'll be all right."

"You didn't answer me."

Frank narrowed his eyes. "I don't have anything to prove." He stopped suddenly.

Scott knew he had something else to say. "Go ahead. Finish."

Frank shook his head. "No."

"Do you want to stay on this team?"

Frank shrugged. "You can kick me off, but it would be a mistake."

"Why? You're hurting more than you're helping at this point."

Frank stared at Scott, who met his gaze for several seconds. There was something very dark lurking behind Frank Jesup's eyes. Scott saw it, but didn't understand what he detected. It mocked him without words and dared him to take another step. He involuntarily shivered. Frank saw the movement and knew he'd won the invisible struggle. He smiled slightly.

"Don't worry," the student said. "We'll pull together. I'll say something to Yvette."

"You'd better," Scott replied. But the words came out of his mouth without any authority.

Kay returned with Yvette, who was embarrassed at her outburst and ready to accept Frank's glib apology so that she could put the incident behind her. Scott could see in Dustin's eyes that he was less willing to forgive and go on. They finished the session without further incident. Frank gave his closing argument for the plaintiff's case in front of the whole group. No one clapped, but Scott was impressed.

The students left, and Scott dropped down in a seat in front of Kay's desk.

"I'm tired. That confrontation with Frank wiped me out."

"How did you convince him to apologize?"

"I didn't. He did it on his own."

"That's a good sign."

"I'm not so sure. Frank does things for his own reasons, and I don't think I know what is really motivating him."

"He wants to prove he's the best and the brightest. He's very competitive."

Scott remembered the look in Frank's eyes. "Maybe, but there is something else going on inside his head. Did you ever talk to his parents?"

"I've left two messages with his father, but he hasn't called back. I don't have a number for his mother."

Scott could get Vivian Jesup's phone number from the file at the office. He made a mental note to give it to Kay. He closed his briefcase, and they walked out of the classroom together.

"How are we going to do on Saturday?" she asked.

"Good. I'd especially like to do well against the team coached by my old adversary from Duke."

"Does that mean we need to win?"

Scott grinned. "Yes."

He walked Kay to her car and opened the driver's-side door.

"After our Tuesday and Thursday sessions are over, when will I see you?"

Kay's eyes met his. "I don't know. I'm going to spend most of my time with Mrs. Willston. Maybe the three of us could get together."

Scott held on to the door. "That wouldn't work. Our threesome is you, me, and Nicky."

Kay smiled. "You're probably right. I couldn't go too long without seeing Nicky. He's special."

"He feels exactly the same about you."

Driving home, Scott didn't dwell on the depths of darkness in Frank Jesup's soul. More pleasant thoughts occupied his mind.

———

The following morning, Scott reported his findings about cousin Kendall to Leland Humphrey.

"Good detective work. Are you sure Mrs. Garrison didn't recognize your voice?"

"Yes, I used my salesman voice."

"Really? Let me hear it."

"Okay, but it will cost you a $500 set of kitchen knives."

Mr. Humphrey chuckled. "I'll pass."

"What should I do next about Kendall?" Scott continued. "I thought about calling him but couldn't come up with a plan of action."

Mr. Humphrey thought for a moment. "If you don't want to talk to him, the next option is to talk to those who know him. Coworkers, family, the police."

"Police?"

"Do a criminal record check on him. If it turns up positive, the local authorities might be willing to talk with you."

"Okay."

"Are you going to meet with Lester before next Monday?" the older lawyer asked.

Scott nodded. "He is coming in on Friday. It's a review session unless something turns up with Kendall. Since there is no plan for Lester to testify, I just want to make sure he understands what is going to happen."

"Do you want me to be there?"

"No, sir. That won't be necessary. Have you looked over the new jury pool?"

Mr. Humphrey patted a thin stack of papers on the corner of his desk. "It's on my list for this afternoon. I'll dictate a memo of my recommendations."

Upstairs at his computer, Scott accessed a public-record database for South Carolina. He typed in Kendall's name and requested criminal convictions within the last ten years and didn't get a hit. Then, he realized he typed in Garrison, not Kidd. Correcting his error, he tried again. The server searched for several seconds then came to life. There was a list that ran to the bottom of the screen. Kendall had been a bad boy and a worse man.

Scott leaned closer. He quickly counted seven misdemeanors and two felonies. The misdemeanors included several drunk and disorderly convictions, two DUIs, a petty theft, and selling a stolen gun. The two felonies were more sobering: an assault with a deadly weapon charge that resulted in five years in prison followed by a serious drug charge involving cocaine. If Kendall was about thirty years old, he had spent three-fourths of the time since he was eighteen behind bars.

Several of the charges had been filed in Union County, South Carolina. Scott dialed the phone number for the sheriff's department and asked to speak to one of the detectives.

"Griffin, here," a gravel-voiced detective answered.

Scott introduced himself. "I'm interested in information about a man named Kendall Kidd. Do you know him?"

"Are you his lawyer?" the detective responded with obvious interest.

"No. I represent a juvenile in North Carolina, and Kidd's name has come up in the investigation."

"I'm interested in information about him myself," the detective replied. "There is an outstanding warrant for his arrest. We've been looking for him since the first of the month."

"What are the charges?"

"He shot up a black church outside Rock Hill. No one was killed, but he wounded a man in the leg."

Scott swallowed hard. "Was anyone else involved?"

"Unknown at this point. Kidd was picked out of a photo lineup by several people who were present at the scene. What are the facts of your case?"

"The same, only no injuries. Do you have a picture of him on file?"

"A drawerful. We photograph him every time he's arrested."

"What color hair does he have?"

"White."

"White?"

"Yeah, dyed as white as snow, but underneath it's black. I've arrested him several times since he was a juvenile. When we catch him, we're going to try him under the three strikes statute and put him away for good."

"A life sentence?"

"Without parole."

"Will you let me know if he's arrested?" Scott asked. "It may be that he should be the one charged in my case here in North Carolina. My client's going to trial on Monday, so call me anytime."

Scott gave the detective his phone number at home and the office.

"We'll catch him," the detective replied. "But maybe not in time to help you."

Scott reported his findings to Mr. Humphrey. The older lawyer was leaning back with his feet on the corner of his desk when Scott came into his office, but by the time Scott got to the information about Kendall Kidd facing a life sentence under the recidivist statute, he was sitting straight up in his chair.

"What do you think?" Scott asked when he finished.

"It's dynamite. We've just got to figure out a way to get it into evidence."

Scott nodded. "Kendall either fired the shots or encouraged Lester to do so. In either case, he's on the scene with Lester helping him break through any resistance to violating the law and jeopardizing the lives of others."

"Kendall's relationship with Lester is a lot like me and you."

"What?" Scott asked in surprise.

"Kendall is mentoring Lester in hate crimes; I'm trying to help you learn how to survive in the courtroom."

Mr. Humphrey rubbed his hands together. "I'd love to cross-examine Kendall about his prior criminal record. Of course, it would be even better if he's convicted of this latest offense. The similarity is beyond dispute."

"And the jury wouldn't have any problem accepting the argument that D.A. Davenport should be prosecuting a hardened criminal like Kendall, not an impressionable teenager like Lester. But that's a fantasy case. Kendall Kidd isn't available for cross-examination or convicted of a church shooting."

Mr. Humphrey leaned back in his chair. "Don't jerk me back to reality yet. I allow myself a few daydreams about cases. If we could write a script for the next few days, I'd recommend a scenario in which Kendall is caught speeding on his way north through Blanchard County. A routine license check turns up the outstanding warrant in South Carolina, and he's arrested. That way he'd be available for transport from our local jail on Monday morning."

Scott grunted. "Maybe in fiction. I'm still in the real world."

Scott met with Lester Garrison on Friday afternoon. He had mailed his client a copy of the jury list to review, but Lester didn't know anything about the people who would decide his fate. His father wouldn't be back in town until Sunday night.

Scott had debated several ways to bring up the Kendall Kidd issue. He decided to ease into it gently. Without Harold present, Lester might be more pliable.

"It's important that I have as much information as possible to give you the best defense," he began. "Do you remember what I told you during our first meeting at the youth detention center? I'm representing you, not anyone else."

"Yeah, and I'm not convinced that I shouldn't be a witness. People are going to wonder what I have to hide."

"Maybe you don't have anything to hide."

Lester's eyes narrowed. "What do you mean?"

Scott made an effort to sound casual. "You could testify about your cousin's involvement in the incident. It would fit with everything else you've told me about your innocence and the testimony of the other witnesses for the prosecution."

"You heard what my father said—"

Scott interrupted. "Your father isn't my client. You are. You told me Kendall fired the shots. That makes him guilty, not you."

"But won't the D.A. ask me why I didn't tell the police about Kendall when they picked me up?"

It was a good question. Lester's late decision to tell the truth would open the door to a string of questions about a self-serving motivation to blame someone else during the trial of the case. Scott had an answer ready.

"Two things. First, I'll notify the D.A. today that Kendall was the shooter and tell her that you will testify against him if he's charged and brought to trial. That way you can tell the jury you were willing to help convict the guilty person before the case began. Second, tell the jury the truth about Kendall as a person."

"What do you mean?"

Scott was blunt. "Kendall is a very dangerous man. It's obvious you didn't mention his name to the police because of what he might do to you. Lester, you are seventeen years old. People wouldn't expect you to stand up to someone like your cousin."

Lester swallowed. "I need to think about this."

"You don't have much time. If I'm going to call the D.A., it needs to be today."

Lester hesitated.

Scott played his last card. "If Kendall is convicted of another felony, he will go to prison for the rest of his life without the possibility of parole. He won't be around to cause you trouble."

"How do you know so much about him?"

Scott used words he'd heard from Lester. "I'm not stupid. I used the Internet and made a couple of phone calls."

"My father told you to drop it."

Scott shrugged. "I did what I thought was best for you."

Lester wavered. "When do I need to let you know?"

Scott looked at his watch. It was 3:45 P.M. "One hour."

Scott was sitting in Mr. Humphrey's office when the receptionist paged him. The older lawyer put the call on speakerphone, and Scott walked over to the corner of the desk.

"I'm here," Scott said. "Do I call the D.A.?"

"No. I'm not going to do it," Lester said.

Scott rolled his eyes. "But that doesn't make— "

"I talked to my father in Mississippi. He's mad at you for snooping around when we told you not to. We don't want to drag Kendall into this."

"He's already in it. You told me he fired the shots."

"Forget I said that. It was a mistake."

Scott looked at Mr. Humphrey for help. The older lawyer shook his head.

"Are you sure?" Scott asked.

"Yes."

"Okay. Be here Monday morning at 8:30. We'll walk over to the courthouse together."

"Should I wear the same clothes as before?"

Scott made a wry smile. "Yes. Your clothes were fine."

"Bye."

The phone went dead.

Before Scott could say anything, Mr. Humphrey spoke. "You can't help someone who doesn't want help. In the future you will have other clients bent on self-destruction for a variety of reasons. You can warn them and try to convince them of a better course of action, but in the end, if they want to jump off a cliff, you can't stop them."

"Right now, I'd like to give Harold a push myself. I think I had Lester talked into it."

"Maybe, but it's not going to happen. You've come full circle. We're at the same place we were before Kendall's name was mentioned. Without a doubt there's a possible pattern of crime, but even with the information you've uncovered, we still don't know the truth."

"You don't think Kendall fired the shots?"

Mr. Humphrey shrugged. When he did, both eyebrows went up.

———

The bomb had not been the work of a night; however, it hadn't been as hard as he first imagined. He was resourceful, and although there had been unexpected delays, in the end he overcame every obstacle in his path.

The field tests had been exciting. He scouted the countryside for a remote place and settled on a clearing in the middle of a huge tract of land not far from a rock quarry. Hunting wasn't allowed on the property, and there weren't any houses for over a mile in any direction.

He'd conducted two tests. No one reported anything to the police because the sound of explosions was part of everyday life in the area; however, several deer resting in a nearby thicket fled in panic when the blasts reverberated through the woods. The real bomb would be many times more powerful.

39

The man that mocks at it and sets it light.
RICHARD II, ACT 1, SCENE 3

S aturday was mock trial regional competition day, and Scott had to put the real battle of *State v. Garrison* on hold. Yvette Fisher arrived late at the high school, and the caravan left Catawba fifteen minutes behind schedule. Scott, Kay, and three parents drove the students. Dustin rode with Scott, and they talked about football. There was still a chance Catawba could make the play-offs if another team lost its final game.

"We made it my senior year but lost in the first round to A. L. Brown," Scott said.

"That's who we'll play if we make it," Dustin said. "They're not as tough this year as they have been in the past, so we'll have a chance. How badly did they beat your team?"

"They killed us. It was 42-0. The last play of the game a tiny guy who hadn't played a snap the whole season burst through the line and sacked our quarterback. It was humiliating."

They arrived at the Mecklenburg County Courthouse in Charlotte. The downtown streets were deserted. The city's focus on the weekends shifted to the suburbs, not the cluster of towers along Tryon Street. Groups of students, coaches, and parents were walking up the sidewalks to the court buildings.

Nervous students dressed in suits and nice dresses lined the long hallway outside the courtrooms. The North Carolina Academy of Trial Lawyers furnished coffee, juice, and doughnuts. Scott and Kay found a vacant area and assembled their group. Scott didn't see the lawyer from Duke.

Each team would represent the injured plaintiff in one round and the defendant driver in another. Three volunteer attorneys would sit in the jury box and grade each team's performance. The two teams that received the top point totals would meet in the championship round later in the afternoon.

"This is our base," Scott said to the assembled students. "You can leave your stuff here, and I'll watch it. We have thirty minutes until we meet in Courtroom 307. Don't eat too many doughnuts. We don't want anyone to have a sugar overload."

Most of the students scattered. Yvette walked up to Scott and Kay.

"I'm sorry about the other night," she said. "I shouldn't have had such a thin skin."

Scott wanted to say that the problem was Frank's thick head but answered, "Nothing you'll face today will be as challenging as the practices we've had at the school. The judges will be very courteous, and the students on the other side will be more nervous than you are."

"I'm pretty nervous."

"Only enough to help you do a good job. You know the problem from every angle. It will all come back to you when you need it."

One of the event coordinators handed Scott the team's room assignment for the first round.

When the students returned, he said, "We're the defense side in the first round. That means Dustin and Yvette will be attorneys for Pete Pigpickin. Once the case is called, no one can talk to them. No stage whispers from the gallery, Frank. It could cost us points."

Frank gave an innocent look. "Don't pick on me."

The other team arrived. With them was a tall, good-looking lawyer with dark hair and wearing an impeccably tailored dark suit.

Kay nudged Scott. "Is that him?"

Scott nodded. "Yes."

"Do you think you could give him my phone number?"

Scott looked down at her. "I'm sure it's highly confidential."

The lawyer saw Scott and waved.

"How are you?" he asked. "Where are you in practice?"

Scott sensed the man recognized his face, but couldn't place his name.

"Blanchard County. How are things in the big city?"

"I'm in the Bank of America tower. It's a great view from the fifty-first floor."

Before Scott replied, the presiding judge and the three lawyers on the jury walked into the courtroom. Everyone scurried to their places. The courtroom was called to order, and the case began. Opening statements are not an opportunity to forcibly argue the case, but a skillful advocate can give a forecast of the evidence that sends the right message to the jury. The plaintiff's attorney for the other team went first, and it was obvious to Scott that the young man was either well coached or had experience in the program. The student was cool and confident.

It was Dustin's job to respond for the defendant. He stood up.

"If it pleases the Court, my name is Dustin Rawlings. Yvette Fisher and me, uh, Yvette Fisher and I, represent Pete Pigpickin, the plaintiff, I mean, defendant in this case."

It was a rocky start, but Dustin quickly recovered. He included a few touches of humor in his opening statement that Scott hoped made the judges forget about his initial miscues.

"Our client, Mr. Pigpickin, is the father of eight children—all by the same wife. He is in the catering business and delivers the highest quality barbecue to gatherings across North Carolina. On the date of this accident, his truck was loaded with over a hundred pounds of prime barbeque and four gallons of homemade barbeque sauce. He was on his way to feed a large group of lawyers and judges and wanted to give them the best food that money could buy. Then tragedy struck."

Looking directly at the student playing the part of the plaintiff, Betty Moonbeam, Dustin said, "Miss Moonbeam, our client is very sorry that you suffered injuries in this unfortunate accident. Nothing that we say here today will take away the pain that you've suffered. Our sincere desire is that you fully recover and fulfill your lifelong dream to become a phlebotomist."

There were several audible chuckles in the courtroom at the mention of Betty's career goals.

Turning back toward the jury panel, Dustin continued, "Nothing that we say today will bring back the pounds of wasted barbeque that lay scattered on the asphalt after this collision occurred. Scores of lawyers and several judges went hungry because their food never arrived."

He worked his way through the opening statement to a more serious conclusion. "We believe the evidence will reveal three convincing reasons why our client should not be found liable for damages in this case. First, Mr. Pigpickin will testify that he came to a complete stop before entering the intersection and obeyed all traffic laws. Second, our client's testimony will be backed up by Billy Bob Beerbelly, the driver of a third vehicle at the intersection. Third, the evidence will show that Ralph Risky, the driver of the car in which Betty Moonbeam was a passenger, was intoxicated."

The Catawba student playing the part of Pete Pigpickin held up well under cross-examination by one of the plaintiff's attorneys.

"Isn't it true that you weren't looking at the road when you approached the intersection?" the lawyer asked.

"I'd been looking at the road all morning long since I left my house in Hogbottom Hollow."

"But when you approached the stop sign, you looked away from the roadway because you'd dropped a barbeque sandwich on the floorboard of your truck."

Pete stared at the lawyer without answering. The lawyer waited, then faced the judge.

"Please instruct the witness to answer the question."

Pete spoke up. "Judge, he didn't ask me a question. He told me what he thinks happened. I only have a fourth-grade education, but I'm smart enough to know that this fellow wasn't riding in my truck on the day of the wreck. I have a policy not to pick up hitchhikers or lawyers."

The lawyers in the jury box laughed out loud. Scott smiled. He had told the witnesses to listen closely and only answer questions, not respond to statements. Pete was following directions.

The lawyer persevered. "Well, isn't it true that you took your eyes off the road as you approached the intersection because you dropped your sandwich on the floor?"

Pete looked at the lawyers in the jury box. "It's true that I dropped my sandwich, but I never took my good eye off the road. I was driving like this."

Pete leaned over in his seat so that he was peering over the edge of the box that surrounded the witness stand and moved an imaginary steering wheel back and forth. "This is how I did it. I've been driving like this since I was eight years old, so it wasn't a problem at all."

"Isn't it true that you have only one good eye?"

Pete squinted. "Yes, and I don't have any problem shooting a squirrel out of a tree from seventy-five yards away."

"Objection, your honor," the lawyer said. "He's testifying to facts outside the mock trial problem."

Yvette was on her feet. "Your honor, the witness is allowed to give an illustration to explain an answer so long as it does not contradict a fact in the case. The facts say that Mr. Pigpickin has a bad eye, but there is no indication of the condition of his vision in the good eye."

"Overruled."

"Thank you." Yvette sat down.

The case quickly progressed to the closing arguments. Yvette took a chance and spoke without notes. Everything went smoothly until she became confused about a twist in the testimony from one of the witnesses and then made an overgeneralization.

"And even though Billy Bob Beerbelly and Pete Pigpickin are second cousins on their mother's side and first cousins on their father's side." She paused. "Wait, maybe it's the other way around. Anyway, Billy Bob said he wouldn't lie for his mother and remember that Ralph Risky's testimony about not drinking is unbelievable. A lot of people drink at high-school parties."

"Objection. There is no evidence before the court about other high-school parties."

"Sustained."

Yvette's face flushed, but she ended without any further snags.

The other attorney was as smooth in his closing argument as his partner had been in the opening statement. The young man bobbled his cross-examination of Pete Pigpickin, but he nailed the closing argument. When he finished, the judge and lawyers left the courtroom to grade the round. The students quickly crowded around.

"I'm glad it's over," Yvette said.

"Don't worry about the objection during your closing argument," Scott said. "The rest of it was great."

Turning to the other students, he said, "You all did well. Dustin, you made some good objections, and I thought Yvette's cross-examination of Betty Moonbeam went smoothly. All the witnesses knew their parts and came across as very believable."

While they waited, the lawyer/coach of the other team looked across the room at Scott and gave him a confident smile. Kay saw the exchange between the two men and whispered to Scott, "Your friend thinks they won."

"He's not my friend, and I'm not so sure. Our kids did pretty well."

Kay quickly squeezed Scott's hand. "They were great."

The judge and jury returned and gave a critique of all the lawyers and witnesses. Their goal was to encourage, but they also pointed out areas for improvement. In each round, a witness and lawyer received special recognition. The panel selected Pete Pigpickin as the best witness, and the plaintiff's lawyer who delivered the flawless opening statement as the best attorney.

"Finally," the judge said, "we have to declare a winner of this round. It was difficult to decide, and we had a sharp debate that kept us in the jury room longer than we expected. However, considering all the witnesses and the lawyers we give this round to the plaintiff."

Scott quickly looked at the team members to see how they took the news. No one seemed upset, and he realized that the students were so relieved to have survived the experience in one piece that they didn't consider themselves losers. Only Dustin walked over to him with a downcast look.

"Sorry, coach."

Scott put his arm around the boy's shoulders. "If we'd been able to play a full game, we would have worn them out."

"On to round two," he said to the whole group. "We switch sides and argue the plaintiff's case."

It had been an advantage for Frank and Janie to watch the other team. It was even more helpful for the witnesses to observe students from other schools portray the characters the Catawba students would assume during the next round.

They left Courtroom 307 and walked down the hallway to Courtroom

303. Their opponent was a team from a public high school in one of the best neighborhoods of south Charlotte. Frank went outside and waited in the hallway. Janie sat next to Alisha. Kay slid into the seat beside Scott.

"What do you think?"

Scott looked at the young man and woman who were arranging their papers at the table reserved for the student lawyers who represented the defense. The young man was dressed in a dark gray suit, white shirt, and red-striped tie. The girl was in a navy women's suit that must have cost five hundred dollars.

"Those two look like attorneys from a big firm in Raleigh that represents insurance companies. I want to see their birth certificates; I'm not sure they're still in high school."

"They're probably seniors."

"Maybe at Harvard."

The judge and three lawyers came into the room. Janie stepped into the hallway to get Frank. Scott suddenly felt butterflies in his stomach.

"I'm nervous," he said softly to Kay.

"You know how good they can be and want to see them do it."

Frank and Janie took their places. Janie had placed everything neatly across their table. The judge, a woman attorney with curly dark hair, called the case.

"Proceed for the plaintiff."

Janie stood up and began just as Scott had taught on the first night of practice. "May it please the court. My name is Janie Collins. Together with my co-counsel, Frank Jesup, it is my privilege to represent Betty Moonbeam, the plaintiff in this case."

Janie's accent immediately captured the attention of the courtroom. It helped that her grammar was perfect, thus debunking for a moment the stereotype that someone from the country didn't know a participle from a preposition. Scott smiled. He was glad he lived in a generation that didn't try to keep women like Janie out of the courtroom. She concluded by looking directly in the faces of the lawyers in the jury box.

"After you have heard the evidence, my client will entrust the decision about these important issues into your hands for your careful consideration. Thank you very much."

Kay elbowed Scott in the side and whispered, "I see that smug look on your face, but remember who recruited her."

Janie's counterpart was the male member of the other team. He didn't give a canned speech, but worked in some direct responses to what Janie said in her opening statement. Scott was impressed. This was going to be an interesting match.

Frank debuted by conducting the direct examination of their first witness. He didn't try to project himself into the center of attention but kept the focus where it needed to be—on the testimony. After a cross-examination that didn't do much damage because of some of the witness strategies developed by Frank, the case moved forward smoothly.

Alisha played the role of Betty Moonbeam. Janie questioned her and brought out the pathos and pain she'd suffered. Alisha had a gift that can be the bane of men in the hands of a manipulative woman—the ability to cry on cue. She shed a tear when Janie questioned her about the effect of her injuries on her life and added a few more when she was cross-examined too strenuously by the male defense lawyer.

When the last witness for the plaintiff stepped down, Frank said, "Your honor, subject to rebuttal, that concludes the plaintiff's case."

The defense lawyers started out with their own version of Pete Pigpickin. It was a strong role, and the young man in the witness chair had a piece of straw stuck behind his left ear as a prop for the part. Frank was scheduled to cross-examine the driver of the barbeque truck. As Scott listened, he realized it would have been better for Janie to take on her fellow countryman, but it was too late to change.

Frank began with some good questions and had Pete back-pedaling down the road until the witness gave an answer Frank hadn't anticipated. Frank's face suddenly grew red, and he said, "I object, your honor, that is, uh, outside the ability of the witness to observe and offer an opinion."

The female lawyer on the other team stood up. "Judge, nothing in the facts prohibits the witness from offering his lay opinion about the condition of the roadway. He testified that he's driven on the road at least once a week for ten years."

"Objection overruled," the judge said.

The setback threw Frank off his rhythm, and a few questions later he committed one of the cardinal sins of cross-examination—he gave a witness the chance to repeat a damaging answer. Pete testified that Billy Bob's car had on its right turn signal, then turned left. This tended to shift blame away from Pete to Billy Bob. Instead of pointing out an inconsistent statement that Pete gave to the policeman who investigated the wreck, Frank asked sharply, "That's not true, is it?"

Pete gave Frank a long look. "Mr. Attorney, I put my hand on the Bible before I started testifying and everything I'm saying is the truth, the whole truth, and nothing but the truth. What I said about seeing the right turn signal before Billy Bob entered the intersection is all of those kinds of truth."

Frank salvaged a few points toward the end of the questioning. Janie cross-examined the other two witnesses for the defense. The female lawyer then delivered her closing argument. It was hard-hitting. Scott decided that in a few more years she might be another Lynn Davenport.

Scott could see Frank's profile. He was staring straight ahead, not watching his opponent. Scott had told him to listen closely enough that he could counter the other side's argument without becoming vulnerable to the logic of the presentation and be psyched out. The defense lawyer finished with a passionate flourish.

Frank stood up.

Scott should not have worried. Rarely referring to the few note cards in his hand, Frank proved his own case and refuted several of the key points made by the other side by quoting almost verbatim from the testimony of the witnesses. The young man had an incredible memory, and the closing argument gave him an opportunity to show what a potent weapon it could be when combined with a sharp, analytical mind. Putting his hands on the railing in front of the jury box, he concluded by asking them to remember what Janie had said during her opening statement.

"Betty Moonbeam cannot make the defendant do the right thing. That power is in your hands. Use it wisely and with compassion."

The judge and lawyers left to discuss the presentation. The coach for the other team, a young teacher about Kay's age, came over to them. With her was an older lawyer with gray hair and small, frameless glasses.

"Is this your first year in the competition?" the teacher asked.

"Yes," Scott replied.

The lawyer introduced himself to Scott and Kay. "I've been coming to these competitions for ten years, and I've never seen a better round than we just witnessed. The only one that comes close would be the state finals three years ago when we lost to a team from Asheville. You did a great job preparing them."

"The girl who played the plaintiff was superb," the teacher added.

Scott returned the compliments, then gathered the students in a huddle and told them about the older lawyer's comparison to the state finals.

"Whatever happens, you can be proud of what you accomplished."

They waited anxiously in small huddles for several more minutes before the judge and jury returned. The room was totally silent. The judge took off her glasses before she spoke.

"I've been trying cases for twenty years and it's rare to see real lawyers as prepared as these two teams. All of you deserve recognition. I've asked my colleagues to speak first."

Once again, the lawyers in the jury box gave a brief critique, followed by the judge's comments.

The judge continued, "Now for the hard part. We frequently have to make decisions as lawyers or judges, but some are harder than others. Picking the best attorney, witness, and team was very difficult, but we have selected Alisha Mason as best witness"—the judge looked down at a piece of paper—"and Janie Collins as best lawyer."

Janie and Alisha were sitting next to each other. They both screamed and hugged. The judge smiled and banged her gavel. "Order in the court! We're not finished. Although the best witness and lawyer are from the plaintiff's side, we give the overall top score to the defense. They were the most consistent from start to finish."

Only Scott's and Frank's mental wheels turned fast enough to instantly read between the lines of the decision. Catawba lost because Frank botched the cross-examination of Pete Pigpickin. Scott looked at Frank, who turned his head toward him at the same time. Their eyes met again. Frank wasn't smiling, and Scott didn't either. He knew there was no use trying to communicate an unspoken message of encouragement that would not be received. Frank left the room without congratulating anyone on either team.

During the ride home to Catawba, Dustin and the other boys talked about the mock trial competition for thirty minutes, then switched back to football. As he listened, Scott realized that the day's activities were just a blip on the boys' radar screen of activities. It had been fun, but nobody in the halls on Monday would be scrambling for news about the results of the mock trial competition.

The car in which Frank was riding arrived at the high school before Scott, and the young man was gone. Janie and Alisha were still there.

"Thank you, Mr. Ellis," Janie said. "I can't wait until next year. Will you be helping with the team again? You're great. I can't imagine anyone being better than you."

Scott hadn't even thought about the future. "Uh, I'll consider it."

"Please do it," Alisha added. "There are some other kids we can recruit for the team now that we know what it's all about."

After all the students left, Scott turned to Kay. "What next?"

"I think we need to have a victory celebration."

"But we didn't win."

"Objection overruled. That's a mere technicality. Didn't you see Janie's face when she was selected best attorney?"

"Yeah, that was one of my favorite images of the day," Scott admitted. "What did you have in mind?"

"Dinner tonight. The two of us."

"Without the kids?"

Kay laughed. "You sound like a guy with toddlers. We'll do something with the students later. Probably during the school day."

"Okay. Where would you like to go?"

"Would it be too much trouble to go back to Charlotte for dinner?"

"No. Where?"

"A surprise, but it's a nice place. Wear a tie and pick me up at six o'clock."

"Sounds fancy."

"It has historical interest."

40

Rarely do great beauty and great virtue dwell together.
PETRARCH

Scott knocked on the door of Kay's apartment and waited. She didn't answer. He knocked again and straightened his tie. Still no answer. Waiting on Kay's doorstep was beginning to be a pattern, and he knocked a third time. He was reaching for the door handle to see if it was locked when Kay opened the door. His mouth dropped open an inch.

"You're gorgeous," he said.

Kay was wearing a long black sheath dress with a silver necklace and earrings. Her hair was done up in a French twist with several wisps escaping around her face. Over one arm was a white wrap. The only missing item was shoes.

"Thanks, come in. I'm almost ready." She disappeared into her bedroom.

Scott stepped into the place where she'd stood and caught a whiff of her perfume. He took a deeper breath and wished he had Nicky's sensitive nose so he could appreciate all the nuances that were floating in the air. When she returned, her high heels brought her closer to eye level with Scott.

"I'm ready."

Kay threw her sweater around her shoulders and went down the steps. Scott followed.

"Let's stop at a mall and let me rent a tuxedo," he said.

"You're fine."

He opened the door of his vehicle for her and caught another hint of fragrance.

"You need a corsage."

"No, I don't."

He walked around to the driver's side of his vehicle. Kay was right. A flower would detract rather than enhance. He got in and started the engine.

"Where to?" he asked.

"Charlotte. That's enough for now."

Kay was going to play this evening out her way. So far, Scott had no complaints. He drove out of the apartment complex and in a few minutes they were on the road to the city.

Kay was in a talkative mood, and after a few minutes, Scott stopped being overwhelmed by her appearance and settled into the conversation. She was full of questions. Nothing about the bomb explosion and the death of Steve Robinson. They'd already covered that territory. She peppered him with questions about his childhood up to the time they'd dated.

"Why didn't you call me when you were home on leave?" she asked. "Everything stopped so abruptly."

"I called, but you had started dating Bill Corbin. He was one of my friends, and I didn't want to create confusion."

"Bill Corbin?" she asked with surprise. "I never dated him."

"Yeah. I talked to your father, and he told me that you and Bill had gone to Charlotte."

Kay laughed. "I remember. We had to buy supplies for an art project. All we did was share a car ride. He took me straight home."

"Oh."

Scott suddenly wondered how different his life might have been if he'd not given up so easily. They drove in silence for a few moments.

"Are you thinking of what could have been?" Kay guessed.

Scott didn't lie. "Yes."

"Don't do it. We've both made mistakes. Mine have been much worse than yours. The important thing is how we're living our lives today."

"*Carpe diem*. Seize the day."

"Yes, only I want to grab what's important, not just focus on surface things."

"Does that mean I can't tell you how beautiful you are?"

Kay smiled. "Thanks, but more than how I look on the outside, I want to be beautiful on the inside."

Scott thought for a second before responding. He suspected Kay meant the way God was changing how she looked at life.

"So, should I say God has made you beautiful?" he asked.

Kay patted his arm. "If you said that to me, it would be the greatest compliment of my life."

When they reached the outskirts of Charlotte, he said, "Time for more directions. Which road?"

"South Boulevard near Uptown."

From its beginning point in the center of the city, South Boulevard crossed over the two abandoned gold mines that had attracted settlers to the Charlotte area in the 1840s. Many of the older buildings in the area had been renovated and converted to expensive condominiums, shops, and restaurants. Farther out, it was less chic.

"Are we going to the South 21 Drive-In?" he asked. "I wouldn't mind eating in the car."

"No."

Two blocks later, Kay pointed. "Turn in there."

It was the Barrymore Restaurant—the place where Scott and Kay ate before the high-school prom.

Scott laughed. "I'm dense. I should have guessed."

"Yes. You're not as smart as I thought. The questions I asked about the past were a huge clue."

The restaurant had valet parking by boys about the same age as Scott when he'd brought Kay twelve years before. Then, it had been awkward giving the keys to his father's car to someone his own age. Now, he didn't give it a second thought. Kay had made a reservation.

When they were seated, she asked, "Notice anything else?"

Scott looked her over again from her head to her hands holding the menu. The diamonds around her neck sparkled in the candlelight. There was a lot to notice.

"Not me," she corrected. "The restaurant."

He glanced around the fancy establishment. White tablecloths, older waiters carrying bottles of wine, a man playing a piano softly in the bar area. Couples like themselves dressed up for a special occasion and a few businessmen on an unlimited expense account.

"No, it looks the same."

"It is. This is the table where we sat. I remembered because it was next to the steps leading up to the bar."

Scott tried to bring back the scene but couldn't capture it.

"I'll have to trust you. It was like tonight. I was so caught up with your beauty that no other details remain in my memory bank."

Kay smiled. "You're much smoother than you were at age eighteen. Actually, you spent a lot of time during dinner talking with Perry Dixon."

Scott grimaced. "Is it too late to apologize?"

"Yes. Do you remember what we ate?"

"Steak?" he guessed. The restaurant was locally famous for its filet mignon.

"Right, but I won't press you for anything else."

The waiter took their order and brought out salads.

"What happened to Linda, the girl who was dating Perry?" Kay asked.

"She's Mrs. Perry Dixon," Scott answered. "They married soon after high school."

"I'm not surprised. While you and Perry were having your long, long conversation, Linda and I talked. She was a senior, and I was a sopho-more, so we didn't know each other at all. I wasn't sure what she thought about you taking me to the dance. I think she had a friend she wanted you to ask."

Scott swallowed a bite of salad. "Oh yeah, Mary somebody."

"Linda and I hit it off, and when we were leaving, she told me we were a 'cute couple.'"

Scott nodded. "She hasn't changed her opinion. I work out at Perry's gym a few days a week. I told him about you, and Linda has been very interested in the whole situation. I think they want us to come over for supper."

"That would be fun."

Their steaks arrived. Scott had a greater appreciation for a fine cut of meat as a man than he did as a teenager. He took a bite. It was perfect.

"This is almost as good as the steak we cooked over the fire," he said.

"There are a few differences," Kay replied. "The chairs are more comfortable, and the smoke from the fire isn't chasing us in a circle."

"Does that mean you didn't like camping?"

Kay cut through her piece of steak. "No, I loved it. I even did some writing."

"When?"

"In the morning while you were washing dishes after breakfast. Nicky visited me in my tent. His paw print is on the edge of the paper."

"What did you write about?"

"About the hike. It was more of a diary entry than anything else."

"What stood out about the trip?"

Kay chewed thoughtfully for a moment. "The overlook where we sat on the rocks. It was a neat place. And the way you didn't get upset when you lost your lures in the stream."

"Really? I wouldn't have thought that was important enough to write about."

"It showed me something about you. I hate it when I have to walk on eggshells around someone because they get angry and upset too easily. After watching you respond to the lost lures, I knew that I could relax with you."

Kay wanted to know more about Scott's work at the office. He told her several stories about his interaction with Mr. Humphrey.

"That's what I wanted you to do with Frank," Kay said. "He needs someone he respects to talk to."

Scott shrugged. "For some reason, I didn't make the cut."

They ate the last bites of meat and shared a strawberry cheesecake for dessert. When it came time to pay the check, Scott reached for his credit card. It wasn't there.

"I must have left my wallet in my car," he said. "I'll be back in a minute."

While Kay waited, an older couple who were leaving the restaurant came by their table. The woman stopped and said, "I have been watching you all evening. You are such a beautiful couple. Is this your anniversary?"

"No, we're not married. We came here when we dated in high school, so in a sense it's an anniversary."

"Have a good evening," the woman replied. "And create new memories."

Kay was pondering the woman's comment when Scott walked up to the table.

"I paid the bill at the front. Who were you talking to?"

"A woman who was like Mrs. Kilgore at Bishop Moore's church."

"The dessert lady?"

"Yes. Only it wasn't the dessert I was thinking about. It has to do with someone who sees things before they happen."

"What did she see?"

"I'm not sure. Maybe the future."

Kay was less talkative during the drive back to Catawba. The lights of the city quickly slipped behind and were replaced by dimmer reflections from the windows of houses along the shores of Lake Norman.

When they arrived at Kay's apartment complex, Scott got out and walked her up the steps to her front door. Kay unlocked the door.

"This has been a great celebration," he said.

Scott hesitated. He wanted to kiss her but wasn't sure if the invitation was open. Kay faced him, and Scott's heart skipped. He felt more nervous than a schoolboy. He cleared his throat.

"Do you remember what I told you about my fear at the overlook?"

Kay nodded and kept her eyes on his.

"Would I be making a mistake if I kissed you?"

"No."

Scott leaned forward, and they leaped together across the chasm from friendship to the first steps of intimacy.

When they parted, Kay said, "Thank you, Scott."

"For what?"

"For helping to bring me back to life."

———

The following morning, Kay opened her eyes to the first frost of the season. The green grass was covered with frozen crystals, and the heat of the earth was sending up a white mist. The few remaining green leaves would soon turn color and fall to the ground. She wrapped herself in her warmest robe and stepped onto her deck. Her breath reached out to the mist rising from the ground.

She arrived a few minutes late to the church. She found a spot by Janie's little brother, who smiled when he saw her. Soon after the music started, Kay was in the place where God's love was both the focus of her attention and the experience of her spirit. When the last notes faded, she stayed still for a few more moments in the river of worship.

When it was time for the sermon, Ben Whitmire took his place behind the black music stand. "My scripture today is from Psalm 116:15. 'Precious in the sight of the LORD is the death of his saints.'

"Seven years ago my mother died. She was eighty-nine years old and lived the last eighty-five years of her life in west Texas, an area that shares a lot in common with the land of Israel. It is hot, dry, and you can see for long distances. But there is something about a barren place that brings perspective, and my mother had a healthy perspective on life and death. For example, one of her favorite sayings was 'human history didn't begin with our birth and won't end with our death.' She believed we are part of something bigger than ourselves. This is especially true if we are part of God's kingdom."

Ben told several stories about his mother that illustrated the life of a twentieth-century person who walked with God.

"One of the greatest lessons my mother taught me came at the time of her death. Now, there is no doubt that death is an enemy. Paul writes that 'the last enemy to be destroyed is death.' However, there is something even more remarkable about death found in the words of Jesus in John 8:51: 'If anyone keeps my word, he will never see death.'"

Ben took off his bifocals.

"This verse troubled me for a long time. I mean, a lot of Christians have died in the last two thousand years. Didn't they have to face death? My mother's last day on earth helped me understand this truth.

"When she was getting very weak, she told me to call my brothers and ask them to come to the hospital. She had a sense that her time to leave us was close at hand, and our family spent her last afternoon on this earth together in her hospital room. About four o'clock, she gave a long sigh and stopped breathing. At that moment a lightness entered the room, and there was peace in the atmosphere and on her face. Immediately, the Lord reminded me of the words of Jesus and spoke to my heart: *She didn't see death. She passed directly from this life to the next.* We all stood around and said good-bye. As one of God's children, she walked seamlessly from this world to the next."

Ben wiped his left eye with his handkerchief.

"Usually, death is only discussed at funerals when everyone is upset at the loss of a loved one, and the message of Christian hope is dismissed by many as a sentimental attempt to help people feel better about what has happened. But I realized something the day my mother died—death is a defeated foe to those who know the Lord in a personal way. If his life is in you, you may stop breathing, but you will not see death. Jesus Christ is Conqueror of death and Lord of life. Let's pray."

Ben's message was a strong affirmation of the freedom from the fear of death Kay had already experienced. Now her focus was on life.

41

Deceive not thy physician, confessor, nor lawyer.
GEORGE HERBERT

Monday morning, the trial day butterflies returned to Scott's stomach. As he sat in his office going over his notes, he realized that he was more nervous about seeing Harold Garrison than facing Lynn Davenport and the twelve people who would serve on the jury. He already knew secondhand that the older Garrison was mad at him. Soon, Harold would be able to vent his displeasure in person.

Mr. Humphrey's fantasy had not come to pass. Kendall Kidd was not in the Blanchard County jail, and Scott had not received a phone call from Detective Griffin that the felonious cousin was in custody in South Carolina. Thus, the most important person connected to *State v. Garrison* would be absent from the courtroom.

Lester and Harold arrived at the office a few minutes before they had to leave for the courthouse. Scott stopped by Mr. Humphrey's office on his way to the reception area.

"They're here," he said.

The older lawyer straightened his bow tie. "I'll come with you in case someone has to sit on Harold."

As instructed, Lester was wearing the same wrinkled white shirt and black pants. Harold was wearing brown pants and a blue shirt that didn't match. Scott decided to proceed as if the discussion of Kendall had never taken place.

"Are you ready to go?" Scott asked.

"I have one question for y'all before we leave," Harold responded.

Scott waited. Mr. Humphrey moved a step closer.

"How long will it take to try this case?" he asked. "Will we finish it up today?"

Caught off guard, Scott hesitated before responding. "I doubt it. It will take two days to select the jury and present the testimony. Then we have to see how long the jury deliberates. Anything else?"

"No. That's it."

The jury pool wasn't as large as the one summoned for the previous week of trial, and the old courtroom was only half full. Lynn Davenport entered, and Scott walked over to her. He didn't want another unanticipated continuance.

"Are you going forward with the Garrison case?" he asked.

She nodded curtly. "Yes."

"Do you have any preliminary matters?"

"Yes."

Scott didn't try to find out how long they would have to wait. They had to stay in the courtroom anyway.

Judge Teasley arrived, and the D.A. began calling cases in which the defendants wanted to plead guilty. Several men and women admitted their guilt to a variety of charges. Judge Teasley sentenced some of them on the spot; others were referred for a pre-sentence investigation and background check. Scott didn't like the jury pool hearing so many people stand before the judge and confess their guilt. It gave the impression that every case involved a guilty person. He glanced at Lester. His client was watching the process very closely.

It was an hour before Lynn Davenport stood and announced, "*State v. Garrison,* case number 76452, called for trial."

The defense team took their place at their table, and the jury selection process began. The clerk of court sounded twelve names, and the persons summoned separated themselves from their peers and entered the jury box to be questioned by the lawyers.

The first time Lynn Davenport addressed a panel of prospective jurors she gave a brief summary of the case.

"Lester Garrison is charged with assault with a deadly weapon with intent to inflict serious injury, assault by pointing a gun, and criminal damage to property. These crimes occurred during a sacred baptism service at the Hall's Chapel Church."

Scott had lived with the case in such close quarters that the events leading up to the charges against Lester had become words on a piece of paper. Now hearing them repeated in open court, the situation was no longer a hypothetical problem but a dangerous incident involving real people. It was chilling. Out of the corner of his eye, he saw Lester squirm in his chair.

Scott introduced himself to each panel the same way. "I'm Scott Ellis. Together with Mr. Leland Humphrey, I'll be representing Lester Garrison in this case. Lester is the young man sitting next to Mr. Humphrey."

Scott adopted a relaxed attitude in an effort to send the jury a subtle message that *State v. Garrison* was not as serious a matter as the assistant district attorney with the northern accent made it sound. Every time Scott mentioned Mr. Humphrey several jurors smiled and nodded in greeting to the well-known lawyer. Scott could see Lynn Davenport making notes of unspoken communication. He doubted any smiling jurors would make the cut.

When it came time to select the twelve men and women to decide Lester's fate, the prosecutor didn't try to strike everyone who knew Leland Humphrey. Her strategy was more relevant to the facts of the case. She targeted white males who might not think there was anything wrong with scaring black folks by firing a gun in their general vicinity and tried to protect African-Americans and the more educated jurors.

Scott wanted to keep a few rednecks, several women who might be sympathetic to Lester because of his age, and clients and friends of Mr. Humphrey. The only juror known to Harold Garrison was dismissed by the D.A. and left the courtroom with a pouch of chewing tobacco bulging in his back pocket.

The sharpest debate over a juror at the defense table involved a man who attended Hall's Chapel Church. He wasn't present on the day of the shooting. Mr. Humphrey and Scott quickly discussed the pros and cons. Scott wished he could flip a coin.

Lester leaned over and hissed, "You're not going to leave him on the jury are you? He said he went to the church."

Scott answered, "He might be good because he'll believe what Bishop Moore and Alisha Mason say about a dark-haired person."

"I don't want him," Lester said, looking at his father.

"Keep him off," Harold seconded.

Mr. Humphrey nodded. "He's gone."

In spite of Lester's preferences, all the African-Americans could not be stricken, and when the twelve jurors were seated, two of them had dark skin.

The judge looked them over and asked the D.A., "Is this your jury, Ms. Davenport?"

"Yes, your honor."

"Mr. Ellis?"

"Yes, your honor."

The judge administered the oath to the jurors, then said, "Ladies and gentlemen of the jury, do not discuss the case among yourselves or with anyone else. Do not attempt to find out about the case from any source. Your decision will be based solely on the testimony and exhibits admitted into evidence in this courtroom. When you return, reassemble in the jury room. The bailiffs can direct you."

He banged his gavel. "The court will be in recess until 1:15."

The jurors filed out of the jury box. In a simple case like Lester's trial, the jury wouldn't be sequestered and were free to scatter for lunch on their own.

Scott, Mr. Humphrey, and the Garrisons walked up the aisle to the back of the courtroom. Outside in the hallway, Mr. Humphrey said, "We have a good jury. I think they will make the state prove its case."

Harold grunted. "I don't trust none of 'em. What was the D.A.'s last offer if Lester pleaded guilty?"

Scott stared at Harold, and Mr. Humphrey cleared his throat so loudly that it sounded like he swallowed something by accident.

"There is no offer," Scott responded. "We turned it down before the case was on the trial calendar two weeks ago, and it's been withdrawn. The prosecution doesn't have to leave an offer on the table."

"What was it?" Harold persisted.

"Six months in a boot-camp program and three years on probation. The conspiracy charges would also be dropped."

"And if he don't plead guilty, what could he get?"

Speaking slowly and distinctly, Scott asked, "Did you hear me? There is no offer to accept. If Lester is convicted, the sentence would be up to the judge. He could give him probation or ten years in the penitentiary. It's a gamble."

Looking at his son, Harold asked, "Well?"

Lester turned to Scott. "Should I plead guilty? What do you think?"

Scott thought both of the Garrisons were crazy. This was not the time to float a plea offer in front of Davenport so she could blow it out of the water.

He pointed out the basic reason why his client couldn't plead guilty. "Lester, you shouldn't plead guilty to something you didn't do. You're not guilty of the crimes listed on the indictment. I advised you to testify to the truth about your cousin Kendall. Since you've decided not to take my advice, I'm ready to try the case."

Lester looked once more at his father, then said, "I want to plead guilty. I couldn't stand it if I had to go to prison."

Scott was speechless.

Mr. Humphrey recovered enough to ask, "What made you change your mind?"

"Watching the people plead guilty this morning got me thinking," Lester answered. "Then, listening to the stuff the D.A. said about the case made me realize that the jury might believe her lies."

"But we don't have an offer," Scott added.

Harold looked at Mr. Humphrey. "You talk to the judge. You know him, don't you?"

Mr. Humphrey answered, "We can talk to the judge, but under the rules we have to bring the D.A. into the conversation."

"She don't carry your clout," Harold said. "Get the deal involving the boot camp and dropping the other charges."

Scott turned to Lester. "But you're not guilty. What are you going to say when the judge asks you if you fired the shots? You heard him question the other defendants who entered pleas this morning. He makes sure the person committed the crime."

"We talked about that while you were selecting the jurors," Lester answered. "I'll tell the judge that I did it."

Not trying to hide his frustration, Scott replied, "But that would be lying. What about Kendall?"

"I fired the shots," Lester replied with a straight face. "All Kendall did was dare me to do it. In the end, it probably won't make any difference."

Scott stopped to digest the information thrown at him by the Garrisons. For such simple, ignorant people, they could be extremely complicated, and the truth was proving more slippery than the oil in Lester's beat-up truck.

Mr. Humphrey spoke. "Lester, your sudden change in story is hard for us to believe. And as Scott told you, there is no deal on the table."

"That's why we want you to talk to the judge before we go any farther into the case," Harold said. "It's time y'all earned the money I paid you."

Scott barely kept himself from laughing out loud.

"What if Judge Teasley won't agree to the deal previously offered by the D.A.?" Mr. Humphrey asked. "What then?"

Harold shrugged. "I guess we'd need to do some more talking."

"Okay," Mr. Humphrey said. "Scott, find out if the judge is in his chambers and ask if we can see him before the jury comes back in."

Lynn Davenport was sitting at the prosecution table writing on a legal pad when Scott reentered the courtroom.

"Don't leave," he said. "We have something to discuss with the judge if he's available."

"What is it?" she asked.

Scott enjoyed being nonresponsive and blunt. "You'll find out when we present it to him."

The door to the judge's chambers was to the left of the bench. Scott went down a short hallway to the anteroom. The judge's secretary wasn't at her desk, so he walked to the open doorway and peeked inside. Judge Teasley was reading the business page of the Charlotte paper. A half-eaten sandwich was on the corner of his desk. A can of Cheerwine sat on a fancy coaster.

"Excuse me, your honor."

The judge closed the paper. "Yes?"

"We would like to meet with you before the jury is brought back into the courtroom."

"All right. Is the D.A. here?"

"Yes, sir."

"I'll be out in a minute."

Scott returned and reported to Mr. Humphrey. In less than a minute the judge, wearing his black robe, came into the courtroom.

"Ms. Davenport," he said, "counsel for the defendant has a matter to discuss before we begin."

Leland Humphrey stood. "Your honor, the defendant would like to discuss the possibility of a guilty plea to certain aspects of the charges."

Lynn Davenport was on her feet in an instant.

"There is no outstanding plea offer. The defendant didn't accept a timely offer and forced the state to prepare for trial."

The judge spun his glasses once. "Go ahead, Mr. Humphrey."

"Thank you, your honor. As you know, Lester Garrison was sixteen years old at the time this incident occurred. He is now seventeen years old. He has no history of problems in juvenile court and is a junior at Catawba High School."

The judge interrupted. "Ms. Davenport, do you have a copy of the juvenile court file available?"

"Yes, sir."

The D.A. took the thin folder up to the bench and handed it to the judge. Everyone waited. The juvenile court file contained information about Lester's background, home life, and any prior run-ins with the police. When the judge finished, he nodded to Mr. Humphrey.

"What is your proposal?"

Leland Humphrey knew it was time to get directly to the point. "Guilty to assault with a deadly weapon without intent to kill or inflict serious bodily injury because no one was hurt. He will also plead guilty to the criminal damage to property. We ask you to sentence him for six months in the boot-camp program for youthful offenders followed by two years on probation under the first offender act with the provision that his record be expunged if he completes all probationary time without incident."

Before the judge could reply, Lynn Davenport said, "The state vigorously opposes this request, your honor—"

"Just a minute," Judge Teasley said, twirling his glasses once. "Ms. Davenport, is it true that no one was injured?"

"Uh, yes, sir. However, this defendant is part of a larger racist conspiracy. The state believes there may be additional charges that will be brought against him. And my withdrawn offer provided for three years on probation."

"How do you respond?" the judge asked Mr. Humphrey.

"When and if any other charges are filed, they will have to be evaluated on their own merits. Today, there is nothing else before the court. The defendant will be in custody for the next six months if the state wants to obtain an indictment, and he can be brought back for trial. Given successful completion of the boot-camp program, two years on probation would be an adequate time to continue supervision."

"Ms. Davenport?" the judge asked.

Lynn Davenport spoke with biting intensity. "Your honor, this was a serious criminal offense. Although no one was hurt, the defendant placed the lives of more than a hundred people, including small children, in jeopardy by firing gunshots in the direction of a large group of people. The sentence suggested by defense counsel is a slap on the wrist. This defendant needs to understand that endangering the lives of other people carries serious consequences. Counsel's request also undermines the state's ability to administer its cases. A plea bargain was offered and rejected. Now, as we are beginning trial, the defendant suddenly wants to turn back the clock and revisit a deal that was previously refused."

Listening to Lynn Davenport's argument, Scott knew what the judge would do. He pulled the legal pad containing the notes for his opening statement closer to him. This had been an interesting interlude, but he'd better get ready to proceed.

The judge nodded and turned to Lester. "The defendant will please rise."

Lester rose to his feet beside Mr. Humphrey. Startled, Scott joined them.

"Mr. Garrison, I have considered the arguments of your lawyer. Do you realize the seriousness of the charges that have brought us here today?"

Lester was appropriately subdued. "Yes, sir."

"Someone could have been killed."

Lester blinked without responding.

"Do you understand the proposal your lawyer has asked me to consider?"

"Yes, sir."

"You've heard the charges against you. Did you fire shots from a handgun in the vicinity of the people at the church?"

Scott looked sideways at his client. Lester was silent for several seconds before answering.

"Uh, yes, sir."

The judge stared hard at Lester, then continued, "Do you realize that if you choose to plead guilty, I do not have to accept the recommendation of your lawyer as to your sentence?"

Harold Garrison blurted out, "Then he ain't pleading guilty."

"Who are you?" the judge asked sharply.

Still seated, Harold answered, "His father."

"Mr. Garrison, stand when you address the court."

Harold lumbered to his feet. "I was just—"

The judge cut him off. "Let your son's lawyers speak for his interests. That's why they are here."

Harold opened and closed his mouth.

Leland Humphrey spoke. "Is the court inclined to adopt our suggestion as to sentence?"

Lynn Davenport stood, but the judge silenced her with a look. He then stared hard at Lester. Scott closely inspected the judge's face, trying to guess what was coming. The glasses remained motionless.

"Having considered the proposal of counsel for the defendant and the arguments in opposition by the state, the court believes that the proposed plea and sentence satisfies the interests of justice and holds out the possibility of rehabilitation for the defendant. Given the defendant's young age, the court is reluctant to send him into an environment with the general prison population and finds that the boot-camp program for youthful offenders administered by the North Carolina Department of Corrections is an appropriate disposition. Defendant's request that his plea be accepted under the first offender act is also granted."

Scott was in shock. He barely heard the judge ask Lester the additional questions required when a defendant enters a guilty plea.

When the judge finished, Mr. Humphrey said, "Your honor, may the defendant remain free under bond until space is available in the boot-camp program? He is living at home and attending school as a condition of the pretrial bond."

The judge looked toward the D.A.'s table. "Ms. Davenport, how soon do you think a place will open up in the program?"

"One or two weeks, your honor. We can call this afternoon. I'm concerned that the defendant—" The D.A. stopped. "That's it."

"Very well. The defendant will remain free on bond upon the same terms." The judge motioned to the bailiff. "When the jury returns, bring them in and I'll advise them that the case has been resolved. I'm sure they'll be happy to learn that they're free until tomorrow morning."

No one spoke on the walk back to the office. Scott had said everything he could think of—twice.

Outside the front door of Humphrey, Balcomb and Jackson, Mr. Humphrey said, "Lester, we'll let you know when you have to report to begin your sentence. You should have at least twenty-four hours' notice."

Scott added, "In the meantime, go to school and stay out of trouble. No fighting."

Lester shrugged. "I'm not stupid."

Scott bit his lower lip and didn't allow himself to debate the truth or falsity of Lester's comment. The facts spoke for themselves. The Garrisons went around the corner to the parking lot. Scott and Mr. Humphrey went into the building.

"Can we debrief?" the younger lawyer asked.

"Of course. Come into my office."

Scott slumped down in a chair.

"What happened? I never guessed Lester would want to plead guilty and was more shocked when the judge went along with the sentence."

Mr. Humphrey ran his thumb down the inside of his right suspender.

"I'm not sure I can unravel Lester, but bravado in the office doesn't necessarily transfer to courage in open court. I've seen it happen in all sorts of cases. The client boasts about a strong case before walking into the courtroom, then reality hits, and he decides to take something certain rather than gamble on the unknown. The judge is easier to fathom. He looked at Lester's age and the fact that no one was hurt. Wayman Teasley is not interested in prematurely increasing the general prison population of North Carolina by adding a seventeen-year-old boy to the mix."

"And Kendall?"

"Is a contradiction wrapped in an enigma."

"What do you mean?"

"Real life isn't always neat and tidy, and the truth doesn't come wrapped with a bow before the commercial break at the top of the hour."

"So, we'll never know the truth?"

"Never is a long time. But there are a lot of unresolved controversies in the closed files stored at the firm's miniwarehouse."

Mr. Humphrey leafed through his phone messages and picked one up.

"This looks interesting. Now that you've increased your criminal law experience you might want to give this man a call. The note says that he's been charged with bigamy. He's been married four times in three counties without bothering to get a divorce in between. Bigamy cases are rare, so this would be a unique opportunity."

Scott grinned. "If it's okay, I'll pass. He sounds like another contradiction wrapped in an enigma."

42

Or have we eaten on the insane root that takes the reason prisoner?
MACBETH, ACT 1, SCENE 3

After his long morning in court, Scott had trouble diving back into routine office work. He wandered downstairs to the kitchen for a drink of water, then went into the room where the firm kept its fax machine, postage meter, and copier. Several incoming faxes were lined up on the counter. He glanced at the cover sheets. When he reached the last one, he stopped. It was from a clinical psychologist in Charlotte to Ann Gammons. The subject of the evaluation—Franklin Jesup Jr.

Scott picked it up and started reading. It was an extensive report. Frank had an IQ that placed him in the top 2 percent of the population. He was moderately depressed, which was not surprising considering the breakup of his parents' marriage. He was angry with his mother and didn't like his little sister very much. But the information that began on page three of the report made the hair on the back of Scott's neck stand up.

In a battery of tests designed to reveal forms of subtle, hidden psychosis, Frank Jesup Jr. revealed a dark side to his personality that harbored the potential for violent behavior. The psychologist didn't rely solely on the results of an initial test. He ran a second series of tests, then a third more sophisticated sequence that contained complicated crosschecks making it virtually impossible to manipulate—even for someone as intelligent as Frank. The results were uniform and consistent.

He concluded that Frank needed immediate psychiatric treatment, possibly hospitalization, and removal from the public school setting. According to the psychologist, Frank Sr.'s influence on his son was very negative, and the relationship between them needed to be monitored closely.

Scott picked up the report and went upstairs to Ann's office. The only female lawyer and a partner in the firm, Ann worked at the opposite end of the building from Scott. Everything in Ann's office was first-class: beautiful cherry desk, original watercolor paintings of scenes from the Outer Banks, a large oriental rug on the polished wooden floor. Leland Humphrey would have been paralyzed in Ann's world. There wasn't a single stack of papers to rummage through in the entire room.

Her door was open, and Ann was on the phone. She motioned for Scott to sit down in one of the blue leather chairs across from her desk while she finished the call. She hung up the phone and ran her fingers through short black hair streaked with gray.

"Weren't you and Leland trying a case today?" she asked.

"The client pleaded guilty, so I'm delivering faxes."

Scott handed her the report.

"Frank Jesup Jr. was one of the students on the mock trial team I coached at Catawba High. I saw this downstairs and brought it right up."

Ann scanned the report. As she did, her eyes grew bigger. Scott waited until she finished and put it down.

"Did you read this?" she asked.

"Yes. I've been around him a lot over the past few weeks. My assessment was that he is a smart kid with a bad attitude. I tried to befriend him but hit a brick wall. Now I know why."

Scott leaned forward and picked up the papers.

Turning to the back page, he read aloud, "Frank has a morbid fascination with death. He views it as a positive event, both for himself and others, thus raising concern of suicidal/homicidal potential. He jokingly acknowledged occasional suicidal/homicidal fantasies involving one or all of the members of his family, but quickly added that it was only an imaginary outlet for the frustrations he'd experienced in the home. Although he does not admit to auditory hallucinations, it would be consistent with his profile and is suggested by some of the test data."

Scott looked up. "Frank would try to kill a member of his family and claim he heard a voice telling him to do it."

"Possibly."

Scott put the report on the edge of the desk.

"What are you going to do with this?"

"Try to get him help, but his father's lawyer may send him to another psychologist who will say there's nothing wrong with him."

"Are they fighting over custody?"

"No, Vivian doesn't want Frank, but she requested an evaluation to back up her claims about the negative influence of Frank on his little sister, Jodie. Vivian doesn't want Jodie visiting her father if Frank is in the house."

"This should help you on that issue. Are you going to notify the school system?"

"And then who would be sued?" Ann asked.

Scott nodded. Ann was right. The report was confidential.

"Yeah, it would be up to the mother to contact the school. What do you think she will do?"

"I don't know. Her focus has been on keeping Frank out of her hair and away from his sister. Her initial goal was to send him to a private school, not the psychiatric ward of a hospital. Since this report contains more than she bargained for, she may have to rethink her position. I'm going to recommend that she limit her contact with him since the most likely objects of his anger would be the members of his family."

"Or anyone that looks at him the wrong way on the wrong day," Scott added.

Still troubled by the report, Scott returned to his office. He had a voice-mail message from Kay.

"Hi, Scott. I've been thinking about you and Lester all day. Let me hear from you when you have a few minutes. Bye."

Scott looked at the clock. Kay would still be in class for another hour and a half. He decided not to leave her a message at the school about Lester's case.

On the edge of Scott's desk were the mock trial materials. He dictated a memo to his secretary to open a file so he could keep the information for use the following year. Scott was hooked. He'd enjoyed working with the students, and Janie's request that he help in the future could not be denied. Kay's involvement was the icing on the cake. Scott had one regret. He wished he'd known the seriousness of Frank Jesup's problems. The young man needed professional help, but Scott wondered if he could have helped by trying harder to reach out to him rather than getting so easily frustrated with the student's attitude. By next year, Frank would be lost to graduation, and it would be up to college to give him the stimulus and challenge that could lift him out of his inner darkness.

After finishing with the mock trial materials, Scott also gathered together the multiple folders that made up *State v. Garrison* in a larger folder. In a few weeks Lester would make the journey to the boot-camp program near Fayetteville, and the pleadings and documents would make a brief trip to the closed file depository. Scott wondered what an extensive psychological evaluation would reveal about Lester Garrison.

———

Larry Sellers, the maintenance supervisor for the school system, found the list while doing a routine inspection after the students left the building on Monday. He opened a cleaning closet and saw a piece of wrinkled paper wedged against the doorframe. When he picked it up to toss it into a nearby trash receptacle, a crude design at the top of the page caught his attention. It was a simple drawing of a human skull. He flattened the crumpled sheet of paper. Underneath the skull was a crudely written list of twelve names.

There was a Catawba high-school yearbook propped between two plastic containers of floor-cleaning compound in the closet. Larry opened it to see if there were students at the school whose names matched those on the list. The first name he checked was a sophomore boy. The second was a junior girl. The third was a junior boy; however, one thing was different. The student's name was printed in the column on the left-hand side of the page, but his class picture was missing from the book. It had been cut out with sharp scissors or a razor blade.

Larry paused. He turned to the fourth name on the list, found the student, but no picture. It was the same with the next four students. The next student's picture was in the book, but the final three were not. He flipped through the yearbook. There were several other pictures cut from the student sections that did not correlate to the names on the list. But the connection between the list and the cutout pictures was too important to ignore. Under the security guidelines issued by the superintendent's office, the sheet of paper had to be reported. The possible connection with the yearbook made the situation more suspicious. He took the sheet of paper and yearbook with him and called Dr. Lassiter at home.

After listening, the principal asked, "Where are you now?"

"In the administrative offices. I have the sheet and yearbook with me."

"Who has access to the closet where you found them?"

"Everybody on the janitorial crew and the faculty or staff members who have a master key. Of course, you know how hard it is to maintain an accurate inventory on keys."

"Yes. I'll investigate it in the morning. Put the items in my office."

Before he left the office to go home, Scott called Kay at her apartment and gave her a factual report of the outcome in Lester's case.

"I don't understand," she said. "How could he plead guilty if he didn't do it?"

"I can't go into it because of attorney-client privilege, but it was a bizarre turn of events at the end. I've learned that the law is not a science; it's a poker game."

"Will Lester come back to school?"

"Yes. Regular school attendance is mandatory until a space opens up for him in the boot-camp program. If he skips out, he will be in a cell at the youth detention center within twenty-four hours."

"Okay. I'll be praying for him."

Scott chuckled. "You are a woman of great faith. If it's okay with you and God, I'm not going to think about young Mr. Garrison or his father for a while."

Scott wanted to mention the information he'd learned about Frank but couldn't think of a way to bring it up. He settled for something general.

"How's Frank?" he asked.

"He was in class today. I thanked him for serving on the mock trial team."

"What did he say?"

"Nothing. I don't remember that he responded."

"Do you think I should try to spend time with Frank?" Scott asked.

"Why?" she asked with surprise. "I thought he shut the door on you."

"He did, but he is such a smart kid, and I know his parents are splitting up. I'd hate for him to take a violent"—Scott caught himself—"uh, negative turn."

Kay didn't notice his slip. "I guess you could give it another try. It would be outside school."

"I might call and invite him down to the office."

"Do you need his number?"

Scott knew Ann Gammons would have all relevant phone numbers. "No, I can get it."

"I wanted to ask you about something else," Kay said. "I'd like to set up a special lunch on Wednesday for the students who were in the mock trial program. Can you fit it in your schedule?"

"At the school?"

"Yes, I think we're having tacos, and I know how much you like them."

Scott paused. "Are you laughing at me?"

"Only on the inside."

He looked at his calendar. "I can come anytime between eleven-thirty and one o'clock."

"That will work. Make it 12:15. I'll meet you at the office."

"I know where to go. I've eaten at the cafeteria more times than I'd like to remember."

"Just meet me at the office."

Scott understood the unspoken message. The students were preparing something for him, and he needed to show up at the right time.

"Okay."

———

Kay spent the evening thinking of a word or two that characterized each student on the mock trial team and writing a few lines of encouragement to share while they ate their meal. Earlier in the day Dustin had perfected an impersonation of Scott that perfectly captured the way the young lawyer acted when showing the students how to question a witness. Janie had written a humorous lyric about the mock trial competition. She and Alisha were going to sing it to the theme song from *The Beverly Hillbillies*. Dr. Lassiter had agreed to attend, and Mr. Humphrey would make a surprise entrance toward the end of the meal. Several mothers were going to bring snacks. Yvette Fisher's mother had baked a cake.

It was going to be a fun day.

43

The die is cast.

JULIUS CAESAR

Recently, Tao had thought about the words he'd heard at the river near the refugee camp and wondered again why he was in America. It was enough to be in harmony with the will of the One who loved him, but deep down he suspected there was something more.

Tao didn't see himself as a man of destiny. Self-centered ambition was not his area of weakness. He was from a respected family in his home village, but the notion that one man could make a difference across an entire society was more American than Asian. Tao saw himself as the part of a larger whole, a perspective that helped him relate to the biblical idea of the church as a group of many members working together.

Thus, it was a challenge for him to be in isolation at the school. He was surrounded by hundreds of people, but they were in a different world. His relationship with the Tuesday group was a hidden secret known only to himself. Thus, his heart's cry for fellowship with others during the workday was not satisfied on a practical level.

He prayed about the situation and the Lord answered by enriching Tao's inner communion with the Lord himself. The janitor enjoyed a relationship with Jesus that filled the void left by interaction with people during the day. Perhaps that was why he came to America, he concluded. In aloneness he found a greater intimacy.

The bomber sat in the parking lot of the high school until the first wave of his classmates flowed through the front doors on their way home. Many of the young people were laughing and smiling. The components of the bomb were hidden under a sheet on the floorboard of his vehicle. It would take three trips to transport everything into the building. The bomber wanted to make his trips at the proper time. He didn't want to attract attention by being so early that the number of people still roaming the halls would make secrecy a problem, and he didn't want to be too late and risk being questioned by a teacher or member of the administration.

When the number of students had dwindled to a trickle, he walked casually up the sidewalk into the building and into the administrative offices. A middle-aged woman with thick glasses and a negative expression sat behind the counter.

"Ms. Laramie needs some paper for the copy machine near her office," the student said.

"That machine was filled up yesterday," the woman replied.

The student shrugged. "I was staying late to catch up on some work I've missed, and she asked me to get some copy paper from the supply closet in the hall. It was locked."

"Of course, it's locked," the woman snorted. "We keep it locked all the time."

The student attempted to be respectful. "Do you have a key I could borrow?"

"Yes, I guess so." The woman selected a key from a pegboard on the wall behind the counter. "Bring it back before you take her the paper. And make sure you lock the door behind you."

The key in his hand, the student walked down the hallway to the supply room. He unlocked the door and went inside. The storage closet contained boxes of paper, toner, and chemicals for all the copy machines in the school. It was located in the center of the buildings that made up the campus and was well stocked with supplies. There must have been a recent delivery. The student took a ream of paper from an open box. As he closed the door, he was careful not to push in the button that engaged the locking mechanism.

Paper in hand, he returned to the office. The aide was on the phone, so he put the key on the counter.

As he was leaving, she hung up the receiver and called out, "Wait!"

The student froze for a second before turning around.

"Tell Ms. Laramie to complete a requisition form for that paper and turn it in to the office tomorrow. We have to account for every sheet."

"Uh, okay."

The bomber returned to his vehicle and put the largest of his three components in an old backpack that he hadn't used in a couple of years. Hoisting it on his shoulders he went back inside the school and walked directly to the supply room. He was about to open the door when a science teacher came around the corner. Their eyes met. The student had sat in the back row of the teacher's class in ninth grade. He could tell the teacher recognized his face and wondered if he had forgotten his name.

"Taking a lot of books home, aren't you?" the teacher asked.

"Yeah, I've been out some in the past couple of weeks."

The student took a few more steps forward, opened a locker that had been left ajar, and pretended to be looking for something. It belonged to a girl who had covered the inside with pictures of herself and her boyfriend. The teacher passed, and the hallway was clear. The bomber returned to the supply closet and went inside. He put his load behind the boxes, then started to leave. He stopped and picked up another ream of paper. Coming from the supply closet empty-handed would be out of the ordinary; carrying paper would not arouse suspicion. Several students passed him in the hallway. No one paid any attention to him.

In a few minutes, he returned with his second load of explosive material. This time he made his delivery without interruption. After depositing the material, he picked up a bottle of toner and walked down the hallway and out of the building to the parking lot. This was his last load. He carefully placed the detonator, the power source, and a digital clock in the backpack. He opened a zippered pouch and put in a screwdriver, pliers, and wire strippers.

Once again, the hall was deserted. He pulled on the doorknob. This time it didn't open. He pulled harder and tried to turn the knob. The door didn't budge. He must have locked the door by mistake. The student silently swore and debated his next step. There was only one thing to do. He had to go back to the office and get the key.

The office aide was still at her post. The student tried to adopt a nonchalant attitude that was completely at odds with his feelings and appearance.

"I'm back again," he said. "The light on the copier that shows that the machine is low on toner came on. I saw some bottles of toner in the supply room when I got the paper."

"We don't give toner to students," the woman replied. "I'll make a note and have someone service the machine tomorrow. Tell Ms. Laramie to use a different copy machine. She can bring the material here to the office if she wants to."

Stymied, the student went back into the hallway. The explosive material was inside the supply room ready to be activated, but without the key he couldn't close the circle of destruction. He went to his locker and opened the door. He considered putting the backpack in the locker until another opportunity. But each day would increase the chance that the explosive material in the supply closet would be discovered. If only he'd made sure not to lock the door.

At that moment the bomber got a break.

A female student came out of the administrative offices and walked directly to the supply closet. The bomber closed his locker door and drew closer. In the student's hand was the key. She unlocked the door and went inside. The bomber appeared in the doorway.

"I need to get some paper for Ms. Laramie," he said.

At the sound of his voice, the student jumped. "You scared me."

The bomber ignored her reaction. "You can take the key back to the office," he said. "I'll lock the door."

The female student left. He went inside and shut the door. Moving the boxes to the side, he sat down on the floor and began connecting the detonator to the two power sources and the packets of explosive. He had practiced the procedure many times in the private place where he kept the components of the bomb, but to do it for real made him perspire. He had memorized the function of each colored wire. It was an exciting moment when he got out the clock and prepared the final connections. Included in the configuration were several dummy wires that served no function and two tripwires that would automatically cause the bomb to detonate if an effort was made to disarm it. He took a deep breath and looked over the assembled device. It was beautiful. Everything was neat and organized. He wired the clock to the detonator and checked his watch. Holding his fingers on the buttons, he advanced the numbers to the correct settings. He released his control. The time flashed and began its downward descent. The bomb was alive.

In less than twenty-four hours the clock would reach zero. There would be a faint click followed by an earth-shattering boom that no one within two hundred feet of the copy room would ever remember. The secondary effects of the explosion farther away from the supply room were harder to predict, but he knew that the effect of falling debris would be significant. Now that the bomb was operational, the student didn't want to leave. He wanted to sit with the bomb, watch the clock, and anticipate the moment of detonation. He carefully double-checked every connection. Three minutes had already passed. He knew he had to leave. He arranged several boxes of paper and chemicals so that everything was concealed. He wouldn't see it again until he stood in the midst of the firestorm that would destroy everything and everyone in its path.

44

A date which will live in infamy.
FRANKLIN DELANO ROOSEVELT

Each day dawns filled with the unknown. Sometimes a day arrives pregnant with anticipated importance. At other times, a routine day takes on a significance that no one anticipated. But most days are neutral—neither good nor bad, notable or memorable.

There had been many Wednesdays at Catawba High School since public education began in Blanchard County. Wednesday usually held no special place in the school calendar. It wasn't a Monday when the week's activities were communicated through faculty memos and homeroom meetings, or a Friday filled with tests during the day and athletic contests at night. Wednesday was a vanilla segment of twenty-four hours.

When Tao arrived at the school, he went to the cleaning closet to retrieve his copy of the yearbook. He'd spent several days praying for the same two students and wanted to ask the Lord if he had another assignment for him. The yearbook was gone. The janitor carefully looked behind the bottles and jugs in the closet but couldn't find it. Puzzled, he went into the break room where the maintenance staff ate lunch to see if he had left the book on the table. It wasn't there either. It was time to begin work. The search for the yearbook would have to wait.

Tao had time to clean two rest rooms before the students arrived for the school day. When he finished, the sinks shone, the floor was spotless, and the mirrors didn't have any streaks. He would clean two other rest rooms after the students left in the afternoon.

Dr. Lassiter had a breakfast meeting with the local Kiwanis club and arrived at the school later than usual. On a chair in his office were Tao's yearbook and the piece of paper left by Larry Sellers. The principal repeated the process of comparing the names on the list to the missing pictures in the book and decided Larry should call a meeting of the janitorial staff and ask about this yearbook.

Lester Garrison returned to school. Before opening his locker, he looked up and down the hallway. No one was paying attention to him. News of Monday's events in court had not yet filtered out into the school population. Soon, what the students at Catawba High School said or thought about him wouldn't matter.

Kay used her morning free period to decorate the faculty dining room for the lunch with Scott and the mock trial students. At 12:05 P.M. she would stop by the dining room for a last-minute check before meeting Scott at the office.

Frank Jesup Jr. called the school office and told the woman who answered the phone that he was sick. It was a true statement. The night before Frank had stayed up late to battle his unseen on-line adversaries. He didn't hold back. There was no use concealing his best strategies any longer, and it was a time of major victory for him. He tracked down his most formidable adversary and cut him to pieces in a deluge of blood-red images. The enemy signed off with a string of profanity and threats about the future. Frank didn't respond. In his mind, success had been a foregone conclusion.

The weakest link in Frank's plan was the possibility that the boxes of paper or supplies might be removed late Tuesday afternoon or early Wednesday morning and the bomb discovered. This almost happened at 10:45 A.M. on Wednesday. The copy machine in the athletic offices was out of paper, and Coach Leonard sent two boys to get a couple of boxes of paper. They stopped by the office to borrow a key.

"Make sure he files a requisition form," the aide said. "I'm tired of people getting paper and not reporting it."

"Yes, ma'am."

"What's her problem?" one of the boys asked when they were back in the hall.

Each student picked up a box of paper. When the second box was removed, it exposed the face of the clock that was resting on the floor.

One of the boys noticed the red numbers and said, "Someone left a clock in here."

"Leave it alone," the other student responded. "Coach Leonard told us to get two boxes of paper. That's it."

They closed the door and returned the key. The door was unlocked.

While Kay made last-minute preparations for the luncheon and Tao helped set up chairs in the gym, the clock connected to the detonator steadily counted down the minutes and seconds. As his last act on the computer, Frank ran a set of several computer projections of the damage the bomb might cause. The results ranged from partial destruction of building A to total destruction of buildings A, B, and the cafeteria. In his mock-up, he also predicted the appearance of the high school from the air after detonation. He left the pages beside his computer.

Frank hadn't seen his father in two days. Frank Sr. was spending almost every night at his girlfriend's condominium. Vivian Jesup had left a message on the answering machine that she wouldn't be bringing Jodie by for her scheduled visit. She didn't give a reason. Frank didn't care what they did. They had no control over him; he held his future in his own hands.

At 11:45 A.M. he walked out of the house carrying a duffel bag that contained an old, single-shot deer rifle that had belonged to his grandfather. He sat in the driveway for several minutes before starting his car's engine. Frank didn't know anything about the list of names on the wrinkled sheet of paper in Dr. Lassiter's office. It had been prepared as a prank by a tenth grader who picked all but one of the names at random and slipped the note into the locker of a classmate whose name he put at the top of the list. That student never saw the page because it fell out of his locker the first time he opened it. It was then kicked around the hallway for a couple of days before becoming lodged in the doorway of the cleaning closet.

Frank could have prepared a list, but his act was general, not specific. If he saw a few individuals that particularly deserved extermination, he would use the rifle. Otherwise, he trusted in the impersonal selection process of the bomb and would fire gunshots at random.

Frank knew that he didn't have to go to the school. The bomb was in place, and the devastation and death it would produce would not be significantly affected by his presence. He could easily dispose of the paraphernalia that might link him to the blast and casually watch the report on the national news shows later in the evening. But Frank didn't want anonymity. He wanted his act to be connected with his name. Frank would be dead, but he knew that after today, his name would not be forgotten. He didn't want to live and read about his deed. He wanted to stand in the fire.

He started the car and backed out of the driveway.

As the morning progressed, Tao became slightly agitated. He took out one of the pictures he was carrying in his pocket and looked at it. It was a young man. He studied the student's features. He was a good-looking boy, but as always the eyes revealed the heart. The eyes told Tao that the student was troubled. How deeply was not clear. So, he prayed. The agitation didn't leave. Tao wanted to be alone, but it was over an hour before his lunch break. He didn't know how to ask his supervisor for permission to take an early lunch.

When Scott arrived at the school, Frank was in the parking lot waiting until the clock ticked down a few more minutes. As the young lawyer walked up the sidewalk to the front door, he remembered the reservations he had about helping with the mock trial team at the time of his initial meeting with Dr. Lassiter. Today, he'd taken a few minutes during the morning to compose a brief speech for the students. He wanted to encourage them to keep believing in what they could accomplish. Frank was at the center of Scott's thoughts. He wanted to say something that would open the door for future contact with the brilliant young man.

It had been an overcast morning, but it was now bright and sunny. Scott pushed open the door and stepped into the broad hallway. It was beginning to fill with students moving from classes to the cafeteria. While he waited for Kay in the reception area of the office, he opened a yearbook that was two years old. It was amusing how much the students had changed in such a short time. In ninth grade, Dustin's ears stuck out beyond his shirt collar, and Alisha Mason was wearing glasses so big they seemed to overwhelm her head.

The door opened, and Kay stuck her head into the room.

Smiling, she asked, "Ready?"

Before Scott could answer, the first shot was fired.

45

Unto the breach.
KING HENRY V, ACT 3, SCENE 1

"What was that?" Kay asked and stepped back into the hall. Someone screamed, and Scott ran to the door. Everything happened quickly and in slow motion at the same time. A second shot was fired, and Scott recognized the sound. It was a high-powered rifle. Students began running in every direction. Scott looked up and down the hallway but in the pandemonium of fast-moving legs, arms, and bodies, he couldn't locate the gunman.

"Get into the office!" he yelled at Kay.

She remained frozen in shock and disbelief.

Crouching down, Scott ran across the hall focusing his attention on the entrance of the building. He still couldn't identify the shooter. A third shot came blazing out of the barrel of the gun. The bullet struck Kay in the head. Scott didn't see her fall. A small pool of blood quickly formed on the shiny floor and mixed with her blond hair.

A fourth shot ricocheted off the floor and into Scott's right calf. He fell down, rolled over, and crawled to the door of the copy supply storage room. He jerked open the door, slid inside, and slammed the door shut. In the darkness he could feel the warm blood running down his leg to his ankle. Grimacing in pain, he reached up and felt along the wall until he found the light switch and flipped it on. He pulled up his pant leg. The wound was bleeding, but it wasn't spurting as if an artery had been severed. He took off his shirt, wrapped it around the wound, and tied it tightly to slow the bleeding. Another shot rang out in the hallway.

Scott didn't know what to do. He desperately called back everything he could remember from his military training. He quickly surveyed the room. The only item that could be considered a makeshift weapon was a pair of red-handled scissors.

Then he saw the clock.

———

When the first shot was fired, Tao was bagging the trash in the boys' bathroom around the corner from the main hallway. The sound of gunfire was not unfamiliar to him. He had fought many skirmishes with Communist troops in the mountains of his homeland. On two occasions he had crept in under enemy fire and rescued a wounded member of the unit composed of men from his village. In America, he would have received a medal. In Laos, he received a simple thank-you.

At the sound of the shot, he stopped and looked toward the door. A boy standing next to him turned to a companion.

"Was that a firecracker?" he asked.

"It sounds like somebody dropped an M-80 in a toilet in the girls' bathroom," the other responded.

Tao was at the door when the second shot was fired, and a stream of male and female students came rushing in screaming.

"Somebody's got a gun!" a boy yelled.

It wasn't difficult for Tao to recall his training. He slipped through the crowd into the hallway and moved along the wall until he reached the corner. He peeked around the edge of the wall and saw the young man with the rifle standing inside the front doorway. The boy raised the gun and fired again. Tao didn't see Kay spin around and collapse on the floor. Tao moved along the wall. The shooter's next shot was too low and went toward the floor. This was the bullet that hit Scott in the leg. Tao saw him fall, get up, and limp into the storage room. Tao kept his focus on the gun. The young man turned around and took a few steps back so he could look out the front doors of the building. He did not seem upset or in a hurry.

In the midst of the students fleeing down the hall, Tao saw a girl turn toward the shooter. He recognized her immediately as one of the members of the prayer group. Her picture had spent many days riding in his pocket. The girl leaned over and yelled several words at the top of her voice. The shooter turned in her direction and put a bullet in the chamber of his weapon. When he could clearly see the young man's face, Tao gasped. The boy began walking toward the girl.

———

Pushing aside two boxes of copy paper Scott saw the rest of the bomb and realized that the clock was a timer for an explosive device. There was exactly one minute and thirty seconds until it reached zero.

After the explosion that killed Steve Robinson, Scott and the other members of his unit were debriefed about the nature of the bomb that snuffed out the life of their comrade and the way it might have been disarmed. It was hard for Scott to relive his mistake, but he had no choice. He learned that the key to disabling every bomb was proper disruption of the power source necessary to trigger the detonator. It was just like the movies. Cut the green wire; the world is saved. Cut the red wire; Armageddon is upon us. The problem lay in making the right judgment when there was limited time to analyze the relationship of the components of the device. In the movies, the hero always makes the right choice. In reality, the odds are less certain. The clock read *1:14*.

Scott's mind began to work in overdrive. He quickly checked the back of the clock. If there was only one wire connected to the timer, he could cut that wire with the scissors, and the bomb would be placed in suspended animation—always waiting for the signal that never came. There were three black wires snaking out from the back of the clock. This meant there was a probable backup power source, the main line from the clock to the detonator, and a cross-connected wire that acted like a switch. If the switch wire was cut, it would connect the circuit in either direction and detonate the bomb. The only way to fool the device would be to cut the two power wires before cutting the switch wire. It would require two right choices without a wrong one in between. The clock read *:55*.

The three black wires were identical. No green, red, and yellow. As soon as they exited the clock they were braided together, making it impossible to sort them out as they entered a small metal box. The box, which Scott guessed contained the batteries and the detonator, was screwed shut with ten screws. Even if Scott had a screwdriver, he couldn't have opened the box and sorted through the jumble of wires and connectors in less than a minute. The wires left the small box on the other side and traveled a foot to a much larger box that contained the explosive material. The clock read :41.

Scott picked up the scissors. He positioned his body so that it was between the large box and the door. He didn't know the nature of the explosives, but if he could save someone else by partially blocking the explosion, he was willing to do it. It was quiet in the hallway, and Scott suddenly realized that the shooter was on a suicide mission, passing time until the bomb detonated. Scott had to decide which wires to cut. There was no time to flip a coin. The clock read :28.

He decided on his strategy. Holding the wire nearest him as it exited the back of the clock, he opened the scissors so that the wire rested against the lower blade. The clock read :21. He held his breath and closed the scissors.

In the hallway outside the storage room, Frank walked toward Janie Collins. He passed Kay's body on the floor in front of the administrative offices. He did not know that his fourth shot had hit Scott in the leg or that the young lawyer was in the storage room. He checked his watch. There were less than thirty seconds until the bomb exploded. He wanted to be at ground zero when the ball of fire came roaring out of the room, vaporizing everything within its path.

"You've shot Ms. Laramie! Please put down the gun!" Janie cried out.

Frank raised the rifle toward her. When he did, he looked into her eyes. The eyes knew him. He hesitated. He wanted the moment to be impersonal, and Janie's presence threatened his detachment.

"Move!" he screamed.

He doubted she could run fast enough or far enough to escape death, but in the insanity of the moment, he decided it was better for the bomb to kill her than for him to put a bullet into her chest. Her eyes wide, Janie backed away toward the corner where Tao waited.

Waving the rifle back and forth, Frank approached the storage closet so he could open the door. He didn't want anything to hinder the fiery hell he'd planned from being released in its greatest horror.

When Scott squeezed the scissors, nothing happened. The wire was either tougher than he'd thought or the metal blades of the scissors were very dull. His first attempt only put a crease in the black insulation. Beads of sweat stood out on his forehead. Blood from the wound in his leg had soaked his makeshift bandage. He felt slightly dizzy. He didn't realize how quiet it had become in the hallway. The clock read *:20*.

He squeezed harder and severed the wire. No explosion.

Of the three identical wires that exited the back of the clock, Scott had cut the wire nearest to him. In the only logic he could muster, he'd decided that the two outside wires were most likely the sources of power, leaving the middle wire as the switch wire. He opened the scissors to cut the wire farthest from him. He would have to squeeze harder. There wouldn't be time for a second chance. The clock read *:15*.

———

Tao saw the shooter's attention directed away from Janie and toward the storage closet. He knew the wounded man was inside the little room. The young man reached for the doorknob. Tao quickly came into the hallway as Frank opened the door.

When he opened the door, Frank saw Scott with a pair of scissors in his hand. A look of shock and surprise streaked across the young man's face. He realized what Scott was attempting to do.

"No!" Frank screamed and raised the gun toward Scott.

The clock read *:09*.

Tao dove in between Scott and the open door as Frank pulled the trigger. The bullet meant for Scott pierced Tao's chest. Scott recoiled from the deafening sound of the gun at such close range. He looked at his hand. It was still holding the scissors. He squeezed the scissors and cut the wire. The last number on the clock face was *:02*. It went dark.

Frank swore at Scott. Their eyes met and rage boiled out of the young man with a level of hate that Scott had never seen in another human face. Frank fumbled in his pocket for another shell.

"I'll kill you and blow up that bomb myself!"

Tao rolled onto his side so that he faced the young man. Blood was already beginning to soak the top of his chest. He reached into the front pocket of his shirt and pulled out a picture of a smiling student with dark hair and eyes. The upper half of the photograph was already red with the janitor's blood. He held the picture out toward Frank, then slowly brought his hands together in the universal sign of prayer. The picture dropped from his fingers to the floor.

Frank took a step forward and looked down. It was his eleventh-grade photograph. Shaking his head to clear it from Tao's gesture and the image of his own smiling face, he chambered the shell that would drill a hole through Scott's heart. He could directly wire the bomb and bypass the clock.

At that moment, the front door of the school opened, and the deputy sheriff assigned to the campus came into the hallway. He had finished patrolling the parking lot and wanted a cup of coffee. He saw Kay's body on the floor and Frank, rifle in hand, standing over Tao. He pulled his pistol from the holster on his hip.

"Drop that gun!" he commanded.

Frank turned and fired. The bullet shattered the glass front of the trophy case. The officer fired back. The bullet hit Frank in his chest. The young man dropped the rifle, staggered backward, and reached one hand up to the place where the bullet had entered his body. His hand came away covered with blood. Puzzled, he looked at his hand and then collapsed on the floor.

His gun still drawn, the deputy ran down the hallway. He reached the doorway to the storage closet and saw Scott sitting on the floor. He pointed the gun at him.

Scott weakly held up his hands.

"I'm Scott Ellis, a lawyer. There was a bomb in here, but it's disabled. Check the janitor."

The security officer examined Frank first. The young man was dead.

Tao was on his side. The deputy rolled him over onto his back. He was still alive. Barely. The officer held Tao up in his arms. The Hmong man opened his eyes, but he didn't see a Blanchard County sheriff's deputy.

He saw the angels.

Standing soberly, shoulder to shoulder, they nearly filled the empty hallway. He recognized some of the heavenly beings from the time around the table in the cafeteria. However, his ability to distinguish their individual characteristics was now heightened 1,000 percent. They weren't uniform in appearance. Like people, each one was unique. Each one beautifully, fearfully different. And in an instant, he knew things about them and the duties they had performed at the command of the Lord they served. Today, their attention was focused on him.

The one to the left of the deputy had been with Tao his entire life. He'd been the guardian whose gentle nudge kept Tao from stepping on a deadly snake when he was a little boy walking down a jungle path. He served as Tao's unseen comrade in arms who warned him not to take a trail that would have led him into a Vietcong ambush. He became the barricade between Tao and the beckoning waters of death in the refugee camp. And during the great journey of spiritual discovery to Bangkok, the heavenly watchman kept sleepless vigil over Tao, whispering the words of heaven into the pilgrim's newborn spirit. Tao saw more examples of the merciful, sovereign hand of God than could be chronicled in a dozen lifetimes.

The other beings in the hall had their own stories to tell. Tao knew they were tales of great faith—adventures involving people of every color and language who loved Jesus and gave their lives for the sake of the Kingdom. The angels showed no emotion as they gazed at him, but there was a reality of love in their faces that filled him with something more life-giving than the blood flowing out of his body.

He was too weak to speak aloud, but internally he asked, "Why are you here?"

"Because you and others prayed."

And Tao knew that prayers offered in faith are not in vain. Evil exists in the world, and bad things happen. But God has not left his people without the right to petition heaven. Faith still moves mountains.

"And to take you home."

Tao was overwhelmed. The glorious messengers were a celestial honor guard sent to usher him into the presence of his King. He had followed his Savior in laying down his life as a sacrifice for others. Now, the time of never-ending rejoicing had come. It was time to go. His eyes fluttered shut, but he didn't see death. He entered directly into the life that never ends.

"He's gone," the officer said.

46

Earth felt the wound.
PARADISE LOST

The deputy laid Tao on the floor and disappeared from Scott's view. The young lawyer couldn't stand up, so he pushed himself forward with his arms into the hallway. The bodies of Tao and Frank were partially blocking the door. He turned sideways so that he faced the entrance of the school.

And saw Kay.

The security officer was kneeling beside her with his hand on her neck.

"No!" Scott cried out. "Is she alive?"

"I don't know! I can't find a pulse!"

The sound of sirens filled the air. Scott forgot about his own injuries. He forgot about the bomb. He forgot about Frank. All he could think about was Kay. The police officers arrived first and secured the hallway. The EMTs followed. Dr. Lassiter and other staff members came out of the administrative offices. There were several students with superficial wounds caused by material knocked loose by one of the bullets. Only one student, a ninth-grade girl, was seriously injured. Frank's first shot had hit her in the right arm, shattering her elbow. A teacher had led her into a classroom. She was screaming with shock and pain.

Scott kept asking about Kay as police and medical personnel began flooding the hallway.

"Is she alive?"

Two men lifted Scott and put him on a gurney.

"The teacher who was shot," Scott persisted. "Where is she?"

"Everyone who was hurt is going to the hospital," one of the men answered.

In the emergency room, Scott was whisked into a cubicle where an IV was stuck in his arm, and he received a shot for pain. Within less than a minute, a doctor who looked younger than Scott came in to examine him.

"I'm Dr. McMillan," he said.

"Do you know anything about the female teacher who was shot?" Scott asked anxiously. "What is her condition?"

The physician unwrapped the bandage the EMT had wrapped around Scott's leg.

"I don't know specifics. Dr. Paynter, the chief of surgery, is taking her to the OR."

"So, she's alive?"

"Yes, but I don't know the extent of her wounds."

Scott closed his eyes. "Thank God."

"I know more about your wounds," the doctor continued. "We need to take some x-rays. You have several pieces of metal and debris in your leg that don't belong there. We need to take them out."

Scott woke up in the recovery room and groggily opened his eyes. He remembered what had happened and tried to fight his way to consciousness, but it was too soon. He lapsed back into an uneasy dream world for another twenty minutes. The second time he awoke, there was a nurse standing beside his bed.

"He's waking up," she said to someone Scott couldn't see. Then she looked down at him. "We'll take you to a room in a few minutes."

She was gone before Scott could ask a question about Kay. When she returned, Scott was more alert. She unlocked the wheels of the bed.

"What about the young teacher who was shot?" he asked.

"She's in surgery. That's all I know."

Scott closed his eyes. Still alive.

When he was in his room, a new cadre of medical personnel attended him. He learned that the bullet hadn't done any permanent damage to his leg. His makeshift tourniquet had helped minimize the loss of blood. He would have a scar and the memory of what happened.

When there was finally a lull in the activity, there was a knock on the door. Scott turned his head. It was Leland Humphrey. The older lawyer came over to the bed and gently laid his hand on Scott's shoulder.

"How are you?" he asked.

"Hurting, but the doctor said I'll recover. I didn't think they were letting visitors in yet."

Leland smiled. "I've never sued the hospital, and they appreciate it."

"Do you know anything about Kay Laramie?"

Leland shook his head. "No. I arrived at the school after all the injured had been evacuated. I didn't know what had happened until I talked to a detective."

"How many people died?"

"I've only heard about two. The Jesup boy and a school employee."

"The janitor," Scott said softly. "He saved my life."

"From what I'm told, you're the hero."

Scott shook his head. The image of Tao bleeding on the floor came back. The look on Frank's face returned. He closed his eyes.

"I'll leave you in a minute," Mr. Humphrey said. "Is there anything I can do for you?"

"Try to find out about Kay. Let me know as soon as possible."

"I will. Anything else?"

Scott thought for a moment. "Yes, I have a close friend who will need help while I'm here."

"Of course. Who is it?"

"His name is Nicky."

After Mr. Humphrey left, two state law enforcement officers from Raleigh questioned Scott about what had happened in the hallway. They asked a lot of questions about Frank. The bomb had been removed and disassembled. Scott's guess about the dual power source and switch wire had been correct.

"Do you want to talk to the media?" the older of the two officers asked.

Scott closed his eyes. "Not now. Maybe later. Can you serve as spokesman for me?"

"Yes, we can include information from you in our official statement."

"Okay. Make sure you credit the janitor."

The officer checked his notepad. "Tao Pang."

Scott repeated the name softly. "Yes, Tao Pang."

Later that evening, Dr. McMillan came into the room.

"How are you feeling?" he asked.

"Dopey from the pain medicine. Any word about Kay Laramie?"

"That's one reason I stopped by. The nurses said you have been asking about her all day. She's going to make it."

Scott closed his eyes and exhaled. He opened his eyes and asked, "What happened to her?"

Dr. McMillan pulled a chair up to the bed and sat down.

"I've seen Dr. Paynter's chart. A bullet hit her in the left side of the face. It traveled along the side of her head until it lodged in her skull behind her left ear. Along the way, it did a lot of superficial damage, but the most serious problems involve the nerves that control her facial functions. Once nerves are severed they can't regenerate to a significant degree. Adjacent nerves can help take up the slack, but her damage was so extensive that it may not correct the problem."

Scott thought about the beautiful symmetry of Kay's face. He couldn't comprehend it marred.

"What will she look like?"

"On the right side there won't be any difference. On the left side, she will have scars that can be helped with plastic surgery, but we don't know the extent of nerve damage. It could be mild or as bad as a severe stroke victim."

"How bad is severe?"

"Her eye might droop, her cheek sag, and her mouth not respond normally, causing slurred speech and difficulty keeping certain types of food in her mouth. A full smile would be impossible."

"Oh, no," Scott groaned.

"It could have been worse. One inch difference and she probably would have died from a bullet to her brain."

Scott knew the doctor was right, but he ached for Kay.

"Does she know any of this?"

"No, she's heavily sedated."

The next morning Scott watched scenes from Catawba on the national news. It was odd seeing news reporters from all the major networks standing in places that had been familiar to him since he was a boy. The most popular spot for the cameras was a flat place by the flagpole in front of the high school. His own picture appeared frequently. It was a pre–law school photo and wasn't his most flattering likeness. His hair was in a military cut, and he looked like he wanted to spit at the camera. It saddened him when Frank's face flashed onto the screen. His parents were in seclusion, but the cameramen filmed the big house where Frank and his father lived.

The photo of Kay was the same one he'd seen in the yearbook in Dr. Lassiter's office. When it appeared on the screen, the announcer incorrectly identified her as a history teacher and said she had "serious head injuries." There weren't any photos of Tao, but the reporters made up for it by talking about the Hmong people.

The public relations director for the hospital came into the room and asked Scott if he wanted him to arrange an interview.

"No. Tell them I don't have anything to add to the official report."

Scott's thoughts were on Kay, not sound bites. He knew that people wanted to hear from the person who disarmed the bomb and was present in the hallway, but he wasn't sure he understood it himself. The sequence of events was clear: shots were fired; he cut the right wires; Tao placed himself in harm's way; Frank died. The reporters didn't need him to tell them the facts, and he didn't feel capable of analyzing what had happened. Something else was going on in those minutes, and Scott didn't have the words to express or explain it.

It was late in the afternoon before he convinced a nurse to wheel him up to Kay's room. It was painful to move his leg, but he pretended it didn't hurt too badly when he made an easy transfer from the bed to the wheelchair. All the weights he'd lifted were having a practical impact besides increasing his shirt size.

Kay was on the next floor. He was nervous in the elevator. The door opened, and the nurse wheeled him down the hall. Kay's mother was standing outside the doorway of the room talking with a doctor. She was the same as he remembered, only grayer and showing the strain of the past thirty-six hours. She saw Scott, stepped forward, and gave him a quick hug.

"Hello, Scott. How are you feeling?"

"Okay. I'd like to see Kay."

"She's asleep, but you can peek into the room."

Mrs. Laramie held open the door so the nurse could push him inside. Kay was lying motionless on her back. The doctor was correct. The right side of her face was perfect. Her cheek was pale, but she looked the same as when they sat across from each other eating filet mignon at the restaurant in Charlotte. The left side of her face was covered with bandages. Scott stared, drinking in her image, glad she was alive.

The nurse started pulling him out of the room. He held up his hand and whispered, "No, not yet."

Kay heard the sound and opened her right eye. She turned her head slightly, saw him, and the light of recognition came on. She tried to smile, and Scott saw that the slight upward curve of her lips stopped toward the left side of her mouth.

"Hi," she said weakly. "Come here."

Her lips didn't close properly to make the *m* sound. He rolled himself forward until he was beside her head.

"You don't have to talk," he said. "I just wanted to see you."

She blinked her eye. "Hold my hand," she whispered.

Once again, the words weren't distinct, but there was no doubt what she meant. Scott reached up and put his right hand on top of hers. Her hand was cool and white against the sheets. It felt so fragile, as if it would crack if he tried to squeeze it. She nodded slightly and closed her eyes.

Scott sat motionless, trying to will the strength that was in him to flow into her. He didn't move until her breathing was deep and even.

47

It is never too late to give up our prejudices.
HENRY DAVID THOREAU

Scott was out of the hospital in two days and back at work by the following week. It was difficult for him to navigate the stairs, but he could make it if he took his time. Kay would be in the hospital for a few more days. She'd already had a second round of surgery.

The media blitz that deluged Blanchard County for the first thirty-six hours evaporated as quickly as it fell. Scott decided not to return phone calls from reporters, and the initial flood of requests reduced to a trickle. On the national level, the incident at Catawba High School became stale news and joined the ranks of statistics on violence in American schools. The name of the lawyer who disarmed the bomb at a high school in North Carolina would soon be a difficult trivia question.

Of course, Catawba itself was still reeling from the threat to the lives of its young people. Some politicians wanted to install metal detectors and use high-school health classes as a forum to give psychological testing that would tip off administrators and identify students with a propensity for violence. The latter suggestion produced the threat of a lawsuit from the ACLU chapter in Charlotte. The purchase of metal detectors was placed on the agenda for the local school board.

Scott was at his desk when the receptionist buzzed him.

"Lynn Davenport from the district attorney's office on line 4."

Scott picked up the receiver.

"I'm not sure what to say," the D.A. began. Her voice was so different Scott wasn't sure it was the same person.

He waited.

"Oh, well, I won't try," she said. "I'm calling because the department of corrections has a space for Lester Garrison. He leaves tomorrow. We'll send a deputy to pick him up at his house. Make sure he's there at two o'clock."

Scott thought for a second. "Could his father bring him to the sheriff's office?"

"Yes, so long as he's here by two-thirty. We have three inmates to transfer to different facilities tomorrow, and they leave at that time."

Scott called the Garrisons' number and learned from Thelma that Harold was on a trip. Lester hadn't arrived home from school.

"Lester leaves for the boot-camp program tomorrow," Scott said in as cheery a voice as he could manage.

"Tomorrow?" the old woman said faintly. "Who's going to take him?"

After a few moments of awkward silence, Scott said, "I'll be by at two o'clock to pick him up and bring him into town. The sheriff's department will take over from here."

"Okay. I'll tell him."

Scott had volunteered to pick up Lester Garrison. In his moment of sympathy for Mrs. Garrison, he'd offered to serve as unpaid taxi driver for one of the two people in Blanchard County he'd rather not see again for the rest of his life.

Shortly before 2 P.M. the next day, Scott left the office. It was a cloudy day, and a few colored leaves clung to the wide variety of hardwoods that thrived in the rich soil and mild temperatures of the Piedmont. In the mountains west of Catawba, the bare trees would be farther along the cycle of the seasons. Scott let his mind drift to a place where huge poplar trees lined the hills of a North Carolina mountain cove. In winter, they looked like giant, gray candelabra.

Enjoying his daydream, he missed the road leading to Thelma Garrison's house but saw the crooked sign as he passed by. The house was easy to locate. Lester's truck was in the front yard.

Scott pulled into the yard and stopped underneath the massive oak tree. A nondescript brown dog charged off the front porch and began barking wildly. The animal circled Scott's vehicle, then began sniffing the tires. Scott rolled down the window and could hear a deep growl coming from the animal's throat. He hesitated. Scott wasn't normally afraid of dogs, but knowing Lester and Harold, he suspected the animal might have a tendency to bite first and refuse to apologize later.

Lester came out of the house and stood on the front porch.

"You can get out. Jack won't bother you now that I'm here."

Scott opened the door and stepped to the ground. Jack came closer and sniffed his leg. The dog had never smelled a Bichon before, and he stopped at the place where Nicky had brushed past Scott's pant leg earlier that day. Satisfied that the intruder was harmless, Jack sauntered over and lay down under the porch. Scott walked gingerly up the steps. Through the open screen door he could see an old woman standing in the shadows of the living room.

"How is your leg where you got shot at the school?" Lester asked.

"It's better."

"Ask him to come in," Thelma called out to Lester.

Lester went back in the house, and Scott followed. Thelma Garrison was in the middle of the floor with white tissues in each hand.

At the sounds of Scott's footsteps, she asked in a shaky voice, "Are you Lester's lawyer?"

"Yes, ma'am."

"Does he have to go now?"

"Yes, ma'am. He has to be at the sheriff's office by two-thirty."

Thelma had been crying. And Scott suddenly saw his client through a grandmother's sightless eyes. The rest of the world might view Lester as a bigoted, hate-filled young man whose future would almost certainly be worse than his past. Thelma Garrison's perspective was simpler—Lester was her grandson who was leaving home for prison. She remembered how he looked as a twelve-year-old before her eyesight faded for the last time. Her heart ached at the thought of what he faced.

"I'm sorry," Scott said. And meant it.

Thelma sniffled. "Do you think he'll be all right? Lester is kind of high-strung."

Scott didn't answer.

"Should he fix a sandwich to take with him?" she continued. "I don't know what they'll be feeding him in that place where he's a-going."

"If he wants to take something to eat on the way, that would be okay."

"I also told him to pack a small suitcase, but he didn't do it," she added. "What do you think?"

"There's no use," Lester said. "When I went to the youth detention center, they took everything away from me and put it in a plastic bag."

"He's right, Mrs. Garrison," Scott responded. "You can't take personal belongings to the boot-camp program. His father can bring him some clothes when he gets out in a few months."

Lester's head was down. The bravado of a few weeks ago couldn't rise up.

"I gotta go, Granny."

Thelma didn't move. Two streaks of tears quickly traced their way down her wrinkled cheeks. Scott didn't know what to say.

"Good-bye, Mrs. Garrison," he mumbled and followed Lester through the door.

His client was kneeling down on the porch talking to his dog. The look on the young man's face was something else that Scott had never seen. Lester held the dog's head between his hands and looked straight in his pet's eyes. For all the darkness and anger in Lester's heart, he had the capacity to love. Scott caught the end of the one-way conversation.

"Stay by the truck and guard it," he said. "Remember the nights that we sat outside and looked at the stars. I'll be back, and we'll do it again."

Lester stood up. "I'm ready."

They rode in silence. The lawyer knew platitudes would bounce off his client's bald head without penetrating his skull.

Finally, he asked, "What's your dog's name?"

Still looking ahead, Lester replied, "Jack."

"How long have you had him?"

Lester stared out the window before answering. "Since he was a pup. A lady down the road gave him to me when he was barely old enough to leave his mama."

"Did he sleep in your bed when you first brought him home?"

"Yeah," Lester grunted. "I had to wait until everyone else was asleep.

My mother was still with us, and she didn't want me to have a dog at all, especially one that came in the house. So, I'd have to sneak him into my room. He would sleep under the covers next to my leg without moving a muscle."

Scott thought about Nicky resting beside his leg in the recliner in the den.

"I have a dog that likes to lie next to my leg and take a nap while I watch TV," he said.

Lester turned toward him. "What's his name?"

"Nicky."

"That's a good name. What kind of dog is he? Jack has a lot of bloodhound in him."

Scott decided not to tell Lester that Nicky was a Bichon Frise, an ancient breed loved by Portuguese sailors in the fifteenth century, French kings in the seventeenth, and traveling organ grinders in the nineteenth. It would require too much explanation.

"He's a little white dog. He stays in the house or the backyard, but he sleeps in a crate in the laundry room at night. I don't let him sleep in my bed."

"Yeah. Jack still has a few fleas he picked up this summer."

They arrived at the jail. There was a parking space in front of the dreary, red-brick building. Blanchard County hadn't reached the place where its jail could be mistaken for a nice motel. A deputy and two men in jailhouse whites were standing next to a van with the sheriff's department name printed on its side. All of the men, including the deputy, were black. The inmates were shackled together with leg irons and wore handcuffs.

Scott glanced at Lester whose jaw was visibly clenched.

"That's the deputy who gave me such a hard time when I was arrested," he said.

Scott's recollection was that Lester assaulted the deputy, but he tried to think of the best way to respond that Lester would understand.

"Don't say anything. You're outnumbered."

The deputy's expression didn't change when he saw Lester walk up.

Scott asked the officer, "Do we need to go inside?"

"No, I'll take care of it, Mr. Ellis," the deputy responded. Almost everyone in town knew Scott on sight. "I have the paperwork with me. Hold out your hands."

Lester responded, and Scott noticed that although Lester's hands were large, his wrists were thin. There was no danger that the handcuffs would chafe his skin.

The deputy opened the side door of the vehicle.

"Get inside," he commanded.

Apparently, Lester would not be chained to the other prisoners. He stepped in and sat in the bench behind the driver. The other two inmates followed him and sat next to each other on the bench seat behind him.

Scott watched. No one said anything. No one waved good-bye. It wasn't like a group of children leaving for summer camp with hugs, kisses, and promises of letters every day. Neither did it bear any resemblance to the day Scott left for the army induction center. His mother had cried, and his father had slipped a note into his hand. Scott still had the note in a drawer at his house. It spoke in simple words of a father's pride in his son. The contrast between the two days couldn't have been more stark. Scott left home with a message of encouragement and affirmation in his hand; Lester had to settle for shiny, steel handcuffs.

The deputy started the engine and pulled out of the parking lot.

Scott drove in silence to the office. Parting ways with Lester Garrison didn't carry the sense of relief he'd expected.

48

Return, ye children of men.
PSALM 90:3 (KJV)

K ay quickly recovered her physical strength after the first rounds of plastic surgery to correct the outward scarring to her face. She left the hospital, and her mother returned to California. The initial paralysis affecting her mouth and eye began to improve, but she didn't have normal function and felt self-conscious about the changes. The exuberant joy that had been her sustaining companion throughout the divorce never got up from the floor at the high school. Scott wanted to help but didn't know what to do. He visited her regularly in the hospital, but Kay wasn't able to communicate well because of her injuries and the residual effects of the surgery. The day before she was scheduled to return to work, she called him.

"Do you have time for lunch today?" she asked.

Her speech wasn't precise, but Scott could understand her better each time they talked.

Scott looked at his calendar. He had an appointment but crossed through it. His secretary could reschedule.

"Yes, my calendar is clear."

"Do you want to meet at the Eagle?" she asked.

"No. I can't go there yet without people interrupting me. It would be worse—" He stopped.

"With me?" she finished.

"You know what I mean," he said awkwardly.

"Let's forget it," she said.

"No, I have a plan," he said quickly. "I'll pick you up at noon."

"Are you sure?"

"Yes. Be casual."

Scott didn't have a plan, but he had an hour to come up with one.

When he knocked on Kay's door, she opened it dressed in a fuzzy green sweater and jeans. Her hair fell straight to her shoulders. The bullet had traveled downward in a sloping line from a point near her nose until it disappeared in her hairline. It left a jagged gash that the surgeon closed and now hoped to conceal. The first time Scott saw Kay without bandages he fought back tears. He hurt so deeply in sympathy for what had happened to her that he could barely stand it, and he knew beyond all doubt the depth of his feelings for her. So far, he'd said nothing to her.

"I'm ready," she said.

They drove to Scott's house.

As they pulled up to the garage, he said, "Nicky wants to see you. He hasn't stopped talking about you since the camping trip."

Kay smiled. It was still slightly crooked, but better than the last one Scott had coaxed from her. Every few days there was improvement in her muscle function and appearance.

"I'd never want to disappoint Nicky," she said.

When Scott opened the back door, the little dog jumped up and down on his back legs until Kay knelt down and rubbed his head between her hands.

"He's glad to see you," Scott said.

"Ditto," Kay responded.

Nicky licked Kay's cheek where the path of the bullet had creased her face.

"Would you like a grilled cheese sandwich?" Scott asked.

"That's your plan?"

Scott continued to stall. "The plan is bigger than a grilled cheese sandwich. It's only the beginning. How would you like your sandwich? One piece of cheese or two?"

"Two with extra butter."

Scott put a skillet on the stove. Nicky trotted into the kitchen with his hedgehog and lay down on the floor. He was working on dislodging the stuffed animal's right ear. Kay leaned against the counter and watched Scott lay the bread out. She saw the scar in his right hand.

"Now, we both have scars," she said.

Scott glanced down. "I've thought about that," he said. "Scars are signs of healing, but underneath the wounds still hurt."

"Yes. That's true."

Scott melted the butter in the skillet and put the sandwiches next to each other.

"Are you ready for school tomorrow?" he asked.

Kay looked down at the floor. "No. I'm not ready to face the place or the people. I know I have to go back, but to see the hallway—" She shuddered.

"I haven't been to the school either."

Scott watched the sandwiches until it was time to flip them over. When he did, he had an idea.

"Do you want to go together this afternoon? We could wait until everyone has left for the day."

"Is that your plan?"

"Yes. I want to be with you."

Kay gazed out the kitchen window into the backyard before answering.

"Okay, that would be the thing to do."

"Good. I'll meet you in the school parking lot at five-thirty."

They had a quiet lunch. Kay told Scott it was the best grilled cheese sandwich she'd ever eaten. He said his secret was using real butter. Nothing fake or artificial.

———

The heaviness that was swirling around Kay accompanied Scott upon his return to the office. He met Mr. Humphrey in the downstairs hallway. "I saw Bishop Moore today," the older lawyer said. "He asked about you." The Sunday service at Hall's Chapel seemed long ago.

"I've been struggling," Scott replied. "Partly me, partly Kay."

"Come into my office," Mr. Humphrey said.

Scott sat down in the leather chair that had been more therapeutic for him than a psychiatrist's couch.

"Kay is going back to work tomorrow. It's going to be difficult for her."

Mr. Humphrey's right eyebrow edged upward. "And you're wondering how to help?"

"Yes. I suggested that we meet at the school this afternoon after hours, and she agreed."

"That's a good idea."

"But something else is bothering me that Kay doesn't know about." Scott took a deep breath. "The psychological report on Frank Jesup in his parents' divorce case. From my contact with Frank in the mock trial program, I knew he had problems. The report connected the dots. If I'd contacted the school, maybe this could have been avoided. Seeing Kay's face today, thinking about the janitor, the girl who was shot in the arm, even Frank—"

The report had been discussed within the firm. Pursuant to specific instructions from Vivian Jesup, its contents remained confidential, and the Jesup file was kept under lock and key. No one in the media knew about its existence.

"I'm glad I hired you," Mr. Humphrey responded.

"Huh?" Scott gave him a puzzled look.

"Scott, you're a hero. There is no way to know the lives you saved, but you're concerned about what you could have done better. That says a lot about you."

Mr. Humphrey was right. The accolades had fallen thickly on Scott's head but hadn't caused it to swell.

The older lawyer continued, "The decision whether to contact the school wasn't yours to make. The report didn't reveal a criminal act that had already occurred; it only warned of a possible danger in the future. The choice whether to release the information was in Vivian Jesup's hands."

"But it's hard not to have regret. Maybe I could have done something to prevent the whole thing from happening."

"Your concern shows your humanity. Only the insane and fanatical rejoice in tragedy." Mr. Humphrey paused. "I talked about the situation in a general way with Bishop Moore today, and he helped me."

"How?"

"Alfred doesn't know the law and probably hasn't read a psychological report in his life, but he knows people. He reminded me that the battle line between good and evil runs through the center of the human heart. Along that line the struggle is won or lost. Frank Jesup was commander in chief of his soul. He made choices that determined the outcome of the conflict. It wasn't your fault—not one bit."

Scott arrived a few minutes early at the school. He didn't want Kay to wait for him. As he sat in his vehicle, he looked at the school building. The most remarkable thing about the brown rectangular structure was its utter ordinariness. There was nothing that set it apart from thousands of other school buildings that dotted the American landscape— except the fact that it had faced destruction and been spared. That made it special.

He looked in the rearview mirror to see if Kay was pulling into the parking lot. When he did, he saw his own face. It, too, was ordinary. With his brown hair and square-shaped head, he was a lot like the school building. There was nothing about him that set him apart from thousands of other young men in America—except that he had faced destruction and been spared. Not once, but twice. Two men had sacrificed their lives so that he could live. Steve Robinson and Tao Pang were gone. He remained.

Why?

It was an important question. Scott wondered if there was an answer.

In the late afternoon sunlight the flagpole in front of the school cast a long shadow that stretched across the edge of the parking lot toward him. Near its top, an intersecting shadow caused by a stop sign crossed it. Scott noticed the configuration.

It was a cross. The sign of ultimate sacrifice.

Scott's heart beat a little faster. He could name two people, Steve Robinson and Tao Pang, who had placed themselves in harm's way for him and paid with their lives. Suddenly, he realized there were three.

"Jesus," he whispered.

The name of the Son of God spoken in recognition of his redemptive purpose opened heaven. Tears appeared at the edges of Scott's eyes, but more importantly, he knew the answer to his question. There was a sacrifice that transcended all others. Its origin was in unfathomable love. It was the ultimate sacrifice given for him.

And in a moment of divine intervention the burden of responsibility Scott Ellis felt to justify his existence rolled away from his soul. He had made mistakes in the past. He would make more in the future. But his worth as a person was based not on his actions but on the sacrifice of the Son of God. A weight heavier than any barbell lifted from his chest, and a tear escaped from the corner of his eye. It wasn't his code of honor or self-discipline that justified him in the sight of God; it was the sacrifice of Jesus that made him clean. He exhaled and drew a deep breath of freedom.

"Thank you," he said louder.

Scott didn't notice Kay's car until she parked beside him. He wiped his eyes and opened the door. She got out and saw his face.

"Are you okay?" she asked.

He remembered something he'd heard from Kay's lips. Now he understood what she'd meant.

"Better than okay."

Kay looked in his eyes, and they experienced what only the children of God can share—the recognition of spiritual life in another person. Kay put her hand over her mouth.

"Scott! Something has happened to you!"

He nodded. Then, in a level voice, he told her. By the time he finished, she had soaked two tissues.

Through her sniffles, she said, "Hearing you restores my own hope. I'd wondered if it could ever return. You've done it again."

"What have I done?"

"You've helped bring me back to life. Thank you."

He stepped forward, and they embraced.

When they parted, Scott asked, "Are you ready to go inside?"

Kay looked up the sidewalk toward the front doors of the school. "Yes."

Scott reached out and took her hand. They walked into the future. Together.

EPILOGUE

The light shines in the darkness, and
the darkness did not overcome it.
JOHN 1:5 (NRSV)

The blood that flowed from Tao Pang's body was removed from the hallway in front of the supply room door. The floor was cleaned and waxed, and Larry Sellers hired another janitor. However, in the ways that mattered most, no one could fill the void left by Tao's absence.

No one with a rag in one hand and a bucket of soapy water in the other stood vigil over the students who prayed in the cafeteria each Tuesday. No one carefully studied an old yearbook and asked the Holy Spirit to reveal young people and teachers who needed special prayer. No one prayed for lockers or praised God while operating a buffing machine. Tao was gone.

But Tao's prayers remained.

True intercession endures beyond this earthly life. *Amen* is not a word of ending but an affirmation of faith for the future. Tao's prayers didn't die when he took his last breath. They remained alive like unseen banners suspended from the cafeteria ceiling and hidden signs posted along the hallways where he'd worked. Nothing God inspires is lost. Nothing his servants do in obedience is wasted.

The Tuesday group continued to meet. Janie healed slowly from the horror of her experience in the hallway. As she did, her compassion and concern for those on the fringes of the student body increased. Alisha's willingness to be a bold witness to her faith became stronger.

The angels who surrounded the table maintained their unwavering watch. Faith in God by human beings who cannot see into the spiritual realm is one of the greatest marvels of the universe, and the heavenly guardians considered it a high honor to serve those who believed in prayer. The light burned brighter than ever. The darkness had not overcome it.

One Tuesday the students in the group were sitting around their usual table.

"Thank you, Lord Jesus, for protecting us from evil," Janie prayed. "Please reveal your goodness and glory in this school. Let each person know how much you love them."

"And thank you for your presence," Alisha continued. "We want you in every part of our school. Touch the lives of all the students and teachers."

A cool breeze blew across their faces.

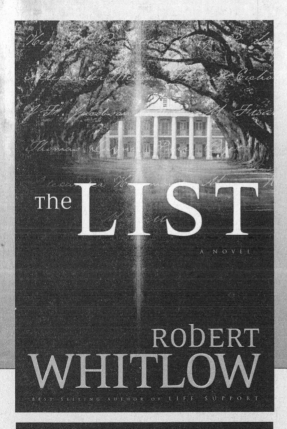

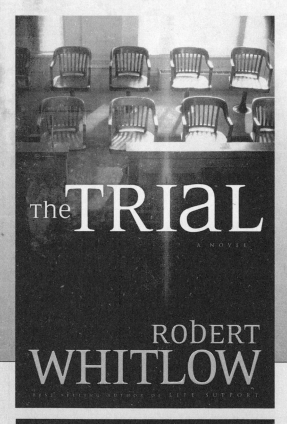